A LONG WAY DOWN

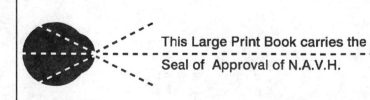

This Large Print Book carries the
Seal of Approval of N.A.V.H.

A RYAN DeMARCO MYSTERY

A LONG WAY DOWN

RANDALL SILVIS

THORNDIKE PRESS
A part of Gale, a Cengage Company

Farmington Hills, Mich • San Francisco • New York • Waterville, Maine
Meriden, Conn • Mason, Ohio • Chicago

GALE
A Cengage Company

LIBRARY OF CONGRESS CIP DATA ON FILE.
CATALOGUING IN PUBLICATION FOR THIS BOOK
IS AVAILABLE FROM THE LIBRARY OF CONGRESS

ISBN-13: 978-1-4328-6878-9 (hardcover alk. paper)

Published in 2019 by arrangement with Sourcebooks, Inc.

Printed in the United States of America
1 2 3 4 5 6 7 23 22 21 20 19

A12007 355277

FOR MY SONS, BRET AND NATHAN,
HEART OF MY SOUL,
SOUL OF MY HEART

MY THANKS, AS ALWAYS, TO
SANDY LU,
LITERARY AGENT PAR EXCELLENCE,
AND TO MY INESTIMABLE EDITOR,
ANNA MICHELS

■ ■ ■ ■

I

■ ■ ■ ■

Come dance with me, the darkness says
when rain shines on the cobblestones
and the bones of memory tick tap tick
like flies on a body three days dead,
and the moon wraps itself in diaphanous
    cloud
like a mourner's shroud around an old
    woman's head.
            — from "3 a.m.," Thomas Huston

When I first spot him, a soft little voice inside my head says Him. He's the one. I have no doubt that voice came from my Guardian. He had come to awaken the magician in me.

Brenner is average size, in his thirties maybe, one of those bland Caucasian faces, and he's walking along so careless and oblivious with his earbuds in that I can't help being amused. He is fast asleep and doesn't even know it.

It's exactly 10:29 p.m., and dark in only the way a city can be dark, with a sky so black and low that the only thing visible in it is a pair of red blinking wing lights. No stars here. And down on the street there are only pools of light from the streetlamps, so that the darkness pooled around those lights looks oily and slick.

So I drive past Brenner and turn at the corner. I wonder if he feels my presence, some strange electricity in the air. The fact that he doesn't stop, look around, change his

9

mind and hustle back to the safety of his cave tells me how numb he really is. He's out for a stroll after a late dinner. And now he's full of chemicals and preservatives, animal fat and gluten, just another slave ignorant of his enslavement.

I check out a couple of intersections along his path and find a corner that looks good. An empty parking space three back from the corner. Not a lot of light. No restaurants or bars that might spill out a patron or two.

So I go walking up to him, not too fast, moving in and out of the light so that I don't spook him. Excuse me, sir. There's something wrong with my car. Could you help me please?

He slows down like he's not sure what to do. He says, What kind of problem are you having?

That's when I get this déjà vu kind of feeling that what I'm about to do has already been done, and that the two of us are here just to reenact it all again. So I tell the guy, like I'm reciting lines from a play, I can't start my car. The key seems to be locked in the ignition. I can't even pull it out.

Okay, he says. I've had that happen too. All you have to do is depress the brake and give the steering wheel a quick turn. You have it in Park, right?

I say, I tried that already. I've tried everything. Do you mind having a quick look at it? I don't know how I'm going to get home otherwise.

And two minutes later he's sitting in the driver's seat. But I'm leaning in from the passenger side like I don't want to miss a thing he does. He turns the key and, surprise surprise, it turns. That was easy, he says.

And then I push my cell phone into his side. And because it's not really a cell phone, he starts twitching and jumping in the seat, even banging his head against the ceiling. I keep zapping him until he falls forward over the steering wheel. Then I grab the tape off the floor in the back, and get it around his face and wrists as fast as I can. When he starts fighting back a little I stun him again, then get the tape around his ankles.

The hardest part of the whole thing is pulling and dragging him into the passenger side and buckling him in. Then I do three more loops of tape over his mouth and nose. And we're on our way.

Honestly, it took no time at all. It flowed like music. I was pure will. Will and intention in a perfect, seamless flow.

He bounces around in the seat for a couple of minutes, suffocating, and then he goes quiet. I've already chosen the place for the rest of it. I park so that the car blocks any possible view of him when I drag him out onto the grass.

It's hard to explain the way I feel when the blade starts cutting. It's like somebody is whispering good good good as the saw rips into him. The saw is Magus's idea. Maximize the horror, he said. Maximize the fear.

I kept waiting to feel bad or sick or something, but I never did. And know I never will. Why should I? He was asleep, and I woke him. He was in prison, and I set him free.

That was the first one. The first step toward Completion. More will follow.

I am Erebus, son of Khaos.

ONE

The sky was ash. Lake Erie was ash. Even with the midday August sun out there somewhere behind the gray, everything De-Marco looked at through the hospital's fifth-floor window was painted in the same monochromatic hue. Even the silence outside the window seemed gray, not an actual silence but that of life tamped down, muted, and capped — the silence of a bottled-up scream.

Ever since he had stepped off the plane, a heaviness in his chest and a mild soreness just above the sternum made him wonder if he was developing some kind of infection. Flying was a notoriously easy way to catch something. He kept waiting for the condition to worsen or fade, but it never did, and he sometimes found himself tapping his breastbone as if that might dislodge the heaviness and allow him to breathe easier.

This was his third visit to Laraine in as

many days, and she had not yet uttered a word to him nor even glanced his way. Technically, he was still her husband, and so felt an obligation to keep trying. Yet what good was he doing here?

After her suicide attempt, she had been admitted on a 302, involuntary commitment for emergency evaluation and treatment. He had received the phone call in Kentucky in the middle of the night, flew back to Pennsylvania the next morning — with Jayme's blessing, thank God. He went straight from the airport to the hospital, but was informed that visitors were not permitted in the locked Behavioral Unit, so he returned to his closed-up home an hour south, where, for the next three days, he relied on long walks in the woods and long telephone calls back to Kentucky to keep him from falling into old habits.

Finally, on the fourth day of Laraine's hospital stay, she was moved to a private room. He arrived just after lunch that first restraint-free day, and found her sitting up beside the bed in a cushioned chair. She would not look at him or respond to his questions, so he sat on the edge of the bed and told her about the case he had wrapped up in Kentucky just a week earlier, the seven skeletons, the summersweet bushes and the butterflies.

He told her about the amateur cold case investigators he had worked with and sometimes against over the past few weeks: Hoyle, the obese retired medical examiner; Vincente, the retired lawyer; and Rosemary Toomey, the retired librarian. He recounted his ordeal in the mountains, and described Cat and Virgil Helm, two of the kindest people he had ever known, despite the fact that Cat had tried to frighten him away with a gunshot, and then, failing to chase him off, had trapped him overnight in an elaborate bear cage.

He told her about the government-hating McGintey brothers and Reverend Royce, the slimy TV evangelist. And about Toad Burl and Dr. Friedl, two thoroughly despicable men. From time to time as he talked, a light seemed to flicker in her eyes, but then she would close her eyes as if to deny him that light. Eventually he surrendered to her silence and returned home to fall asleep in his chair with the television on.

On his second visit, he returned to the hospital around 2:00 p.m. This time she was in her bed, so he sat beside her in the cushioned chair. And this time he told her about meeting the writer Thomas Huston the previous summer, and the horror that

15

befell the Huston family that fall. "It was rough," he said, "finding a friend like Tom, and then losing him so quickly." And he told her about Jayme, how she was helping him to recover from all that, and had convinced him to take the RV trip to Kentucky. "Can you picture that?" he asked. "Me in an RV? It was touch and go between us for a while, but she hung in there. And now I'm not drinking like I used to. Getting more exercise too. Watching what I eat."

And finally, because the more he shared with her, the easier it became, he told her about the dreams he had had of his and Laraine's son while in the mountains of Kentucky. "Those dreams have helped me probably most of all," he said. "Seeing him half-grown-up like that, not a baby anymore. I can't even describe how much good it's done me."

When he spoke of Ryan Jr., she had turned her face to the window. He watched her reflection in the glass, her mouth in a scowl. Did she resent him for having those dreams, and for finding some comfort in them? When he touched her hand, she jerked it away. And so he'd left her again.

And now, on his third visit, as he stared across the gray parking lot at gray water melting into a gray sky, he had all but resolved that the best way to help her was to leave. They shared a wound that would never heal, and he knew that her ache was just as deep and fresh as his, but the loss of a child was more often a divisive ache than a binding one. Her ache was all grief and anger, his grief and guilt. Deep in his heart he wanted no relief from the pain because he deserved none. So how could he ever do her any good? On the other hand, why had she given the hospital his telephone number? Was it only so that he would suffer more?

It was unlike him to give up so easily. After all, he had remained married to Laraine for over a dozen years despite their estrangement. Despite her silent treatment all that time and the way she regularly punished him by sleeping with men she barely knew. One of those men had hung around long enough to call 911 after she used the blade of her scissors to etch diagonal lines across both slender wrists, just as DeMarco's mother had done a quarter century earlier. He wondered if that was Laraine's way of saying *First you killed your mother, and now you're killing me.*

Over the past three days, he had been her only visitor. He wanted to question the head nurse's advice to him an hour earlier, but doubted his own judgment, and his own motivations.

To the window, he said, "I want to stay, because I want to be here for you. But . . . according to Nurse Ratched out there, your doctor thinks maybe I'm the cause of your . . . lack of communication. Seeing as how you respond to everybody else except me."

She sat in her bed and stared expressionless at the wall, the ceiling, the window — anywhere but into his own eyes. Did she even know anymore why she behaved this way? If a nurse came in to administer a pill or take her pulse, Laraine would smile, answer a question, come quietly alive again for those brief moments. But if DeMarco spoke to her in the nurse's presence, his words were ignored; they left no trace on her.

Yet he stayed. He talked until he had nothing more to say. Sat beside her, stood at the window, leaned against the wall. When her eyes closed, he simply looked at her, remembered how she used to be. Remembered the laughter of the early years and the insatiable hunger they had felt for each other. Other than his mother, Laraine was the first woman he had ever loved. And how different those two loves were, just as his love for his baby son was different, and now his love for Jayme.

It was a funny thing, love. It could take so many forms. Could be so freeing, or imprisoning.

He felt tied to each of them. Least of all to his mother, the one longest gone. Still, he wished he had been with her on her final night. Instead he had been in Panama, barely a man, reducing a neighborhood to ash.

And he would always be tied to Ryan Jr. too, although, strangely, less so to him as well, ever since those dreams in the Kentucky mountains. Or no, not less, but differently. Much of the heaviness had lifted. When he thought of his son now, he saw him less frequently as a baby, and more often as the twelve-year-old in his dreams. And his chest was warmed not by grief and guilt but wonder and hope.

But seeing Laraine like this, knowing that he, ultimately, was to blame for her condition . . .

"So I guess I'm going to go," he told her. "Not because I want to. But because I want what's best for you. I want you to be happy. I want you to move on. If I can, you can."

A few moments later he turned away from the glass, hoping against all odds that she would be looking his way. But she was staring at the far wall — seeing, he knew, all the way through the cement blocks, probably all the way back to the last time they had been in a hospital together, the day her love for him had turned to ash.

He walked around the foot of the bed, lingered for a few moments at her side. Then leaned down to where her arm lay against her body. He kissed the tape around her wrist, expecting her to pull her arm away. But she didn't. So he kissed the soft skin on the inside of her elbow. Rose slowly to kiss her cheek, his hand light on the back of her head. He waited for a response, any kind of response, but received none. Then he stood, sniffing, blinking, and turned away.

"You can call me anytime you want," he told her, his eyes on the floor. "Anytime."

And he walked to the door.

She said, her voice too soft, and unfamiliar, "Do you remember that time you made the crab-apple wine?"

He turned. Her head was lowered, her gaze going down toward her knees, her cheeks wet. He said, "I picked that little tree clean, didn't I? Thousands and thousands of tiny, sour apples."

A small smile. "You kept adding sugar and

adding sugar. Bag after bag of it." Her voice was soft and hoarse, the same as his.

"Until I could taste the juice without puckering up."

"And when it was ready, oh boy." Her smile widened by a few degrees. And then her head turned. And her eyes met his.

Where had all the blue gone from her eyes? They were gray now, a shimmering smoke. He crossed to the bed. Pulled the chair up close, sat, and took her hand. "I swear it was three hundred percent alcohol. What a kick it had!"

"It was good, though."

"Best wine I ever made."

She kept smiling, looking into his eyes. And then her smile faltered, and her gaze slid away, over his shoulder and to the door. "Have you made any since then?"

He shook his head no. "Lost the urge, I guess. Lost a lot of urges."

She gripped his hand. And again met his eyes. "We could move on together."

He was startled by that. Startled and stabbed. He said, "We would always remind each other of everything we lost."

"I don't think I can keep going by myself," she said.

"Yes you can. You taught a dumb trailer park kid to love Beckett and Camus. You're a miracle worker."

Another small smile. Her fingers loosened their grip. "Did you really see our boy?"

"Twice. Two nights in a row. Exactly when I needed him most."

"Why didn't he come to me when I did this?" she asked, and lifted her arms, and looked at the tape wrapped from wrist to elbow.

"Maybe because he knew I would."

She nodded. "I just want to be with him."

"You are," he told her. "He's with both of us."

"I wish I could see him again. He was grown?"

"A good-looking boy. Handsome and quick."

"How could that be?" she asked.

"I don't know."

"But you believe it really happened? That it was real?"

"It was the realest thing I've ever felt."

"I want so badly to see him again."

"Tell him that," DeMarco whispered, his voice so hoarse now that he could speak no louder. "Keep asking. I bet he comes."

And he held her hand awhile longer, as long as he could, until her tears subsided and the pale light through the window crept into the corner of the room.

TWO

Going down in the hospital elevator, De-Marco felt the descent in his knees, felt them wanting to bend, so he held to the metal rail and stared at the buttons on the panel and struggled against the urge to hit Stop. He had never been good with relationships. Things were good with Jayme despite his clumsiness, his many bad decisions, but things had been good with Laraine too, until another bad decision, a brief lack of attention.

Women remained a mystery to him. He understood the criminal mind well, and had a knack for predicting its simple turns and convolutions. But the mind of a woman in love — no law of physics could account for the complexities of such a mind. For every action there was never an equal and opposite reaction. The rate of change was never directly proportional to the amount of force applied. And an object at rest, if that object was a woman in love, seldom remained at rest until acted upon by an external force.

Still, it was as clear as crystal to DeMarco that without a woman in his life, he had no balance, no center. His mother, then Laraine, and now Jayme. The periods between those three remained dark in his memory. Not dark as in unseeable, for they were all too visible to him even yet, but dark with resentment. Dark with anger. Dark with the grim resolve to feel nothing, let no one in, allow no light into his tight-fisted heart.

But he had tasted that light, and was hungry for more. The moment the elevator bell dinged and the doors slid open, he stepped out into the lobby, needing to hurry lest he turn and ascend again to the fifth floor. He wanted to return to Jayme as quickly as possible, even though he thought of that desire as a selfish one, whereas staying with Laraine was a duty, an obligation to fix what he himself had broken.

He had his head down when he stepped into the lobby, and nearly ran into a man waiting to board. "Sorry. Sorry," DeMarco muttered, then offered a quick glance and apologetic smile as he stepped to the side.

"S'all right," the man said, and squeezed

past him into the elevator.

DeMarco continued toward the front entrance, but slower now, because the man's face had seemed vaguely familiar, someone he should know.

Behind him, the elevator doors slid open again. "Twenty-seven!" the man said.

The number on DeMarco's high school football jersey. He turned. Looked across the fifteen feet of tile at the man holding the door open: a bald, goateed black man wearing the uniform of law enforcement, the smoke-gray jacket, charcoal epaulets, gold star and buttons. Mahoning County Sheriff's Office. Ben Brinker.

DeMarco retraced his steps to the elevator, smiled and held out his hand. "Eighty-six," he said. "It's good to see you again, Ben."

The sheriff gripped his hand, held it firmly. "Damn, Ryan, you're getting old."

"At least I still have most of my hair."

"I do too, around the sides anyway. I just moved it down here on my face where everybody can see it better. Vee started leaving boxes of Uncle Ben's rice on the bathroom sink. I finally got the hint."

"And now you have a kind of Samuel L. Jackson vibe going," DeMarco told him. "It suits you. And how is Miss Veronica these days?"

"On cloud nine. We just had our second grandchild. A boy this time."

"You buy him a football yet?"

"You better believe it."

"Figured," said DeMarco. "And how's business on your side of the border?"

The sheriff shook his head. "You know the answer to that. Short on manpower, long on crime. Some of our neighborhoods still have the highest crime rates in the country. We shove one demon back into Pandora's box, and three more jump out the other side."

"I hear you," DeMarco said. "Three at a minimum."

The sheriff finally released his hand. "So what are you doing in this place? Not having any health problems, I hope."

"My wife, Laraine. Opened up her wrists a few nights ago."

"Oh God, man, I'm sorry. But I thought you two got divorced a long time ago."

"Separated."

"And this is a, uh, reconciliation?"

DeMarco blew a thin stream of air over his lower lip. "Apparently when they brought her in, she asked for me. Still had my number on her phone."

"Good thing you were so close."

"I was in Kentucky," DeMarco told him. "With a friend. I've been on medical leave the past month."

"Medical as in . . . ?"

DeMarco shrugged. "Needed a mood adjustment. That case last fall. Don't know if you read about it or not."

"Sure I did. The writer. Lost his whole family in one night."

DeMarco nodded. "The man was my friend."

"That's rough, partner. It's good you were able to clear things up for him."

DeMarco offered a small smile, but no other response.

"Listen," Brinker said. "You have time for a coffee? Maybe a sandwich? It's on me. There's a little café right over there."

"You were on your way upstairs."

"My sister's boy. Soccer player, of all things. Torn meniscus."

"I don't want to keep you from seeing him."

"He won't miss me. He's probably entertaining a couple of candy stripers at this very minute."

"Takes after his uncle," DeMarco said.

The sheriff grinned. "Don't ever say anything like that around Vee. She'll tear

27

both of our heads off."

"It would be nice to see her again. It's been a long time."

And then he winced to remember it — the funeral for Baby Ryan. He had let a lot of old friendships die after that.

"Let's plan on it," the sheriff said. "Meantime, how about that coffee? I got something I wouldn't mind running past you."

DeMarco groaned. "I hate when people tell me that."

Brinker laid a hand on DeMarco's shoulder, turned him toward the café. As they walked, he said, "I can't help wondering about meeting you here like this. You ever think that maybe some things happen for a reason?"

"The question is," DeMarco said, "is it a good reason or a bad one?"

"You remember that double homicide the summer we graduated?"

DeMarco looked back through the fog. It was the summer his life first changed. In late June he'd gotten into another fight, sent the kid to the hospital with a broken nose and fractured jaw. On July 5, a judge gave DeMarco the option of army or jail. Five days later, he heard about the murders while on the bus ride to the New Cumberland Army Depot processing center. And now he said, "That mob guy and his lawyer. Cut into pieces."

The sheriff nodded. "We think the guy who did it might be at it again."

THREE

Jayme awoke to a thump. She had been dreaming about a huge, vicious dog prowling the backyard, and about trying to find her handgun but not being able to locate it. So when she awoke suddenly in her grandmother's bedroom, the windows gray with predawn light, she needed a few moments to remember where she was. A sound like distant rain could be heard, and the soft hum of the ceiling fan. Had she dreamed the thump? She listened for another one and tried to quiet her racing heart.

She sat up, looked to the open window. A pinkish hue to the gray of dawn. *Maybe 5:30,* she told herself. If rain was falling, it was farther out, had not yet reached her window.

And then, another thump. Not a dream. Someone rummaging around downstairs?

She slid quietly out of bed, turned to the bedside stand, laid her left palm atop the holster, and was relieved to find it where she had left it. She slid the .380 free and, with her left hand, felt around for her cell phone but couldn't locate it. Must have left it in her jeans again, which were now stuffed into the laundry basket.

She thought for a moment about covering DeMarco's long T-shirt with a robe, but that would require opening the squeaky closet door, a noise that might alert the intruder. So she went to the door and into the hall, stood with head cocked, goose bumps on her arms and naked legs. When she smelled the scent of fresh coffee brewing in the kitchen, she also recognized where the sound of rain was coming from: in the guest shower twenty feet down the hall.

She lowered the handgun and raced down the hall and into the bathroom, where she paused only long enough to place the .380 on the toilet seat before throwing open the shower door and plunging inside.

FOUR

The kitchen was warm with a bright Kentucky morning, still fragrant with the scent of bacon and toast and scrambled eggs that had filled their now-empty plates. Jayme took a sip from her coffee mug, then reached out to rub a naked foot over DeMarco's. "So breakfast is over," she said. "Where's this present from Pennsylvania you've been saving for me?"

He said, "I don't recall using the word *present.*"

"Pretty sure you did. So now you owe me one."

He pushed his plate out of the way, slid the laptop close, and opened the screen. "If this is a present," he told her while scrolling through pages, "it's not a very nice one. Sorry."

She stood and crossed to sit sideways on DeMarco's lap.

"There," he said, and leaned back, reached

for his coffee cup.

She read to herself from the digital edition of the Youngstown *Vindicator.* The article was dated ten days earlier:

Cottage Grove man third victim of copycat torso killer?

The body of Cottage Grove resident Jerome Hufford, 51, was discovered early Sunday morning in the parking lot area of the Campbell farm market and swap meet. Hufford, a divorced father of two adult children, was employed as a machinist at Crescent Industries.

The only detail police have released is that the condition of the body was consistent with those of two earlier victims this month, 20-year-old Canfield resident Samantha Lewis, a student at Heaton-Young College, and the first known victim, 36-year-old Justin Brenner of Smokey Hollow. According to the sheriff's office, all three victims died by means similar to those recorded in the Cleveland Torso Murders some eighty years ago. This has caused some to speculate that a copycat killer may be responsible for the recent tragedies.

The official number of victims attributed

to the original Cleveland Torso Murderer is twelve, all of whom died between 1935 and 1938. The actual number could be as high as 20, with victims from as far away as New Castle and McKees Rocks, Pennsylvania (1936 and 1940 respectively). All victims were decapitated, some with their arms and legs amputated; male victims were usually castrated.

The Cleveland Torso Killer might also be responsible for the Murder Swamp deaths; from 1921 through 1939, several dismembered bodies were found in the swamps outside New Castle.

Famed Untouchable Eliot Ness, best known for his work in sending gangster Al Capone to prison, oversaw the Cleveland Torso Killer investigations from 1935 to 1938 in his capacity as Cleveland's director of public safety. Although multiple suspects were questioned in regard to those murders, none was ever prosecuted for the crimes.

More recently, in July 1988, the bodies of Jared Brogan, a lawyer, and Alan Talarico, president of the Youngstown Firemen's Credit Union, were dismembered and later discovered on a fairway at Fonderlac Country Club. Although the murderer or murderers were never identified,

Talarico's rumored affiliation with organized crime led police at the time to state that those crimes were unrelated to the Cleveland Torso Murders except in regard to the condition of the bodies.

Police are unwilling to comment upon any possible relationship between those murders and the three most recent ones.

The Mahoning County Sheriff's Office, along with the Youngstown Police, are asking for the public's assistance in identifying the murderer of Hufford, Lewis, and Brenner. Anyone with any information whatsoever is asked to call 911 or the tip hotline established for this investigation: 1-800-255-8888.

"Whoa," Jayme said after she finished reading. "That's a lot of bodies."

"Youngstown's crime rate is almost twice the national average."

"And now three in less than a month?"

"With nothing apparent in common. Brenner was a CPA, Lewis a college student."

"Did you know the part about Eliot Ness?"

DeMarco sipped his coffee, then nodded. "He cleaned up Cleveland back in the thirties. Got rid of a couple hundred crooked cops. Rumor is he spent the rest of his life haunted by his failure to solve the Torso Murder case."

"Who wouldn't?" Jayme said.

"There's a photo of him on Biography .com. He looks like a grown-up version of Alfalfa from *The Little Rascals.*"

Jayme leaned back against him. "Don't make fun, babe."

"Just saying."

"So this is my present?" she asked. "A serial killer working thirty miles from home?"

"I ran into the Mahoning County sheriff at the hospital. We played high school football together. Name's Ben. Ben Brinker."

She twisted around to face him. "Two cold cases, one thirty years old and one eighty, both tied somehow to this new stuff? How can that be?"

"That's mostly the media's work. But the sheriff thinks there might be a link between the last two. The 1988 murders and the new ones. Lots of similarities, he said. Thought maybe we could provide a fresh look on things."

"Hmm. Let's say the killer was eighteen to thirty in 1988. That would make him . . . fifty to sixty-two years old now. Okay, I guess it's feasible. But it doesn't seem very likely."

DeMarco said nothing.

"So how come the sheriff is looking for outside help? Why not call in the FBI?"

"They've already helped with forensics and database searches. But you know how it is with local police. There's a lot of pride involved here too."

"Ben would rather have a local hero involved?"

"Hardly a hero. But yes, a local boy."

She turned to look at him again. "So we pack up the RV and head north?"

"I vote no."

"Really? And why is that?"

"Because you couldn't participate in the case and still go back to your real job. And because eastern Ohio is no sunnier than western Pennsylvania. And because the RV we're still paying for will sit in the driveway and turn to rust."

"First," she said, "who says I want to go back to my real job? As for the RV, we'll sell it or stick it in a garage. As for the lack of sunshine, I'll buy you a sunlamp and a bottle of vitamin D."

"You would really consider it?"

"Twenty dollars for the lamp, five for the vitamins. Big deal."

"Seriously," he said.

"You're not bored doing nothing?"

"Not at the moment. Are you?"

"I can't sit on your lap forever, Ryan. You have bony knees." She wiggled her butt atop his thighs. "Are you telling me that a case like this doesn't get you even a little bit excited? And what about going back to where you came from? Back to where you sowed all your wild oats."

"Thomas Wolfe says I can't go back. He wrote a whole book about it. *You Can't Go Home Again.*"

"Writers lie," she said. "Besides, the sheriff asked for your help, didn't he?"

"Our help. Apparently he heard one of the newscasts about how you took down the Kentucky Toad Man."

She grinned. "Sweet. So we're big news in Youngstown?"

"You are. I'm just the gimpy sidekick."

"I like that," she said. "Unfortunately, your limp is barely detectable now."

"We'd get a per diem. A thousand a week max. Plus we'd split the quarter-million-dollar reward if we bring in the killer."

"I'd get the same as you? I like that too."

"You're the brains of the outfit," he told her.

"So we're an outfit now?"

"We're a team."

She smiled. Laid a hand on the back of his neck. Rubbed a finger across his hairline. She said, "Want to hear about this weird dream I had last night?"

"Love to," he said.

"So I was in this big house . . . mine, I guess."

"Not ours?"

"Mmm, I'd like to say yes. But honestly I don't remember you being in the dream."

"Bummer."

"But you must have been because I had a baby. He was just a toddler. In another room, sleeping."

DeMarco rolled his upper lip under his front teeth. Bit down briefly. "Okay," he said.

"And I was in the upstairs hall and came to a door I hadn't noticed before, so I opened it and went inside, and the entire room was painted in a glossy pink. Very glossy. Like a smooth, shiny shell of pink on all the walls."

"Remind me not to ask you to pick the color next time I paint a room."

"Shut up," she said. "It was a huge room, and it sort of folded around itself, and kept opening up to other spaces. And in one of them there was an antique baby grand piano, and a harpsichord without any legs, and just trunks and trunks full of old stuff. And I remember thinking that I had forgotten all about this room, and how happy I was to discover it again."

"Sounds like a pleasant dream."

"Until I heard the dog. It was a huge, deep, vicious growl, like out of a horror movie. The sound the monster makes when it bites into one of the characters. So I went to the window and looked out and there it was, as big as a bear almost, and it was ripping a smaller dog to shreds. And I thought about the baby and went flying out of the pink room and down to the nursery, and the crib was empty. So now I'm running around crazy all through the house, can't find the baby, can't find my handgun, and what if the back door is open . . . And then *thump!*"

"Thump?" he said.

"I'm thinking it was you shutting the door on the shower stall."

"I woke you up?"

"I'm glad you did. It had turned into a *horrible* dream."

"Happy to be of service," he said.

She kissed the side of his head then, and remained in that position for half a minute, holding him close. "What I can't forget is how terrified I was that the dog was going to get my baby. And the love I felt for my baby. It was *huge.* So powerful. I don't even know how to describe it."

"You don't have to," he said.

Again she touched her lips to the side of his head. "Before you had your son," she asked, "before you knew you were going to be a father, did you even realize how empty a part of you was?"

"I did. Just didn't know which part. I sure knew afterward, though."

"Then you know what I mean."

"I do," he said.

Neither of them spoke for a while. He thought he could predict where the conversation was going, and hoped he was wrong.

She said, "Before I came downstairs this morning, I googled the meaning of pink in a dream."

"I bet it means you ate too much pizza before bed."

"It symbolizes the love of God. Also sensuality and moral purity."

"So it was a good horrible dream."

"Except for the dog. A vicious dog in a dream symbolizes inner conflict."

"There must be a lot of people dreaming about dogs."

She smiled. Stroked the back of his neck.

Said, "What would you say if I said I would love to have a baby with you?"

Beneath her hand, the muscles of his neck tensed. "Where did that come from?"

"You don't know where babies come from?"

"When did you start thinking about having a baby?"

"Since our first night in the RV. And then that dream, it was so powerful. The clock's ticking, you know. For both of us."

He shifted in his seat. Tilted his head just slightly away from hers. "Still," he said.

"Are you saying it's out of the question?"

"I'm saying let's slow down a little."

"Until I change my mind."

"Until we're sure. I mean . . . we were talking about a serial killer here. And now suddenly you want to have a baby? It's jarring, to say the least."

She sat there motionless for a few moments, then abruptly slid off his lap and stood. She gathered up the breakfast plates and carried them to the sink, set them down noisily, so hard he was certain something was going to break.

"Jayme," he said, "I'm almost fifty years old."

"You're a child," she said, and turned the hot water on full blast. He could feel the angry little droplets bouncing out of the sink to spit against his neck.

FIVE

After silently drying the few dishes Jayme had vehemently scrubbed clean before stalking upstairs, he pulled the plug to drain the water, then rinsed out the sink, wiped the counters and table, and stood looking out the kitchen window for ten minutes. The day was bright, every color vivid. He could feel the heat coming through the glass.

He asked himself, *What are you so afraid of?*

That was an easy one. He was afraid of another wound that would never heal. Sometimes he could actually see the one he carried now. Would wake in the middle of the night after a troubling dream and see his soul standing there before him, gray smoke in the form of a man, a wide gaping slash across the chest, precisely where his chest ached each time he thought of his son.

He asked himself, *What if you lose her over this?*

Not as easy to answer. Would it be better for her to be free of him than to remain caught in the updraft of his darkness? She would find another man, younger and full of light. But what if she did not? What if she were ruined too?

He asked himself, *Who says this is your decision anyway?*

When he closed his eyes he could see himself on the Amish rocker he and Laraine had bought at a yard sale, the perfect chair, she had said, for breastfeeding Baby Ryan. She used it during the day, but it was his and his son's at night. At five weeks old Ryan developed colic, and would start crying every night around 1:00 a.m. DeMarco would slip out of bed at the first cry, pick up his son and carry him to the rocker. The only way to console the infant was to hold him aloft, tiny feet dangling, his armpits cupped between his father's thumbs and index fingers, DeMarco's elbows braced on his knees. Within a minute or two the boy would be asleep, and DeMarco would slip easily into a mood unique to those moments, a contentment so warm and complete that it was closer to bliss than any he had ever imagined.

DeMarco had never before and never since felt such contentment, though moments with Jayme came close — lying together while sunlight streamed through the window, for example, or falling asleep with her hand in his, her breath warm and regular against his chest.

What were the chances he could feel true bliss again, with a woman he adored, a child he cherished?

And what made him think he had the right to deny Jayme that bliss?

After a while he went upstairs and into the bedroom. Jayme was at the bathroom mirror, flossing. She gave him a glance, no smile, then turned away. He started making the bed.

"I've had a couple of thoughts," he told her.

"Two?" she said. "This is a big day for you." And she spit into the sink.

He smiled. Tucked the sheet and light comforter under the mattress on Jayme's side of the bed, because she liked to feel swaddled and properly nested. He didn't like the confinement, preferred his blankets free so he could stick his feet out at night. "How do you feel about me calling Hoyle? I figure it couldn't hurt to pick a medical examiner's brain a bit."

When she offered no reply, he said, "If we can stand the mental whiplash, that is. Brilliant man, but his brain moves like a gerbil on a . . . a . . ."

She looked at him, her face expressionless, and swished mouthwash from cheek to cheek.

He said, "I was trying to think of something that would have a gerbil jumping from place to place, but I'm drawing a blank."

She leaned toward the sink and spit out the mouthwash. Turned on the faucet for a few seconds. Turned it off, wiped her lips, and looked at herself in the mirror.

"Maybe meet him for lunch?" DeMarco said. "What do you think?"

She turned away from the mirror and came to the threshold. Leaned one shoulder against the doorframe, her body a long, graceful diagonal, hands clasped and hanging below her waist, ankles crossed. Gave her head a little toss. "People have to eat," she said.

He stood with a pillow in hand, smiling. Many times he had remarked that Jayme reminded him of a thoroughbred, though she never seemed to understand the analogy, his allusion to stature and grace and elegance all tuned to perfection. There was something indelibly summery about her. Whereas he was a rock in the shade, cold and inflexible, buried up to his neck in the dirt of memory, she remained as frisky as a foal in a sun-drenched meadow. "Maybe it's that mane of hair," he said, thinking out loud.

"Just graduate from non sequitur school?" she asked.

God, she was something. He loved the way she stood up to him. Hit back and never flinched. "My second thought is . . . having a baby is a very big decision. A huge decision. It's not to be rushed. So I suggest that we first decide whether or not we're going to take the case in Youngstown —"

"There it is," she said.

"And if we do, we give it our full attention."

"You are so predictable," she said, and turned back to the sink and mirror.

"But afterward . . ."

Her head slowly pivoted his way.

"Afterward," he said, "if you want, you could maybe stop taking the pill, and we could maybe leave the big decision up to . . . you know."

"Up to who?"

"Fate," he said. "If there is such a thing. Destiny. Whoever or whatever makes the decisions about making babies."

"God?" she said.

48

"Something along those lines. A higher power."

"You mean, like, our station commander?"

He chuckled at the thought. "I just want us to be sure it's the right decision."

"I am sure. But okay, fine, I can wait a couple weeks. Because it's always going to be two to one against you. Me and Big Mama, we've already made our decision."

"That's what you call God? Big Mama?"

"I do now," she said. "So put the pillow down, please."

"Why?"

"Do you always have to be so disobedient? Lay it down."

He placed the pillow against the headboard, heard the first footstep, turned just as she leapt into the air but too late to brace himself. She flew against him and knocked both of them onto the bed.

Six

They arrived at the diner twenty minutes late, Hoyle's pick for a meeting and early lunch. At 11:20 a.m., the gravel parking lot was nearly full. The building was monochromatic on the outside, dull chrome panels and filmy glass, but its crowded, noisy interior was a chaos of bright red. Red counter stools, red vinyl booths, red Formica tabletops, red shirts on the servers, and a tube of red neon light encircling the ceiling. The black-and-white checkerboard floor exacerbated rather than softened the assault of red. A Hank Williams tune playing from ceiling speakers was intermittently discernible above the babble.

Hoyle, in his usual black suit, had commandeered the expansive booth that ran across the full rear of the narrow building. He sat in the center of the bench seat, leaning over an iPad, a smorgasbord of plates covering the rest of his half of the table.

"Looks like he ordered for us," Jayme said as they made their way down the aisle.

DeMarco scanned the plates. A large omelet, creamed chipped beef over grits, two sausage patties, four strips of bacon, hash browns, a bowl of cubed fresh fruit, a smaller bowl filled with pink yogurt, a chicken-fried steak, a wedge of quiche, a sliced avocado covered with salsa, a large mug of coffee, and a glass of water with a wedge of lemon floating inside. Every serving had already been sampled.

Across from these plates, in front of two empty chairs, were two menus, two coffee cups turned upside down on the table, and two red napkins rolled around silverware. "That's all his," DeMarco whispered.

But Jayme, now just a step from the table, had noticed something else. Hoyle had not yet looked up from the iPad to see them approaching because he was scrolling slowly through the profiles on a dating site.

They stood behind the empty chairs for a few moments. Then DeMarco said, "How's the creamed chipped beef, Doctor? I haven't had that since I was a kid."

Hoyle slipped the iPad off the table and laid it screen down beside him. "Superb," he answered, and offered them his version of a smile. "Just as both of you appear to

51

be. Please, have a seat." He waved to the nearest server carrying a coffee carafe. In a moment she was at DeMarco's side.

"Coffee for you two?" she asked.

Both turned their cups upright.

"Like his or regular?"

DeMarco glanced at Hoyle's mug.

"Bulletproof," Hoyle told them.

Jayme said, "Excuse me?"

"It's called bulletproof coffee. Coffee, butter, coconut oil, and cream, blended to a velvety consistency."

"Sounds disgusting," DeMarco said.

"A staple of the keto diet," Hoyle told them. "And surprisingly tasty. The lingering film of oil on the palate is the only drawback I can detect."

Simultaneously Jayme and DeMarco looked up at the server and said, "Regular, please."

She filled their cups. "I'll give you a minute to look at the menus," she said before hurrying away.

Jayme nodded toward Hoyle's array of dishes. "You're on the keto diet?" she asked. "Watching your carbs?"

"In my mind, I am. Still striving to convince my stomach to play along. I have, however, lost one full kilo since I last had the pleasure of your company."

"That's impressive," Jayme said.

"An abundance of water taken with lemon, several times a day, including with every meal, is the key to effective peristalsis and an expeditious removal of carbohydrates from the system."

"Seriously?" Jayme said. "That's how you rationalize grits and creamed chipped beef?"

A blush rose in his ample cheeks. His meager smile widened. "You are indeed a pistol, my dear."

"Fully loaded," DeMarco added.

When the server returned, DeMarco told her, "I'll have the creamed chipped beef, please. On whole wheat toast. Plus," and he pointed at Hoyle's slice of quiche. "Is that spinach?"

"Spinach and bacon," the server said.

"Delightful," Hoyle added.

"And that," DeMarco told her, ignoring the heat of Jayme's gaze on the side of his face. "With some hot sauce, please. And a glass of water. With lemon."

Hoyle smiled approvingly. Jayme did not. DeMarco was supposed to be watching his calories *before* they went into his mouth, not after. Just to drive that point home a little harder, she ordered an egg white omelet and a small bowl of fresh fruit.

For the next several minutes, Jayme and

DeMarco watched Hoyle eating. His movements were, as Jayme had noted at earlier meetings, decorous and precise. He took small bites and chewed slowly, sometimes with eyes closed. After every third or fourth bite, he took a sip of water.

After their orders arrived, Hoyle asked the server to clear his plates, even though half of every dish remained uneaten. "So you are considering another case already? The last one nearly crippled you," he said to De-Marco, then turned his gaze to Jayme. "And nearly got you shot, my dear. Which of you is the glutton for punishment?"

DeMarco smiled at the word *glutton*. Jayme, with her hand beneath the table, squeezed his knee. Then said, "That would be both of us, I guess. Just can't resist the challenge."

"Understandable," Hoyle said, and dabbed at his mouth with the napkin. "It is a fascinating case. No fewer than three suspects identified for the original Cleveland murders, but none charged. Each now likely deceased or too feeble to continue the carnage. Which leaves us in Youngstown, Ohio, with an emulator. Perhaps an admirer of the original miscreant. He kills two men in 1988. Two men and a young woman more recently. Obviously someone with a familiarity with the more distasteful elements of the Cleveland crimes."

DeMarco said, "The only connection between the murders in 1988 and the Cleveland Torso Murders is the dismemberment and decapitation of the victims. But the Youngstown police do think the 1988 killer could be the same one at work now. Whether he's a fan of the Torso Killer or not doesn't seem particularly relevant to me."

Hoyle nodded, sipped his buttery coffee. "A copycat twice removed," he said.

"Twice, three times, four times removed, it really doesn't matter," DeMarco said. "The police have a suspect. The same suspect they've had since 1988. They just can't find enough evidence to make a case against him."

Hoyle nodded, unfazed by DeMarco's impatient tone. "Can we assume competence regarding the earlier as well as the most recent investigation?"

DeMarco answered, "We shouldn't assume anything."

"We know the basics of sociopathy," Jayme told Hoyle. "We're hoping you could take us a little deeper than that."

"I would suggest," Hoyle answered, "that you will be looking not for a sociopath but

55

a psychopath. Although the two types do share qualities in common — a proclivity for violent behavior, lack of remorse, lack of a moral compass — the sociopath tends to be un- or underemployed, easily agitated, prone to fits of rage, whereas the psychopath maintains an emotional detachment. He's intelligent, cunning, manipulative, quite possibly a very successful and charismatic individual. The sociopath is a loner; he tends to act spontaneously, often in a chaotic or disorganized manner. Which means he can get sloppy, is more likely to make mistakes. The psychopath is a meticulous planner. And, considering the penchant for dismemberment, one with a knowledge of human anatomy."

"So," Jayme said, "around one percent of fifty or so million men. In this country alone."

"A rather large field to interview," Hoyle conceded. "But considerably smaller if we tighten the scope to psychopaths from Youngstown and its corporate limits. Not that all psychopaths grow up to be serial killers. Some make very successful car salesmen."

"Or lawyers," Jayme added with a smile.

"Politicians," Hoyle said. "Doctors. Professors. Intelligence agents."

"Hollywood producers."

"Wall Street tycoons."

"Probably even medical examiners," Jayme teased.

"Oh, quite probable indeed," Hoyle said.

DeMarco was growing restless. "Back to the dismemberment," he said. "We're not talking about deboning here. Head and limbs. Anybody who has carved a turkey can cut up a body. Especially with a Sawzall."

Hoyle asked, "A reciprocating saw is known to be the instrument used?"

"For the three in Youngstown, yes," De-Marco said. "Also, we can't limit our parameters to Youngstown. He could come from outside the area. Maybe he's just using Youngstown for his hunting grounds."

"Possible," Jayme said. "But he seems to know the neighborhoods well enough to move bodies around in them without being seen."

DeMarco said, "I know the neighborhoods well enough to move a few bodies around."

"Case solved," Hoyle said with a grin.

Only Jayme smiled. Hoyle, seeing DeMarco's scowl deepen, continued more solemnly. "Your individual enjoys all aspects of his crime. Choosing his victim. Lying in wait for just the right moment to strike. Dismembering the body. Are you aware that some of the Cleveland victims were still alive when decapitated?"

DeMarco nodded. "I read that, yes. But Cleveland is irrelevant."

"Were any of the recent victims still alive during decapitation?"

"We don't know that yet," Jayme told him. "But we'll find out."

"Do," said Hoyle. "The psychopath enjoys carnage in all its forms. If he happens upon the scene of an accident, he will stand by and watch the victims suffer rather than come to their aid. Most likely, he will photograph their pain."

"Too bad we can't stage an accident and see who turns up," Jayme said.

Hoyle appeared to take her joke seriously. "I have often thought it unfortunate that all newborns aren't subjected to an MRI before they get sent home. Psychopathy has its beginnings in the womb. A failure of certain parts of the brain to fully develop."

Jayme asked, "And that can be identified with a scan?"

"Indeed," Hoyle said, and dabbed the napkin to his lips. "Psychopaths show markedly different levels of brain activity compared to non-psychopaths. Less activity in the amygdala and ventromedial prefrontal cortex, for example, and heightened activity in the insula and striatum."

"Meaning what?" DeMarco asked.

"Decreased empathy for the plight of others, decreased fear of consequences."

"But sociopathy," Jayme said, "is more likely to be the result of childhood trauma, neglect, repeated abuse of one type or another. Am I right, Doctor?"

"You are," he said.

"So I wonder if any current subjects could be compelled to undergo an MRI?"

"How would that tie anybody to the murders?" DeMarco asked. "And even if somebody were charged, it would provide a great defense. My deformed brain made me do it."

"Understood," Hoyle said. "The neurology is not your concern."

"I prefer to stick with what we know," DeMarco told him. "The 1988 murders were committed the same night, apparently when both men were together. The recent three took place one at a time over the course of a month."

"With no similar events in the intervening years?"

DeMarco said, "I'm assuming we'll learn that in the briefing. If their suspect has lived in Youngstown continuously from 1988 to the present. If there have been any similar homicides in other parts of the country during any years he might have been away from Youngstown. And if those incidents can be tied to his known whereabouts during that time."

Hoyle nodded. "And if not," he said, "you're wondering about the hiatus."

"Is it realistic?" DeMarco asked. "Two killing sprees thirty-two years apart, with nothing in between?"

Hoyle said, "We have to allow for the possibility of two wholly different motives."

"By the same killer?" Jayme asked.

"Taking a life," Hoyle told her, "is an extreme action. It requires a trigger. One might go an entire lifetime, or only thirty-two years, before that trigger is pulled."

"The first two victims have a possible link to organized crime," Jayme said. "But only the first two. In 1988."

"Which means they might have been assassinations," Hoyle said. "Murder for hire. Thirty-two years pass, and the killer, much older now, reflects fondly on what may have been the high point of his life. His crowning achievement, so to speak."

"And he decides to do it again," Jayme said. "Just for the kicks."

"To prove to himself he can still do it," DeMarco said.

"Or maybe this time the trigger was a midlife crisis," Jayme suggested. "Loss of a job. Loss of a spouse or lover. Or, possibly, the new ones were murder for hire too. By someone with a grudge against all three victims."

"Maybe he just wants to go out with a bang," DeMarco said. "Make his sick mark on society while he still has the strength for it."

They all were silent for a moment, then Jayme said, shaking her head, "Too many possibilities."

Hoyle took a long sip of water. Dabbed at his lips again. And said, theatrically, "*Nothing* is impossible, my dear."

"That's an interesting attitude for a scientist," DeMarco said.

Hoyle leaned back in his booth and crossed his arms over his belly. "Science is an approach, sir, well-suited for the examination of cadavers. But limited, at best, for the examination of a subject as infinitely paradoxical as life."

SEVEN

The RV headed northeast from Aberdeen, Kentucky, at six in the morning, driving into the sun. Jayme took the first and third three-hour shifts at the wheel. Now, late in the day, with the sun well behind them but still too bright in the side mirror, DeMarco, on the fourth shift, drove on cruise control while Jayme slept in the bedroom. His neck and back were tight, his right shoulder aching with occasional searing stabs of muscle pain. Yet he felt good. Strangely content. Maybe it was the act of coming home. Maybe the prospect of a new investigative challenge. Maybe it was the syrupy, quicksand voice of Rachael Yamagata on Sirius radio singing "Meet Me by the Water," or the thought of Jayme's smile as she slept, or the lulling hum of rubber over concrete. Maybe it was everything in total, the known and unknowable, the moment itself. He felt a little dopey with contentment, even though he knew it would not last.

A while later, Jayme came wandering out of the bedroom, moving unsteadily toward her captain's seat. She kissed the top of his head before sitting down. "I can take over early if you want me to, babe."

"I'm good," he told her.

"Rolling down the highway."

"Rolling like a river."

Neither spoke for a while. But he was aware when Jayme leaned forward in the seat to read a highway sign. Aware when she looked up at the directional indicator in the corner of the rearview mirror.

"Babe?" she said.

"Hmm?"

"Did you miss a turn?"

"I don't think so."

"You're way too far east of where we ought to be."

"Really?" he said.

"We should be heading north on 79 by now. We should be close to Morgantown."

"You mean we're not?" His satisfied smile gave him away.

"All right," she said. "What's going on here?"

"I booked us a room in Berkeley Springs."

"I thought you wanted to get home tonight."

"Tomorrow's good. Or maybe the day after. We'll get there eventually. And then we'll visit the sheriff and tell him we're on board."

"This isn't like you."

"Who is it like?"

She turned sideways in her chair and leaned toward him. "What's your plan, Strangelove?"

"Tonight we'll get a nice dinner and sleep in a big comfortable bed. I scheduled you for a spa treatment tomorrow morning at nine. Manicure, pedicure, facial scrub, mud bath, hot rocks massage . . ."

"Hot rocks?" she said.

"Maybe it's cold rocks, I don't remember. I know it involves rocks. You're getting the whole megillah."

"I never had a megillah before, but it sounds wonderful. And what will *you* be doing all day?"

"A long, hot sauna is all I ordered. But that mud bath is starting to sound kind of appealing too. Maybe even the acupuncture treatment."

She reached out to rub his shoulder. "I would love to be covered in mud with you. But why are you doing all this?"

"It's going to get crazy soon."

"In other words, you're warning me that

you will get crazy soon."

"I've been told that I sometimes develop tunnel vision when working a case."

"I wonder who told you that."

"Someone who cares," he said.

The afternoon light was low and soft, the sky clear, the road ahead flanked by fields of corn. The RV's shadow ran ahead of the vehicle, showing the way. Van Morrison's "Caravan" was playing on the radio now, and DeMarco felt as if his own body was on cruise control too. He powered down his window halfway, inhaled the warm, fresh air.

He said, "I think this might be what happiness feels like."

EIGHT

The tranquility Jayme and DeMarco enjoyed during their day of spa treatments stayed with them for most of forty hours, precisely until 9:00 a.m. Monday morning, when Mahoning County sheriff Ben Brinker paused before opening the conference room door on the fourth floor of the justice center.

"Just so you know," he said, speaking first to Jayme, then to DeMarco, who had already begun to frown, "Detective Olcott is perfectly okay with having you guys on the team. He's a very mellow guy. Sort of bookish; some might even say nerdy. Very smart. Plays everything close to the vest."

"But?" DeMarco said.

"Fascetti is, uh, a little put out right now. But he'll come around. Just give him a chance to get to know you. Maybe take them both out for a couple of beers some night soon."

"Judging by the way you're looking at

me," Jayme said, "I'm guessing that the operative word regarding Fascetti is *misogynist*?"

Brinker sucked air in through his teeth. "So maybe 'Old World sensibility' would be the best way to describe him."

"I won't take any crap from him," Jayme said.

"Wouldn't want you to," the sheriff answered.

DeMarco stepped closer to the door. "Let's get this over with."

Inside the room, cold air was blowing through the ceiling vents, bright morning light streaming through the large tinted windows. The solar film coating the glass gave the world outside a greenish hue.

Detective Olcott, fortyish and fit, clean-shaven and blue-eyed, with thinning blond hair combed straight back from a prominent widow's peak, rose from his seat near the center of the long table. Detective Fascetti, older, broader, and at least five inches shorter than his slim, five-foot-eleven partner, remained seated at the far end, arms crossed over his belly. He had a full head of curly black hair, and a pencil moustache that was inexpertly trimmed, higher on the left, which made part of his upper lip look slightly swollen, and endowed him with the appearance of a perpetual sneer. A pair of wire-rim bifocals rested near the tip of a fleshy Roman nose. Both men were dressed in black slacks and white shirts, though Fascetti's looked slept in, Olcott's fresh from the closet. Olcott wore a perfectly knotted blue-striped tie, Fascetti's mud-brown, with both tie and shirt loose at the neck.

Lined up atop the table were four file storage boxes of sturdy white cardboard. Written in black marker on the side of each box was a case name: Hufford, Jerome; Lewis, Samantha; Brenner, Justin; Brogan/Talarico 1988. All four boxes looked new.

Brinker made the introductions. Detective Olcott shook first Jayme's hand, then De-Marco's. Fascetti greeted both with a small nod.

Olcott said, "It's good to meet you both. I followed the Huston case, Sergeant. What a horrible thing that was."

DeMarco glanced at the man's left hand, saw a gold band. "You have kids, Detective?"

"Two boys. Though mine are older than Huston's were."

"Still," DeMarco said, "you *know.*"

"Just the thought of it sends a chill down my back."

DeMarco nodded, thought, *I like this guy.*

68

Then he returned his gaze to Fascetti.

They locked eyes for a few seconds, then Fascetti regarded Jayme. His gaze traveled down her body, then up again. He said, "How tall are you?"

"Taller than you," she said.

His wince was barely detectable, a quick tightening around the eyes. "You weren't involved in that case, were you?"

"If she had been," DeMarco answered, "we'd have solved it in half the time. She was instrumental in the Kentucky case. Not only took down the perp but saved his life afterward."

"A real Wonder Woman," Fascetti said.

And Jayme said, "So you're into comic books, Detective?"

Fascetti sat motionless but for one finger tapping the conference table. "For the record, I'm not in favor of employing outside help."

"That's not your call," Sheriff Brinker said. "So let's all just settle down and play nice. Everybody have a seat."

He pulled out the chair at the near end of the table, facing Fascetti, and sat. DeMarco waited for Jayme to take a seat next to the sheriff, but instead she moved three chairs down to sit beside Fascetti, who gave her a

69

long, scowling look that only broadened her smile.

Oh boy, DeMarco thought, and took the seat across from Olcott.

"Here's how this game is going to be played," the sheriff said. "DeMarco and Matson will be working the case as independent private investigators temporarily attached to the office as consultants. Any new leads or other information they come across will be shared ASAP. Everybody reports to me. I expect full cooperation on all sides. I'll make sure each of you has everybody else's cell number, but just keep the egos in check. We have three new victims and three new families waiting for closure. I think if we keep that first and foremost in our minds, we can all behave professionally."

Jayme put a hand on the nearest box. "Can we get copies of these files to take home with us?"

"Those are your copies," the sheriff said. "We have the originals. And by the way," he said with a glance at Olcott, then one at Fascetti, "let's keep all this on the down low for now. As of this moment, the only other people who know about our new recruits are Chief Davis of the municipal police, and Colonel Mesco of the highway patrol. I'd like to keep it that way for as long as we can."

DeMarco said, "The first time we flash our IDs or introduce ourselves . . ."

"Understood," Brinker replied. "And given your high profile, Sergeant, there's bound to be some kind of fallout when the word gets around. Could be negative, could be positive. Probably a little of both. But it's best to postpone the fallout as long as possible. So *nobody* talks to the press until this thing is over."

Fascetti said, "You two rock stars licensed to work in Ohio?"

The sheriff spoke before DeMarco could. "Their PI applications were endorsed and faxed to ODPS this morning. These two have fifteen and twenty-five years of law enforcement experience respectively. Their records are superlative."

Hearing this, DeMarco smiled at his old teammate's hyperbole. Jayme's record was superlative. DeMarco's had a blemish or three, not least of them his recent extended medical leave, which, apparently, the sheriff had not chosen to share with the detectives.

Olcott asked, "Does this mean you're done with the staties?"

DeMarco told him, "We'll be wrapping that up this afternoon."

"What does that mean?" Fascetti said.

Again the sheriff was quick to respond. "Tend your own garden, Detective. Everybody. Tend your own garden, and don't be trampling on anybody else's tomatoes. Understood?"

"Roger that," Olcott answered.

"Yes sir," said DeMarco, and was echoed by Jayme.

Fascetti rolled his eyes.

The sheriff leaned forward across the table. "If four is too many for this case," he said, "I can make the necessary reassignments."

Fascetti's sagging cheeks glowed red. "I started on this case, I'm going to finish on it. Besides, we're close. We know who did it."

The sheriff looked from DeMarco to Jayme when he said, "We think we know. We just don't have enough to charge him yet."

"We have hair," Fascetti said. "We have means and opportunity. We can link him to the double homicide in 1988."

DeMarco said, "I'm guessing he'd be in jail now if you had DNA."

"We have two hair shafts found on the girl," the sheriff told him. "No follicles, so no DNA."

"And even if we did," Olcott said, and

72

shrugged. "A few years back, the FBI tossed a lot of its database of results from hair analysis. Turns out DNA identification from hair isn't as accurate as we used to think."

"But protein matching through hair is a promising science," the sheriff added. "Just not promising enough yet."

Fascetti said, "We have a witness."

Both Jayme and DeMarco reacted to that statement with raised eyebrows. DeMarco was about to ask *Then what are we doing here?* when the sheriff said, in a slow, deadpan tone, "We have a child who claimed, in 1988, that he saw the subject at the scene around the time the bodies were deposited. But the boy was five years old at the time. Watching from a second-floor window in the middle of the night."

"And he's still around?" Jayme asked. "Still stands by that story?"

"He's not so sure anymore," Olcott said.

Fascetti said, "The subject knew the victims. He was employed by a rival mob boss."

"He was ground floor at best," the sheriff said. "A glorified errand boy."

"Button man," said Fascetti. "According to Koenig."

"And Koenig is . . . ?" Jayme asked.

"Detective," Fascetti said. "Retired. He

put more bums behind bars than you two rock stars can even imagine."

"He led the investigation," the sheriff explained.

DeMarco pointed to the box marked Brogan/Talarico 1988. "It's in there?"

Sheriff Brinker nodded. "He lives in Naples, Florida, now. You can Skype him if you have any questions."

"From what I recall," DeMarco said, "the Youngstown organization wasn't into slicing and dicing. Car bombs were SOP. Occasionally a bullet to the back of the head, and on rare occasion a ligature."

Jayme glanced at her notes. "I still don't understand how," she said, and quickly scanned what she had written. "This guy you're looking at for the three recent homicides. He would be . . . how old now?"

"Fifty-eight," the sheriff said. "Goes by Freddy Costa, a.k.a. Frederich Constantine."

"Is that Russian?" DeMarco asked.

"Townie, actually," the sheriff said. "Born and raised. Grandfather was an immigrant."

Olcott said, "All in all, there are more differences than similarities between the murders."

Fascetti continued to scowl. "It's the freaking media trying to tie all three together, not us. Sells papers, that's all. Nobody in his right mind is thinking that the Cleveland Torso Murders are in any way related. Talarico and Brogan, plus these recent three? That's a different story."

Jayme spoke directly to Olcott. "What similarities and differences?"

"The Torso Murderer had good knife skills," Olcott told her. "Not so much the 1988 guy. The new guy? A little of both. Brenner's and Hufford's decapitations were fairly neat. But his hand seemed to get a little shaky on the female. Didn't finish the job. Additionally, the Cleveland victims were all indigents and transients. Drunks, vagrants, and prostitutes. The ones from 1988 and now were all middle-class or higher. Several of the first batch were still alive when decapitated. As were Talarico and Brogan."

Jayme cocked her head. "But not Brenner, Lewis, or Hufford?"

"Asphyxiated," Olcott answered. "Residue from a wide tape such as duct tape or Gorilla Tape was found around the wrists and ankles of the male victims, though none was discernible on Samantha Lewis. A plastic bag was found under her body."

"Fingerprints?" DeMarco asked.

"Plenty. But none in the databases. No

signs of recent blunt trauma, no defensive wounds or other signs of struggle on any of the three. We have what appear to be stun gun marks on Hufford, none visible on the other two vics."

"That doesn't rule out stun guns for them," DeMarco said.

"It does not. Hufford was by far the biggest of the three, so it probably took multiple and longer jolts to subdue him."

"What about the state of dress?" Jayme asked.

Ben nodded. "Most of the Torso Murder vics were at least partially denuded. Males were often left wearing nothing but their socks, which is exactly how Brogan, Talarico, Brenner, and Hufford were found. All with four limbs and head completely separated from the body. Again, just like the Torso Murders."

"Castrated?" DeMarco asked.

"Yep. All four."

"And Samantha?" Jayme asked.

"Completely dressed, partial decapitation."

"Sounds to me," Jayme said, "like the new guy took more pleasure from killing the males. He liked to see them suffer, and spent some time denigrating the bodies."

"So you're a psychologist now," Fascetti said.

She smiled. "Master's degree. Six credits short of the doctorate."

Fascetti turned his head, looked out the window at the green-tinted clouds.

The sheriff said, "Detective Koenig figured Costa as a copycat. Maybe a fan of the Cleveland murderer. As to why he handled Lewis differently, if, in fact, it was him —"

"It was him," Fascetti said.

"If it was," Brinker continued, "who knows why he treated her differently? Maybe his paternal instinct kicked in."

DeMarco asked, "He's lived in Youngstown all this time?"

"Koenig put him away for four years on assault," Brinker said. "After that it was straight back home again. He lives in a duplex on the north side. Brier Hill, to be exact. Or what's left of it."

"And there have been no similar murders since he returned?" DeMarco asked. "Other than the recent three?"

"Multitudes of every other kind," the sheriff told him, "but no, none the least bit similar."

Jayme said, as she bent forward over her notes again, "How certain are you that the hairs found on the girl belong to Costa?"

"They're a possible match," the sheriff told her. "Color, age, but without DNA . . ."

"Even with," Olcott reminded him.

"So," she said, "your only evidence against Costa . . . is hair that can't be positively tied to him, and the testimony of a man who can't or won't affirm what he said he saw as a child?"

"He freaking cuts his victims to pieces," Fascetti argued. "MO is just as telling as DNA in my book. It was good enough for Koenig, it's good enough for me. And would be for you if you'd get your heads out of your asses."

DeMarco watched his old teammate take in a long, slow breath. Saw those big hands that used to haul in high passes now go flat atop the table. So DeMarco pushed his chair back, turned to Jayme, and said with a smile, "Sounds like we have a good place to start, partner. Let's see how the subject and witness react to a couple of new faces."

"Show them your press clippings," Fascetti said. "I'm sure Costa will drop to his knees and confess to everything."

Jayme smiled. "He never did that for you, Detective? Must be because you have such a friendly face."

Everyone else sat motionless for a few tense moments. Then DeMarco said, "For the sake of clarity, anybody mind if we run through all this one last time?"

Fascetti grinned. "Memory starting to fade on you, pops?"

DeMarco returned the smile. "Anxious to hit the playground, junior?"

"It's all in the reports," Fascetti told him.

DeMarco kept smiling. "I like the sound of your voice."

Now Fascetti turned to Jayme. "Did you know his gate swings both ways?"

"Enough," Sheriff Brinker said. He shook his head, clicked his teeth together. Then he let out a breath, and turned to DeMarco. "Where do you want to start?"

"Power tools," DeMarco said. And to Olcott, "Specifically?"

"In all likelihood, a reciprocating saw," Olcott told him. "Long bimetal blade, what they call a demolition blade. Cuts through flesh like butter but can leave a lot of bone fragments behind."

"And did you find those bone fragments?"

"Yes sir. Killer did the butchering, spread the pieces a few feet apart, and drove away. Except, as you know, in regard to the girl. She was the only one intact."

"So he didn't scatter the pieces after dismemberment?" Jayme said. "That's unlike the '88 murders, isn't it?"

"It is," Brinker said. "Those bodies were dismembered in the woods, approximately forty yards from where the pieces were then laid out on the short grass."

"Why treat the girl differently?" DeMarco asked. "No dismemberment, only partial decapitation. No evidence she was bound before death."

The sheriff shrugged. "The blade broke. The battery died. Somebody came along and spooked him. He didn't have the stomach for chopping up a girl. Maybe he knew her, liked her. Maybe she reminded him of somebody. Take your pick."

"If he knew her . . ." Jayme said.

Olcott answered. "We interviewed all known associates. But remember, she was a college girl. Over a week's time she could have come into contact with any one of the thirty-two hundred students, faculty, or staff on campus. Or it could have been somebody from her high school, her hometown. Somebody she used to date. Somebody who wanted to date her but couldn't get her interest. Could have been a clerk from the damn convenience store where she bought her coffee."

"If it was somebody who knew her," DeMarco mused, "that would change everything. It would make her the centerpiece.

The pivot on which all three murders turn."

The sheriff said, "We have no way of knowing if it was personal or not, or why she was handled differently. Could have been for a mechanical reason. Could have been as simple as an interruption."

"And you can't find a single thing that ties all three victims to each other?" DeMarco asked.

"Totally different worlds."

Jayme said, "Then it had to have been random. Son of Sam–like."

Olcott said, "Except that Berkowitz shot and walked away. Our guy hung around long enough to cut up the bodies. And they were found in places where public visibility at night was very low, but high during the daytime. So that part wasn't random, wasn't by chance."

"So maybe he picked the victims at random," DeMarco said, "wherever he saw the opportunity. Then got them into his car somehow —"

"Ted Bundy," Jayme said.

"Right. He got them into his car, used a stun gun, secured them, transported them to places he'd already picked out. And that's where he killed and butchered them."

"Planned randomness?" Jayme asked.

DeMarco, thinking out loud, said, "He

went out to kill. Just didn't know who. But he already had his butchering place picked out. He just needed to sit and wait, build up his courage, wait for that demented little voice in his head to tell him when to get busy."

Fascetti scowled, Olcott sat with one eyebrow cocked, and Sheriff Brinker said, "Could be. Could be. Or maybe not."

DeMarco asked, "As far as you can tell, he didn't take any souvenirs?"

"Apparently the killing and butchering was enough for him."

"That's unusual," Jayme said.

Fascetti told her, "Berkowitz didn't take trophies."

"But he visited the victims' graves. The graves were his trophies." Again she turned her eyes to Sheriff Brinker.

"We have cameras up where we can," he told her. "Some from a long way off. Still haven't caught anybody visiting the graves."

DeMarco said, "This guy's a strange one."

Fascetti, looking bored, rolled his eyes. "Any nutcase who kills and butchers human beings is a strange one."

"Can't argue with that," DeMarco conceded.

"Look," said Fascetti. "Costa does a job for the mob in 1988. Talarico's pissed somebody off. The boss tells Costa, there's too much heat on us already, so make it look like some weirdo did it. So he takes out Talarico. The lawyer's in the way so he gets the same treatment. And guess what — Costa gets away with it. But maybe, with the beheading and all, he's gone a little too far even for the mob. They want nothing to do with him after that. Thirty some years later, his life's shit, he's turned into a cat lady, and who does he blame for that? The cops. He's been stewing in that same juice all this time. A couple of months ago he starts thinking, why not have a little more fun before I die? Watch the cops chase their own tails again."

"So why pick a girl this time?" Jayme asked. "And why treat her body differently?"

"Because he's a twisted son of a bitch, that's why. My guess is he was going to rape her. Probably hasn't dipped his wick since the turn of the century. But somebody came along and spooked him before he had the chance to drop his drawers."

"He planned to rape her *after* partially decapitating her?" Jayme asked.

"What part of *twisted* don't you understand?"

Jayme ignored the remark. She asked the sheriff, "Do we know where she was prior to her death?"

"We do not."

"Her family has no idea?"

"Brother and father are all she has. And they say no, they don't."

"Have they been told about the gray hair?"

"We haven't released that detail. Unfortunately, the decapitation detail leaked out about Brenner. Naturally, the public is assuming it happened to all three victims."

"If Samantha's family was informed about the hairs, it might help them determine where she could have been that evening."

Brinker thought for a moment, then said, "If you want to pursue that, discreetly —"

"Now wait a minute," Fascetti said. "We can't be releasing proprietary information to the public just because Nancy Drew here has a question."

Jayme turned to him. "You think if word gets out the killer has gray hair, he's going to start dyeing it? If he has a handful of functional brain cells, he's dyed it already."

Olcott said, "All we can tell from the hair is race. Caucasoid. At least middle-aged. Costa has been asked for a hair sample but has refused. Last time I saw his hair, it was that ugly yellowish red you get from Grecian Formula."

DeMarco shook his head. "None of it

holds together," he said. "There's not a single piece of the puzzle that fits another piece."

"That's why you two are here," the sheriff told them. "Find the rest of the pieces."

Then Brinker turned to Olcott. "You mind giving our new colleagues a hand with these boxes?"

"No sir, I do not."

"Then we'll leave you to it." Brinker stood, turned, and went to the door. With a hand on the doorknob, he paused to turn his eyes on Fascetti, who was still stiff in his chair, arms across his belly. "Detective?" the sheriff said, and held the door open.

By slow degrees Fascetti pulled his arms apart, raised his hands over his head, laced his fingers together and cracked his knuckles. Eventually he stood and, walking behind Jayme, touched a hand to her shoulder. "Happy reading, Trooper," he said. "If you run into any big words in there, give me a call. I'll explain them to you."

She reached up to pat his hand. "Very pusillanimous of you, Detective. I'm so pococurante right now."

The crooked look on Fascetti's face made him appear as if he'd just inhaled a rotten frog. It was the prettiest sight DeMarco had seen all morning.

Olcott was able to stifle his laughter only until his glowering partner was out the door.

NINE

They were back inside the car, waiting for the air conditioner to do its magic, the four file boxes lined up on the back seat, when Jayme said, "So what did you think of Fascetti and Olcott?"

"Fascetti is a real piece of work, isn't he? He reminds me of that guy from *Seinfeld*. George somebody. The obnoxious short one who's always complaining."

"You're lucky there are reruns," Jayme said, "or I wouldn't know who you're talking about half the time."

"How can you not know the characters from *Seinfeld*?"

"I was a child, and my family wasn't interested in a show about New Yorkers. I'm still not."

DeMarco pulled the harness over his shoulder, then slipped his left arm through it so that only the belt held him in place.

"What were those big words you threw at him?"

"Pusillanimous means cowardly. Poco-curante is an Italian word. To be indifferent."

"I've never loved you more," DeMarco said.

She grinned. "I wish I could see his face when he looks up the definitions. Why are you wearing your seat belt like that?"

"The shoulder harness gives me a stiff neck."

"Since when?"

"Since this morning, I guess."

"Did the thought of coming here this morning make you tense?"

"Nothing makes me tense." He put a hand on the gearshift, checked his mirrors, started the engine, and flashed her an exaggerated grin. Then pulled away from the curb.

"You mind if we don't head home just yet?" Jayme asked. "I showed you my childhood playground in Kentucky. So how about you show me Ryan DeMarco's Youngstown."

"You're not going to find butterflies and summersweet here," he told her. "Unless we hit the MetroParks. I could go for that. Being in the woods makes me horny."

"Breathing makes you horny," she said.

"Show me where you used to live. Where you and Ben played football and made all the cheerleaders swoon."

"Nothing's where it used to be."

"Just do it," she said. From the console she took her MP3 player and plugged it into the car's sound system. "You want to start with Springsteen's 'Glory Days' or Mellencamp's 'Small Town'? No, wait — how about 'I did it my way!' "

"Like that's on your playlist."

" 'Memories,' " she sang, " 'from the da da dada da . . .' "

"I miss Fascetti already."

TEN

From the justice center, DeMarco drove south, crossed the Mahoning River, merged smoothly with the heavy traffic. Jayme was less interested in looking at the passing buildings than in watching his face and eyes for subtle indications of his emotions. He had grown quiet since leaving the parking lot, and sat hunched slightly forward in his seat. And that exaggerated grin after he said he wasn't tense — he knew he was lying and so did she.

And now she wondered about the source of that tension. Taking on another case? Being back in his old hometown? He had grown up only forty minutes from his house in Pennsylvania, but she had never thought to ask how frequently he returned to Youngstown. Did he ever visit old haunts, drop in on old friends? If so, he kept those excursions to himself. Her knowledge of his past couldn't fill a Post-it Note.

"Gibson Park is over that way," he said without expression, and nodded to his left. "South Side Park is off to your right."

"That's where you played as a boy?"

His brow wrinkled. "Played what?"

"Games," she said. "Tag. Hide-and-seek. Whatever you and your little friends played."

He shook his head. "No."

Several minutes and red lights later he pulled to the curb. Off to the left, thirty yards beyond a cyclone fence with a no trespassing sign attached to the gate, was an impressive three-story granite building, its windows boarded shut. "That's my old high school," he told her.

"It's a beautiful building. Can we get out and walk around?"

"You see the sign, right?"

"I just thought that somebody of your standing . . . former All-Conference football star . . ."

"All-City," he said.

"They must have surely put up a statue to you."

"One in every hallway. Have you seen enough?"

"What's your hurry? Tell me what it was like back in the olden days."

He rolled his eyes at the word *olden*. Then answered flatly. "It was school. Nobody likes school."

"Lots of people like school. You must have enjoyed something about it."

He pursed his lips. Thought for a few moments. "Around back there's an entrance to the park. I used to love running the trails in there. Just running for the fun of it."

"You want to do it now?" she said. "I'm game."

"Too hot. Too many bugs."

So she said nothing for a while. Stole glances at his face as he continued to gaze across the street.

Finally he said, "So that's the nickel tour."

"Wow, a penny a minute. I think I overpaid."

He didn't even look at her. Smiled a melancholy smile. "As long as we're in the neighborhood," he said, "you mind if we visit the dead?"

"Isn't that what we've been doing?"

"I mean the cemetery."

At first she thought he meant the cemetery where his son was buried, then realized that he was probably referring to his parents' graves. They, of course, would have been buried in Youngstown. Yet in all the time she had known him, he had never once mentioned their graves. But now he wanted to visit them? To share them with her? She didn't know whether to be nervous or happy.

She said, "I'm not sure I can stand much more excitement."

"Let's find out," he said.

After five additional minutes of low-speed zigzagging through the neighborhood, De-Marco drove down a short entrance road into a cemetery. Many of the stones nearest the road were lopsided, the faces eroded, engravings indecipherable.

He shut off the engine and removed the keys. "We have to walk from here."

At the front of the car, she took his hand. "How long since you've been here?" she asked.

"It's been a while."

His parents had separate gravestones, his father's a flat, grass-level stone of gray granite, approximately the size of a shoebox, his mother's four times larger and five years newer, a slant marker with a polished black face. His mother had borrowed the money for her husband's stone, which listed only his name and the dates of birth and death. DeMarco had purchased his mother's stone with army pay, and had added the two-line inscription, *Devoted Mother, Peace At Last.*

Both graves were surrounded by over-grown grass, dandelions, and slender weeds growing out of the dead, matted leaves. The smaller stone was coated with a thick layer of dust and old grass clippings. When De-Marco sank to his knees to clean up around his mother's stone, Jayme did so too. In silence they pulled and cropped the grass on all sides. DeMarco finished by using a handful of dead leaves to scour the polished face bright again, then blew bits of leaf out of the engravings, and gave the face a final brush with his hand.

He leaned back and looked at it for a moment, then stood. "I'm ready to go when you are," he said.

Jayme looked up at him. "We're not done yet, are we?"

"Looks good to me."

"But don't you think —"

He interrupted. "I'll get the car cooled off," he told her, and walked away.

Jayme spent the next five minutes clearing the weeds and debris from around his father's headstone. When finished, she filled her hand with a ball of leaves and grass and scoured the face as best she could. His first name was Francis. Francis Joseph De-Marco. She had never once heard Ryan utter his father's name, and only a few times refer to him at all.

And now she remembered Ryan's comments earlier at his old high school, when he had pointed to the woods and said he loved to run the trails just for the fun of it. At the time she had thought, *for the joy of being young.* But now she amended it to *the joy of forgetting.*

She leaned forward, close to the gravestone. "Whatever you did to him, Frankie," she said, "I hope you are appropriately ashamed of yourself."

Then she rose, brushed off her knees, and returned to the car.

ELEVEN

After leaving the cemetery, Jayme asked to visit the mobile home park where DeMarco had lived with his mother and sometimes-father. "There's nothing there anymore," he told her.

"I'd like to see it. How far can it be?"

"It no longer exists."

"So what's there now?"

"What does it matter? The same thing that's all around us. Take your pick."

"You haven't been back, have you?" she asked.

He gave her a *Can we drop this?* look, then turned his eyes to the road again.

She leaned closer, took hold of his arm. "I challenge you to tell me. Exactly what is there now where your trailer used to sit?"

"A car wash," he said.

"Hogwash. In fact, are you sure they even had trailers back then? Maybe you lived in a log cabin."

He tried to hold back his smile. "Maybe you'd like to walk to Pennsylvania."

She squeezed his arm. "Thirty years, Sergeant? And you've never once been back?" She could not comprehend such a possibility. If she lived within forty minutes of the place she grew up, she would return every weekend. To be so close yet keep so distant — it could only be a deliberate choice.

"All right," he said. "I did come back once. It was a couple years after I buried my mother."

"And?"

"What are you, the Grand Inquisitor?"

"Why did you come back? And what did you see when you came back?" She heard the insistence in her voice, knew what it would do to him, so she kneaded his arm while assuming a comical sinister tone. "Answer fully and completely or I will have you toasted like a marshmallow."

Again he smiled. She felt some of the tension go out of his arm. "I came back with a belly full of Jack Daniels, a can of gasoline, and a book of matches. Unfortunately, the place had been razed. Nothing but dirty concrete pads. I have no idea what was later built there, if anything."

She was startled by the image he'd

painted, but tried not to show it. "And you're not the least bit curious to know?"

"Could not care less," he said.

She continued to hold his arm throughout the rest of the drive, and tried not to think of that angry young man coming upon the empty lot, his moment of revenge stolen. All those memories he had wanted to burn to the ground. And what had she done but to unearth those memories again?

Surely one of these days he would share them with her. She had to be patient, let them come at his own pace. Another good reason to avoid the baby discussion for a while? Or a good reason to speed it up?

TWELVE

Their arrival at the barracks thirty minutes later was no less solemn. They spoke briefly with two other troopers, who greeted them like returning heroes, apparently unaware that Jayme and DeMarco had come to finalize their retirement from the state police. Jayme had sent a text to Captain Kyle Bowen, the station commander, alerting him that they would be stopping by, but he must not have shared that information yet with the troopers.

She and DeMarco walked down the short hall to Bowen's office. His door was halfway open. Jayme peeked inside.

Bowen sat behind his desk, leaning back in his chair, frowning as he met her gaze. He shook his head from side to side. He was younger than both of them, and now looked even more boyish than the last time she had seen him — but currently not a happy boy.

Jayme pushed the door open and led the way inside.

Still no one spoke. They sat side by side in the pair of brown vinyl chairs facing his desk.

Finally DeMarco said, "I take it Sheriff Brinker placed a courtesy call."

"Courtesy?" Bowen said. "This is anything but a courtesy."

DeMarco said, "I've been doing this long enough. I need a change. I'm sorry."

"You I can understand," Bowen told him. "I freaking hate it, but I can understand it. But you," he said to Jayme. "This is like treason to me. I can't lose you both."

"My heart's just not in it anymore," she said.

"You don't have to tell me where your heart is. I know where your heart is. But do you understand what you're doing here? Do you understand what you're throwing away?"

"If it's any consolation," DeMarco said, "I've told her the same thing. She's obstinate."

Bowen laid his head forward, placed both hands over his face. When he lowered his hands, dragging them down over his chin and neck, he then spoke directly to Jayme. "He's old," he told her. "He's cranky and mean and emotionally constipated. He's probably even impotent. Does he have you drugged or something?"

Jayme smiled with tears in her eyes. "We love you too," she told him.

DeMarco stood, leaned forward, and put out his hand. Bowen stood, took DeMarco's hand in his. "Tell you what," DeMarco said. "How about if she calls in a domestic disturbance every week or so? You and the boys can come over and rough me up a little bit."

"That would almost be worth it," Bowen said.

Thirteen

After a tedious hour with Human Resources, and another twenty awkward minutes working their way toward the front entrance while one trooper after another wished them well, DeMarco and Jayme walked toward his car in the parking lot. "How are you feeling?" he asked. He had never before noticed the soft crunch of the gravel chips beneath his feet.

"A little strange," Jayme said.

"You can always go back, you know."

"I know. How are you doing?"

They reached the car, and stood side by side by the passenger door. He said, "I just now realized that nobody will ever call me Sergeant again."

"I will."

"I can't tell if what I'm feeling is emptiness, or freedom."

"It's probably both," she told him. "We've given up one of the ways we've defined ourselves."

He placed a hand between her shoulders, leaned forward to open her door. "So you're saying I no longer have a definition."

She slid past him to sit down. Looked up at him and smiled. "Your definition was blurry to begin with. Whoever drew you didn't color inside the lines."

Before returning them to his house, DeMarco swung by the post office to pick up his recent mail. Among the accumulation of junk mail was a cardboard box big enough to hold five reams of printer paper. It was wrapped in brown paper and sealed shut with several yards of clear shipping tape, with a return address he recognized.

He placed the box and the bundle of mail in the back seat, then climbed in behind the wheel. "What's in the box?" Jayme asked.

"No idea. It's from Tom's mother-in-law. Rosemary O'Patchen."

"Another Rosemary," Jayme said.

He looked in his side mirror, then the rearview mirror, then pulled away from the curb. "Excuse me?"

"Rosemary Toomey. The librarian? Da Vinci Cave Irregulars?"

"Sorry," he said, "my mind was elsewhere. But yes, another Rosemary."

"And what has Rosemary O'Patchen sent you? Copies of Tom's books?"

"Maybe," DeMarco said. But it hadn't felt like books. Felt heavier. Denser. More portentous than books.

He pushed the feeling aside. Drove home. Parked in front of his garage, across the dirt alley from his backyard, where a day earlier they had parked the RV beside Jayme's silver Nissan, which was now blanketed with weeks of gray dust, windblown grass clippings, and hardened bird droppings.

Before climbing out, Jayme told him, "I'm going to run home and pick up a few things. And get my own mail. I'll help you carry in those files first."

"No, you won't," he said. He took the keys from the ignition and held them out to her. But she didn't reach for them.

"I'll take my car," she said. "Run it through the car wash while I'm at it."

"See you in a bit."

She returned some ninety minutes later, arms loaded with clothes on plastic hangers, to find him sitting on the living room sofa. The contents of Rosemary's cardboard box, a dozen cheap composition books and stacks of loose paper, were spread over his coffee table. The look on his face struck her as somewhere between annoyance and panic.

"What's all this?" she asked.

"Tom's papers."

"Okay." She laid her clothes across his La-Z-Boy. "And why are they here?"

"Apparently Tom's audience is clamoring for more. According to his publisher. So Rosemary wants me to sift through all this and . . . put together a book."

She lowered herself beside him. Leaned forward to survey the papers. The cover of each composition book was inked with a range of dates, month/day/year–month/day/year, the pages filled with Tom's handwriting. The loose papers appeared to be printouts of emails, advice to students and strangers, ideas for stories, screenplays, novels, essays, short poems, reflections on random subjects . . .

"Nothing personal," Jayme said, still thumbing through the pages, "but she knows you're not an editor, right?"

He lifted up a notebook, slid from beneath it a single sheet of cream-colored stationery, Rosemary's letter, and handed it to Jayme. She read quickly, scanning the lines:

the big brother he'd always wanted . . . would want you to do it . . . wouldn't trust anyone but you . . . the man who held him in your arms when he died.

"Oy," she said.

"Double oy."

"On the other hand . . . all she's asking is that you," and she looked at the letter again, and read, " 'choose the pieces that show who Tom truly was.' "

"I knew him for less than half a year."

"She just wants you to winnow it down, that's all. Then it will go to the editor."

"I have no idea how to do that. I've never even been to college."

"College is overrated," she told him. "Binge drinking, sex parties, it gets tedious after a while."

He smiled. "I'm barely literate."

"You're more literate than ninety-eight percent of the people I know."

He blew out a slow breath. "It's intimidating. It will be like working two cases at the same time. Three cases counting the one from 1988."

"We can read to each other at night. We'll pick out the pieces you like best. It could be fun. Could maybe even wash the taste of a bad day out of our mouths, so to speak."

"Tom wasn't all happiness and light," he told her.

"Sounds like somebody else I know. Which is probably why Rosemary picked you."

He thought for a few moments. "There *are* bad days coming," he told her. "Four boxes full on the dining room table."

She patted his thigh. "You're preaching to the choir, babe."

FOURTEEN

When Jayme awoke that night and found the other half of the bed empty, then looked at the little clock, 3:21, at first she thought she was still in her grandmother's house in Kentucky, and wondered why the night smelled differently, why the perfume of the summersweet bushes was undetectable, replaced by a vague staleness of air. Then she remembered: *Ryan's house.*

If he had gotten up to work, to get an early start on the files the sheriff had given them, she should smell coffee, but didn't. The bedroom door stood halfway open, with no light beyond. *He lives in such darkness,* she thought. She slid out of bed, picked up the sherpa blanket she had dropped at the foot of the bed five hours earlier, wrapped it around her shoulders, and went into the hallway.

The house was silent. In the living room, where she had hoped to find him asleep on his recliner, the only sign of life was the blue readout on the cable box: 3:23. The kitchen, too, was empty and dark, illuminated only by another digital readout, this one on the range and more greenish than blue. She stood there with head cocked, not even aware that she was staring at the clock until it clicked and changed: 3:24.

Then she felt the soft, warm breeze on her legs. The kitchen door stood open, screen door closed and colored black with darkness.

He was sitting out there on the edge of the low porch, hunched over, elbows on his thighs. She pushed the screen door open softly, let it softly close, crossed to sit beside him. Slipped a hand around his arm. "What's going on in that head of yours?" she asked.

"Nada y nada, bella."

"Liar," she said, and laid her head against his shoulder.

A couple of minutes passed before he spoke. "I can't shake the feeling that maybe this is a mistake."

"What is, babe?"

"Coming back to all this. Especially that business in Youngstown."

"So we're having second thoughts?"

"Tenth and twelfth thoughts."

"Are you sure it's about the homicides? Not that box of stuff from Tom? Or maybe it's about Laraine?"

He shrugged. Watched the stars awhile. "There were more stars in Kentucky," he said.

She turned her head against him, kissed his shoulder through the T-shirt.

He lowered his gaze. Studied the darkness. In the distance there was a screeching sound, a speeding car taking a turn too fast. Then nothing but a kind of high-altitude rumble.

He said, "All those years with nothing like this, you know?"

"Nothing like what?"

"It was all just so routine. Car wrecks, drunken husbands, hour after hour with a radar gun. Busting a drug dealer here and there. But nothing like this. Three high-profile homicide cases in a row — bam bam bam. Why now?"

"Maybe the universe was waiting until you were ready for them."

"I'm not ready, that's the thing. Maybe it was waiting for you."

"Waiting for the team."

"That day at the spa?" he said. "I almost suggested that we not come back. Just turn ourselves around and drive as far away as we could. I had finally gotten used to not being armed everywhere I went. At first I felt off-balance, was always feeling for it, then surprised when the feeling wasn't there."

"I know," she said. "Me too."

He chewed his bottom lip.

"If we did just take off and go somewhere," she said, "where would we go?"

He thought about it, envisioned a map of the United States, a red line moving straight across it, then suddenly veering left. "Mexico maybe. Baja. The Sea of Cortez. I have visions of us all suntanned and salty, barefoot on the beach with our surf rods and wide-brimmed hats."

"I didn't know you like surf fishing."

"Never tried it. Looks relaxing, though."

"We can pack up and leave in the morning," she told him, then waited a long three minutes for a reply.

He did not want to tell her that he was afraid. That when they had thumbed through the case files before going to bed, a chill of fear had possessed him. She would laugh, say *you aren't afraid of anything.* But that was not true. Some dark assignation lay ahead of him. He could smell it in the air, a vague but distinctly slaughterhouse reek. And he feared it. Did not know the nature of that assignation, only knew that what waited for him was more powerful than he was, and would find him no matter what he decided to do.

"Thing is, I hate backing out of something I agreed to," he told her, and tried for a lighter tone. "Plus I wouldn't want Fascetti thinking he scared us away."

"I keep thinking about the girl. Samantha Lewis. So young and beautiful. Her picture reminds me of my friend MaryKyle, the one who died when I was in high school. I told you about her, right?"

"Mmm-hmm."

"What was done to Samantha . . . and to the men too, all of them . . . If it were me that happened to, I'd want somebody willing to go to the mat for me. Wouldn't you?"

"There's going to be more," he told her. "More violence of some kind. I can feel it in my bones."

"Not if we stop him, there won't."

He said, "How much of this baggage can we carry?"

She took in a slow breath. Released it just as slowly. "We can do whatever you want," she told him. "Wherever you want. What would make you happy?"

"Something more . . . I don't know. Productive. Meaningful."

She wasn't going to argue with him. Better to let him think his own thoughts. He would bring himself around to a decision eventually. Besides, it was nice out here with him and the stars. Everything so hushed and still.

"When I was a kid," he told her, "the only thing I really wanted was to understand."

She waited. When it seemed he had no intention of continuing, she asked, "Understand what?"

"Why life is so ugly. People so cruel to each other. Every chance I got I'd head for the woods in one of the parks, or over to the railroad tracks or down along the river. Figured if I just kept walking, sooner or later I would see or hear something. Some explanation, you know? I felt like I should know it already . . . used to know it. Just needed to find it again. Thing is, and I never realized this until now, but I never looked for that explanation from *people.* Only by getting as far away from people as I could."

She said, "You're still looking for that explanation, aren't you?"

"And beginning to think I've been looking in the wrong direction all this time."

"You mean you *should* be looking to get it from people?"

He shook his head side to side, then

surprised her with what he said next. "The funny thing about those dreams I had in the mountains," he told her, and paused again before he continued. "They felt more real . . . No, that's not right. *I* felt more real. More real than I do right now."

"I'm not sure I understand what you mean."

"I don't know how to express it."

She waited.

"It felt like it was life at a deeper level," he told her. "More meaningful than this one. But in a way I can't quite get a handle on."

She smiled despite the dampness in her eyes. He hadn't meant to offend her or to diminish the importance their relationship. He would never do that.

He made a kind of chuckling sound, a tiny grunt deep in his chest. Then said, "You know I never had anybody I could talk to the way I can with you."

"Not even Ben or one of your other buddies? Not even a girlfriend?"

"I didn't really have friends. Just people I knew."

"Not even your mother?"

"My mother . . . lived on the surface of things. Life was too slippery for her. Never could keep her footing. It was all I could do just to hold her upright."

She searched for her own words then, but soon told herself, *Be still, just listen.*

"Sorry," he said, and smiled to make light of himself. "I don't mean to be so metaphorical. My night sickness, I guess."

"You must have been so lonely as a boy. All alone against the world."

"I guess I never admitted that to myself. Wouldn't let myself admit it."

"You're not still lonely, are you?"

He slipped his arm around her shoulders. Pulled her close. "It's one thing to be alone and lonely," he told her. "And a whole other thing to be lonely with you."

She understood. Remembered the gawky, gangly, lonely girl she used to be. Knew exactly what he meant. And let her silent tears soak into his shirt.

Gawky. Gangly. Jayme hated those words and all of their synonyms. From fourth grade all through high school, those words had defined her. She heard them not only from teachers and classmates but also from her own family. Only her oldest brother, Galen, and her friend MaryKyle refrained from using those words. She never doubted that her family loved her, never doubted that she was bright, a quick learner, but when you are raw and unformed, even love is not enough, and intelligence runs a distant second to pretty.

In college, when finally the boys were taller than her and had no knowledge of her as an awkward child, they said she was beautiful, she was elegant, she took their breath away. She smiled at the compliments but never believed them. Only the mirror told the truth. The child you were never leaves the mirror.

That didn't stop her from trying to erase the child. Too many surrogates for Galen. Too many for MK. Their professions of love left her empty. Only later, years later, did she understand why. To truly love her was to love the gangly child that lived in her. To *see* that child, and to adore her as she was.

She would always remember the moment she met Ryan DeMarco. Her first day with Troop D. He had returned to the barracks late that afternoon, long after everybody else had been introduced to her. She had approached him as he came down the hall with his eyes lowered, held out her hand, said, "Hi. I'm Jayme."

When he looked up and their eyes met, the feeling was immediate. Just like every cliché in every love song ever written. Electricity when their hands touched. A heavy thump deep in her chest. She recognized herself in him and knew that he had recognized himself in her.

"Welcome," he'd said, then looked away, strode away without another word. And every day thereafter, she found herself trying to get close to him. She knew he was still in mourning, estranged from his wife, their only child long dead, but she also knew he felt the pull between them too, knew that was why he always looked at her with hooded eyes, always kept their conversations brief. But she was patient. And finally made her way into his bed. Only to have him pull from her even harder. To suppress every feeling in himself that was healing and good.

Until finally, a mere ten months ago, he had mustered the strength to break from his wife. And turned to who in his emptiness? To Jayme. Where he had always belonged.

Because she knew herself, she knew him. They were two halves of the same whole. The seam that joined them was not smooth, however. His childhood had been far more damaging than hers, had left his edges ragged and torn. His years as a soldier carved other scars, so that the seam between them was tentative in places, the whole always in danger of tearing apart.

So she could never let that happen. To do

so would be to let the gawky, homely, lonely child claim the mirror again. She would always be there in the background, and Jayme was okay with that now, always gave her a smile and a nod, but the foreground belonged to the other Jayme, and that one was determined to rearrange DeMarco's mirror too, to guide that dark and frightened and angry little boy deep into the background where he belonged.

FIFTEEN

It was past noon before they finished going through the four boxes of information. Five hours of sifting through Fascetti and Olcott's reports, the older files pertaining to Brogan and Talarico, the coroner's reports, newspaper clippings and photographs. Both DeMarco and Jayme had copied essential information into their notebooks: names, ages, dates of birth, home addresses, places of employment, times and dates of death, places and times where the bodies or first parts of the bodies were discovered. The cause of death was the same in the three most recent cases: asphyxia.

Talarico and Brogan, on the other hand, were probably both alive when they were butchered in the summer of 1988. Both were killed in the woods alongside the twelfth fairway of the Fonderlac Country Club south of Youngstown, their body parts then scattered across the fairway and green, where the first foursome of the morning discovered them beneath a cloud of raucous crows.

Learning such intimate details of the victims' last minutes, and layering this information atop the pre- and postmortem photos, weighed heavily on both Jayme and DeMarco. The dining room felt small, the padded chairs no longer comfortable. The only windows faced north, and though the small front yard lay in full sunlight, the room felt dim yet too warm.

Jayme pushed herself away from the dining room table and stood. "You want another cup?"

"God no," DeMarco said. "I feel like an acid volcano ready to blow."

Her nose crinkled, and the corner of her mouth twitched in a wince. "That's a pretty picture."

"Sorry," he said.

"So now what?"

"Food."

"I'm not eating anything that's been in your refrigerator for the past three weeks."

"I was thinking croissant sandwiches at Burger King."

She glanced at the clock on the range. "They stopped serving breakfast two hours ago."

"I feel like I need eggs. Something soft and bland."

"Grab your notes," she told him as she picked up her own notebook. "We'll swing by Eat'n Park, then find an empty gazebo somewhere. Wear your walking shoes."

He raised both hands to the ceiling, tried to stretch the kinks out of his back. "Brilliant," he said.

Sixteen

They had avoided discussing the case while eating their egg sandwiches and fruit-and-yogurt bowls at a shelter in Memorial Park. Instead they reread their notes, watched a few joggers, watched people walking their dogs, watched the dogs pooping in the grass. DeMarco thought he might like to have a dog. He'd had a puppy as a boy, but only for a day, until his father came home and found it and silenced its whimpering for good.

Now they were walking. The asphalt path they followed made a wide loop around the park, a little over a half mile in length. They were finishing the first lap when DeMarco started the conversation.

"Three victims. Three different neighborhoods. Three different ages. Two different sexes. Three different lifestyles. No friends or known acquaintances in common."

Jayme read from a pocket notebook with

a yellow cover. "Victims one and three, Brenner and Hufford, both decapitated and emasculated. That matches both Brogan and Talarico. All four were stripped naked except for their socks. That matches victim two from the Cleveland murders."

DeMarco said, "I thought we were leaving Cleveland out of this."

"I don't know if we can. Costa appears to have been following the Cleveland model when he killed Talarico and Brogan."

"If we accept that it was Costa."

"Correct," she said. "For the sake of argument. He then followed the same pattern for Hufford and Brenner."

"But not for victim #2, Samantha Lewis."

"Right," Jayme said. "She's the anomaly. She was almost decapitated, but not quite. Fully dressed. Body wholly intact. That doesn't match any of the other victims."

"Something spooked him when he was working on her."

"Or he just had a hard time cutting up a girl. She's his only female."

"So he went back to a male for number three."

"So in every case except Samantha's," Jayme said, "the killer has got to be covered in blood, no matter how sharp the blade is supposed to have been. How does he get away without anybody seeing him? In 1988, I can understand. But today? With all the security cameras and smartphones around?"

"However he did it, all five victims were abducted. That's not like Cleveland either. The Torso victims were probably killed where they were first encountered, in alleys and empty lots and so forth. But the five most recent victims were abducted and killed somewhere else. Whether they went willingly or by gunpoint, stun gun, or whatever, they were subdued, taken somewhere private, killed and dismembered."

"Except that Hufford and Brenner were all taped up and asphyxiated before dismemberment. But no tape residue on Lewis. Plastic bag. The records don't say anything about tape residue on Brogan and Talarico either."

"Plus they were bled out. Still alive during the cutting."

"He took it easier on the three new ones," DeMarco said. "Because he's older now? More mellow? Lost his taste for torture?"

"The first two, mob hits. The next three, for the pleasure of killing again."

They walked in silence for half a minute. Then Jayme said, "The girl weighed a hundred and two. So maybe he cut the males up to make them easier to move. He's a lot older now, not as strong as he used to be."

DeMarco shook his head. "He got them into and out of his car without cutting them up. He cut them where they lay."

It felt odd to be expressing such thoughts in full, unfiltered sunlight. Felt as if they were playing a game of some kind, working out a riddle. Two geese and four mallards floated across the park's little pond. A long-legged jogger in a white tank top and red yoga pants, her ponytail bouncing, ran past them, so close that DeMarco could hear the music from her earbuds and smell her perfume.

Jayme said, when the girl was well past, "Who wears perfume when she's jogging?"

"Never know who you might run into."

They walked for a while. "I think he's definitely opportunistic now," Jayme said. "Picks his victims at random."

DeMarco raised his eyes, shrugged, said nothing.

"Unless," Jayme said, and thought for several seconds before finishing. "Maybe this time he's trying to stay truer to the Cleveland pattern. And that's why he picked a female. Except that he couldn't finish the job."

DeMarco had no response. They walked

on. Then he shook his head, apparently in answer to a question he had been asking himself. "No evidence of semen on Samantha Lewis. But the coroner's report does indicate that she probably had sex prior to her death."

"And Hufford and Brenner still had their wallets and cash and phones on them."

"So we rule out robbery as any kind of motive, even a secondary one. But can we rule out sexual gratification in Samantha's case?"

"The killer might have used a condom," Jayme suggested. "Or used a Kleenex or a rag or something."

"It's possible. What's a big word for somebody like that?"

"Mmm," Jayme said, "fastidious? Punctilious?"

"Punctilious," DeMarco repeated with a smile. "Can't wait to drop that one on Fascetti. We should make a list of big P words. Hit him with them whenever we can. The fact that they all start with a P will drive him crazy, make him think we're up to something that we're not."

"Interesting," she said. "What if that's what the killer is doing — making us think that things are important that really aren't?"

"Then he's definitely a psychopath."

Up ahead, where the walking path made a wide turn to the right, in a small shelter in a grove of tall oaks, a teenage boy sat on the edge of a picnic table, a young girl leaning into him.

"So if there was sexual gratification involved . . ." DeMarco said. "Was there anything in the files about Costa being gay?"

"Not that I recall. So are we ruling out sex as a motive or not? At least in regard to the males?"

"Sex," DeMarco said, "but not arousal."

"Nonsexual arousal?"

"What if he denuded the men to humiliate them? So his arousal would have been, I don't know, the way a real estate agent feels when he gets a commission on a million-dollar sale? Or like when an accountant goes on safari and brings down a rhino?"

"The thrill of the big kill."

"That moment of triumph. Feeling all-powerful."

Jayme nodded, leafed through her notes. She read to herself while they walked. Then closed up the notebook and shoved it into a hip pocket. "Here's what I don't get," she said. "If Brogan and Talarico were mob assassinations, why go to the trouble of copycatting the Cleveland murders?"

"It doesn't seem necessary, does it?"

"Unless they weren't sanctioned hits. They were personal."

"In which case he would do what he could to muddy the scent. The Youngstown mob was still getting a lot of attention back then."

They walked silently for the next ten minutes. At the end of the second lap, De-Marco paused a few feet from his car. Jayme stopped too. She said, "Are we done walking?"

"Let's get to work," he said. "Where do you want to start? With Costa, or the witness who used to be a child?"

SEVENTEEN

DeMarco kept the speedometer needle around twenty. The street was full of potholes, broken glass, plastic and paper litter. Jayme waited for DeMarco to comment on it, but he didn't. He drove without speaking, turning his gaze from one side of the street to the other.

Occasionally they passed a neat home with a small yard and well-maintained flower beds, but these buildings were outnumbered by those with peeled, faded paint, rotting clapboards and buckled siding. Some buildings were abandoned, windows shattered and doors missing, others boarded shut. In one lot nothing remained but a set of concrete steps where three young Black men stood, watching, motionless, as DeMarco's car approached and then moved by.

While DeMarco drove, Jayme read from her phone. "Brier Hill gets an F for crime, employment, and housing."

DeMarco said, "I remember when it was a solid D+."

And then he became talkative. "The old-timers say Black Monday was as bad as Pearl Harbor. September 19, 1977. Every bit as devastating, they said. The day the Sheet and Tube works shut down. Beginning of the end for Youngstown steel."

He nodded toward the Saint Anthony of Padua Church a block ahead on Jayme's side, then slowed to a crawl, his foot riding lightly on the brake. The building sat atop a knoll, its past and present conjoined, one era embodied in a long trapezoid of red brick and gray concrete with a steeply slanting roof. It was attached by a low gallery to an older two-story rectangle, painted white, with a flat roof and shingled eaves. A single freestanding wall of red brick maybe fifteen feet long and six stories high stood in the building's front yard, three heavy bells suspended in a square opening near the top. Attached to the narrow front face of the wall, a simple cross extended another ten feet into the sky.

"When I had the money," DeMarco said, "I used to come here for a pizza. The best in town. They make it in the church kitchen."

"A pizza shop in the church?"

"Not every day but, you know. They grew the tomatoes and peppers behind the church."

She said, teasing, "Did you eat the whole pizza yourself?"

"Sometimes. And sometimes me and my mom. She loved Brier Hill pizza."

The vehicle stopped for a few moments as he gazed at the church through Jayme's window. She powered the window down and leaned back in her seat.

Ten seconds later he faced the windshield again. Blinked once. Lifted his foot off the brake. And they crept forward once more.

"It will be on this side," Jayme told him. "An even number."

"Yeah," he said. She knew then that he wasn't searching for Costa's place but still layering the past atop the present. How much had the neighborhood changed over the years? His eyes kept moving from one side of the street to the other, taking it all in, but his mouth remained the same, lips closed in a thin line that might have been the beginning of a smile but could also have been a frown about to fall.

Whatever he was feeling, she felt like an intruder and didn't want to interrupt. Costa could wait.

Near the end of the street, an old Black

man who looked close to ninety with his stooped back and headful of bristly white hair was standing in the center of the street, overturning a tall bag of black asphalt mix into a pothole in DeMarco's lane. Two full bags sat atop the curb.

When DeMarco pulled the car abreast of him on Jayme's side, the old man was tamping the asphalt down with the flat head of a sledgehammer.

The man looked up, surprised to see a car where none had been, and a pair of white people looking at him through the open window. "You two lost?" he said.

DeMarco said, "Just wondering why you're doing the city's job for them, sir."

The old man straightened a bit and rested his palm on the tip of the handle. "That would be 'cause the city ain't likely to do it, and my granddaughter don't appreciate ruining the tires on her little red car when she comes to visit."

"You plan to pave the whole street?" De-Marco asked.

"As much as I have to."

"Doesn't seem right to have to do it at your own expense."

"Hasn't for the last fifty years, far as I can tell."

"Well," DeMarco told him, "we know

somebody who knows somebody. We'll see if we can't get this street taken care of for you."

" 'Preciate it," the old man said. "But I won't be holding my breath waiting for it."

DeMarco gave him a nod and a smile. "You mind if I turn around in your driveway?"

"You want to drive over this minefield again? You're better off making a turn at the corner."

Jayme said, "We have some business back fifty yards or so."

"If it will get this place cleaned up some, you go ahead and do it, missy."

DeMarco pulled ahead to the driveway, made a slow turn, and said out his window as he passed the old man, "Have a good day, sir."

"Whenever I can, young fella."

A few seconds later, Jayme looked back through the rear window. The old man was dragging a second bag of asphalt into the street. "That's kind of sad," she said.

"Did you see the size of his forearms? I bet he used to be a steelworker."

"Why won't the city take care of the street?"

DeMarco shrugged. "Remind me to mention it to Ben later."

He slowed the car and eased it up to the curb alongside a wide, two-story house with cement-block pillars holding up the tilting porch roof. The porch and pillars and three-inch clapboards were all painted the same shade of faded lime green. An unpainted wooden stairway, looking none too stable, ran up the side of the building to a second-floor apartment.

"You can wait here if you want," he told her. "Those stairs look more than a little sketchy."

She popped open her door. "Want me to run up and down them a couple times? Just to make sure you won't hurt yourself?"

He shut off the engine, opened his door, and climbed out. "I was trying to be a gentleman," he said.

"You're not very good at it, are you, babe?"

At the bottom of the stairs, he stood aside. "Youth, beauty, and intelligence first."

"So much better," she told him.

He followed two steps below her, and told himself, *The view is better from here anyway.*

EIGHTEEN

Despite the open windows in Freddy Costa's apartment, the air was still and heavy. The only thing blowing in through the dirty screens was the scent of poverty, a scent DeMarco recognized and remembered, of dirty concrete and littered yards, old garbage and despair and a simmering outrage for everything at once and nothing in particular.

Native to the room was also a beery odor and the thick stench of cat litter in need of disposal. From Freddy himself came the sour stink of sweat.

"So you're not the police," Costa said, and leaned away from the IDPI card DeMarco held out to him. Jayme had ordered leather PI wallets for both of them, complete with mini-badges, but until they arrived in the mail, the simple cards she had designed online and printed on glossy white card stock would have to do. DeMarco felt a little foolish showing the homemade card, so he displayed it only for a couple of beats, then slipped it into his shirt pocket again.

Costa's living room was dim and sparsely furnished. A gray thrift-store sofa with a black cat curled atop the center cushion. A green vinyl recliner with the footrest extended and cocked at an angle, a white long-haired cat curled against the armrest. A small gray cat watching from the windowsill. A scarred end table holding an unlit light made from a cast-iron hand pump and a too-small beige shade. A small flat-screen TV mounted precariously atop a pair of blue plastic crates, the volume loud. On the screen, Johnny Depp lay in the sand, his face painted white with black streaks, a stuffed raven, wings spread, mounted atop his head, his dark eyes studying action off-screen. The booming background music suggested something ominous about to happen.

"You mind turning that off for a couple minutes?" DeMarco said.

Costa looked at him, then at Jayme. He bore the appearance of a super middle-weight boxer gone soft and paunchy, naked arms flabby in a black tank top furred with three colors of cat hair, vein-gnarled calves extending below the red basketball shorts.

He was five ten, with a round, battered face, his thin gray hair slicked down and combed straight back from the forehead.

Jayme smiled and said, "Please? It's a little loud."

He said, "You think I'm loud, you oughta hear the assholes downstairs when they wake up, which thank God won't be till suppertime or later."

She leaned forward, still smiling. "I'm sorry; could you say that again?"

He gave a nod, turned and crossed to the recliner, picked up the remote, and muted the TV. "It's crap anyway," he said. "He's supposed to be Tonto. Looks like he came straight from one of them pirate movies and stuck a crow on his head."

He waved a hand at the sofa. "You might as well set down. I'm going to. Don't worry about Connie. She won't hurt you." He picked the white cat off the recliner, flopped onto the seat, lifted his bare feet to the cockeyed footrest, and lay the cat across his lap.

He didn't wait until DeMarco and Jayme were seated. "They can't find anything on me, can they? Because I didn't do nothin'. That's why you're here, isn't it?"

While Jayme brushed the cat hair off her cushion, DeMarco sat and took out his notebook. Flipped through the first couple of pages. Connie studied Jayme for a few moments, then crawled onto her lap.

"July 11, 1988," DeMarco said. "Between 11:00 a.m. and 4:00 p.m."

"Fuck, man," Costa said, and scratched one naked foot with the other one. "Didn't they give you a report to read? There's gotta be a dozen of them by now. Why do you have to bother me with this shit again?"

Jayme said, "We just need to know if you have anything to add."

"Add to what? You think I'm gonna change my mind about it? I wasn't there. I wasn't there in 1988, and I wasn't there for any of them people this past month. How many times does a guy have to say it?"

"So where were you?" DeMarco asked. "July 11, 1988. Between 11:00 a.m. —"

"Ah for chrissakes," Costa interrupted. "I was with a guy in Canfield. His car. Sussing out some houses."

DeMarco told him, "It says in the reports you can't remember where you were."

"Fascetti and me don't like each other," Costa said. "I like her." And he gave Jayme a wink.

"You were looking for a house to rob?" she asked.

"No, to give them a Publishers Clearing

138

House check for a million dollars."

"Were you looking for anything in particular?" said DeMarco.

"Personally, I was hoping to score a computer or two. Everybody was talking about them back then. I wanted to see what all the excitement was about."

"So this was freelance?"

"It's what I did. Me and Zero and a couple of other guys. We hired out when we could, but those jobs were few and far between."

Jayme said, "Did you find a house you liked? That night in Canfield?"

"Shit," Costa said. "We were so drunk and high we were lucky to find our way home. Zero blacked out and put us in a ditch. I did the last mile and half on foot, left the dumb bastard there to sleep it off."

"Zero being . . . ?" Jayme asked.

"Jimmy Skirowski. But you already know that, don't you?"

"What route did you take back from Canfield?" DeMarco asked.

"Didn't I tell you we were too drunk and high to see straight?"

DeMarco looked at his notes. "You used to know."

"625 and 62, okay? You happy now?"

"Did you stop anywhere along the way?

Either coming or going?"

"You think we were stupid? We knew what we were doing."

Jayme said, "Is that why you were drunk and high?"

He grinned. "You got a sharp little tongue on you, don't you? I gotta be honest; you're turning me on a little bit."

DeMarco said, "We're having so much fun here, I'm thinking I should call Fascetti and have him join us. That okay with you, Freddy?"

Costa rolled his head from side to side. "I am so fucking tired of you people. If you had anything on me, I'da been in jail a long time ago. But I'm not. Koenig couldn't do it, Fascetti couldn't do it, and neither will you, no matter what you try to pin on me. Times like now, though, I almost wish I *was* in jail. So how about you just get the fuck outta here and go ruin somebody else's life? You've done all the damage to mine you can. Prison would be a freaking vacation for me."

DeMarco closed up his notebook. "What would you say if I told you that gray hairs were found on the victims? Gray hairs that match your own?"

Costa laughed. "I'd say you're grasping at straws that ain't there. How dumb do you think I am?"

Jayme said, "You seem a little angry, Mr. Costa. Were you angry the nights you killed Hufford and Brenner?"

Costa laughed another sour laugh. He shook his head and stroked the white cat. Then he leaned toward Jayme, looked her in the eye. "Sweetie, you're a good-looking girl. When I look in those pretty eyes of yours, I don't see stupid. So you should be smart enough to understand this. The guys I used to work for are all either dead or locked up or senile, and none of the younger ones will have anything to do with me. I'm supposed to be the nobody who wasted a couple of big earners. You think the bosses would've let me live to see 1989 if they believed it was me?"

He kicked his heels against the footrest a couple of times, but it would not go down. "Take a long look at my life. This shithole and these cats are all I got. I don't go nowhere, I don't do nothing but open cans of cat food and watch TV. But if you want to float me a loan of, I don't know, a thousand dollars or so, I'll be out of here before you can whistle Dixie."

DeMarco leaned back, slipped the notebook into his pocket. He stood. "Why'd you beat the crap out of your friend?" he asked.

141

"What did Zero do to you?"

Costa settled back against the chair cushion. Raised his eyes to the ceiling. Stroked the white cat between the ears. "All he had to say was that I was with him up until he put us in a ditch. All he had to do was tell the truth and back me up. But what did he say? He couldn't remember. Didn't even remember leaving town that night, he said. Couldn't remember driving into a ditch. Thought probably he was alone all night."

"So you put him in the hospital for that?"

"Fucking Koenig," he said. "One of your people. Turned my only friend against me."

"Is that why you're so angry?" Jayme asked.

"I'm closing my eyes now," he said, and did.

DeMarco nodded to Jayme. She slipped her hands under Connie, lifted and laid her aside. Then she stood.

DeMarco said to Costa, "You mind if I hit the john before I go?"

"Knock yourself out," Costa said without opening his eyes. "Check the bedroom too if you want. You're not going to find anything in there either."

As DeMarco headed for the bathroom, Jayme picked a few cat hairs off her arm. "You know, Mr. Costa," she said, "I get the feeling you possess a lot more information than you're willing to share. If you were to try a little harder to cooperate with us, we could return the favor and help you."

Still with his eyes closed, he lay motionless for a moment. A smile spread across his mouth, but it wasn't a pretty one. He opened his eyes and turned his head her way. "You think somebody's going to help *me*? That ain't the way it works, and you know it."

"How does it work?" she asked.

"I'm an old heterosexual white guy with a criminal record." As he talked, his voice grew louder, his body more rigid, until he was sitting up and leaning over the armrest to shout at her. "Four strikes against me. Nobody's going to throw a bone to me or anybody like me. They got too many so-called oppressed minorities to satisfy first. I can whine and complain just as loud as any one of them damn minorities, but it's like screaming down the crapper in an outhouse. You know the only good thing about liberals? If they get their way, every last one of us will be living in a third-world dictatorship, and it will serve them right for being so goddamn stupid. The whole fucking country will end up looking like this neighborhood."

"I'm not sure I understand," she said. "Are you blaming the liberals for your situation?"

"I'm saying they're ruining this country! They think they can do better? Where were they when this country was being built? Hell, you know who really built this country? Organized crime, that's who. Think about it. What would Chicago be without Al Capone? What would Vegas be without Bugsy Siegel? LA without Mickey Cohen? Miami without Trafficante? You remember the Industrial Revolution? You think J. D. Rockefeller wasn't a crime boss? You think J. P. Morgan wasn't? Andrew Carnegie? Every single one of them and a hundred more, they all had their crime families. They all killed and stole and lied and murdered their way to the top. Even the little guys like me, we did our share too. Every truck I jacked meant the factories had to produce more. I made a little money selling it to this guy, he made a little money selling it to that guy, and so on and so on. Every time I picked up a collection, the guy we shook down had to work that much harder to break even again. Crime incentivizes productivity. Organized crime is good for the economy. It's a proven fact, sister! People downtown, they think Youngstown is a nicer place now that they broke up all the families. And I say it was the mob that held this city together. I mean okay, we got a little crazy with the car bombs for a while, but that was internecine war, that's all it was. Life was better back then! Better for everybody but the people getting blown up. Learn your history, for God's sake! And just go away and leave me the fuck alone."

He sank back in the recliner, turned his head away from her, and stared at the wall.

A few minutes later, DeMarco met Jayme beside the car, where she was still busy picking black cat hairs off her clothes.

DeMarco brushed at the front of his shirt. "That was a nice little conversation you and Freddie had."

"A bit one-sided," she said. "See anything interesting in the bathroom?"

"I can confidently report that the bathroom, bedroom, and closet are all thoroughly devoid of interest."

"But not of cat hair, I bet."

He chuckled. "You want to go see what the child witness has to say?"

"Do we really need to hear him repeat what's in the latest report?"

"So let's call Koenig. Maybe he's in the mood for a chat."

"How about finding us a car wash first,"

Jayme said, and picked a cat hair off her tongue. "I feel like I need to be hosed down."

NINETEEN

In lieu of a high pressure soaping and rinse, they remained parked at the curb, the air conditioner blasting cool air. Jayme called the Naples, Florida, number of former detective Gene Koenig. He answered with a breezy hello, then listened as she introduced herself and DeMarco and inquired of his availability for a short conversation via Skype.

"No can do," he said. "I'm standing on a dock in Pelican Bay, waiting to step onto a refitted Regulator for an afternoon on the Gulf. What's this about?"

"Freddy Costa," she told him. "The Talarico-Brogan murders."

"That guy again," he said. He then shouted to someone to hold their horses. To Jayme he said, "What's so important about Skype?"

"Sheriff Brinker suggested it. Probably figured you'd want a look at our creds before we start talking."

"I can give you five minutes right now," he said. "Then I'm shutting this thing off for a while."

"You mind if I put you on speaker? I know that Sergeant DeMarco wants to get in on this too."

"Have at it," he said.

She tapped the speaker icon and held the phone toward DeMarco. He asked, "What are you fishing for, Detective?"

"Call me Gene. Pompano, grouper, wahoo, whatever's biting. It's less about catching fish than sitting in the sun and drinking beer, if you know what I mean."

"Sounds like paradise," DeMarco said, and received a look of reproval from Jayme.

"To cheeseburgers like us, I guess it is. So what do you want to know?"

"We've read the reports," DeMarco told him, "but we were hoping there might be a videotape. Of the interview with the boy."

"Didn't make one," Koenig said. "It was conducted impromptu. In the kid's house with his parents watching."

Jayme asked, "So there was no child forensic interviewer present?"

"What did I just say? It was impromptu. Besides, we didn't do that back then." He paused for a moment, then continued, his tone a bit softer. "Listen, I know there's a lot of extra hoops you've got to jump through these days, but thirty years ago, we concentrated on getting the job done. And we did. And in a lot less time than it takes you folks now."

Jayme flashed DeMarco a quick look — eyebrows raised, mouth in a wide grimace — then leaned toward the phone again to ask, "What led you to the boy in the first place?"

"Door-to-door query. A couple of houses on the west side of the road had a clear view of the trees on the edge of the fairway. Costa would've had to park his car along the shoulder to get into those trees. The entrance gate gets locked after the clubhouse staff leaves. Which was around 11:10 that night. Still, there's no way to drive a car close to the fairway. Nearest approach is through the trees."

"And the boy claimed to have seen Costa?" DeMarco asked.

"Pretty much nailed his description, as I recall. Impressive for a five-year-old."

Jayme asked, "What was a boy that age doing up at such an early hour?"

"Getting a juice box, he said. According to his mother, he would sometimes have a bad dream, get out of bed and go get something to drink."

Jayme looked to DeMarco and mouthed, *Sounds like you.*

DeMarco said, "The report is a good summary, Gene, which is how I do mine most of the time too. It says that the child could not provide a description of the vehicle, but accurately described Costa's height, weight, and build."

"What do kids know about cars?" Koenig said. "Unless you're into them, I guess. Which he wasn't."

Jayme said, "His bedroom window overlooked the street?"

"He had to stand on his headboard to look out, yeah. One of those bookshelf types. His mother said he did it all the time, even during the day. Only child, you know? Apparently didn't have a lot of friends."

"His parents didn't see or hear anything?" DeMarco asked.

"Said they didn't. No reason not to believe them."

DeMarco scowled at the phone, his forehead pinched. When he raised his eyes to Jayme, she recognized the look. It said, *This doesn't feel right.*

Jayme said, "Do you happen to remember, sir, the boy's demeanor during the interview? Specifically, did he often look at one

or the other of his parents before responding to your questions?"

Koenig said. "You expect me to remember
who he looked at? Thirty years ago?"

"It's just that it could be indicative of why
he answered as he did."

"How so?" Koenig asked.

"He would have wanted his answers to
meet with the approval of his mother or
father."

"And they wanted him to tell the truth.
Besides, kids don't lie. Not five-year-olds
anyway."

"Actually," Jayme said, "the research
doesn't really support that. Even toddlers
will lie for a number of reasons."

"Such as?" Koenig said.

"To avoid punishment. To win approval.
To impress somebody they admire. Somebody like a police detective, perhaps."

"That might be so in some cases, but this
kid wasn't lying. You been in the job as long
as I was, you learn to sense these things."

DeMarco said, "Do you remember how
the boy became the focus of your questioning? You probably asked the parents first,
right? I'm sure you didn't go there expecting to interview a child."

"Of course I —" His answer was cut off
by a short blast from a small air horn.

"That's for me," he said. "I have to get moving here."

"Can you talk on the boat?"

"Whether I can or can't isn't the point. Let's wrap this up."

Jayme said, "What we're looking for, sir, is an idea of how the questioning went. If, for example, you asked the boy, 'Tell me what you saw.' Or if maybe you asked him, 'Did you see a man getting out of a car?' "

"I know what you're insinuating," Koenig said.

"Sir, I apologize if it seems that I'm insinuating anything. It's just that with children, the manner of questioning is of utmost importance."

"You got to be careful with kids, you think I don't know that? I raised four of my own, so I know. Sometimes you have to give them a little help. You can't push a kid that age or he'll start crying. He starts crying, the interview is over."

Jayme leaned away from the phone, met DeMarco's gaze, and gave her head a slow shake.

DeMarco leaned in. "Just one last thing, Gene, if you don't mind. Was Freddy Costa a person of interest when you started the investigation? Before questioning the boy, I mean."

"Him and a handful of others, sure. Known criminal types. Especially those likely to be involved in wet work."

"My understanding was that Costa was little more than a button man."

"We'd looked at him a few times before. Just couldn't make anything stick. Not enough to satisfy the DA anyway."

DeMarco took a single breath. Held it.

Koenig said, "I'm wasting sun here."

"Thanks for your time, Detective," DeMarco told him. "Good luck catching your limit."

Jayme ended the call, palmed the phone and laid it between her legs. She gave DeMarco what he teasingly called her Howdy Doody face: eyebrows raised, mouth upturned in an exaggerated grin, perfect teeth pressed tightly together.

He said, "So what did you hear?"

"I heard, 'Did you see a man getting out of the car? Was he about your daddy's height? Did he look strong? Were there two other men with him?' "

DeMarco nodded. "I heard that Costa was on Koenig's radar even before the bodies were found. Like maybe our good detective was out to put him away for something — whatever came along. Costa as much as told us the police were out to get him."

"So where does that leave us?" Jayme asked.

"Not a place I'm enjoying."

"We all have our blind spots."

"The police were doing their best back then to clean up the city," he told her. "Even I got caught up in it. Hauled in for a friendly fight."

She smiled. "So friendly that you broke his jaw."

"I really liked the guy. Threw in a busted nose just to show how much."

"Aren't you the sweetest palooka," she said. "Can we get some lunch now and decide our next move?"

"Let's see if Ben's hungry too," he suggested, and held out his hand.

She slapped the cell phone into his palm.

The call was answered on the third ring. DeMarco said, "Did you have lunch yet?"

"Not to my way of thinking," Brinker said. "Some crackers and a cup of yogurt."

"In that case Jayme would like to buy you a late lunch."

"Sounds great. As long as you're not going to be there too."

"No, I'm heading over to see Vee instead."

Brinker laughed. "Where we meeting?"

"What are you in the mood for?"

"I'd kill for some barbecue, but I always

end up with half of it on my shirt. How about Carmela's, on Fifth between Rayen and Lincoln? It's cafeteria style, so it will be fast, and there's usually an outside table we can grab. The carne frita and mofongo will knock your socks off."

"How soon?"

"I'm walking now," the sheriff told him. "Walking and drooling."

"See you in ten. Try to keep your shoes dry."

TWENTY

The fried pork chunks were crispy but tender, seasoned with lots of garlic and adobo, and the mashed plantains with their sofrito of peppers, onions and tomatoes, all sitting in a pool of garlicky chicken broth and topped with a couple of cracklings, kept DeMarco and Brinker silent for the first fifteen minutes but for the muttered *oh*s, *mmm*s, and *yeah*s from each of them.

Jayme sampled DeMarco's pork, but otherwise enjoyed her chicken pastelillo and cod fritters. "You two sound like you're having sex," she told them.

Brinker said, "My wife says the same thing."

DeMarco cooled his garlicky tongue with a sip of iced tea. "You don't know what you're missing," he told her.

Only when their plates were nearly empty did the conversation grow serious. "I'm guessing you didn't want to meet just to watch me eat," the sheriff said.

DeMarco said, "We made contact with Detective Koenig."

"That's good. Or is it not?"

DeMarco looked to Jayme. "Why don't *you* tell him? He's less likely to punch you."

She gave the sheriff her sweetest smile. "Freddy Costa," she said. "We don't think he did it."

"You talking 1988 or now?"

"Sort of both."

He laid his fork on the plate. "Based on what, specifically?"

DeMarco answered. "From what we can tell — and we're just extrapolating here — Detective Koenig might have . . . suggested certain responses when he was interviewing the boy."

"He told you that?"

"He told us he gave the boy a little help," Jayme said.

"And, according to Costa," DeMarco added, "Koenig was hot to pin anything he could on him."

"So you talked to him too?"

"Before we called Florida."

"Yeah, well, Freddy Costa has never been what I would consider a credible source."

"Fair enough," DeMarco said. "But let me ask you this. Those two gray hairs you took off the girl. Did they have hair gel on them?"

"There was nothing about that on the lab report."

"Costa has a big jar of it in his bathroom. Appears to use it liberally."

Jayme said, "And you know about Costa's cats, right? He has three of them. And they all shed. Liberally."

DeMarco added, "It would be impossible for him to touch Hufford or Brenner or Lewis without getting cat hair all over them."

"Maybe he showered first," the sheriff said. "Somebody was very careful with those bodies."

"Yeah, well," Jayme said, "Freddy doesn't seem all that fond of water. I would guess it's been a couple of weeks since he stood in the shower."

"And fastidious, he's not," DeMarco said.

Brinker sat there staring at his dirty plate, shaking his head back and forth. "I don't want to hear this."

"Nobody does," said DeMarco.

The sheriff leaned back in his seat. "You spoiled a perfectly good lunch."

Jayme said, "We'd like to take a different tack. Go a different direction than Detectives Fascetti and Olcott are going."

"You have any idea what that direction might be?"

DeMarco said, "Ask us in a day or two."

Sheriff Brinker shook his head. Took a sip of tea. "I respect your observations," he told them. "Do what you need to do. But I'm not pulling Fascetti or Olcott off the scent they're tracking."

Jayme said, "Freddy's scent is a hard one to forget."

DeMarco slid his hand closer to Brinker's plate, tapped the table a couple of times. "I have some questions about the security cameras."

"In particular?"

"How extensively did your guys check them? The only reference to a camera is in Samantha Lewis's file."

Brinker made a popping sound with his lips, three little pops as he considered the question. Then he said, "Give me a lift back to the office. You can ask them yourself."

TWENTY-ONE

In the conference room, Brinker sat at one end of the long table, Fascetti at the other. Jayme and DeMarco sat facing Olcott, who had brought along a tall, thin bottle of sparkling water. Fascetti nibbled from a bag of smoked almonds.

In answer to a question from DeMarco, Fascetti said, "What do you think we did? We checked every camera available."

"But what were you looking for?" Jayme asked. "Were you looking for Costa? Because if that was your focus . . ."

Fascetti licked the salt from his lips, then turned his eyes on DeMarco. "You think you're hot shit, don't you? You think because you got lucky on a couple of cases you can come in here and tell us how to do our job?"

Olcott didn't wait for DeMarco's reply. He told him, "There are no cameras outside Hufford's place. It's all blue-collar, lower-middle-class residential. The cameras outside Brenner's apartment are aimed mostly into the parking lot. We have him exiting the building, but then we lose him half a minute later. It could be the killer picked his victims for that very reason."

"But not Lewis," DeMarco said.

"We have her car leaving her home — the whole neighborhood is covered with personal security cameras — and then we pick it up on the street a couple more times. Once she leaves town, though, we're blind."

DeMarco knocked his knee against Jayme's.

"So that's the thing," Jayme said. "That difference. Even though you weren't able to follow the course of her vehicle that night, she's the only one of the three who lived in a neighborhood with lots of cameras. The only one who came from an affluent neighborhood. And she's the only female. The only one under thirty. The only student. The only one who was fully dressed. The only one on which gray hairs were found. The only one asphyxiated with a plastic bag and not tape. The only one who wasn't dismembered."

"He did start the decapitation process," Brinker said.

"But couldn't finish it," said DeMarco. "Why not? Why her and only her?"

"Because he was interrupted," Fascetti said. "We already covered this crap, didn't we?"

"That's speculation. Nine distinct differences have to be important," DeMarco answered. "Jayme and I want to focus on her. Just her."

The sheriff asked, "You're suggesting she had a different killer?"

"She's the anomaly," Jayme said. "In every way. Which might mean that she had a different killer. Or might mean that there was something special about her. Special *to* the killer. Maybe she was the true target. Brenner and Hufford were killed just to get us all looking in the wrong direction."

They sat in silence for a few moments. Fascetti scowled and shook his head.

"At least it's something," Brinker told her. "Her family is holding a memorial for her Friday night. You might want to check it out. At her old high school in Canfield."

"She went to public school?" Jayme asked.

Brinker nodded.

Olcott said, "I can meet you there if you want."

Fascetti jerked back as if slapped. "So you're throwing in the towel on Costa too?"

"I don't see it as an either/or situation."

"So go," Fascetti told him. "Go to the

dark side. I could care less."

"You *could* care less?" Jayme asked with a smile. "Or you couldn't care less?"

In an instant the room grew hot for everyone except Jayme. Her smile remained cool and confident.

DeMarco asked Olcott, "Is your face well-known in that area?"

The detective wagged his head back and forth. "Yeah, maybe. I hear what you're saying."

"Thanks for the offer, though," DeMarco told him. "We'll probably get around to interviewing her family before then, so we won't be total strangers either. But still, the lower the profile, the better."

DeMarco turned to Jayme. "So that's it, partner. We have our assignment."

"Yeah," said Fascetti. "One you made up for yourself."

"Detective," Sheriff Brinker told him, "eat your nuts."

TWENTY-TWO

They had to go back to the beginning. Treat it like a new investigation. Forget the Cleveland Torso Murders unless a very clear link presented itself. Forget Freddy Costa. Look harder at the case files. What wasn't done that should have been done? What could be done differently?

Visit the victims' homes. Talk to the families. Ask all the usual questions and several unusual ones and check against the earlier answers for inconsistencies. Push harder. Look through the victims' rooms, journals, laptops, social media. Confirm family members' alibis and timelines. What wasn't asked that should have been asked? What wasn't searched that should have been searched? Push harder.

Check the victims' phone logs. Review cell phone tower data.

Check arrest records for anyone who could fit the profile. Any parolees in the area at the time of the murders? Any media accounts of similar killings elsewhere in the country?

Ask the sheriff's office if any cars were pulled over around the estimated time of the murders and placement of bodies. Anybody pulled over and/or captured on security camera who fits the rather ambiguous profile of a serial killer? Of a sexual predator? Of a, what else . . . scorned lover?

Double-check DNA taken from victims and crime scenes. Any areas of the scenes where DNA should have been collected but wasn't?

Push forensics to zero in on type of blade used for dismemberment of bodies. Is it possible to discern a specific brand? If that brand is available locally, get purchase info from merchants. Push harder.

Push harder.

Push *harder.*

After running through all this in his head during the drive back to Pennsylvania later that afternoon, DeMarco summarized his thoughts for Jayme. She was seated with her laptop open, reading Samantha Lewis's Facebook page while ignoring Interstate 80's usual high-speed parade of eighteen-wheelers rumbling past, shaking the sedan in their back drafts. "We need to start at the beginning," DeMarco told her. "Treat it like a whole new investigation."

"Which in a way it is," she said. "Change the perspective, change the way the information looks."

He nodded. Glanced at the laptop. "Getting to know our girl?"

"Not as well as I would like to. She hasn't posted anything in a couple of years."

"Years?" he said. "That seems odd. Maybe it's all on her private page."

"The only photos or events on her timeline are from her first week of college. And she would have been a senior this fall."

"Interesting. The case file said her mother is deceased. Do you remember when that happened?"

"Not the exact date, but I remember it said she was a junior in high school."

"So sixteen or seventeen years old. Bad time to lose a mother."

"The thing is, most young people use social media *more* when they're distressed, not less."

He shook his head. "Just what we need — another enigma."

Jayme closed her laptop and watched him for a few moments. "You seem tired," she told him. "Are you all right?"

"I'm good," he said.

"No . . . I can hear it in your voice. You're hiding something from me. What is it?"

It took him a while to answer. "I've been feeling a little short of breath lately."

"What do you mean? You're having chest pains?"

"No, nothing like that. I just can't seem to get my breath sometimes. Just a heaviness, you know?"

"How long have you had this?"

"I guess I noticed it not long after we came back to Pennsylvania."

"You need to see a doctor," she said.

"You know how I feel about doctors."

"I'm going to make an appointment for you."

"I won't go."

"You'd rather die than have a doctor listen to your heart and lungs?"

"You see? I never should have told you. It's not a big deal."

She kept looking at him, her mouth grim.

"Tell you what," he said. "Baby aspirin is supposed to be good for you. I'll start taking one every day."

"Baby aspirin," she repeated. "Well, I guess that's appropriate, isn't it?"

"I'm fine," he told her, and softened his voice. "My heart's strong, lungs are clear. Blood pressure is maybe a point or two above normal, but otherwise I'm an amazing specimen of perfect health."

She scowled but said nothing more on the subject. They returned home, where she took a long, tepid shower while he lay on the bed and stared at the ceiling. Then he showered while she made a salad for dinner. They listened to Bob Dylan's *Fallen Angels* on the CD player while eating, and sometimes commented on the music, of the strangely hypnotic effect of that nasally, gravelly, often mumbling voice paired with the orchestral harmony of vintage love songs. But neither DeMarco nor Jayme seemed interested in discussing the case any further that day. After dinner they silently watched two episodes of *Mindhunter* on Netflix.

Not until they were undressing for bed, after she watched him match up the seams on his khakis, fold the slacks in half and lay them over the back of the chair, did she ask, "Is it because I started talking about having a baby?"

"What do you mean?" he said.

"Your chest pains."

"I told you, there's no pain. Just . . . a little soreness and heaviness. I must have pulled a muscle somehow."

"I know it's stressful for you. Because you

don't want one."

"That's not true."

"Subconsciously," she said. "Deep down in your heart of hearts. You don't want another baby, do you?"

He smiled. "I'm not conscious of anything my subconscious is doing."

She did not return the smile and continued to frown at him until he went into the bathroom to brush his teeth. He closed the door and looked at himself in the mirror. And asked himself, *What if?*

Twenty minutes later, they delved into the box of Huston's papers for the first time. Jayme had never met Thomas Huston, had seen him only briefly the previous summer when he came to the barracks to do research for a novel. But she remembered the way DeMarco had changed as his and Huston's friendship bloomed over the next few months, how much mellower he seemed after every lunch with the writer, then how obsessed he became when Huston's family was slaughtered, and how broken he was when he returned from holding his dying friend in his arms. Jayme knew all this, and now, with the box between them on the bed, she felt like an interloper.

She and DeMarco sat side by side against

the headboard, pillows stuffed behind their backs, Jayme in a silky maroon shorts and cami set, DeMarco in black basketball shorts and a gray T-shirt, the box wedged between their hips. Just before they began, a few minutes after ten, she expressed her doubts.

"I haven't read nearly as much of his stuff as you have," she told him. "Just the last novel."

"You said you liked it."

"I did. But you have to admit it was kind of depressing."

"I thought it was a very hopeful novel. Considering what the characters went through."

"Okay, you're right," she said. She lifted a composition book from the box and tossed it onto his lap. Then took out the next one for herself. "All I'm saying is, maybe my reactions to his writing won't be as well-informed as yours."

"Yours will be more objective. Which makes them better than mine."

"If you say so," she said, and laid a small box of sticky colored flags within reach. "I'll use the yellow flags, you use the green. Full go for your choices, caution for mine."

"Actually it should be the other way around."

"Do you want to argue or do you want to read?"

"If you don't want to do this . . ." he said.

"Shut up. I'm reading."

They read.

Near the end of the first half hour, DeMarco told her, "I'm out of green flags."

"So go blue," she told him.

Twenty minutes later, he said, "I'm so tired I can't tell if these two pieces are supposed to go together or not."

"We can quit if you want to." The tone of her voice was smoother now, without the earlier strain. "Though I'm enjoying this more than I expected."

"Can I read these to you? They're not long. The first one is dated, but the second one isn't. And they're separated by a blank space."

She marked her page, then closed the composition book. "Let's hear it."

"Okay, here's the first one," DeMarco said. And he read:

In a letter to Aldous Huxley's older brother Julian, Huxley's wife Laura wrote of the writer's final hours as he died of cancer, and how she, with his permission, administered LSD to ease his transition, which she described as "beautiful and peaceful and easy." The process leading to his final breath, she wrote, "was not a drama at all, but like a piece of music just finishing so gently in a sempre più piano, dolcemente."

A piece of music finishing more and more slowly. If only death could come to each of us as a song.

"Gee, that's not depressing at all," Jayme said. "What's the second one about — hellfire and damnation?"

He read:

What I have come to understand is that this life is not about this life. It is about the true life — the life of spirit. We must learn to look at each of our actions here in that light: How does each of my actions affect my spirit, and what will all too soon become of it?

"Hmm," Jayme said. "I don't think they go together, if that's what you're asking. Don't they sort of contradict each other?"

"Maybe each one is an isolated observation. He does that a lot."

"Yeah, in mine too. You said it's dated?"

"The first one is. Third of October last year. Why?"

"It almost sounds as if he knew he was

going to die soon."

DeMarco peeled off a little blue arrow and stuck it to the edge of the page. "Aren't we all?" he said.

And a chill shot up her spine.

TWENTY-THREE

In the dark of morning, but with the eight candle-flame bulbs of the chandelier hanging above the dining room table providing a chapel-like illumination, Jayme, sitting, and DeMarco, standing behind her, both highly caffeinated, again studied the display they had taped to the wall.

The display was divided into thirds, with more or less equal space accorded to each victim: Justin Brenner, Samantha Lewis, Jerome Hufford. At the top of each space, the victim's pre-mortem photo. Below that, an index card with, printed in Jayme's neat block lettering, DOB, date, time, and place of discovery of body. Beside that, a photocopy of a postmortem photo, date, and approximate time of death.

Below that, more index cards: names of family members, names of friends and known associates. Most of the names had a red checkmark in the corner of the card, meaning that their alibis had been corroborated. Those corroborated by only one individual, whose own alibi was corroborated only by the individual whose alibi they corroborated, bore a question mark. Those individuals who claimed to have been alone at the time of the murder were marked by a double question mark.

Phone data had established that the cell phones of three of those questionable individuals, at the approximate time of their friend's or associate's death, were in places significantly distant from where the victim was last seen and where the body was later deposited. The remaining five phones were, at those times, located somewhere near that individual's home.

"Which might or might not support the alibis," Jayme said.

"Somebody as careful as the killer has been," DeMarco said, thinking out loud, "would know to leave his phone at home."

"So we start with those five. And get their alibis for all three dates."

DeMarco nodded. "And anybody with three uncorroborated alibis goes under the microscope."

Jayme, still on her first cup of strong coffee, turned the mug in her hands. "What are the odds," she asked, "that we'll find the killer on this board?"

"Zero to zero point oh oh one percent."

"You're still convinced it's a stranger."

"If a single thread tied the three victims to each other," he said, "I might think differently."

"So we made all this for nothing."

"Art is good for the soul," he said.

She raised a hand beside her head, touched him, then lightly scratched his chest. "I can hear the cogs turning."

"In my chest? No you can't. My cogs are elsewhere."

"Art is good for the soul? That tells me you're optimistic. And that tells me you have an idea."

He kissed the top of her head. "How does a frittata sound?"

"Excellent. I'll be your sous chef."

She followed him to the kitchen, where she took a green bell pepper and the remaining half of a foil-wrapped sweet onion from the vegetable bin in the refrigerator. He gathered two Idaho potatoes from the bag in the cupboard, scrubbed and rinsed them at the sink. Then he plunked two sweet Italian sausages from the freezer into the deep cast-iron skillet to brown, then set to grating the potatoes while she chopped and minced. The conversation continued with intermittent pauses while they built and seasoned the frittata and watched it cook.

"So," he said, "working from the premise that the 1988 killer was familiar with the Cleveland Torso Murders. But not the same person."

"I thought we were going to forget about 1988 and Cleveland altogether," she said.

"We are and we aren't. We can also assume that the new killer was familiar with the 1988 killer's work."

"But yet another different person?"

"Correct."

"And just what," she asked, "makes us so certain of that?"

"Something I read last night in Tom's papers."

"Are you waiting for me to guess?"

"Sorry," he said. "It was advice to one of his students. A boy who was upset because the grade on his first story was so low. Tom reminded him that he was a student, not a professional. But that he could expect to get better the more he practiced. That even thinking about writing, imagining himself as a successful writer, would speed the process."

"And this applies to us . . . how?"

"If it were the same killer," he explained, "what's he been doing for the past thirty-two years? He's either been killing . . . if not here, somewhere else, even some other country . . . or he's been in prison . . . or he's been hiding in plain sight as an upright citizen."

"But?" Jayme said.

"But he hasn't shut off his brain. He hasn't had his . . . what parts did Hoyle say?"

"The amygdala and prefrontal cortex."

"So he hasn't had those fixed, right? He still wants to kill. Has at least been thinking about it. Fantasizing. Over and over and over until he just couldn't stop himself from actually doing it again."

"Like a pedophile masturbating to photos. Soon or later he's going to have to have the real thing."

"Not an appetizing image for the breakfast hour," DeMarco said. "But accurate."

"And you're suggesting that just by thinking about killing, he would have gotten better at it?"

"Tom told his student that wretched prose is not forever fixed in its wretchedness. He said that evolution of craft is inevitable. Maturation alone will account for some of it. Practice and intent will account for the rest."

"I don't know," Jayme said. "Our guy does

seem pretty good so far."

"Knife skills," he told her. "Compare 1988 to now."

She paused. Looked at the blade of the knife in her hands. Said, "From fixed blade to electrical power. So the only evolution is technological."

"He couldn't even finish the job with his second victim. And made a real mess of her neck."

She nodded. "So it's positively absolutely a different guy. He's smart; he's cunning; but, in the words of Gordon Ramsay . . ."

" 'Your knife skills are bloody wretched, mate.' "

She smiled. "Your British accent could use some tweaking, babe. Just saying."

"I do Sean Connery better. Five more minutes on the frittata."

She went to the cupboard for the plates.

He said, turning down the heat, "So maybe our new guy hasn't been practicing his knife skills, but he *has* studied up on at least the 1988 murders, if not the Cleveland ones too."

"Easy enough," Jayme said. "Both are all over the internet."

"But let's just say," DeMarco mused. "Let's say he was concerned about having that information on his hard drive. Whoever this guy is, he hasn't left any tracks so far. *That's* his forte."

"He'd have to hit the library."

"And so should we. The same one he would have."

"If we can get access. And we probably can't."

He shrugged. "Gotta try. You mind if I brown up some of this ham too?"

"From the freezer?"

"Meat compartment."

"What's the expiration date?"

"We're close," he said.

"Close close or close over?"

He held the open plastic container to her face. "Here, smell it. It's still good."

She sniffed, and wrinkled her nose. "It's iffy at best."

"The heat will kill the bacteria."

She took the container from his hand. Carried it to the trash bin. Popped open the lid and dropped the ham inside.

"I better look at your cheese too," she said.

"Don't let the blue scare you. It's like free penicillin."

TWENTY-FOUR

They waited in the parking lot, inside De-Marco's car, until the library doors were unlocked at one minute after ten. The morning was no longer soft, the air no longer sweet. DeMarco looked up at the sky as if it had insulted him. It was going to be one of those gray flannel days that keep promising rain, with black squall lines in the distance that never get any closer, and flaming tempers that threaten to combust everything in the vicinity, and muscles that feel like pasta cooked five minutes too long. The kind when the air tastes and smells and lays in your lungs like your high school gym socks after a week of hard workouts. By noon women's makeup will be running and their hair hanging limp. Everybody will unbutton their shirts as far down as they dare, and then a button or two farther. People who work outside won't be able to see for the sweat in their eyes, and will accidentally massacre the hedges or run their equipment over a dog sleeping in a patch of shade, and will be too exhausted to care. Everybody will avoid conversation and hardly anybody will have the energy to raise their eyes more than four feet off the ground. People who work inside will cling to their air-conditioning like a suffocating Methodist clings to the Holy Spirit.

That's the kind of day it's going to be, he thought. Hot. Triple digits hot. Humidity a hundred percent. Already half the people in the city would have sold their souls for an ice bath. By nightfall there would be power outages over a third of the county. People would climb onto their roofs in their underwear, lie spread-eagled in their yards as if that might make the breathing easier. All it would make easier was the mosquitos' and ants' and gnats' ingress into their choice of human orifices.

Inside, he breathed a little easier, and recovered a few degrees of hope for the future of the world. Two reference librarians were seated behind the large round counter on the second floor of the Youngstown Public Library, each at her own computer station. The room was spacious and cool, hushed and well-lit, still fresh with the lemony scent of the janitor's night work.

The younger librarian, tall and thin and probably no older than twenty-five, smiled up at Jayme, who stepped close to the desk and said, "We'd like to take a look at any newspaper articles from July 1988. Could you point us in the proper direction for that?"

"Let me guess. The Talarico murders."

"It's a popular search?"

"Most of last month. So many that we've catalogued the sources together for easier access."

"Actually," DeMarco said, and stepped closer to the counter while reaching for his credentials, "what would be most useful are your records for which patrons accessed that material prior to the Justin Brenner murder."

The older librarian, smaller, petite, swung around on her chair and allowed her colleague no chance to respond. "You know we can't do that," she said after a long look at his ID.

DeMarco shot a glance at her name tag: Meghan Bauer. Then he turned a faded smile on her, and lowered his voice. "I understand. But we're dealing with a serial killer here. The information could help us identify —"

She was already shaking her head no.

" 'Library records or patron information shall be released in the following situations: (a) in accordance with a subpoena, search warrant, or other court order; (b) to a law enforcement officer who is acting in the scope of the officer's law enforcement duties and who is investigating a matter involving a matter involving public safety in exigent circumstances.' Section 149.432 of the Revised Code."

"We are aware of the code," he told her.

"But you don't have a search warrant and you aren't a law enforcement officer."

Jayme took out her ID and showed it to both librarians. "We are employed as consultants by the Mahoning County Sheriff's Office."

"Then perhaps the sheriff would like to make the request. In person."

"You're going to force him to come over here?" DeMarco asked.

"I will be happy to look up the number for you."

"I have it," he told her, and pulled his phone from his pocket. "But thanks so much for your assistance."

While the reference librarian, seated behind the circular table, copied information from her screen onto an index card, Olcott looked across the room to where DeMarco and Jayme stood side by side, feigning patience, with their backs to the windows. He gave them a wink.

"He's such a mellow guy," Jayme said.

"Detective Mellow," DeMarco said.

She put a hand to his back, pinched the skin through his shirt. "What did we talk about?" she asked.

"Don't be mean," he said. "Sorry."

"You miss your badge, don't you?"

He grunted. Scowled. Tried a smile. Let it fall.

"Just don't take it out on Olcott," she told him.

"He's a wonderful human being. He has the patience of Job and a beautiful head of hair."

She pinched him again. "No more snark!"

He stretched his back, pulled away from her hand. "I get it, okay? You're right. Please stop pinching me."

Half a minute later, Olcott approached them. He held the card out to DeMarco. "I feel stupid that we never thought of this ourselves."

Jayme said, "You have a suspect already."

DeMarco read silently. There were two names on the card: Dr. Terence Gillespie, Mr. Daksh Khatri. Gillespie had visited the library once, nine weeks before the first of the triple homicides. Khatri had spent three consecutive afternoons with the relevant microfiche reels, beginning two days after Gillespie's visit. Each name was followed by an address.

To Olcott, Jayme said, "You done good."

"Meghan and my aunt Sarah are friends." He grinned at DeMarco. "She's not fond of you, by the way."

"Your aunt Sarah?"

"My aunt loves you. Doesn't know you from Adam, but she loves you anyway. She's like that."

"And what did I do to earn Miss Meghan's ire?"

Olcott merely smiled. He placed a fingertip atop Gillespie's name. "He's a professor at Heaton-Young College. Religion. Lives very close to here."

"And Khatri?" Jayme asked.

"Struck out on him. Just the name and address."

DeMarco mused aloud. "Why would a professor of religion be researching a thirty-year-old double homicide?"

Olcott said, "Hard to say, isn't it? My aunt Sarah is religious, and she's the sweetest person on the planet. Other religious people think they have a moral obligation to slaughter the infidels. But a professor of religion? I guess it all depends on how he professes it."

Jayme said, "Why don't we all drop by for a chat? Let the good man explain himself."

"Would love to join you," Olcott told her. "But my partner would accuse me of fraternizing with the enemy."

To DeMarco, Jayme said, "You really do rub people the wrong way, don't you?"

Olcott said, with a laugh, "Pusillanimous? Really? And what was that other word?"

"Pococurante," she said.

"Right. He is never going to forgive you for that."

DeMarco told him, "I lose so many friends because of her."

Twenty-Five

On the short, halting, noisy drive to the professor's house on the edge of the small college campus, DeMarco realized how far from the city he had grown, and how much he longed to be surrounded by undisturbed greenery and trees, where the loudest sound came from crows or geese and not from car horns. As a boy wandering farther and farther from his home, he had always been excited to discover a new street or bridge or a new route to the river, though even then he did not love the fabrications of man, no matter how he marveled at them, but only wondered how vast the city really was and if he would ever find a way out of it.

Later he discovered that Youngstown was not infinite at all, only seemed so to a boy on foot, and that there were innumerable cities bigger and noisier and brighter than his hometown, but that none of them held what he needed either. And now, driving from stoplight to stoplight, impatient and hungry and annoyed, he was reminded of a phrase Raymond Chandler had used: *the big sordid dirty crooked city.* Chandler's Marlowe preferred it over small-town life, but DeMarco was no Philip Marlowe, and he knew it. Any similarities were only skin-deep. He was more like Chandler himself, a man whose spirit and heart were gradually crushed by the city.

And now, for the first time, DeMarco thought about the quarter of a million dollars in reward money he and Jayme might share if they could bring the killer to justice. Most of the reward had been contributed by the father of Samantha Lewis, a county commissioner flush with old money. A quarter mil could get DeMarco and Jayme away from the cities of this world forever, even if it caused him a stab or two of guilt for profiting from other people's misery. And that was when he started thinking how nice it might be to live in a log home on the slope of a mountain somewhere in the Dakotas or Idaho or Wyoming, anywhere humanity was not crowded together so tightly that people continually ground and grated against one another. He thought that Jayme would probably like that too.

"There it is," Jayme said, and pointed to her left.

It took him a few seconds to come down off the mountain and back to Youngstown. Gillespie's prairie box house, three blocks north of Wick Park, was one of the few old, stately homes on the street that hadn't been claimed by the university for administrative offices. It sat at the rear of a long, narrow lot bordered on three sides by firs, maples, and thick walls of well-established lilac bushes, all of which gave the building an isolated, imperious appearance. The home was constructed of large blocks of red sandstone, their faces rounded and polished. On the top floor, dormers were visible on at least three sides. A front porch ran the width of the building, its shingled roof supported by four white pillars on sandstone block foundations. A long gravel driveway of white limestone chips led to the attached garage.

"We need a big house like that," Jayme said.

"Made of logs," he answered.

"You mean the ones in your head?"

"You don't like log homes?"

"For ski trips," she said.

He winced. He had forgotten about skiing. If he lived in the mountains he would have to learn how to ski. Just thinking about it made his bones creak.

They unbuckled and climbed out of the car. Immediately the heat rose up off the pavement and into his face, a dirty, unpleasant scent that made his eyes sting. When he came around the front of the car to meet Jayme, she said, "Just curious. Have you always been so competitive?"

His forehead wrinkled. "What are you talking about?"

"Back in the library. You didn't like it that Olcott got information the librarian wouldn't give to you. Because you don't have a badge to flash anymore."

"Badges?" he said with a bandito accident. "I don't need no stinkin' badges." But he heard himself and knew there was more sadness and anger in the joke than humor, knew there was no humor in his eyes or in the tightness of his mouth, and because he did not want Jayme to know it too, he turned away briskly and walked ahead of her and onto the professor's porch.

He rapped on the door three times, waited five seconds, and rapped again, harder.

Jayme came to his side, laid a hand against his back. "Slow down, babe. Take a breath."

For some reason his body had gone into guerilla mode, and he didn't like it, didn't understand it. It was a simple interview, for

191

God's sake.

He nodded. Saw a shadow approaching from inside. Then took a half step back from the door and told Jayme, "You talk."

The door was opened by a very pretty young woman of twenty or so, barefoot in a pink midriff tank top and gray gym shorts, with short brown hair and green, wide-set eyes, a small nose and pouty lower lip.

"Hi," Jayme said. "Is your father home?"

"You mean . . . Dr. Gillespie?"

"I'm sorry, I just assumed . . ."

"It's okay. He lets us study here sometimes. Because it's so quiet. But no, he isn't available just now. And who are you?"

Jayme showed her ID card. DeMarco stood smiling at parade rest.

Jayme said, "We're working with the county sheriff's office," and watched the girl's eyes. And there it was, that momentary lift of the eyebrows. "And what's your name?" Jayme asked.

"Kaitlin," the girl said. "What, uh . . . what do you want to talk to him about?"

"Your last name?" Jayme asked.

"Mahood." She gave it up like she was surrendering the car keys to a parent: petulantly.

"Do you know where we can find Dr. Gillespie right now?"

The girl stood motionless for a few seconds, then said, "I'll see if I can reach him."

She closed the door, softly, without engaging the latch.

Jayme turned to DeMarco and whispered, "Did she seem a little spooked to you?"

"She's a child," he said. "They spook easily."

"You mind if I turn up the heat a little?"

"I thought you wanted me to turn the burner down."

"Don't you think she was dressed a bit too casually to be in her professor's house for a study hour?"

"I have no idea," he said. "She looks like a little Daisy Mae to me. Farm fresh."

"Daisy Mae?"

"You know, from *Li'l Abner.*"

"You really do need to update your analogies."

The door came open, and the girl stood there with cell phone in hand. "He's out walking at Mill Creek this afternoon. Around the lake."

"Cohasset?" DeMarco asked.

"Actually it's the Lily Pond. He usually does the loop four times."

"When did he start?" DeMarco asked.

"He's on his second lap."

"Tell him to keep walking," DeMarco

said. "We'll meet him there. Thanks for your time."

He gave Jayme a nod, then walked away from the door, expecting her to follow. But she remained facing the girl. DeMarco stopped walking but kept his back to Jayme.

"Is Mrs. Gillespie home?" Jayme asked.

"I wouldn't know," Kaitlin said. "Seeing as how she lives in Columbus."

"They're divorced?"

"More or less."

Jayme smiled. Nodded. "Dr. Gillespie is an older man, correct? In his sixties or so?"

"Hardly even fifty," Kaitlin said. By now the insincere smile was fading from her mouth.

"And you're comfortable dressing like that around him?"

"Dressing like what?"

"No bra. Butt cheeks hanging out. It looks more like you're here for a slumber party than a study hour."

The girl's face flushed scarlet. She reached for the door. "He's not even here now."

"So you brought a change of clothes for when he does show up?"

The girl said nothing. Began to ease the door shut. Seemed ready to slam it but knew she shouldn't.

"The girl from campus who was mur-

194

dered," Jayme said. "Samantha Lewis. Did you know her?"

A pause. *Too long,* Jayme thought.

"I might have seen her around a couple of times. I wouldn't say I actually knew her."

Jayme nodded. Let her own smile fade. Gave the girl a steely look. "A study hour, huh? You're not fooling anybody, you know."

"Like I care," the girl said, and brought the door closed. She pushed it into the frame. Slid the dead bolt, hard.

Out on the sidewalk, DeMarco looked up at the sky, and smiled. Then started walking again.

They did not speak until they were both inside the car. "She's still standing behind the door," Jayme said.

"Frightened little bunny. I think you ruined her afternoon."

"Better than ruining her life."

"Of course she might have been telling the truth."

"Summer classes ended five days ago."

"You looked it up?"

She lifted her bottle of water from the cup holder, took a drink, then gave him a smile.

"Aren't you clever?" He pulled his seat belt into place and started the engine. A few minutes later, he felt her lingering gaze on the side of his face.

"What?" he finally said.

"Daisy Mae?" she asked, and laughed. "*Li'l Abner?* Farm fresh? You kill me sometimes, DeMarco."

He looked in the mirror, saw the wrinkles around his eyes. He *was* getting old. She wasn't. And she wanted to have a baby? Problem was . . . maybe he did too.

TWENTY-SIX

"That's him," DeMarco said as he drove toward a wooden sign and information board posted near the shore of the Lily Pond. A tall, broad man wearing a floppy-brimmed Aussie bush hat and holding a six-foot walking stick was doing stretches near the sign. A quarter-mile trail circled the pond, some of it boardwalk, some hard-packed earth, all surrounded by trees thick with summer foliage, the reflection of which painted the water with a bright-green surface.

"Where are the water lilies?" Jayme asked. "It should be called Goose Pond."

Not a single water lily was in sight, but at least a hundred black-necked Canadian geese, plus mallards and a solitary great blue heron, floated or waded along the water's edge. Perhaps a dozen people, singles and couples and a few children, lingered close to the water or continued their strolls around the shore.

Jayme squinted into the glare on the windshield at the large man stretching, rather theatrically, near the information board. "What makes you so sure that's him?" she asked. "The hat?"

"Walking stick."

"Maybe he's going off trail."

"Not a chance," DeMarco said as he eased the car to a stop. By the time he had parked and they both climbed out, the man was striding back and forth in front of the sign.

"Sandals," DeMarco said. "Earphones. And you see how he struts around like he owns the place? What do you bet he's listening to Vivaldi? Not because he likes it, but just in case somebody asks."

She chuckled. "You're probably right."

"And the way he walks. How would you describe that walk?"

She studied him for a few moments. His strides were long and deliberate, shoulders back, chin high, arms cocked at his sides, as if he were strolling down the center of Broadway during a one-man parade. "Sort of a sashay?"

"Funny walk for a religious scholar."

"How would you expect a religious scholar to walk?"

"A little more religiously, I guess. Aren't

religious men supposed to be humble?"

She watched him awhile longer, then said, "He's a professor of religion. That doesn't mean he's religious."

DeMarco took a quick look around the parking lot. Five other vehicles — one coupe, a sedan, a pickup truck, and two SUVs. A man Gillespie's size would not enjoy lowering himself into and out of a sedan or coupe, and DeMarco could not picture him in a truck. "Be right back," he said, and hustled over to the charcoal gray Volvo Momentum. An HYC faculty parking permit hung from the rearview mirror.

He jogged back to Jayme. "The man has a $50K ride. Just in case you're looking for a sugar daddy."

"Keep it up," she told him, "and I might be."

Gillespie was not a small man, and grew larger as they drew closer. Six three, De-Marco guessed. Two hundred fifty pounds or more on a wide frame. Not quite fat, but not at all muscular. He was wearing neon-blue bicycle shorts so tight that his body from navel to midthigh seemed carved for a smaller, fitter man, and pushed the flesh out both ends so that it bunched up atop the waistband and below the leg openings. Thick, hairy legs led down to a pair of fatsoled hiking sandals. On his pumpkin head sat the bush hat and a pair of aviator sunglasses, and over a faded black Bowie 1972 world tour T-shirt he wore an unbuttoned cream-colored safari shirt with the sleeves rolled to his beefy elbows.

DeMarco, hoping his smile did not appear too mirthful, walked up to the professor, whom he was already thinking of as a show dog with a nasty habit of licking its own butt.

Gillespie smiled in greeting, pulled the earbud from his left ear, and said. "The detectives have arrived!"

DeMarco said, "You must have been, what, ten years old when you bought that T-shirt?"

"My father bought it, actually. My only inheritance. Shall we continue the peregrination? I've been maintaining my heart rate with stationary exercise."

DeMarco smiled. "Smashing idea," he said.

Because of the narrowness of the path, Jayme and Gillespie walked side by side, DeMarco close behind. It was not an arrangement DeMarco liked; he preferred to sit or stand facing his subject. Body language could be very revealing. Also facial gestures, tics, eyes that darted from side to side. But walking tended to absorb the energy that might have been directed into fidgeting or finger tapping, especially when the walking speed was dictated by the subject. Gillespie's legs were thick and long but he walked like a model on a runway.

DeMarco had seen the type before. Arrogant and supercilious. Blind to his own faults. The kind of guy some people hate without ever talking to. His smile oozed something invisible. Something you didn't want to inhale or light a match close to.

"I take it you're familiar with the unfortunate incidents of the past month," DeMarco said.

"Acutely," said Gillespie. The tip of his walking stick struck the trampled earth with every second slap of his left sandal, a regularity that soon became irritating to De-Marco.

Jayme asked, "Did you know any of the victims?"

"Fortunately, no."

"Why fortunately?" she said.

"Intimacy," the professor said. "The pain, the fear, the anger. It would all be so much more intimate were I to know the victims personally. Anguish is troubling enough in an amorphous state, but when it afflicts us personally — utterly debilitating."

"Brenner graduated from HYC," Jayme said. "And Lewis was a student at the time of the murder."

Gillespie nodded. "Indeed."

"Neither one of them a student of yours?"

They walked for two clicks of the walking stick. Gillespie said, "My classes are large, very popular. Faces I usually remember, but names too often elude me."

Another click. "I could look it up online," he added. "I should do that."

DeMarco leaned forward just enough to shoot a glance at Jayme. She responded with a tiny nod.

"What do you make of the murderer's . . . style of execution?" DeMarco asked.

"Ah!" Gillespie said, and gazed briefly at the sky. "The modus operandi."

He enunciated the phrase as if it were a mystical incantation. DeMarco resisted the urge to roll his eyes.

"You suspect a religious undertone," Gillespie said. "And *that* is why you have sought me out."

"Do you detect a religious undertone?" Jayme asked.

"One might call the decapitation ritualistic," Gillespie said. "But fragmentary at best. No pun intended." And now he turned his head toward Jayme and offered a beaming smile. "You've heard of my theory, I take it."

"Bits and pieces," Jayme lied. "I would love to hear it in full."

"Well then," Gillespie said. Another click of the walking stick. "It wasn't until the death of the girl that I began to wonder of a correlation. Are you familiar with Hypatia?"

"I'm sorry, no," Jayme said.

Gillespie turned to DeMarco. "And you, sir?"

"Sounds like a nasty scalp condition."

Gillespie chuckled. "Hypatia may have been the first of the *Gnostikoi* martyrs."

"Gnostikoi?" Jayme said.

"From the Greek. Those who have gnosis. Knowledge of the truth."

DeMarco asked, "And what truth are we talking about here?"

"You should sign up for one of my classes," Gillespie said. "Law enforcement so seldom considers the underlying cultural influences on the criminal mind-set."

Too busy putting the criminals in jail, DeMarco thought.

Gillespie continued. "The Gnostics were, and remain, very difficult to pin down. Other than the Nag Hammadi scrolls, all we know of them is what their critics wrote.

203

Their critics being overwhelmingly Christian."

"Any chance you could boil it down for us?" DeMarco said.

"Any summary account runs the risk of being misleading," Gillespie told him, "but suffice it to say that the Gnostics, and their predecessors the Pagans, rejected the divinity of the Old Testament God, Jehovah. Also known as Yahweh or Yaldabaoth. To the Gnostics he was an inferior god, wholly demented, a personage not to be obeyed but actively disobeyed. As such they also rejected the Christian doctrine of salvation through faith alone. Enlightenment, they believed, could be achieved only through experiential knowledge, a personal experience with the divine."

They walked for a few moments in silence but for the click of the walking stick, the buzz of insects, and the chirp of birds. Then Jayme asked, "And Hypatia was martyred because of her beliefs?"

Gillespie nodded. "Near the end of the fourth century AD, a mob of Christians torched a temple dedicated to the god Serapis and burned it to the ground. At the time, Hypatia was quite probably a student of the Mysteries, as they were called, though initiates are often also referred to as Pagans —

erroneously, in the modern sense — so this might have been her first exposure to the violence of the Christians. Three years later, Pagan rituals were outlawed by the state. In due time, Hypatia became a revered teacher of the Mysteries. By all accounts she was an exceptional woman of legendary beauty and intelligence. She even drove her own chariot!"

"You go, girl," Jayme said.

"Precisely!" said Gillespie. "Which made her an obvious target for the Christians, which, as I'm sure you know, is in every way a patriarchal religion. Unfortunately, one day Hypatia entered a public square filled with a gathering of Christians. She was pulled from her chariot, stripped of her robes, and beaten to death. Some accounts also have her being raped. The mob not only tore her limbs from her body, but used oyster shells to scrape the flesh from her bones. As a final display of their mindless fury, they burned her bones to ashes."

"Oh my God," Jayme said.

Gillespie smiled. "And so the near-total suppression of the Pagans, the Gnostics, and the Mystery schools began in earnest. The rest, young lady, is Christian history."

DeMarco said, "And this has what to do with the death of Samantha Lewis and the others?"

"My theory," said Gillespie, "is that much contemporary criminal behavior is the result of a collective social and cultural memory."

"Cultural memory," DeMarco repeated.

"And in many cases, a subconscious one. Writ upon our DNA, if you will. Which prompts in those individuals lacking in the necessary intellect and strength of will to resist the urge to reenact or continue crimes of the otherwise forgotten past."

"Interesting," DeMarco said. "Let me see if I understand this. You're saying that the murders we're investigating were all committed by someone subconsciously influenced by events that happened thousands of years ago?"

"The phenomenon is called 'the intergenerational transmission of collective trauma.' We already know that profound trauma in a previous generation can be passed along to subsequent generations via the genetic material. The gene marker, to be exact, rather than the gene itself. The term for that is 'epigenetic change.' As in Holocaust survivors and their descendants, for example. We can also point to the intergenerational trauma suffered by Native Americans. African Americans. Asian Americans. Virtually every ethnicity unlucky enough to encounter those of the Caucasoid persuasion. Most especially, the Christianized version."

"So your theory," Jayme said, "is that our three recent murders —"

"Plus the 1988 murders," Gillespie said, "and the Cleveland murders, and innumerable previous atrocities."

"— were all subconscious reactions to historical traumas perpetrated by white Christians?"

"No, no, no," Gillespie said. "A *continuation* of these traumas. It stands to reason, don't you see? If trauma can be written on the DNA, so can the hatred that engenders trauma. Hufford was a Black man, Lewis a female, Brenner a Jew. Although it is true that Talarico, from 1988, was Catholic, his lawyer was an avowed atheist, and probably the real target."

"And the Torso Murders?" Jayme said.

"The dregs of society. Drunkards, whores, you name it. All despised by Christians."

DeMarco said, "I thought Christians were compassionate and forgiving."

"Ha!" said Gillespie, impassioned by his own words. "Look at their history, my friend. Christian terrorism is part and parcel of the religion, from the days of Moses onward. 'Do not leave alive anything that breathes. Completely destroy them — the Hittites, Amorites, Canaanites, Perizzites, Hivites, and Jebusites — as the Lord your God has commanded you.' Deuteronomy 20:16–17. Just one of many such commands."

"Whew," Jayme said.

Gillespie turned to her and smiled. "It does take one's breath away, doesn't it?"

"It's a bit of a broad sweep," said DeMarco.

"But a wonderfully probable explanation," Gillespie answered. "You must concede that."

"Probable or possible?" DeMarco asked.

"Trust me," Gillespie said. "I have researched this subject front and back. Earlier this month I made a very well-received presentation at the annual True Crime Conference in Cleveland. Very well-received. I have a videotape if you would care to watch it. I'm sure you would find it enlightening."

"Any chance you could email it to me?" Jayme said.

"Of course. Just text me your email account."

DeMarco said, "Send the video to the Mahoning County Sheriff. You can find the email address online. Any chance you could do that today?"

"The minute I return home."

They were coming to the end of the loop around the pond, approaching the parking lot again. DeMarco took two long steps forward, squeezing past Jayme, then made an abrupt turn, so that Gillespie had to pull up short and stop as well. DeMarco said, "I understand that you're divorced, Professor?"

"Estranged, actually. Four years now."

"Children?"

"Two boys. Eleven and eight."

DeMarco nodded. Looked toward his car. Thought, *Your boys were seven and four when you left them.* He winced, then turned back to Gillespie. "That young woman at your house we talked to? Kaitlin? She said she was doing some cleaning for you?"

Gillespie blinked. "That's right. Yes. I like to help out my students whenever I can. Student debt being what it is."

"Of course," DeMarco said. "You might suggest that she dress a little more appropriately, though. Some people might get the wrong impression."

"I, uh . . . I wasn't there when she arrived. But I will certainly make mention of it to her."

"Excellent," DeMarco said. "We'll let you

209

continue with your peregrination now." He turned away, walking briskly.

Jayme said, "Thanks again for your co-operation," and followed DeMarco to the car.

DeMarco climbed inside, started the engine, and turned the air conditioner to its maximum setting. Then he climbed back out and waited beside the open door. Jayme opened her door, then looked over the roof to DeMarco. She took a glance to make certain Gillespie was out of range. He had passed the information board and was striding toward the first turn in the loop, his walking stick clicking even more vehemently now.

"Did you follow all that?" she asked.

DeMarco said, "I once heard a guy argue that 'Mary Had a Little Lamb' was about Mary and Jesus and the separation of church and state."

"And that is relevant how?"

"It's possible to twist just about anything around to make it say what you want it to say."

"So you're not buying his theory?"

"He's a pompous ass."

"That doesn't necessarily mean he's wrong."

"Or right," DeMarco said.

"Truth is, the moment I saw that walking stick, he became a kind of joke to me."

"It's not a walking stick. It's a phallic symbol."

"A pretty obvious one."

"Isn't that the point?"

She chuckled. Then said, "I notice you chose not to mention his library research."

"The timing corresponds to the presentation he made at the crime conference. Precedes it. We should be able to tell from the video if he used the research for his presentation."

"And in the meantime, let him bask in his own self-importance?"

DeMarco nodded. "I've had academics at number three on my list of narcissistic jerks, right behind politicians and lawyers. But I don't know. After listening to Gillespie, I might have to bump them up a notch to number two."

"He deserves it," she said. "But be fair. There are some good teachers too. Lots, in fact."

"Right again," he said.

Mr. Kassis, she thought. Advanced biology. Instead of chewing her out for skipping classes during the dissection unit, he had merely asked, "Was it the frog or the freeze-dried cat?" And she had answered, "Both."

He nodded, asked nothing more, and didn't count those twenty-five points against her final grade.

She and DeMarco climbed into the car then and shut the doors. Both sat still for a few moments while the vent breezes dried their skin. Then Jayme thought of something else, and wrinkled her nose. "That thing about using oyster shells to scrape Hypatia's flesh off her bones? I don't think I can ever eat oysters again."

"When you eat an oyster, you are eating its stomach, intestines, gonads, heart, mouth, digestive gland, and anus. Raw."

"God, Ryan."

"Just sayin'," he said. "Let's grab some lunch."

TWENTY-SEVEN

On the terrace of the little restaurant attached to the park's visitor center, with a narrow but long view of Lake Glacier framed between two walls of lush greenery, DeMarco alerted Sheriff Brinker of the professor's forthcoming video attachment, and asked that it be forwarded to Jayme's account as soon as it arrived. Over club sandwiches, chunks of fresh fruit, and iced tea, they discussed the interview.

She asked, "Do you trust him?"

"I do," he said. "Every bit as much as I trust a TV evangelist with his zipper down and lipstick stains on his underwear."

"Well," she said, and squeezed a lemon wedge over the ice in her glass, "I don't like him either. Kaitlin said she was studying at his house, but he went with your assertion that she was cleaning. Nice trick, by the way. There's no doubt he's a first-class jerk. Too bad that's not a chargeable offense."

DeMarco scowled and juked his head back and forth, which made her laugh.

"So what do you think of his theory?" she asked.

"I guess that's what they call white guilt."

"Lucky for us we don't have any of that."

"I have guilt," he told her. "But I earned it, and not because I'm white. It's about taking responsibility for our own actions, not our great-great-great-great-grandparents'. We are who we let ourselves be."

She was glad to hear him say that. It suggested that maybe he was in the process of reappraising his guilt, deciding what to hold on to and what to let go. Ever since his few days in the Kentucky mountains, he seemed changed in a way she did not yet understand. He was gentler with her than he had been, and teased less often. Even his voice seemed pitched a few degrees softer. He had always been a man of few extraneous movements, but lately she sensed less anger in that control, as if his stillness was genuine and relaxed, and not the stillness of a coiled spring. On the other hand, perhaps the anger had been supplanted by sadness or resignation. Before Kentucky, an urgency had always driven his actions, but any urgency now was barely detectable. More

214

than ever, she found him gazing into the distance. She was afraid to ask where he went at those times, how far his thoughts had moved from her. And so she said nothing. She watched and waited, and prayed he would not disappear from her completely.

Over the next thirty-five minutes, they ate slowly, smiled at each other, and responded to each other's remarks, but otherwise seemed content with their own thoughts. Then Jayme's cell phone beeped to signal a new email.

She tapped the screen, read the header, and said, dramatically, mocking Gillespie's opening statement, "The video has arrived!" She clicked the file open. "Looks like it's . . . not all that long. You want to take turns with the earbuds?"

There were only two other tables occupied on the terrace, but the terrace was small. He said, "Let's do it together in the car. So if it's boring, I can take a nap."

Maybe that's it, she told herself. *Maybe he's just tired.*

The professor's nineteen-minute presentation extended beyond boring into sedative. Jayme balanced the laptop on her knees, with the volume turned up high to compete with the car's air conditioner. DeMarco's brow wrinkled a half minute into the video, which caused him to lean back in his seat and close his eyes. She hit pause. "You don't want to watch it?" she asked.

Without opening his eyes, he said, "I don't want to watch him. I can listen better this way."

His forehead remained pinched all through the presentation. Jayme scribbled notes on her pocket notebook. Only near the end of the brief Q&A, when Gillespie called for security, did DeMarco open his eyes, but too late to see anything other than Gillespie's triumphant grin. Seconds later, the video ended and the screen went black.

"What just happened there?" he asked.

"I'm not sure," she said. "It seemed to jump from a friendly Q&A to him calling for security. You want to see it?"

"If you didn't understand it, I won't. That's already, what, twenty minutes of my life I'll never get back. He said all that stuff in the park, right?"

"That might be a bit of a simplification, babe." She flipped back to the beginning of her notes and read aloud. "Pre-Christian Pagans and Gnostics . . . do what thou wilt. Hermetic Order of the Golden Dawn. Rabelais. Lord Dashwood and Ben Franklin, the Hellfire Club. Aleister Crowley, founder of Thelema. Sex magic and sexual spirituality. Dionysian indulgences in women and wine. Creation out of destruction, life out of death. Daemons and the Ouroboros."

DeMarco said, "What's he have against Matt Damon?"

She chuckled. "I might be mispronouncing it. It might be demons. But anyway, in a nutshell, his theory is that most unsolved murders can be traced back to the way Old Testament Christianity screwed up our DNA."

DeMarco sat up straight, stretched his back, and shook his head. "This is what kids are being taught these days?"

"You should watch the part at the end where the camera cuts to the audience for a second. Which wasn't huge, by the way. Maybe ten or eleven people in all."

"What did I miss?"

"Just a young man standing up. Then it cuts to Gillespie pretending to call for security."

"I didn't hear anybody else's voice on the video."

"There isn't. Just that awkward jump. Something's been edited out."

"I'll watch it tonight," DeMarco told her. He looked out the side window and exhaled through his mouth. "You have that card Olcott gave us at the library? With the other guy's name and address?"

"We can do it tomorrow if you've had enough for the day."

"Do ain't done," he said.

"Excuse me?"

He turned to face her; smiled. "Something my mother used to say. Her parents were pretty much hillbillies. One of their sayings probably."

"And it means . . . ?"

"When she wanted me to do something, clean my room or take out the garbage or whatever. If I hadn't done it, I'd say I plan to do it, or I'll do it in a while, something like that. And she'd say, 'Do ain't done.' Which meant do it now. Get it over with."

Grinning, she removed the card from the back of her notebook. Read what Olcott had written. "Daksh Khatri. #17 Tremont Apartments, 109 Liberty Street, Garrettsville."

"Looks like we're going up the country," DeMarco said. "I'll head us north, you check him out on Facebook."

"Babe, you sound tired."

"Spinning our wheels," he told her. "It always wears me out."

But she knew it was more than that, more than fatigue, more than frustration. He had a weariness that went deeper than muscle and bone. Was she a part of it? When had she first noticed it in him? When she mentioned wanting a baby?

Another chill ran up her spine, and this time she couldn't hold back the shiver. Fearing he had noticed it, she turned the air conditioner down.

TWENTY-EIGHT

Ryan's comment about narcissistic academics had started Jayme remembering, and thinking about the many other fine teachers she had known. Dr. Burnette, for example. Susan. Small and blond and pretty, barely thirty, as fine-boned as a sparrow, as delicate as a sigh. Introduction to Sociology. Her perfume was White Diamonds. Her lipstick, Covergirl Cherry Cordial, their palest shade.

Jayme's personal sociology was making a big change that year, thanks to the very noticeable changes to her body. They all seemed to occur between leaving home in June and arriving at her grandmother's place in western Kentucky a day later, though in truth the changes had been happening since she was thirteen, the new fullness in her breasts and hips, the bouncy, awkward stride that now, at seventeen, was smooth and graceful. Her grandmother's greeting had been, "What a beauty you are!

You're like a whole different person!" Her Aberdeen friends all reacted the same way, especially the boys. They looked at her, spoke to her, treated her differently than they ever had before. It was all very unnerving for Jayme.

Her grandmother insisted that she enter the Peach Festival Princess competition, which was nothing more than a lineup and Q&A before the mayor and a few women from various agencies and organizations. Jayme was both mortified and thrilled when she won. And ten weeks later, when she returned home and started her first semester as a commuter at the local college, she was still struggling to adjust to the way males behaved around her.

It was after her second sociology class that Jayme found herself boxed in by three freshman boys, all six feet tall or more, all wearing T-shirts marked *Property of* the school's athletic department. What's your name? they wanted to know. Where you from? What dorm you staying in? Wanna go to a mixer tonight? They peppered her with questions but didn't allow a chance for her to answer them, each boy speaking louder than the previous one, each trying to crowd closer to her, until she felt as if she were drowning.

Dr. Burnette, tiny as she was, waded into their midst and pushed them aside. "You boys go lift some weights or something. Ms. Matson and I have a meeting to attend."

Alone in the room, Dr. Burnette pulled a chair close to her desk and invited Jayme to sit. "They can be exhausting, can't they?" she said.

"The boys back in high school never treated me like that."

"And where was that?" From her big canvas bag Dr. Burnette produced two oranges and two paper napkins. She set one of each in front of Jayme, then started to peel her own. Her fingers were thin and long, Jayme thought, for such a small person. Her fingernails were painted the same color as her lips. And the napkin she handed Jayme smelled pleasantly of White Diamonds.

Within a week they knew nearly everything there was to know about each other. They would sometimes walk the grounds together, or sit in the gazebo if the day was wet. Sometimes on the weekend they would meet for brunch and a movie; sometimes they would take a drive in Dr. Burnette's yellow Beetle to Rosemont Park, often singing along with the radio all the way there and home again, or to the reservoir spillway to watch the carp crawling over each other for the stale bread visitors tossed into the water.

When she found out that Jayme was an accounting major and planned to work with Cullen, the youngest of her three brothers and the owner of an insurance company in town, their usual lighthearted mood turned serious. "Why accounting?" the professor asked.

"I don't know. It's easy for me. And Cullen is doing pretty well for himself. He says he needs the help."

"Is that something you love, working with numbers?"

Jayme shrugged. "It's okay, I guess. Like I said, my brother says he can use my help."

Dr. Burnette nodded. Her smile was always soft, always melancholy. "The thing about settling down in the place where you grew up," she said, "is that you never really do grow up. You will always be the person other people remember you as. Everybody who knows you will know your past, and will maybe even take advantage of you because of that. Your past can box you in. And a person like you, Jayme . . . my God, you have so much *blooming* to do. I really can't envision you sitting behind a desk every day. I would so love to see you do some traveling before you decide to settle down. Europe, Asia, Australia . . . you should see the world. That's the best education there is for a person like you."

"That would be nice," Jayme said. "My father hasn't been well lately, though. There are a lot of bills."

"I understand," the professor said. "I say silly things sometimes. But if the opportunity ever presents itself . . . please promise me you will grab onto it and run."

"Carpe diem," Jayme said.

And then came a Saturday morning brunch near the end of the semester when Dr. Burnette did not show up. Nor did she answer her phone the several times Jayme called. Nor appear for class the following Monday. The secretary from the Sociology Department was there to announce that Dr. Burnette had a family emergency that made it necessary for her to return to Houston. A graduate assistant would finish out the semester for her.

Jayme was stunned, then furious. *She couldn't even call me? She couldn't even pick up the damn phone?*

At home she was either sullen and silent or short-tempered and brusque. In her classes, she sat with eyes down, never raised her hand to answer or ask a question. After a while she started accepting invitations to socialize, started drinking through the week with people she had known in high school. She got drunk, got high, did things she preferred not to remember the next morning. None of it mattered. All was deceit and betrayal anyway. Nobody could be trusted.

And then one day during semester break, while doing some filing in Cullen's office, she caught a scent of White Diamonds. It came out of nowhere as she was slipping a folder into the filing cabinet. She turned, looked at a couple sitting there waiting to talk to her brother. And then, for some reason, her heart started racing, her throat became constricted. But she could not isolate the scent. Throughout the day it would come and go, there but not there. She kept looking toward the door, kept waiting.

At home that evening, a card-sized white envelope addressed to her lay on the kitchen counter. Again her heart stuttered. The handwriting was feminine and familiar. Inside the envelope was a small sheet of stationery. Jayme unfolded it, saw the neat typing, and breathed in White Diamonds as she read.

My dearest, dearest Jayme,
We never used the word love,
you and I, although I am sure
you know that I felt it. You
know too that there are different kinds of love. Any
kind, I believe, is good. I
hope you can believe that too.
Yet I felt it would have been
wrong to speak of love with
you. Either you would reject
my love, and that I could not
bear, or you would return it,
and that would only cause you
grief in the end. So I gave
you my love with every breath,
but I kept it silent. I have a
condition called hypertrophic
cardiomyopathy. Simply put,
my heart can stop at any moment. In fact it has stopped
on several occasions, though
prompt medical attention has
started it again. But each
time, damage was done. So I
always knew this day would
come, but I never knew when. I
am with my family and doctor
as I write this note to you.
We are waiting for a new heart

to become available. If it comes in time and the surgery is successful, I have a 94 percent chance of living another seven years or more, in which case you will be receiving a different kind of letter from me. But if you are reading this letter, well then . . .

Soon you will receive a letter from my lawyer, and that letter will include a check. A penny for each of the breaths and heartbeats I will never be able to share with you. Please hear my heartbeats when you listen to music and sing along with it as we did. Please hear my breath when the wind blows through your beautiful hair.

Bloom, sweetheart. See the world. Love life, love yourself, love your gifts. And bloom!

In shaky blue ink, she had signed her name. *Susan.*

Jayme sank to her knees at the kitchen

counter, too weak and hollowed out to stand.

Two weeks later, back at school, she changed her major to undecided. The following summer, she bought a Eurail pass and backpacked through Belgium, the Netherlands, Germany, England, Ireland, and Wales, then returned to continue her education at a school four hundred miles from her hometown. She started her sophomore year as a psychology major, and spent the next summer driving a rented car from Houston to Mexico City to Costa Rica. After her junior year, she spent the last of Susan's gift in Australia and New Zealand. Someday, with luck, she would walk across the Great Wall of China.

So no, Ryan, she might have told him. *All academics aren't narcissists.* But he had his experiences, and she had hers. Maybe someday she would share hers with him. But later. When she was sure he would understand.

Twenty-Nine

"Whoa," Jayme said several miles outside of Garrettsville.

DeMarco lifted his foot from the accelerator. "Whoa as in stop?"

"Whoa as in you are going to find this very interesting." She turned the laptop so that DeMarco could take a glance at Daksh Khatri's Facebook page.

"Attends Case Western University," he read with the first glance. Then, "Works at Dairy Queen and the Humane Society."

He faced the road again. "Sounds like dog hair in the ice cream to me."

"The photos, knucklehead."

All eight photos, two rows of four, showed the same thin young man, Indian or Pakistani, mugging with other youths.

"Okay," he said after a couple of glances. "And the interesting part is . . . ?"

"It's the guy from the video," she told him. "The one who stood up just before

Gillespie called for security."

"Carumba," he said softly.

Fifteen minutes later, DeMarco rapped four times on the door of apartment 17. The Tremont Apartments were comprised of a single yellow-brick building, two stories, a blacktop parking lot, and a half acre of browning grass. Most of the cars in the lot were compacts, few late models, several with rusting dents and smashed taillights. "Definitely not Millionaire's Row," DeMarco had said when he pulled into the lot.

Now they stood midway down the second-floor balcony. Competing genres of music could be heard coming from other apartments, accompanied by a baby crying, a mother down below screaming at a child. But no sounds emanated from Khatri's apartment.

DeMarco glanced at his cell phone. "Just after two in the afternoon. I vote for the Humane Society."

"I'm surprised," she said. "I figured you for the Dairy Queen."

"Oh, we're going there. The perfect way to cap the day."

"With chocolate syrup, I'm sure."

THIRTY

A dozen dogs howling, barking, whining in the background. The scents of dog fur, dry dog food, dog urine and feces and bleach and Khatri's half-eaten box of Thai noodles. All this hit their senses simultaneously as first Jayme, then DeMarco entered the lobby of the Humane Society's rescue center. The ripe air scratched at their throats. Daksh Khatri, seated on a high stool behind a short counter, cradled a small, sickly looking dog in the crook of his left arm, a wire brush in his right. He looked up when the door opened and smiled hopefully.

"You wish to adopt?" he said, his voice soft and lilting, enunciation precise. He nodded toward the dog. "This is Layla. New yesterday. Part Yorkie and part Maltese, I think. With maybe some Pomsky thrown in. Very loving and calm, as you can see. Or were you looking for something bigger?"

Jayme stepped forward to the side of the counter, leaned down and petted the docile dog. "Hi, baby. How are you? Are you feeling okay?"

"Three children," Khatri told her. "Always pulling and throwing her around. A doggy wasn't made for that. But she will be fine. I am fixing her up. Two, three days at most. Then you can take her home with you."

DeMarco showed his ID. "We didn't come for a pet, Daksh. We just have a couple of questions for you."

The young man appeared startled by that, but quickly regained his composure and retained it until the end of the conversation. DeMarco warmed up with the usual questions about his whereabouts on the nights of the three recent murders. Each time, the answer was "At the Dairy Queen." As assistant manager, he closed up six nights per week. Jayme took notes, including the name and contact information for Daksh's supervisors at both places of employment.

"You checked out some library material a few weeks before the first incident," DeMarco said. "Information about the Talarico/Brogan murders, as well as the Cleveland murders."

"Yes, sir, I did that."

"For what purpose?" DeMarco asked.

"I was attending a conference the following week. I like to prepare myself so that I am properly informed of the subject to be discussed."

"Would that have been Dr. Gillespie's presentation at the True Crime Conference?"

"Yes, sir, it was."

DeMarco had noticed a brief dilation of Khatri's pupils just before he answered. He asked, "Did you enjoy the conference? Find it as informative as you had hoped?"

Now Khatri looked down at Layla, ran two fingers over her skull. "It was very good, yes."

"How do you know Dr. Gillespie?"

"From the presentation advertisements, I think. Or maybe . . . yes, maybe I heard his name before that. Yes, probably so. When I attended HYC."

"You were a student there?"

"Three semesters, yes. Before I transferred to Case Western University. I am a sociology major. With a concentration in crime, law, and justice."

He could no longer meet DeMarco's eyes. Stroked the little dog almost continuously now.

"If I were to look up your transcripts for your time at HYC," DeMarco said, "would

I see that you were a student of Dr. Gillespie's?"

"No, sir. No, I do not think you would."

DeMarco said nothing now. Both he and Jayme kept their eyes on Khatri. The young man's strokes down Layla's back were becoming longer and slower. Finally his hand stopped moving. Jayme asked, "How old are you, Daksh?"

"I am twenty-eight," he said. "In November, twenty-nine."

"That's a very interesting tattoo on your wrist."

He held up his right arm, turned his hand so that she could see the underside of the tattoo as well. It depicted a cobra coiled around the wrist and entwined around itself. "This is Vasuki, the serpent Lord Shiva wears around his neck."

"It's beautiful," she told him. "What does it symbolize?"

"The endless cycle of birth and regeneration. But also the ego. Which, once tamed, can be worn as a decoration. It is a constant reminder to me. To strive always for humility, and to be of service to others."

"What a lovely thought to wear on your wrist," she said.

He looked up at her now. "I took his Comparative Religions course my third semester. But I did not finish. I withdrew."

Jayme asked, "From the class or the university?"

"Both. Same time."

She nodded. Reached out to scratch between Layla's ears. "And he's the reason you withdrew?"

Again he nodded. "We disagreed."

DeMarco let a few moments pass. Then said, "The man's a total ass, am I right?"

Khatri's head swung around, his eyes as wide with hope as they had been when Jayme and DeMarco first entered the building. "You have met him?"

"We listened to him yammer for most of thirty minutes. I found it difficult to stay awake."

And now Khatri smiled. Turned to Jayme again. "He says many inappropriate things to females. With you as well?"

"He undressed me with his eyes a couple of times. But I think he knew I'd punch him out if he actually said anything."

DeMarco asked, "Why did you really go to that conference, Daksh?"

Ten seconds ticked by before the young man answered. "He humiliated me in front of my classmates. Because I disagreed with him. I had no choice but to go elsewhere."

"So you attended the conference," De-

Marco said, "to try to humiliate *him*?"

"The man is a charlatan. Forgive me but it is true. He twists everything around to suit his purposes. His knowledge of Paganism, Gnosticism, Hinduism, everything he discusses, is superficial and incomplete. Love is the law, not disobedience and violence. Do what thou wilt, yes, but with *love*. Love is the law. This part he always cleverly forgets."

"And you confronted him about this at the conference, didn't you?"

Khatri shrugged. "I only wished to correct his errors. As always, he would not listen."

Jayme asked if Khatri was aware that the presentation had been videotaped. He said, "I saw the camera, yes."

"We watched the video," DeMarco told him. "A minute or two appear to be missing from the Q&A portion. All we see of you is the part where you stand up. Then him laughing and calling for security."

"Again he humiliates me!" Khatri said. "He mocks everything I say. I asked why he does not quote the doctrine of Thelema as it is written. Why he perverts the truth and encourages violence."

"He does?" Jayme asked. "You've heard him call for violence?"

"He is too careful to say that word, but

his meaning is the same. Resist all authority, he says. By any means necessary. I try to show him that Thelema says no such thing. He will not listen. The truth is of no consequence to him."

"What *does* matter to him?" DeMarco asked.

"A few students. He favors them. Because they worship him."

"Which you never did," Jayme said.

"Nor would I fear him. Not until the killings began. Especially the girl."

DeMarco moved closer to the counter. "Are you referring to Samantha Lewis?"

Khatri nodded. "She was one of his."

"Excuse me?" Jayme said. "Samantha Lewis was one of Gillespie's students?"

"Oh yes. One of his pets. Maybe his favorite."

Just then the door swung open, and everyone stopped talking. An attractive young woman in her thirties held the door open as a boy of eight or nine, wearing metal leg braces and using crutches, made his way inside. His smile was huge as he looked up at Khatri.

"She has been waiting for you," Khatri said to the boy. "Go ahead and bring her out."

The boy moved as quickly as he could, his

mother following. DeMarco watched until both disappeared down the hallway to the kennel area. Then he kept staring at the empty doorway.

To Jayme, Khatri whispered, "The boy has muscular dystrophy. He comes each day to play with Fanny. She is a cockapoo, very old. We should put her down . . . but for the boy. It would be impossible for them to take her home. The mother has so much to do already. So the boy comes here every day."

"That's so sweet," Jayme said. DeMarco was still gazing into the empty doorway. She turned to him and said, "We should probably go."

He nodded, turned away and, without another word, headed for the door.

Quickly Jayme handed Khatri a business card, told him they might need to contact him again, and asked him to call if he had any additional information about Gillespie that might be useful. Then she followed De-Marco outside.

THIRTY-ONE

DeMarco moved slowly, heavily to the car. They climbed in and buckled up and headed south out of Garrettsville. Jayme kept waiting for him to say something about their conversation with Khatri, the revelation that Samantha Lewis had not only been one of Gillespie's students but possibly something more. But DeMarco said nothing.

Finally she said, "You're being awfully quiet over there. Have you gone into a trance or what?"

"What a sad place that is," he said.

"The Humane Society?"

"It's like death row for dogs."

"Did you want to look at the dogs? Get one to take home?"

He shook his head no.

She knew that he wasn't thinking about taking a dog home with them, and that he didn't want to talk about Khatri or Gillespie or Samantha Lewis yet either. Something had jarred another memory loose.

She waited to see if he would pull in at the Dairy Queen but he did not, didn't even glance out the side window as they passed. Instead he said, "Do you know the song 'Sky Blue and Black' by Jackson Browne?"

"I've heard it, yes."

"Could you pull it up on your laptop for me? It's been a long time since I listened to it."

"Are you sure? As I recall, it's a pretty sad song."

"It's about forgiveness."

She took a chance and asked, "Is there somebody you would like to forgive?"

He said nothing. So she opened her laptop and found the song on YouTube and let the music fill their space through the car's stereo system.

When the song ended, she said, "Do you want to hear it again?"

He shook his head no.

She reached out, laid a hand atop his leg. "Who is it you want to forgive, babe?"

He didn't answer that question but shook his head and said very softly, as if speaking to himself, "I wish I could. But I can't."

Again he had shut her out. Lost in his own

darkness. Sometimes she just wanted to scream.

■　■　■　■

II

■　■　■　■

Come dance with me, the darkness says
when the night breeze scrapes down
　　every street,
and the invisible people who can find no
　　friend in sleep,
no friend in light,
cling like lovers to their blackened
　　doorways
and fill their souls with the smoke of
　　night.
　　　　　　　— from "3 a.m.," Thomas Huston

For the first time ever, I am seeing life as it truly is. Seeing people as they really are. Magus said only blood could wash the scales from my eyes, and he was right. Experience is what matters, not theory, not faith. Doing, not talking. To think that I used to admire Dashwood and wanted to please him, even be like him. He's no better than a mini-Yaldabaoth. Preaches salvation but it's all demented ego. Just one gross slob of ego.

I need to start looking for another lamb. Different neighborhood, Magus says. The person isn't important but the place is, got to get in and get out without being seen. Even the sheeple are alert now. Can't be too careful this time. The first one was to get everybody's attention, mission accomplished. Fear is like caffeine to a drunk, Magus said, though that doesn't seem like a great analogy to me. Caffeine doesn't sober you up at all. Good for a hangover but that's about it. But fear does open up the eyes for a while. A few days, maybe a week, two at the most. Then the drunks get drunk again, zone out, go back to being deaf and blind.

Me, I'm as clearheaded as I've ever been. Snuffing out a life is so easy. Which gives a good indication how insignificant a life is. We're all bugs, nothing more unless we transform ourselves, do a reverse Kafka. Go to bed a cockroach, wake up a warrior. The warrior is always free, even in defeat. The coward is always in prison, even in victory. Because his victory is an illusion, that's why. His life is without meaning when there's no True Will involved. It's just like Crowley said. "A man who is doing his True Will has the inertia of the Universe to assist him."

That's why the thing with Venus has everybody rattled. I let myself be a puppet, and now I have to redeem myself. Magus says I have to write about it sooner or later, have to process it, same as he is doing, trying to figure the best way to use it to further the cause. Nothing happens by accident, he says. Everything is a gift. A man of True Will takes that gift and puts it to use. The sheeple just blink, eat some more grass, piss and shit and screw their lives away. They go back to their invisible insignificant lives, thinking they matter, having their little accomplishments and romances, getting their meaningless degrees and going to their meaningless jobs and filling up their pretty little boxes with all their meaningless toys.

Not me. I'm ready now. Magus wants another lamb, I'll give him another lamb. Let the blood flow over the altar. Let the tabernacle drown in blood.

I am Erebus, son of Khaos.

THIRTY-TWO

"Do you think we should include the poetry too?" DeMarco asked.

"Sure. Why not?" Jayme said. They had been reading in silence for nearly an hour, sitting in bed with the box of composition books between them, the house dark but for the two small lamps on the bedside tables, quiet but for the rustle of paper and their own movements and the muted hum of the air conditioner when it clicked on to blow a cooling breeze through the ceiling vents.

"There are also little snippets of fiction," he said. "Anyway I think it's fiction. He seldom marks them one way or the other."

"Just include anything you like."

"That's the problem. I like everything. It's as if he's sitting across from me talking."

"Did he used to recite poetry to you?"

"No. It's just the quality of his voice I remember."

She laid her own composition book aside,

reached out to rub her hand up and down his arm. "I wish you'd had more time together. It's hard to lose your best friend."

He touched her hand with his fingertips. "I have another best friend now."

"It's not the same though, is it? I miss my best friend too. Something closed up inside me after MaryKyle died. Something she had opened."

He nodded. Laid his hand flat atop hers.

"Read me the poem," she said. "Before I start crying."

"It doesn't have a title."

"Titles are overrated."

He smiled. Looked down at the composition book that lay open beneath his other hand. And he read:

A tree knows how to listen,
has heard and whispers
all the secrets of time.
And so I listen to the trees.

You must become as us
is the first thing they tell me.
So I clothe myself with bark
impervious to all rain.

That isn't what we mean, they say.

So I send roots deep into the earth

and twist them around rocks
that will not be budged.

That isn't what we mean, they say.

And so I spread my branches wide,
sprout leaves that block the sun,
cast shade on all below me.

That isn't what we mean, they say.

And so I rise and stretch toward heaven,
imperturbable and grand.

That isn't what we mean, they say.

And so, in surrender,
I bend before the wind.
I tremble and shiver and
drop my leaves.
I creak and fall,
succumb to ants and rot.
I turn to brown dust
that children kick when
they run past laughing.

Now you're getting it,
all the trees that fell before me say.

Jayme sat silent for a while, thinking about

the lines. "Definitely include," she said.

"I wish I knew more about poetry. I was big on Rilke and Yeats a while back, but I don't know anything more recent."

"You're not expected to be a critic."

He nodded. Then marked the page with a sticky blue arrow.

"You want to call it a night?" she asked.

"Sure." They laid the composition books back inside the box, and DeMarco lifted the box aside to set it on the floor. Almost simultaneously they turned off their lights, then rearranged their pillows and lay beside each other, holding hands.

In the darkness, she said, "You haven't said a word about Samantha Lewis and Gillespie."

"Still trying to piece it together and figure out how it's relevant."

"I had a bad feeling about Gillespie from the get-go."

"He's a narcissist for sure, and probably fooling around with at least one of his students. I'm not sure I can see him as a serial killer, though."

"We at least need to interview him again," Jayme said. "Or better yet, let's talk to little Kaitlin first. She must have known Lewis, or at least knew of her. She might even be Lewis's replacement in Gillespie's bed."

He nodded and gave her hand a squeeze, as if to signal the end of the conversation. She rolled onto her side and leaned against him, and closed her eyes.

"Do you ever hear a thump in your head?" he asked.

Her eyes came open. "On my head or in my head?"

"Inside. Back at the Humane Society," he told her, "right before we left, I heard this loud thump inside my head. I've heard it a couple of times before too. It comes out of nowhere. Sounds like a door slamming shut. But it's inside my head. It's jolting, to say the least. You've never experienced anything like that?"

She pushed herself up on one elbow. "Not inside my head, no. Are you sure it's not a real thump? Like the wind blowing a door shut, something like that?"

"Ninety percent sure. The first two times happened when I was in bed, and I actually got up and checked all the locks. Creeping around in the darkness with a gun in my hand."

She touched the side of his head. "Does the thump hurt? Or is it just the sound?"

"I do feel it, but there's no pain. More like the change of pressure you feel when a heavy door slams shut."

"Oh babe," she said. "I'm worried about you."

"It's nothing to worry about. Just annoying is all."

"Are you still having difficulty breathing?"

"My chest feels heavy sometimes, but it's no big deal."

She put a hand to the mattress, pushed herself into a sitting position. "You don't know if it is or not. It could be blood pressure or, I don't know, something serious. *Please* go to a doctor and get yourself checked. Please tell me that you will."

"We'll see," he said.

"I'm going to call in the morning and make an appointment for you."

He smiled. Said, "Lie down, it's okay. It's nothing to worry about." He closed his eyes and said nothing more, waited for her body to ease next to him again. And asked himself, *What kind of door would keep slamming shut inside my head?*

THIRTY-THREE

The next morning, she was up early. When he came downstairs forty minutes later, a cup of coffee was waiting at his spot at the kitchen table. As he pulled out the chair to sit, she, with the laptop open before her, said, "Good news. I found your slamming door online."

"Seriously?" he said, and lifted the cup to his mouth.

"It's called exploding head syndrome."

"Oh, that sounds healthy."

"It's supposed to be harmless. As many as a fifth of all people experience it."

"Okay, that's a little more comforting. What causes it?"

"Nobody's sure, but the general consensus is that it has to do with neurons discharging, for whatever reason neurons discharge."

He thought about that for a moment, then shook his head. "Neurons are electricity. And there's nothing remotely electrical about the sound. I know how lightning sounds, and I know how an electrical explosion sounds. I know how a frying wire sounds. None of them sounds like a door banging shut."

"There are a few other explanations, if you want to hear them. They aren't exactly scientific."

He cocked his head and stared at her.

"You took a hit from an energy weapon," she said.

"From who?"

"The CIA. NSA. Shadow government. Take your pick."

"Fascetti!" he said, but his grin was half-hearted.

"Not a possibility for you?"

"Next option."

She laid a hand to her face, stretched her mouth into a cringe. "Evil spirits?"

"Thank you, but no. I don't need no evil spirits mucking around in my brain."

"I guess that leaves alien abduction."

"Hmm," he said. "That might be interesting."

"You wouldn't mind being abducted?"

"Depends on the alien. They obviously know more about reality than I do."

"Whatever," she told him. "I still want you to get a checkup."

"You said it's harmless."

"I also said that nobody knows for sure what causes it. Just the name scares me. Exploding head syndrome."

"Tell you what," he answered, and took another sip of coffee. "You find me a doctor who is up-to-date on alien abductions, and maybe I'll give it a shot."

He felt the fraudulence in his grin, and knew she could detect it too. But how do you tell the woman you love that you fear you are falling apart, and in more ways than one?

THIRTY-FOUR

Two hours later they climbed into their cars and headed west into Ohio. The sky was a scorched blue but with strange-looking stacks of clouds here and there, each one looking like piles of whipped cream layered on top of each other and flattened out, each with an ominous gray underbelly.

DeMarco had called the Canfield home of Mahoning County commissioner Grant Lewis III, father of Samantha Lewis, and arranged for a 9:00 a.m. meeting at his office in downtown Youngstown. In the meantime, Jayme sought to surprise Kaitlin Mahood, she of the skimpy Daisy Mae outfit, at the three-bedroom apartment she shared with two other students on the eastern edge of Arlington, just a few minutes from the HYC campus.

Only one roommate was home, a pink-cheeked blond of five seven or so. The oversized Browns jersey she wore did nothing to flatter her stocky figure. Jayme flashed her ID and said she was working with the county sheriff's office. She asked for Kaitlin and was told by the roommate that she hadn't been seen in two weeks. Jayme nodded and walked past the stunned girl and straight to the center of the room, where a fake granite counter separated the kitchen space from the living room.

The young woman closed the door but remained beside it. "Don't you have to have a warrant or something?"

Jayme smiled. "I'm not searching anything." She made a quick scan of the room. "Besides, warrants are for people trying to hide something. Are you hiding something?"

"I don't even know why you're here."

"Let's start with your name," Jayme said as she removed a notepad and pen from a pocket. She continued to hold her smile, but it was the smile that said, *You don't want to mess with me.* She had at least half a dozen smiles in her arsenal, each with a different message.

"Amber," the girl said. "Bertell."

"One *r,* two *l's?*" Jayme asked as she wrote. "Like the insurance guy on the billboards?"

Amber nodded. "We're not related."

"Why don't you have a seat," Jayme said,

and moved to the window, her back to the light.

Amber gave a half turn to one of the stools pushed against the counter, and sat facing Jayme. She kept her knees tight together, the heels of her bare feet hooked over the stool's top rung. "Did Kaitlin do something illegal?" she asked.

"Two weeks since you've seen her," Jayme said. "Is that an approximation?"

"I guess. Yeah."

"Can you be more specific?"

"I don't know, it was, uh, I think the day after her friend was killed."

Jayme looked up from her pad. "Samantha Lewis was Kaitlin's friend?"

"I guess so."

Now Jayme came away from the window. Paused beside one of the lightweight recliners facing the TV. Ran her hand over the headrest. "These are nice," she said.

"They're called zero gravity. The cushions come separately."

Jayme slid the chair over the carpet, turned it to face Amber directly, and eased herself down. "Very comfortable," Jayme said. "I just might get myself one of these."

Then she leaned forward, gave the girl an encouraging smile. "I really need you to be as specific as you can, Amber. You're telling me that Kaitlin and Samantha were friends, and Kaitlin left here the day after Samantha was killed. And you haven't seen Kaitlin since that day. Is that correct?"

Amber nodded, kept her hands and arms close to her body. "She said she was going to go home for a while. Maybe the rest of the summer."

"And were you and your other roommate friends with Samantha too?"

"We didn't know her. Never met her."

"She never came here to visit Kaitlin?"

"Not that I'm aware of."

Jayme cocked her head slightly, her gaze fixed on the girl. "Doesn't that seem odd to you?"

Amber shook her head. "We're just roommates. It's not like we're close or anything. She's a year ahead of Jenna and me."

"Kaitlin is?"

A quick nod. "We all have different friends we hang out with."

"But Kaitlin mentioned Samantha by name as her friend?"

"Um. I'm not really sure about that."

"I need you to be sure, Amber. How often did she refer to Samantha? And in what context?"

"It was just that one time. We were all sitting around in here talking about the murder, the three of us and a few other kids. Then Kaitlin started crying and went into her bedroom. I went in after a couple minutes to ask if she was okay, and she was stuffing some clothes into her backpack. That's when she said something like, 'A friend of mine has been murdered. I need to get out of here for a while.' "

"Were those her exact words?"

"Pretty close anyway. I mean, it's what I remember her saying."

Jayme smiled. Closed up her notepad. "I need to take a look at her room, Amber. You're okay with that, right?"

Amber's forehead became pinched, her mouth puckered. "I don't know . . ."

"Here's the way it works," Jayme told her, and spoke more softly now, her smile more motherly. "You say it's okay, and the only place I look at is Kaitlin's room. If you don't say it's okay, then I call the police, they get a warrant, and thirty minutes from now, I and two detectives do a full-scale search of the entire apartment. And if we find any kind of weed or pills or anything like that, even beer or wine bottles in your trash, if you're under twenty-one, and I think you are . . ."

Amber sat with her entire body bunched up and tight, as if she had to urinate. "I

261

guess if you have to it's okay."

"Thank you," Jayme said.

She remained in Kaitlin's room for over fifteen minutes, but found nothing that tied her to Samantha Lewis. When she returned to the living room, Amber was standing at the second-floor window, palms pressed to the glass. When Jayme spoke, the girl jumped as if jabbed with a pin.

"There seems to be a lot of stuff missing in there," Jayme said. "Clothes and toiletries and so forth. A lot more than would fit into one backpack."

"She might have come back when we weren't here," Amber said. "Me and Jenna both work four to ten at Barry Dyngles."

Jayme nodded. Gave her a *thanks, you're doing well* smile. "So as far as you know, Kaitlin is at home with her parents?"

"She lives with her dad mostly. He's closest."

"And where would that be?"

"Akron."

"Have you taken any classes with a Dr. Gillespie?"

Amber's eyes widened. "No," she said.

"Why did that question surprise you?"

"It just . . . I don't know. What does it have to do with Kaitlin?"

"I didn't say it has anything to do with

her. I just asked if you've taken any classes from him."

"I haven't," Amber said. "Neither has Jenna."

"His classes don't interest you?"

"I mean, they might but . . . He's supposed to be hard to get an A from. Most people are lucky to get a C."

"How did Kaitlin do in his class?"

Amber shrugged. "Pretty girls always get As. Everybody knows that."

And suddenly Jayme felt like throwing an arm around the girl, pulling her close. Instead she froze for a moment, then stood, took a business card from her pocket, and held it out to the girl. "You call me when you see Kaitlin again, will you?"

Amber looked at the card, nodded, looked up at Jayme.

And Jayme, before turning to the door, said, while wishing she had something more inspirational to offer, something wise and true, "Young beauty fades. But the beauty in here" — and she tapped her chest — "it just keeps growing."

She was moving down the hallway when she heard Amber at the apartment door. "I forgot about the thing tomorrow night," the girl said.

Jayme turned, walked back. "What thing?"

"I guess there's a memorial kind of thing at the Canfield High School."

"Right, for Samantha Lewis. I heard about that."

"I don't know if Kaitlin will be there or not. But she might."

"Thank you," Jayme told her. She wanted to say more, something encouraging and empowering, but she had always resented the platitudes of others, those who had told her as a teen that she would grow into her long legs, that her sharp features would soften. They had been right, of course, but such words had done her no good at the time. So she ended her conversation with Amber with a nod and a smile.

And for the next few moments, as she walked down the hall to the elevator, Jayme remained puzzled by the urge she had felt to embrace and comfort Amber. She thought she had taught herself to keep emotions out of her work. In the academy, cadets were taught to moderate emotions when dealing with both perpetrators and victims. Neither anger nor pity serves a law enforcement officer well in the line of duty. Emotion tends to cloud the brain.

Jayme had initially thought this philosophy an oxymoron. Didn't one choose a career in law enforcement precisely because of a desire to help others? Some did and some didn't, she came to understand. There were also those who joined for the uniform and gun and what they represented, what they made possible. They endowed one with an authority the individual would never have otherwise. A self-image otherwise impossible to achieve. And for others, the rules and guidelines of law enforcement provided a definable framework for living.

Liabilities accompanied all of these motivations. The most rigid of the by-the-book individuals could make life miserable for others, and often found themselves with rebellious children of the same ilk as preachers' kids. Those who joined for the power trip learned that they were seldom top dog, always subject to the authority of others, and so took out their hunger for power not only on suspected criminals but also on the innocent, most often their wives and children. And those with an overabundance of empathy for the oppressed often became victims of the bottle and other medications to numb their depression and suicidal thoughts.

DeMarco, she knew, was of the sympathetic type. When younger, he had also needed the discipline of the profession. But even that wasn't enough, after his son's death, to keep him from climbing into the bottle every night. She liked to think that her love was instrumental in keeping him out of the bottle.

She had never really studied her own influences and motivations as closely as she had DeMarco's. But that surprising and nearly overwhelming empathy for Amber threw it all into bright light. Amber, she realized, was Penny, just as Penny had been Jayme.

Penny Unger. Even her last name was homely. They had been in eighth grade together, sat side by side in social studies. Penny was as short, dark, and chubby as Jayme was tall, fair, and stick-thin. Neither had a boyfriend. Neither got asked to the school dances. Neither ever won a lead role in a school play.

In eighth grade, the play was *Inherit the Wind.* Both Jayme and Penny tried out for the role of Rachel Brown, but of course it went to a prettier girl. Jayme did get a nonspeaking role in scene 1, which, in their middle-school version, opened with a classroom of twelve students. When Penny failed to find her name on the call list, she erupted in convulsive sobs and hurried away to hide in the restroom. All day long Jayme had ached with sympathy and an incessant throb of the injustice of the situation. Both she and Penny were top students. Both had pleasant, clear voices. Both had already memorized all of Rachel Brown's lines. But Penny was overweight, and Jayme towered over Billy George, who, as everyone expected, was given the role of Rachel's fiancé, Bertram Cates.

Near the end of the day, in study hall, Jayme asked Mrs. Fazio if she could give her role to Penny. "I'm too fidgety," Jayme explained. "She's better at sitting still and being quiet." And when, six weeks later, on opening night, Jayme saw Penny sitting straight and happy and inconspicuous on the stage, all of her regret disappeared.

In a peculiar, elliptical way, that was why Jayme had gone into law enforcement. Because life isn't fair. Because the meek do not inherit the earth — not unless the non-meek lend them a hand. You wouldn't get any applause for that, seldom any thanks at all. But what a beautiful way to get revenge.

THIRTY-FIVE

Commissioner Lewis's complexion struck DeMarco as no less gray than the front of the Boardman Street building that housed his office. The man, at five six and maybe a hundred and forty pounds, seemed swallowed up by his office and the wide windows at his back. But DeMarco knew the look: it was grief that had swallowed him — the awful weight of grief that kept him in his seat as DeMarco came forward to shake his hand, and that made every movement slow and ponderous. Even his speech seemed laborious.

"I'm so sorry for your loss, sir," DeMarco said when he took the man's hand.

Lewis nodded, then slipped his hand free and gestured toward the matching leather chairs facing his desk. As DeMarco took a seat, Lewis told him, "Call me Buddy, please. Everybody does."

"All right," DeMarco said.

"Sheriff Brinker tells me you're a Youngstown boy. When did we lose you to Pennsylvania?"

"When I came out of the army. Twenty-two years old. Both parents were gone, so . . ."

"And now we have you back again."

"For a while anyway," DeMarco said.

On the far corner of the desk was a framed photograph of Lewis with his family: Lewis and his Vietnamese wife seated on straight-backed chairs, holding hands over the armrests, while Samantha stood behind her father's right shoulder, and her twin brother, Griffin, stood behind his mother's left shoulder. All four individuals were dressed in black slacks and white shirts.

DeMarco nodded toward the photo. "How old were your children in that picture?"

"Fourteen," Lewis said. "That was taken only eight months before Linny died. Not long after we found out about the cancer."

"I'm sure that was very hard on all of you."

"On everyone but her," Lewis said. "She was so serene about it. Her name, Linh, L-I-N-H, it means spiritual woman. And she certainly was that."

"How did the two of you meet?"

"I did some traveling when I was young," Lewis said. "And I just fell in love with the

269

country. The people. I'm tall over there." He looked away from the photo finally and smiled at DeMarco.

DeMarco returned the smile. Waited for a moment. Then said, "I know that you and Griffin have already met with Detectives Fascetti and Olcott, sir, and I've read transcripts of those interviews. But my partner and I are moving in a slightly different direction with our investigation."

"How so?" Lewis asked.

DeMarco considered how much to say. He certainly did not want to use the words *dismemberment* or *decapitation.* "We're just throwing a wider net, is all. And we're hoping that maybe you've thought of something new since you spoke with the detectives. Someone new Samantha might have met. Some new place she might have started going. A new club or hangout, anything like that?"

"Both she and Grif have always been homebodies," Lewis said. "Except for their classes and activities, they didn't socialize much. Especially since their mother passed."

"Neither had part-time jobs?"

"No. I discouraged that. Maybe it was wrong of me, I don't know. But we kept to ourselves, for the most part. I always made sure that they had everything they needed right there at home."

DeMarco noticed Lewis's use of past tense. "Does all that still hold true for Griffin?"

"I, uh . . . I guess. Yes."

"You're not sure?"

"It's hard for me back there now. Just being there. Most nights I sleep right here."

"Your son is okay with that?"

"He's like me. We pull into ourselves when we're hurt. I mean, I check on him, you know? I call, leave a voice message, and he replies, usually by text. It's still a painful, painful time for us."

"I'm sure it is," DeMarco said. Again he waited, as if a few moments of time could soften the intrusion of his questions. "So Griffin still lives at home?"

"Of course," Lewis said.

"Do you have any live-in help?"

"The gardener and the maid each come once a week."

"And as far as you know, how is your son spending his time? Did he take any classes this summer?"

Lewis shook his head no. "I know he drives around a lot. He likes to take Sammy's car. I know he lies on her bed sometimes and listens to her music. I can't imagine what it must be like to lose half of yourself. I mean I can in a way. I've lost more than half of myself. But there's a special bond between twins, you know? Even fraternal twins. They were always so close. And he's a sensitive boy. I wish to God I could help him somehow, but I'm so mired down myself. So deep in my own damn misery . . ." Lewis lowered his head, put his hands over his eyes. His body tightened as he fought to suppress the sobs.

DeMarco knew he wasn't going to learn anything here. The man's grief blanketed his every thought. His kind of grief, De-Marco knew, was like a thick blanket of black snow; it smothered everything except the pain.

Soon Lewis looked up again and wiped the tears from his eyes. "I'm sorry," he said. "It just overwhelms me sometimes."

"Don't apologize," DeMarco told him. "I apologize for being here. I know what an intrusion it must seem."

Lewis waved a hand through the air, shook his head no. Sniffed, then cleared his throat. "Is there anything else I can help you with?"

"I hate to even ask, but it would be very helpful if my partner or I could have a look around your daughter's room."

Lewis winced. "The detectives already did that."

"I understand. We'd like to take another look."

"How would that be helpful?"

"It would give us a better sense of exactly who she was. And with luck, we might learn something that will point us in the right direction."

"What kind of something?"

"Sir, I can't say exactly. Information about her plans for that night. Maybe some new connection that nobody knows about yet."

"You're suggesting that this wasn't a random thing. That she was killed by somebody she knew?"

"I don't mean to suggest anything, sir, other than possibilities. As it stands, the entire department is up against a brick wall. Sometimes what seems the least significant fact can turn everything around."

Lewis seemed to shrink even further into his seat. He leaned toward the edge of the desk. "Do you want to do it now?"

"Is that possible?"

"I can call Grif and see if he's there. He could let you in."

"I would appreciate that."

"I've never allowed her room to be touched. Not even by our housekeeper."

"I promise you that nothing will be disturbed."

Lewis was looking at the surface of his desk now, unable to lift his gaze. He nodded. Said, "Do you have a number where I can contact you?"

DeMarco stood. Took a business card from his pocket. Laid it near the center of the desk.

Lewis put a fingertip to the card and slid it toward himself. Sat motionless for a few moments. Then cocked his head and lifted his gaze to DeMarco. "I appreciate your efforts," he said.

DeMarco knew there was nothing he could say to ease the man's burden. Time would not ease it, nor would arresting his daughter's murderer. Eventually he might learn to shift the burden from shoulder to shoulder, but he would carry it forever.

THIRTY-SIX

The text came before DeMarco reached his car. Grif will meet you there at 12:30, followed by the address. Immediately DeMarco phoned Jayme. After her hello, he said, "What are you doing right now?"

"Sitting in the car looking at the clouds. Plus taking a few notes. Kaitlin was a no-show."

"You live such a glamorous life," he said. "No info on Mahood?"

"Whereabouts unknown. But get this. She knew Samantha Lewis. It appears that both of them were Gillespie's students."

"*That's* the most interesting thing I've heard all week."

"Thanks a lot, cowboy."

"Of a non-amorous nature."

"Good save," she said. "So what's up with you?"

"Can you meet me in Canfield by . . ." He glanced at the time. "High noon?"

"Name the place."

"Thano's Restaurant on Tippecanoe Road. We'll leave your car there and proceed to the Lewis residence together. I'll have an iced mocha latte waiting with your name on it."

"And I get souvlaki after?"

"Anything your heart desires."

"You silver-tongued devil," she said.

THIRTY-SEVEN

The five-bedroom, six-thousand-square-foot house on Paddington Rowe elicited a small gasp of envy from Jayme. "I think I'm going to run for county commissioner," she said.

"Old money," DeMarco told her. "Grant Lewis I was a ruthless coal baron. Which might be why his grandson likes to be called Buddy. And why there's no Grant Lewis IV."

"I'd let you call me Buddy for a house like that."

The white-brick building sat on just over two immaculately manicured acres, with low hedges in the front and miniature fruit trees in the rear. One-story wings with gable roofs on both sides of a massive two-story, flat-roofed box, with a three-story chimney at the end of each wing, gave the place a fortresslike air that was further enhanced by the lattice windows.

DeMarco parked on the circular drive just shy of the front door. As they walked to the door, Jayme whispered, "How much do you think this house would sell for?"

"On Paddington Rowe? Half a million or so. In southern California, ten mil easy."

"I'll try not to slobber on anything," she said.

The doorbell echoed through the house like the midday chimes of Big Ben. Half a minute later the heavy door swung open to Griffin Lewis's scowl of annoyance.

Barefoot in baggy tan chinos and a gray-and-orange Under Armour tee, the long sleeves pushed up to his elbows, Samantha's twin brother stood at a muscular five five, his thick black hair casually mussed, clipped short on the sides and much longer on top. His mother's Vietnamese heritage was readily apparent in his dark skin tone and, behind the black-framed glasses, the full, slightly almond-shaped eyes, but the crook of disdain on his mouth was his very own, neither the warm smile DeMarco had seen in photos of his sister and mother nor the sorrowful frown of his American father.

"I need to see your IDs," Griffin said in greeting.

Jayme and DeMarco showed him their credentials. "So you're not really cops," he said.

DeMarco told him, "We're working with

the county police. But your father already told you that, right?"

"You realize I have no obligation to let you inside."

DeMarco smiled. "The only reason you wouldn't is if you aren't interested in finding out who murdered your sister."

The young man's expression did not change. DeMarco suspected that Griffin was high, though he could detect no lingering scent of cannabis, and the lenses in his glasses lent a small magnification to his eyes. After ten seconds, the young man turned away and crossed the foyer toward the staircase. He walked with a loose, arm-swinging stride, which struck DeMarco as a fairly good pantomime of nonchalance. The soles of his feet made soft squeaks on the marble tile, but otherwise the house seemed eerily silent, even hollow, despite the array of fine furnishings visible on all sides. The walls and most of the furniture were white — not eggshell white or vanilla white, but as white and starched as a pleated tuxedo shirt.

"If you could point my partner to your sister's room," DeMarco said, "maybe you and I could have a brief talk here in the living room."

"I thought you just needed to see Sammie's room."

"And talk to you," DeMarco said.

"I already talked to the police. Didn't they write up a report you could read?"

"Up these stairs?" Jayme asked.

"We read the report," DeMarco said.

"I'll just go up and find it myself," Jayme said. "It shouldn't be hard to locate."

"Wait a minute," Griffin said, and threw an arm in front of her.

"Do not touch me," Jayme told him.

"I need to go up there with you."

DeMarco said, "You need to let us do our work. Let's you and me sit down and have a little talk."

"My father wants me to make sure you don't disturb anything in her room."

"We're adults," Jayme said with a smile. She pulled a pair of thin white cotton gloves from her back pocket and slipped them on. Then started up the stairs.

Griffin moved to follow her. "I should be up there with you."

"Why?" DeMarco asked. "Is there something you don't want us to see?"

"That's my sister's fucking room!"

DeMarco stepped in front of him. "Griffin, listen," he said. "You do care. That's nice to see. And I understand. But give us a little credit here. We respect what that room means to you and your father. Nothing will be disturbed. So come on, let's have a seat. We'll be out of here in fifteen minutes."

Griffin stood in place, watching Jayme go up the stairs. She paused in front of the first door on her left, and reached for the knob.

"Two doors down on your right," Griffin told her. "The door's open."

She released the knob, but not before giving it a twist and finding the door locked. Then she continued down the hall and entered Samantha's room.

DeMarco took a seat in the white wing chair directly facing the staircase and with a view to the upper floor. "Relax," he said, and motioned to the snow-white sofa directly across from him.

Reluctantly, Griffin sat in the corner of the sofa. Only by turning at the waist could he watch the second floor. He ran a hand over the back of his neck, over his cheek, then over his neck again.

DeMarco took out his notebook and pen. "Eyes over here," DeMarco told him, and waggled a finger at his own face. "I need your attention now, Griffin. The sooner you answer my questions, the sooner we're gone."

The boy seemed to have lost his nonchalance. The twist of disdain on his mouth was beginning to resemble a snarl.

"First of all," DeMarco told him, "try to chill, okay? I know you feel like this is a violation of some kind —"

"You're damn right it is. We don't want her room *touched.* Ever. The same with my mother's room. You have no idea what that means to us."

"I've lost people too," DeMarco told him. "Mother. Father. Son. Friends. So yes, I do understand."

The boy said nothing. He took another look at the second-floor hallway. Then brought his eyes back to DeMarco for a moment, long enough for DeMarco to see the glimmer of tears. Then Griffin turned his gaze to the windows to his right.

"What we're looking for," DeMarco said, speaking more softly now, "is anything new that might have occurred to you since you spoke with the detectives."

"Like what?" Griffin asked.

"Any of your sister's acquaintances you didn't mention before? Anybody who might have wished her harm?"

"Everybody loved her."

"From the looks of her Facebook page, she didn't have many friends."

"She had as many as she wanted."

"Okay," DeMarco said. "Do you remember when she first left the house that evening?"

"I wasn't here. I already told you guys that."

"That's right, you did. Sorry; I forgot. Remind me where you were that night."

"Just driving around. I like to get away by myself sometimes. Just to get out of the house for a while."

"Your father mentioned that. I do the same thing sometimes. Just go out to the country and drive around and listen to my music. Do you do that too? Put the windows down and turn up the music?"

Griffin nodded. "I loaded my sister's playlist onto my phone."

"This was after, you mean? After she was gone?"

Another nod.

"That's cool," DeMarco said. "What did she like to listen to?"

"Seal. Taylor Swift. Adele. Coldplay . . . Lots of oldies too. And a bunch of independent artists. Hollow Coves, Laurel, George Taylor, Zoey Lily, Radical Face, Juke Ross. Plus two whole Beatles albums."

"Let me guess," DeMarco said. "*Sgt. Pepper*?"

Griffin smiled. Nodded.

"And . . . *The White Album*?"

Griffin shook his head no. "*Rubber Soul.* She was crazy for 'Norwegian Wood.' "

"It's a great song," DeMarco said.

He let half a minute pass in silence. Then he noticed Jayme peeking around the corner of the upstairs hall. "Just one more question, Griffin. I'm sure you must have told the detectives this too, but refresh my memory, if you would. When you went out driving that night . . ."

Jayme tiptoed down the hall, testing all the doors. All locked.

"Where exactly did you go?" DeMarco asked.

"I was just driving around," Griffin said.

"I understand. But we usually go to a certain point, right? And then turn around and come back. Especially out in the country, where you're not weaving in and out of streets. So where did you drive to before you turned around?"

"I don't know. I wasn't really paying a lot of attention to places."

"But which direction did you go?"

The boy thought for a moment. "South, I guess."

"Okay, good. And did you head out of town on 62 or, what, maybe 11?"

"62."

"Yeah, that's a nice quiet ride. Especially

if you stay south. Which means switching to 9 down around Salem, right?"

"Right," Griffin said.

"And about how long do you think you drove before you turned around and headed north again?"

Jayme came to the top of the stairs, looked down at DeMarco. He gave her a little nod.

She tapped her knuckles against the handrail before continuing down the stairs. The sound caused Griffin to swivel around in his seat.

"Just an estimate," DeMarco said. "About how long, do you think?"

Jayme smiled at Griffin.

"I don't know," he said. "A couple of hours probably. Maybe a little more."

"And then you came back home?"

Griffin turned to face him again. "Yeah."

"Excellent. That's it, then. Oh, wait a minute. Did I ask what time you left the house that evening? To start your drive?"

The boy cocked his head. Blew out a breath. "Man, I don't know. Just before dark, I guess."

"Okay," DeMarco said, and wrote in his notebook. "Somewhere between 8:30 and 9:00. Close enough."

He flipped up the cover on the notebook, stood, and said, "We really appreciate your cooperation, Griffin. And again, our apologies for disturbing you here at home."

The boy stood and turned away, crossed to Jayme at the bottom of the stairs. "So?" he said.

"It's a very nice room," she told him. "And such a beautiful house. Thank you for your time." With that, she crossed into the foyer and out the front door, with DeMarco close behind.

THIRTY-EIGHT

On their way back to the Greek restaurant, Jayme filled him in on her search of Samantha Lewis's room. While she talked she used a USB cord to attach her phone to the laptop. "The girl was neat to the nth degree," she said. "Every little thing was perfectly organized. Books, CDs, even her panties in the drawers. Folded on top of each other according to color. Black in one stack, pink, white, yellow. It was kind of awe-inspiring."

"That might have been the housekeeper's doing."

"Maybe," Jayme said. "But I mean everything. Dolls, stuffed animals, you name it."

"In other words, nothing illuminating?"

"Hold on a minute. Let me pull up this photo I took."

DeMarco leaned forward, tried for a quick glance at the screen.

"Give it a second," Jayme said. "And

maybe you'd like to pull over instead of wrapping us around a telephone pole?"

Immediately she regretted her words, which had made DeMarco flinch. No telephone pole had been involved in the accident that killed his son, but still . . . "I'm sorry," she said.

"Nope," he told her, and eased the car onto the shoulder. "You're right. Absolutely right." He pulled the gearshift into Park and punched on the four-way flashers. She turned the screen in his direction.

He saw a low bookshelf with four shelves, the top shelf empty, the other three holding books and wire-bound notebooks stacked on top of each other. "What am I looking at here?" he said.

"The entire bookshelf is devoted to the textbooks from all of her classes. Arranged chronologically. First and second semesters on the bottom, up to the fifth and sixth, the last ones she completed, on the top shelf. She kept a separate notebook for each course. Each stack represents one semester. From top down they go text, notebook, text, notebook, text, notebook."

"Okay," he said. "She kept all of her textbooks. Never sold any back. And this means something to you?"

"Click to the next picture."

He did. A close-up of the second-semester stack. He stared for a few moments. Leaned closer. A large truck sped past his car, its horn shrieking. He sat up quickly, glanced through the windshield. "That's not fifty-five miles per hour," he said.

"Like you drive the speed limit? The picture, Ryan."

He looked again. "I don't know. Whatever it is you want me to see, I'm not seeing it."

"That's because you're looking at what's there. You need to look at what isn't there."

Twenty seconds later he said, "A notebook is missing."

"Exactly."

"Which one?"

"Take a guess."

He knew of only one of her courses. "Gillespie's."

She smiled. "Can I get a carumba?"

"Muchas carumbas," he said.

"So two questions. Who took it and why?"

DeMarco sat back in his seat again. Checked in the rearview mirror, the side mirror, punched the flashers off, put on his turn signal and pulled out onto the highway. "Her father said that nothing in her room has been touched. He insisted on that."

"So he doesn't know."

"Which leaves either Griffin or the housekeeper. With the gardener a remote possibility."

"Very remote."

"However," DeMarco said. "Also according to the father, Griffin sometimes lies on her bed and listens to her music. Maybe he also reads her notebooks."

"Should we go back and ask?"

He thought for a moment, then shook his head no. "Let's think this through first. Let's find out if Griffin took the same class. Or plans to take it. That would give him a viable excuse for having the notebook."

"You didn't mention Gillespie to him?"

"I did not. Or anything about the memorial tomorrow night. If I asked about Gillespie, and Griffin was one of his students, he might warn his professor. I want to see if Gillespie shows up tomorrow night. And how they both react if they see us there. Also how they react if they don't."

"Nice," Jayme said. She closed the lid on her laptop. "So what's your read on the boy in general?"

"Spoiled rich kid, for one thing. But does he have something to hide? Maybe he's just full of grief and anger. Grief is like gravity; it grounds us in reality, but too much of it can crush a person flat."

She raised her eyebrows at that. Did he

know whom he was really talking about?

He said, "Maybe he was just genuinely ticked off to have us invading his space. His and his sister's."

She said, "How was he when I was in her room?"

"Antsy. Kept sneaking glances up at the balcony."

"Every other door upstairs was locked."

"I did promise the commissioner we would limit ourselves to that one room."

Jayme pursed her lips. Leaned her head against the headrest. "Amber Bertell," she said. "I can turn her. I get the feeling she can give me something on her roommate Kaitlin. She's not fond of pretty girls."

"Then she must have hated you," De-Marco said.

"Nice try. But you're still buying me souvlaki."

THIRTY-NINE

That afternoon they spent a couple of hours adding to their information on the dining room wall. DeMarco checked in with Sheriff Brinker and brought him up-to-date. At the end of their telephone conversation, Brinker said, "Vee wants me to invite you and Jayme over to dinner some night. Like soon. I think she misses your ugly face."

"Probably wants to find out if she still has a shot with me," said DeMarco.

"You're risking a shot talking like that. Maybe a full clip."

"We should hit the firing range some time," DeMarco suggested. "All four of us. Loser buys dinner at Aqua Pazzo."

"I have an astigmatism and you know it. Let's deal with one dinner at a time. How's Saturday night for you guys?"

"What can we bring?"

"Just tell Jayme to bring somebody other than you. Better yet, she should come alone.

Four's a crowd, you know."

A part of DeMarco enjoyed this reconnection with his former teammate. As a young man he had never allowed himself to feel close to anyone. It still did not feel wholly natural, but he no longer felt a compulsion to run from any possibility of friendship and its responsibilities. Every relationship came with its burdens. Recognizing this, he experienced a wash of guilt for not tending more carefully to his most important relationship.

"What do you say we call it a day?" he told Jayme after relaying the sheriff's dinner invitation. "I'm sorry I've been like a donkey turning a millstone."

"If you have, so have I. So what do we do with the rest of the day?"

"The yard needs mowed. You know how to drive a lawn tractor?"

"You know how to wash and dry and fold laundry?"

"Flip you for it," he said.

"Flip yourself. I'll put a load of laundry in, then go in town and grab a movie for tonight. My choice. Just because you've been such a donkey."

FORTY

It was a few minutes after six that evening when somebody knocked on the front door. DeMarco was in the shower, Jayme downstairs in the kitchen, where she was building her version of Mexican spring rolls: flour tortillas stuffed with shredded cabbage, chopped Vidalia onion, sweet red peppers, and sharp cheddar cheese. She placed the fourth one in the casserole dish, then covered all four with salsa verde and crumbled queso, and failed to hear the first knocks because she was also dancing barefoot in a periwinkle summer dress and singing along with the Cars' "Just What I Needed" playing on the stereo in the living room. Then came the second set of knocks, slightly louder, five quick raps.

Quickly she slid the casserole into the warm oven, went into the living room and turned down the music, then to the front door. She opened the door to an attractive woman in her late forties, wearing beige slacks and a yellow long-sleeved blouse, her dirty-blond hair cut short and neatly styled. Jayme's first thought was that she should have known the woman but didn't — and then suddenly recognized her from the photos in a box in the closet.

Laraine's smile was as pale as her skin. "You must be Jayme."

Jayme's smile was equally wan, though her heart, she guessed, was beating faster. "Laraine. It's nice to meet you."

"I don't mean to interrupt your evening, but is Ryan here? There's something I wanted to tell him."

"He's upstairs in the shower."

Laraine nodded. "May I come in for a moment?"

"Of course," Jayme said. "Of course." And she stepped aside, held the door as Laraine entered, then left the door standing open.

Laraine came forward two steps, then stood there looking around. "It hasn't changed much, has it?" she said, still with a small smile on her pale lips.

"We, uh . . . we don't spend a lot of time here."

Laraine looked toward the stairway. "Do you think he'll be long?"

"He just stepped into the shower a few

minutes ago, and then he likes to shave —"

"And brush his teeth," Laraine said, "and pick out his clothes, and iron out the wrinkles. Maybe I should just tell you?"

"Sure," Jayme said. "Would you care to sit down?"

"Thank you, no," Laraine said. "On second thought maybe you could ask him to call me. I think he has my number."

"I'm sure he must."

"Tell him that I have a message for him from a friend of mine. From our boy."

"Oh," Jayme said, startled, unsure of what else to say. *A message from their boy?* "Okay."

And then another shock. Laraine reached out to take Jayme's hand. "You're very pretty," she said. "I hope you make each other happy. I don't intend to interfere with anything."

The only thing Jayme could think to say was, "Thank you."

Laraine smiled and squeezed her hand once, then released it, turned away and walked outside.

Jayme stood leaning against the edge of the door, watching as Laraine crossed to the curb and climbed into a white sedan and drove away. Then, still holding the door, Jayme turned toward the stairway. The water could still be heard in the shower. The music from the stereo was soft but somehow jarring.

Finally she released the door and crossed to the sofa and sat down. She could not remember if she had taken a breath since first opening the door, but knew it would be a good idea to take a few breaths now.

FORTY-ONE

When he stepped out of the bathroom naked and saw her sitting there on the edge of the bed, he turned quickly, grabbed the wet towel and wrapped it around his waist, then immediately headed for the dresser. But her crooked smile and dazed look stopped him in his tracks.

"What's wrong?" he said.

"We had a visitor a few minutes ago."

"Who was it?"

She paused before speaking. Raised her eyebrows. Crinkled her nose. "Laraine."

He wasn't sure he had heard her correctly. Replayed it in his head. Then said, "Oh lord."

"No," Jayme said. "She was perfectly nice. Sweet even."

"Really?"

"She must think I'm an idiot."

"And why's that?"

"Because I acted like one."

"How so?"

"Like . . . like an idiot," she said.

He crossed to the bed and sat beside her. Took her hand. "Just tell me what happened."

"Nothing happened. She wants you to call her. She has a message from a friend of hers. From your boy."

"What?" he said.

"That's what she said."

"What friend?"

"I didn't ask."

"About Ryan Jr.?"

"She said *from.* From a friend. From your boy."

"Oh lord," he said again. He stood and crossed to the dresser, picked up his cell phone, scrolled through his contacts list, pressed the call icon and stood there listening to the phone ring. Then said, "Laraine. Hi. Jayme said you came by."

"Yes," he said. "She is. Thank you." And he returned to sit beside Jayme again, listening.

And listened for thirty seconds more. Then said, "Well, who is this woman?"

And then said, after an audible sigh, "All right. I should have some time free tomorrow, late afternoon. How about five-ish? We have an appointment in Canfield at seven."

He listened awhile longer, then said, "Just so you're doing okay. I mean, if that's what it takes. If you really believe it's helping you."

He listened, nodded, and finally told her, before hanging up, "Okay. Text me the address. Take care of yourself."

He turned to Jayme. She sat smiling crookedly at the bathroom door. He said, "I need to go talk to a psychic tomorrow. Please tell me you'll come along."

"Ah," she said. "The message from your son. A warning to stay away from me, I bet."

"I guess we'll find out, won't we?"

"I doubt that I'm invited to this meeting."

"Doesn't matter," he said. "If I'm going down that rabbit hole, you're going with me."

FORTY-TWO

The next morning, during breakfast, De-Marco said, "Is there anything you want us to tackle this morning? We have a busy afternoon and evening ahead."

"You want to take the morning off? Rest our brains a bit?"

"I was thinking of visiting the cemetery."

"You don't want to wait till Sunday? That's your usual day, isn't it?"

"What's usual anymore? I feel the urge to go today."

She knew that the visit from Laraine had upset him, the message even more. Had started him wondering, worrying. "Then go, babe. Spend some time with your boy."

He left soon after that, and for the remainder of the morning she didn't know what to do with herself. Her brain, instead of resting, went into overdrive, composing one worst-case scenario after another. While she cleaned up the kitchen, then vacuumed the carpets upstairs and down, then reorganized the walk-in closet, her body felt tense and restless. Finally she dumped half a box of Epsom salts into the tub and filled it with hot water, then lay with the water up to her chin, and only then felt her racing heart begin to quiet. Ryan was not the kind of man to let some message from a psychic drive them apart. Yes, he cared about Laraine's health, but the marriage was over; it could not be revived. There was nothing to be worried about. Everything would be fine. She laid a hand over her navel and told herself to relax. Too much glutamate in the amygdala, that was the culprit here, the only thing wrong. Too much adrenaline and cortisol, the chemistry of fear. She was too sensitive to everything, and that was the estrogen and progesterone's fault. If she wanted to cry, so what? She was already wet, the water was already salty. What would a little more hurt?

Forty-Three

At the cemetery he sat in the car with the doors closed and the front windows down, and for a while he watched an elderly woman some thirty feet away as she filled a plastic milk jug with water from the faucet outside the little equipment shed. He watched her carry it off to her right, leaning from the eight-pound drag on her bony arm, past half a dozen graves until she came to a gravestone with three pots of chrysanthemums beside it. With difficulty she eased herself down on one knee, set the milk jug aside, went down on both knees, and picked up a trowel that she had apparently brought with the mums.

There had been thunder that morning, but the sky was quiet now. Not even the distant jet could be heard, a half-inch glimmer of chrome, its long vapor trail crisscrossing other trails already diffusing outward. DeMarco watched the jet for half a minute before turning his attention to the woman again. She was taking her time replanting the orange flowers, patting the soil firm and watering the plants and cleaning up the area around the gravestone. He wished he knew if she was mourning a husband or a child, and how long the grief had been with her, and if it was still as sharp and strong as the day it began.

He held the silver locket with a few strands of his son's hair in it and hoped the grief would never lose its sting. The grief was their connection now, the grief and love, and he wanted neither to ever ease their grip on him.

After the old woman finished tending to the grave, she wiped her hands on the grass, then leaned to the side and sat on one hip, right hand flat on the ground beside her hip, other hand to the ground two feet forward, in the same posture as the thin young woman in the painting by Andrew Wyeth, except that instead of gazing at a farmhouse on a distant hill, the old woman gazed at the gravestone only two feet away.

He had read somewhere that the real woman depicted in the painting was actually in her midfifties and suffered from a rare and incurable disease. But to DeMarco's mind, that information was incidental and only detracted from the painting. What mattered was the longing insinuated by the woman's pose. The nameless, wistful, unrelenting ache.

DeMarco climbed out of his car and closed the door as softly as he could. He didn't usually talk to his son when he came to the cemetery, but this time he knelt to the side of the stone and put a hand to the corner of it and spoke in a whisper.

"I wish I could say that I believe it all really happened, my son. That you really came to me in those mountains. That I wasn't just feverish or dreaming or whatever. I wish I could say that I really did see your face and your smile and that I know what you look like now. I wish with all my heart I could say that."

The stone was cold and rough under his hand, the locket warmed in the palm of his other hand. "Either way," he said, "I want you to know that I have never stopped missing you. That you're the best part of me and always will be."

He sniffed. Looked up toward the woman. She hadn't turned to look back at him. His voice was not too loud.

"But if it was really you," he said, "could you give me another sign?"

And he sat very still for a while, both

hands motionless. Then he closed his eyes and remained unmoving, saw only a lingering image of the gravestone in the dull glow of sunlight coming through his eyelids. Then he looked up and across the field of stones and hoped he would see something significant and startling, but he did not.

"Okay," he said after a while, and patted the corner of the gravestone. "I'll always be your dad, my son. I will always love you with every breath and every beat of my heart. And I hope you will forgive me someday. I hope you can."

He had to lean against the gravestone then to push himself to his feet. He slipped his hand into a pocket and let go of the silver heart. Then, just before turning back to the car, he cast a last glance toward the old woman. She had turned at the waist and was looking in his direction, smiling.

He gave her a nod, a smile of recognition, and continued on his way.

FORTY-FOUR

Jayme had a light lunch prepared for them when he returned from the cemetery. He came in through the back door to find her seated at the table with her laptop open. Also on the table was a round platter, covered with plastic wrap, holding raw carrots and celery sticks, Kalamata and green olives, and a bowl of tuna salad.

She smiled to see him but did not ask how his morning had gone. He was always somber when he returned from the cemetery, and she wanted to respect his need to keep those hours to himself. She said, "Tuna salad okay for lunch?"

"Excellent," he said. "I'll get the bread."

"If that's what you'd like."

He paused, midturn.

"No bread for me," she told him.

After another pause he crossed to the cupboard and took out two plates, then two forks from the drawer. Brought them to the table. Set them in place. "Water?" he asked.

"Perfect," she said, then closed her laptop and pushed it aside.

He fetched two bottles of water from the fridge and joined her at the table. As he peeled the plastic wrap off the platter, he asked, "What were you working on?"

"Just doing some research. How's your exploding head these days?"

"Non-explosive."

They forked mounds of tuna salad onto their plates, added some raw vegetables. She said, "I considered slicing up the olives and putting them in with the tuna. Do you like it that way?"

"Either way is good."

She watched him scoop up some tuna with a stick of celery. Waited until he had chewed and swallowed. "If you really want to make a sandwich," she said, then left the sentence unfinished.

"This is fine. I eat too much bread anyway."

She nodded and smiled. Had a few bites. A drink of water. They were being so polite to one another. So very distant and polite. He had spent the morning with his sadness, and she with hers. They needed to come together again.

She asked, "Are you still having difficulty

breathing sometimes?"

"Not really," he told her.

"Sometimes, though?"

He gave her a smile. "It's only there when I think about it."

She nodded. "As it turns out," she said, "according to WebMD, it might be because of high blood pressure too. That and the exploding head both."

He tried to spear an olive with his fork, but it kept skimming away around the plate. Finally he trapped it against the tuna salad. "I'll get it checked next time I go past the Rite Aid."

"That would be good," she said.

They smiled at each other and had a few more bites of lunch. "Know what I think is causing it?" he asked.

"What, babe?"

"Too much bread."

She smiled, but it felt false, knew it must look false to him too. There were things that had to be said. But when would there be a right time to say them? The clock was ticking, every tick a little louder, just like the beating of a telltale heart.

FORTY-FIVE

Two hours later, DeMarco awoke feeling sluggish and dull, as he always did after an afternoon nap. At such times the word *logy* would come into his consciousness, a word he had never read anywhere else but in Hemingway's work, which seemed a shame because it was such a useful and descriptive word: to feel like a long-submerged cedar log half-buried in mud. It would take him a while to rise fully to the surface again.

Jayme was still asleep, still breathing her soft, whispery breath that sounded like a hushed conversation a few decibels below discernible. Her face was perfectly still and composed, her eyelids pale and perfect, every pale freckle across the bridge of her perfect nose perfect, even the pillow beneath her head perfectly molded to the perfect contours of her perfectly sleeping face.

He reached for his phone on the night table, checked the time, 3:16 p.m., and laid the phone facedown again. He would have to wake her soon. They needed to be in Erie by five.

The drive to meet with Laraine's psychic would take an hour. With luck the appointment would last only a few minutes. Afterward they would grab some dinner, then head southwest for the 7:00 p.m. memorial for Samantha Lewis at the Canfield High School. Then home again to Pennsylvania. A round-trip of two hundred miles in an itinerary shaped like a drunken South Dakota standing on its eastern border.

DeMarco remembered the shapes of all fifty states. As a schoolboy he had scored high on spatial recognition, low on his ability to follow directions. "I test very high on insubordination," Philip Marlowe had said in Chandler's *The Big Sleep.* The quote had always pleased DeMarco. As did Nabokov's observation that curiosity is insubordination in its purest form.

As male representatives of the human species, Chandler, from DeMarco's view, was more worthy of admiration than Nabokov, the latter, according to his critics, self-promoting and priggish, a misogynist and all-around rat bastard, the former a man who always felt like an outsider, and who was, like his father, an alcoholic, and who tended to fall apart when not with the woman he adored. Throughout his life, Chandler remained fully aware of his many flaws, and did his best to be, in the words of his alter ego, "as honest as you could expect a man to be in a world where it's out of style."

DeMarco saw himself in much the same light. At the age of fifteen he had first figured out that sometimes you have to do bad to do good. In his early years as a trooper, he had tended to go by the book, mainly out of a sense of insecurity driven by the ambition to prove himself a useful human being. After the accident that took away his son, he needed the rule book to help him maneuver through every hungover day. But now, stone-cold sober and with Jayme at his side, he found himself investigating crimes much as Chandler had written his novels, as one who, in Chandler's words, "cannot plan anything, but has to make it up as he goes along and then try to make sense out of it."

But what do we do when there's no sense to be made? DeMarco asked himself. And supplied his own answer: *You keep plodding along until the sense shows itself.*

So he was both a plodder and a free-wheeler. An oxymoron, as detectives tend to be. With the right and left hemispheres of their brains always battling for supremacy, an imp of the perverse whispering in one ear, Saint Teresa admonishing in the other.

That thought made him smile too. Chandler was also a late bloomer who sabotaged most of his early attempts at success. He didn't write his first novel until he was fifty-one. But with only a handful of novels, he was able to change how mysteries were written.

That thought brought back to DeMarco a conversation he had shared with Thomas Huston, the first and so far only person to suggest to him that investigating a crime was a lot like writing a novel. Huston had explained that Chandler chose not to write typical mysteries, those in which the only thing that matters is the resolution, the solution to the mystery, but instead to write mysteries in which every scene matters, because every scene adds another layer to the main character.

A four-hundred-page novel, Huston told him, cannot justify its existence solely on the final few pages, but on page after page of individual scenes that deepen the reader's understanding of and empathy for the characters. The best stories, Huston had explained, aren't about what happens to the world as the plot unfolds, but what happens inside the character and the reader. Chandler's goal, said Huston, was "to exceed the limits of a formula without destroying it."

Just like solving some crimes, DeMarco told himself. *Before you can get to the resolution, you have to peel away layer after layer of character, because sometimes the motivation is buried deep. The smart criminals know how to hide it. Fortunately, most criminals aren't smart. This one, however . . .*

DeMarco looked at the afternoon sunlight soaking through the curtains like golden blood. God, how he missed Tom Huston. Their every conversation had made De-Marco feel that he was learning something new. More than once Huston had teased that he was going to turn DeMarco into a fictional character. To which DeMarco always said something like, "I could stand to be a little more interesting."

In truth, he would not have minded being a Thomas Huston character. Or a Raymond Chandler character. But both authors were dead now, so the chances for DeMarco's transformation were remote.

Or were they? What if he really was nothing more than another Huston character? The thought made him smile. And brought to the surface another conversation he and Tom had had, a discussion on the nature of reality. DeMarco had always been what Tom called a materialist, believing that the observable physical world was, if not the all and the everything, at least the most significant part of reality. The rest, if it mattered at all, was too ephemeral to be fully grasped. But Tom disagreed with that paradigm. He had argued something like this:

"If it is true, as more and more theoretical scientists concur, that mind creates matter, thought creates reality, and that this reality is neither more nor less than the dream or conceit of a higher mind, then why is it not also true that the characters and worlds I create in my novels are as real as I am, though in a slightly lower or perhaps just different dimension than the one I inhabit? That would make me a kind of demented god, wouldn't it? One who burdens his creations with every pain and tragedy and calamity conceivable! All for personal satisfaction and, with luck, financial gain! Is the true reality nothing more than a hall of mirrors in the labyrinth of a single mind, each of us a story within a story within a story ad infinitum?"

DeMarco had laughed at the look on Huston's face, a wide-eyed expression of mock horror. But now he wondered if there might be something to that theory. A hall of mirrors, each reflecting the thoughts portrayed on the previous mirror . . .

"Ad infinitum," he whispered to the light-soaked curtains.

"Excuse me?" Jayme said.

He rolled his head in her direction, saw her watching him, smiling.

She asked, "What did you say, babe?"

"Just thinking out loud."

"About what?"

"About how long to let my Sleeping Beauty sleep."

"I guess you can stop thinking," she said.

He moved closer; kissed the tip of her nose. Felt his body press against her. "You smell the way the *Moonlight Sonata* sounds on a rainy night. What's that fragrance?"

"Soap. With aloe and cocoa butter."

"Every woman should wear it. Every man too. I'm going to start wearing it so that I can have you on my skin."

"Or you could just carry a bar of soap around with you wherever you go."

"But then I'd have a big lump in my pocket."

"Not as big as the one you have in your boxers."

"I would love to pursue that line of discussion," he told her, "did we not have a couple of obligations to fulfill. You ready to log some miles?"

"Depends. Are we getting paid by the mile?"

"No such luck."

"Then screw this job. I'm going back to sleep." She closed her eyes and made snoring sounds.

"You know how my father would wake me up sometimes?" he asked.

She snored louder.

"By dripping a cup of cold water on my face."

She opened her eyes. "So cruel!"

He leaned closer and kissed her mouth, a long and tender kiss. When he pulled away, she said, "That was a sweet kiss. What was it for? Because I said your father was cruel?"

He shook his head. "Because a kiss never tasted is a kiss forever and ever wasted."

She slipped her arms around his waist. "Did you just now make that up?"

"Billie Holiday sang it, Sam Lewis wrote it. In the song 'For All We Know.'"

"You know what I know?" she asked, and pulled him closer.

"The same thing I know," he said, and wished he could remain in that position forever, always breathing her in, their world in quiet suspension, everybody loved, everybody safe, the perfect end for a novel. But if he were a Huston character, if this were a Huston story, such an end would not be possible. Thomas Huston did not write that kind of story. He knew too much of the world beyond the curtains.

DeMarco, with a smile, leaned away from her. He reached into his boxers, rearranged his erection. "I'll make us some coffee," he said.

FORTY-SIX

The address Laraine had sent by text led DeMarco along a twisty narrow dirt lane to a small cottage on a windblown bluff overlooking Lake Erie. He parked behind a yellow Volkswagen and a pale blue Subaru wagon, shut off the engine and looked at the clock. 4:58.

The afternoon light had grown soft behind a low sky. Through the windshield he could see across miles and miles of gray water to the flat charcoal clouds sitting above Canada. He said, "I wonder what they're doing in Port Royal today."

Jayme peered through the glass. "That's what's over there?"

"A whole other country. That's always seemed remarkable to me."

"How many miles?"

"As the crow flies? About twenty-four."

"That would be one tired crow," she said.

"A few years ago some guy swam it. All I

remember is that he was fifty-five years old at the time."

"So you're not as old as you think, are you, babe?"

He knew her implication. Or thought he did. And no, fifty was not too old to become a father. He would be sixty-eight when his son or daughter graduated from high school. Seventy-two for college. Maybe seventy-five when he became a grandfather. That's when things would start looking bleak, if they hadn't already.

He gazed out the side window. The shrubbery around the cottage had been left in its natural state, tall and scraggly and wind tossed, Queen Anne's lace and raspberry vines entwined with wild roses. A hot gust of air rocked his vehicle and caused Jayme to put her hand on the dashboard.

"Kind of windy up here," she said.

DeMarco asked, "Am I supposed to pay her afterward?"

"I don't know. Probably."

"What do you pay a medium?"

"More than you pay a small, but less than a large."

He gave her a look.

"You seem nervous," she said.

"I feel like I'm being set up."

"By Laraine?"

He nodded. Inside the house, a dog started barking.

"Great," he said. "One of those yippy little rat dogs I hate."

"Relax, sweetie. It's probably just an angry spirit looking for somebody to possess."

"You are an enormous help."

"Love you too, babe. We going in or not?"

"We came this far," he said, and popped open the door.

FORTY-SEVEN

The scent of incense. Maybe some cannabis. Something cooking in the kitchen. He could smell tomatoes, garlic, and . . . peanut butter? It struck him as a strange combination.

The young woman who had answered his knock and ushered them into the small foyer smiled at the look on his face. "Sweet potato and peanut soup," she told him. "For tomorrow. We like it served cold."

She was only a little taller than an average twelve-year-old girl, delicate in every feature. She had a wide, beautiful smile, her perfect teeth a brilliant white, skin the color of liquid chocolate. Her eyes were full, dark yet glimmering, her black hair in tight cornrows. She wore a sleeveless summer dress of red, yellow, and purple that hung to three inches above her bare feet. No jewelry of any kind.

Her eyes remained fixed on DeMarco's,

held his gaze with their depth and insinuation. They were playful eyes, challenging, suggesting that she had heard all the world's lies and had invented the best ones herself.

He felt himself warming to her, meeting her smile with his, then warned himself to take it slow, don't fall for a pretty face.

Then the young woman turned slightly and made a little bow to Jayme. "I'm Lathea," she said. "Welcome to our home."

Jayme would have reached out to shake hands but Lathea kept her own hands clasped below her waist. "I'm Jayme. It's a pleasure to meet you."

"Come in," Lathea said, and turned sideways to the next threshold. "Would you like some herbal tea?"

"I'm good, thanks," DeMarco said.

"Me too," Jayme told her.

"Then follow me, please."

In the next room, two young men and another young woman, all late twenties to midthirties, seated at desks along three different walls. The first male, a Caucasian, was leaning close to a thirty-two-inch computer monitor, sliding a wireless mouse in a jerky crosshatch motion over the mouse pad. The young woman, African American, was sketching on an iPad, and the second young man, possibly Hispanic, was turning an agate bead beneath a large magnifying glass, delicately shaping the bead with an emery board. A miniature cocker spaniel sat between the young woman's bare feet and watched the strangers enter.

As Lathea crossed through the room, she pointed at each in turn. "Jessie, Taylor, and Matthew," she said. "My partners. And that guy down there is Geraldo. The world's worst watchdog."

"*Hola, ciao,* how's it going," her partners said in turn. Geraldo tucked in his neck and lowered his chin to the floor.

"We can sit in here," Lathea said from just inside the next room.

As Jayme entered the room behind Lathea, she said, "It's so nice that you all get to work together like this. What business are you and your partners in?"

"We're not business partners," Lathea told her. "Life partners."

"Oh," said Jayme. "Oh, sorry. That's great!"

DeMarco resisted taking another glance back at the three. He kept his eyes on the room just a few steps ahead, which appeared to be lighted only softly. *Such a cliché,* he thought.

As he stepped inside, Lathea said, "Would you mind closing the door, please?"

He did so. The room's only illumination came from a wall sconce on each of three walls. The light was cast upward from each sconce in pale-yellow funnels. The room itself was furnished with several cushioned chairs, a chaise, and a love seat. The floor was carpeted, unlike the previous rooms. Heavy drapery hung over the windows.

Lathea took a seat in a red fanback chair against the far wall, then pulled a small table close to her. DeMarco could not yet discern what objects lay atop the table.

"If you would sit directly across from me," Lathea told him. "And Jayme, why don't you sit beside him?"

DeMarco slid one of the slipper chairs close to Lathea's table, then pulled another alongside his for Jayme. The moment they were seated, Lathea smiled at each of them in turn. "I'm sure you must have some concerns or questions for me before we start."

He asked, "How long have you been seeing Laraine?"

"Three times so far. A client of mine is a nurse. She suggested to Laraine that she might like to visit. And I'm glad she did. She's getting stronger. Finding her center again."

"Good," DeMarco said. "Good." He felt a

warm flush of resentment go through him, just as he had when he'd been forced to meet with a psychologist after shooting Carl Inman. He did not like feeling so exposed to anyone. Did not like having the door to his secrets pried open.

"We don't have to talk about anything you don't want to talk about," Lathea told him.

"I wouldn't," he said.

"I think it's good for Laraine that you came. She wants to help you. Lots of people want to help you."

"Lots of people?" he said.

She smiled again, then reached to the center of the table for what he now saw was a small black bag, not much bigger than a cell phone. She opened the drawstrings and poured out several polished stones of various shapes and colors, the smallest the size of a marble, the largest the size of a shooter. He'd had a big bumblebee shooter as a boy, black with yellow stripes, plus a bagful of aggies and jaspers and a single cat's eye. He had never played marbles with anyone, though, because he had no friends until high school and also didn't want anybody to know he had shoplifted the marbles. But he had liked to hold them in his hand at night before he went to sleep, liked to feel the cool glass warming in his fists. More than once he had fallen asleep with both hands stuffed, and in the morning had to search among the covers and sheets to gather the marbles up again.

Lathea said, "These are just my chakra stones. Holding them helps me to cleanse and center myself before contacting Spirit."

"Okay," he said.

"Do you meditate, Ryan?"

"No."

"It's a very healthy discipline." She looked to Jayme. "Good for both of you, in fact."

"I've thought about starting," Jayme said.

"Have you?" DeMarco asked.

"Several times."

Lathea picked up the amethyst then, closed it in her palm, and fixed her eyes on Jayme. "It would be very good for you right now," she said.

Jayme pressed her knees together. Felt her stomach muscles twitch. "May I ask you a question?"

"Of course," said Lathea.

"Have you ever heard of anybody getting a sound inside their head like that of a door slamming shut?"

DeMarco had not wanted to turn and look at her so quickly, but it happened. Lathea glanced at him, then back at Jayme. "It's more common than you might think.

From a spiritual point of view, it means that Spirit is trying to wake you up. Has this been happening to you?"

"No," Jayme said. "No, I was just curious, that's all. It's not a symptom of having a stroke, or a seizure, or anything like that?"

"If it happens frequently, or has severe pain associated with it, it's something you should get checked."

Jayme looked peripherally at DeMarco. "I don't know how, uh, frequent it is . . ."

Then she and Lathea remained silent. Jayme tried not to look at DeMarco.

And finally he said, "Maybe three times in two years. No pain. Just a sudden bang."

Lathea nodded. "It's an emphatic nudge. For you to wake up."

"I wasn't sleeping," he said.

"That's not what I meant."

More awkward silence. "Okay," Jayme said, hoping to ease the tension in the room. "That's more or less what I read online. So thanks. It's good to have that confirmation."

Lathea turned to DeMarco. Smiled warmly. "What has Laraine told you?" she asked. "About why she wanted you to come here."

It took him a moment to speak; it would sound so foolish. "She said you had a message to convey. From our boy. Ryan Jr."

Lathea held the amethyst a few moments longer, then laid it atop the table, picked up the red malachite, and enclosed it in her hand. She closed her eyes briefly. Then opened them and said, "The way this works is, I don't hear voices in my head. Some mediums do, but I don't. Usually I get images, and typically the images are metaphors. Symbols. Open to interpretation. And because I'm also an empath— I read feelings and emotions — the image might be accompanied by a strong emotion. So I might cry, I might get a stabbing pain in my back or stomach. It can be anything."

"Okay," DeMarco said.

She nodded. Cocked her head. Seemed to be listening intently. "He says you're not going to like this."

DeMarco said nothing. Felt his body tense.

"Just so you know," she told him, "I don't tell my clients only what they want to hear. I tell them what Spirit wants them to hear. But you have the choice to tell me if you don't want to hear anything at all."

He told her, "Go ahead."

Again she cocked her head as if she was listening. Nodded. Smiled. And said, "He's holding his hands cupped together, holding something . . . oh my." She chuckled.

"What is it?" DeMarco asked.

She said, "He wants you to know that guilt is poop."

Jayme stifled a laugh.

DeMarco held his mouth tight, jaw stiff.

"Shall I continue?" Lathea asked.

"Why not?" he said.

Several seconds passed. "Okay. Yes, I think I have it. He's letting me see that you are like a toddler who is so proud of his first poop in the toilet that he has to carry it around and show it to everybody. And that you need to stop."

This time Jayme laughed out loud, a short gasp of surprise she smothered with her hand.

DeMarco sat motionless for a moment, holding every muscle tight. Then he stood with the least abrupt movement he could muster. Very softly, his voice tight, he said, "Please tell Laraine that I'm in favor of anything that makes her stronger. But that she shouldn't feel the need to include me in any of it. And that what I particularly do not appreciate is her using my son for her own purposes, whatever the hell they are."

He turned away and headed for the door, but paused for a moment, still facing the door, when Lathea spoke.

"Not all dreams are messages, Ryan. But

many of them are."

He remained perfectly still for three seconds, then continued forward and walked out past Lathea's three partners without taking his eyes off the next doorway, then out through the foyer and to his car.

To Jayme, who was still half-turned in her chair, looking out through the empty doorway, Lathea said, "People who ignore their dreams are ignoring a very important part of their lives."

Jayme turned, and started to rise. "I'm so sorry about that. He's just . . . he's struggling."

"And you?" Lathea said.

"And me what?"

"You and I can talk, if you wish."

"Thank you, but I don't want to be talking about him behind his back."

"Not about him. About you. Do you have any questions? Anything you would like to discuss?"

"Me?" Jayme said. "No, there's nothing . . . nothing I can think of right now."

Lathea cocked her head and smiled.

"Okay, I do have a question," Jayme said, and sat down again. "Did Laraine tell you about the dreams Ryan had in Kentucky? In the mountains?"

"I really can't discuss anything she and I

talked about."

"Well, he had two dreams about his son. And in both of them, Ryan Jr. looked to be twelve years old or so. The same age he would be had he lived. How is that possible?"

"It's more complicated than this, but, to put it simply, Spirit comes to us in the form best suited for its purposes. To appear as a baby wouldn't have served Ryan Jr.'s purposes. Plus, we don't stop growing when we pass into Spirit, and I don't mean that just in a physical sense. Spirit is ageless, so it can appear however it chooses. It takes a lot of energy to do that, though. And Ryan Jr. has a lot of energy."

Jayme sat very still, her eyes on the edge of Lathea's table, forehead furrowed.

Lathea said, "I know it's not easy to understand. Would you like to borrow a few books on the subject? I have a pretty good library of material."

"No," Jayme said, drawing out the word. Then she looked up and offered a smile. "Things are really busy right now, so . . . some other time maybe." She stood again, and so did Lathea.

"Are you sure you don't have anything else you want to talk about?"

"I would but . . . we have an appointment

in Canfield this evening."

Lathea came around the corner of her table. "Are you sure?"

Jayme looked over her shoulder. Saw the doorway still empty. Inhaled.

The car horn blared outside, making her jump.

She reached into a pocket. "Let me pay you something for your time."

"I don't take money for this," Lathea told her. She turned and reached back across the desk, slid open a drawer, took out a card and handed it to Jayme. "My number's on here. Call me when you have time to talk."

Jayme looked at the card, nodded, palmed it, and turned to the door.

"Jayme?" Lathea said, and Jayme looked back. "There is a reason for everything."

"Okay," Jayme said.

"I want you to know that. And remember it."

"There is a reason for everything."

"God bless you," Lathea said.

And for just a moment, the tiniest blink of time, Jayme saw Lathea not as a petite young woman but as very old, and while not physically large, immense and ancient. It was a dizzying impression, a rush of warm, scented air across her face. And then it was gone.

FORTY-EIGHT

He had his head back and eyes closed when she climbed into the car. Cold air was blasting through the air conditioner vents. Her body felt odd. Everything felt odd. Vivid yet dreamlike.

She said, and heard the odd slowness of her voice, "Was that really necessary?"

He opened his eyes but did not look at her. Stared straight ahead. "Sorry. I bumped the horn."

"Long bump," she said.

He put his hand on the gearshift but did not pull it into Drive. Squinting, he gazed out the windshield, out across the gray water. Finally he said, "The smartest thing a person can do is to learn to identify the difference between people who are more intelligent than you and the people who are too stupid to realize how dumb they really are."

She snapped her seat belt into place. "Are

you talking to me or to yourself?"

He did not reply.

She said, "I hope you take your own advice."

She said nothing for most of the next hour, until they were off the interstate, halfway down OH-11 and still speeding south. There was too much to think about, too much to process. The portentous quality of Lathea's last statement. The melancholy smile that accompanied her blessing.

DeMarco was driving faster than usual. Passing every vehicle they encountered. As if he intended to blast his way through space and time. Whereas Jayme felt strangely stilled. Suspended in a bubble of motionless time.

She really did not want to break that suspension, but it was difficult to sustain with DeMarco so tight and tense beside her. Lightly, she said, "So what about that whole thing with Lathea's life partners? I mean, four of them? A *ménage à quatre*?"

He looked at her. Looked back at the road. Looked at her again. And apparently saw something that made him blink. Made him shake his head and blow out a breath.

She watched his hands on the steering wheel, saw his grip relax. Saw his elbows come down. He said, "There are all kinds of people in this world, I guess."

"But what do you think of a situation like that?"

"I don't think anything of it."

"How do you think it works? One on one? Two on two? Three on one? Every man for himself?"

He smiled. "It's trouble no matter how you look at it. People are too complicated for something like that. Too unpredictable."

"I agree," she said. Then added, a few moments later, "They all seemed fairly happy, though, didn't they? Peaceful, even."

He glanced in the rearview mirror. Glimpsed her out of the corner of his eye.

She said, "I'm not saying I need a foursome to be happy. I'm just saying, if that's the kind of setup they all need to be happy, then why not? It seems to be working for them. So why the heck not?"

He rolled his shoulders. Stretched his back.

"Oh no you don't," she told him. "Don't you do that."

"Do what?"

"Listen to that little voice inside your head that's telling you all the wrong stuff." She reached across the seat to lift his right hand off the steering wheel, then pressed her own hand atop his. "I have everything I need," she told him. "One wonderful man is more than enough for me."

He laced his fingers between hers. "So I'm still wonderful?"

"You're on probation. But I swear, if you ever beep at me again . . ."

He nodded. Kept his eyes on the road, his face stern. Then, when her hand relaxed in his, and he felt more of the tension draining away from him, he said, softly, like a hungry little bird, "Beep."

FORTY-NINE

At the restaurant where they stopped for dinner prior to the memorial for Samantha Lewis, DeMarco continued to study the menu. He had already sent the server away twice with, "A couple more minutes, please."

Finally he laid the laminated menu flat in front of him. "What are you having?" he asked.

"Grilled salmon salad. You?"

He shrugged. "I'll just get the same thing."

She didn't think it wise to bring up the meeting with Lathea yet, the message from Ryan Jr., or what Lathea had told her privately. So she said nothing.

He said, "I wish somebody would invent a pill so that we didn't have to eat. Most of the time it's just a nuisance."

There was something going on with him other than what Lathea had told him. Something that had started earlier. The heaviness in his chest. The exploding head. The general weariness in everything he did. Usually an investigation got his adrenaline flowing and filled him with a relentless energy. She had seen only glimmers of that in the past few days.

Maybe, she thought, it started when he came back to check on Laraine. Then lifted when he returned to Kentucky, then befell him again when they crossed from West Virginia into Pennsylvania. Maybe spending so much time in Youngstown had churned up too many memories. In any case, she wasn't going to question him. He didn't like being questioned. Didn't like being probed.

Still, what if there was something physically wrong with him? Something potentially lethal? She said, "This case is really sapping my energy. I could use a couple days of R&R."

He nodded, but absently, his gaze on the far wall.

"Maybe we should think about some downtime," she told him. "After we see how things play out tonight."

He did not reply.

"Gee," she said, trying for a lighter tone. "There we were with a psychic, and we didn't even think to ask who the murderer is."

Still he offered no reply. Neither spoke until the server arrived again and asked, "Are we ready?"

He nodded to Jayme, who ordered the salmon salad with raspberry vinaigrette and a glass of water with lemon.

"And you, sir?"

"Same," he said. "With balsamic, please."

He usually ordered the blue cheese dressing, or at least some crumbles. Usually iced tea or coffee. She couldn't help but to search his face for some indication of illness, an unhealthy pallor, or eyes that refused to focus. But there was no visible sign.

For the next ten minutes she continued to try to read him, alternating her study of his hands with long looks toward the other customers, then a glance at his mouth, his eyes, the tabletop, the painting of three waterfowl on the wall. But always her gaze came back to his eyes, and finally lingered there too long.

He turned his head slightly. "Why are you staring at me?"

"Because I love you," she said.

When he offered nothing in return, she said, "Please don't go away from me like this. It scares me."

"I don't know what you mean," he told

her. But the sadness of his smile stabbed at her heart.

She said, "What's going on with you, babe?"

He lowered his gaze. Used his fingertips to straighten the edge of the place mat. "I guess a part of me just wants to walk away from all this."

She felt suddenly hollow and nauseated.

He said, "*With* you, of course. Walk away with you. Always with you."

"Then let's do it. Let's just walk away right now."

"I wish it were that easy."

"Why isn't it?"

He shrugged. "I don't quit things. It's a bad habit to start."

She considered reminding him that he had recently quit his job with the state police. But what good would that do?

Then the server arrived with their salads. "Anything else I can get you folks right now?"

DeMarco had turned at the young woman's approach, and now kept looking intently into her eyes. He didn't speak, didn't look away. Finally the server broke eye contact and spoke to Jayme, a bit nervously. "We okay?"

"It looks great," Jayme told her. "Thank

you." She watched DeMarco watching the server walk away.

Finally he turned to Jayme. "How old do you think she is?"

"Early twenties probably?"

"Such a child," he said, and let his gaze sweep the room. "They're all children, aren't they? We're all children, every one of us. We have no idea what lies ahead."

"Babe," she said. "You're really scaring me now."

His eyes went into a squint. He seemed puzzled. But it lasted only a few seconds. Then he smiled, unfolded his napkin, and spread it over his lap. "Preprandial depression," he told her, and picked up his fork. "There's another p-word to try out on Fascetti. Pass the pepper, please."

FIFTY

"Quite a crowd," Jayme said.

From the corner of the visiting team bleachers, they looked out across the football field twenty yards below, where some two hundred people were gathered at the nearest end zone. Many of them held a paper cup in which a small candle burned, even though the sky was still bright with evening light. The crowd was compressed near the front, where it formed a half circle close to a display of photos and mementos. It widened and separated at the back, where it had broken into small pockets of a few people each, those who had shown up out of curiosity or a sense of obligation. On both sides of the crowd a handful of smokers had stepped aside to inhale whispers of their own deaths.

A murmur of voices could be heard, as could occasional bursts of laughter from the back of the crowd. The most prominent voice was male and emanated from the end zone. "That sounds like the commissioner," DeMarco said.

Jayme asked, "How do you want to do this?"

"We should be able to spot Gillespie from here. How many people are six three? I'm betting he's near the front."

"There he is," Jayme said a minute later. "Left of center."

DeMarco nodded. He glanced at his cell phone. "7:19. Let's hold off till it winds down a bit."

Twenty minutes later they approached from the rear, then skirted the crowd from the far side. By this time Samantha's father and two other individuals had finished their remarks. Music from a suitcase-size boom box in front of the photo display was playing, with most of the crowd singing along and swaying back and forth. Others sobbed and held to each other.

Miley Cyrus's "The Climb" began just as DeMarco and Jayme eased into the edge of the crowd a few yards behind Gillespie. She whispered, "Want me to scout ahead?"

"Roger that," DeMarco said.

She moved unobtrusively along the outer edge, close enough finally to look across the faces in the front row. A few minutes later she turned and walked, head bowed, back to DeMarco.

"I could make out both Kaitlin and Griffin in a small group of students at the very front," she told him. "Gillespie is a couple of rows behind them."

"Like a mother hen watching over its brood?"

"You might say that."

"We need to do this in the parking lot," DeMarco whispered. "Can you keep an eye on the kids from the bleachers? I'll take Gillespie."

"What if they break up?"

"Stick with Kaitlin, I guess. If you can keep Griffin from seeing you, all the better. We'll chat with him and the other ones later."

They turned and retraced their steps. Jayme stationed herself at the corner of the bleachers, from which point she could look down almost directly onto the front of the crowd. DeMarco crossed back to the parking lot behind the other end of the bleachers. From there he walked the rows until he spotted Professor Gillespie's charcoal Volvo Momentum. He then hurried back to his own car, and moved it to a slot facing the rear of the SUV.

And he waited. Switched from one radio

station to another. Fiddled with the air conditioner vent. Then reset it to its original placement. Moved his seat back forward a notch. Too straight. Took it back two notches. Uncomfortable. Moved it forward one notch. Just right.

It was well after eight before people started returning to their vehicles. Gillespie was not among the first rush, nor in those who trickled past throughout the next ten minutes. Only twenty or so cars remained in the lot when DeMarco saw Gillespie approaching. He turned off the radio, shut off the engine.

Ten yards from his own vehicle, Gillespie used a remote starter to fire up the SUV. DeMarco popped open his door. "Professor!" he said.

Gillespie turned, smiling. The smile was short-lived. "Well hello," he said. Then mustered a different kind of smile. "Such a sad, sad occasion," he said, and opened the vehicle's door.

"It is," said DeMarco. He paused adjacent to the rear door of the SUV, less than three feet from Gillespie, and leaned against the car's hull. The scent of pine air freshener seeped out of the car. And underneath it . . . was that cannabis smoke he smelled?

"I'm a little surprised to see you here,

Professor," DeMarco said. "Considering that you couldn't remember if Ms. Lewis was a student of yours or not."

Gillespie looked at the electronic key in his hand. "You jogged my memory. It was over two years ago."

"Even so," said DeMarco. "A student gets brutally murdered, a close friend of the student who cleans for you, and it takes me to jog your memory?"

Gillespie now considered the roof of his vehicle. Rubbed a fingertip over a smudge of dirt. "I deal with hundreds of students every semester. I tend to remember their faces, but seldom their names."

DeMarco nodded. Knew that Gillespie had spoken with Kaitlin by now, probably with Griffin too. So he stood there smiling, giving the professor a bit more time to get nervous. Then he said, "It's an interesting coincidence though, don't you think?"

"What is?"

"You do research on the Talarico/Brogan murders, then one of your students happens to be murdered in a fashion similar to those. And not long before that, you made a presentation to an audience of law enforcement personnel and amateur criminologists, in which you proposed that both the Talarico murders and the Cleveland Torso

347

Murders were perpetrated by some kind of weird religious fanatic? A subject that just happens to be your academic specialty."

He smiled broadly at Gillespie then, and said, "It does make a man curious."

Gillespie said, "I am a scholar, sir. The extremes of religious thought move like dangerous currents through man's history. For you to insinuate for even a second that I had something to do with that poor girl's death . . ."

DeMarco waited, kept smiling. But Gillespie had temporarily run out of words.

"Is there any chance you have a book you're trying to get published?" DeMarco asked.

"You," Gillespie sputtered, "you —"

"Naw, never mind," DeMarco told him. "Every academic has a book he's trying to get published, right? I'll just ask around, see what I can find. Save you the trouble of answering. Nice to see you again." With that he straightened and took a step away from the vehicle.

Gillespie remained frozen in place, face pinched, nostrils flared.

Three steps from the SUV, DeMarco paused. He didn't want to let Gillespie off the hook yet. Wanted him to swallow the hook. Wanted the hook to rip his guts out.

DeMarco made a quarter turn and looked back at Gillespie. "I was wondering, though," he said. "University policy."

"What about it?" Gillespie managed.

"In regard to a female student cohabiting with a male professor. Is that something you have to file a formal request for? Some kind of holy dispensation type of thing?"

"Miss Mahood . . . I assume you are referring to her . . . is employed as my housekeeper. I already made that clear to you."

"Yeah, that's another thing. Because what she said is that she was at your house to study. Though she looked to me like she had just rolled out of bed."

"She does not live with me. That's absurd. Sometimes she brings books with her, she studies a bit, does some cleaning . . ."

"Except that the last summer classes are already over. So what was she studying? *The Kama Sutra* maybe?"

Gillespie lurched forward, shaking his finger at DeMarco. "I treat my students with the utmost respect! My students *admire* me! For you to suggest such a thing . . . I . . . I don't even know how to respond to that."

"Her campus roommate hasn't seen her for weeks. Coincidentally, not since her friend, and your former student, was murdered."

"How does that involve me?" Gillespie demanded. "There is no correlation. In fact, as I recall, Kaitlin mentioned that she went home for a while. Spent most of that time with her family."

"I'll check that out," DeMarco said. "It will be interesting to hear what her folks have to say. What do you wanna bet they think she's been in her apartment all this time?"

Gillespie's stiff finger of indignation was now limp at his side, long arms hanging down. He stared at the pavement just in front of DeMarco's feet.

"But hey," DeMarco told him. "She's a legal adult, right? No harm, no foul." He looked up at the sky. "It's going to be a nice clear night after all. Crescent moon. Good night to lie in the grass and ponder the stars. You have grass back at your place, right?"

Gillespie lifted his head. He looked at De-Marco with a sneer that was probably permanent by now, probably born in his childhood thanks to an overly critical mother or abusive father. But he was no child now and long past the time when one has to start taking responsibility for his tendencies, whether it is narcissism or meanness or just a sneer that seems to be begging for a punch in the mouth.

DeMarco asked, "Do you sleep well, Dr. Gillespie?"

"Most nights. Do you?"

"I used to like to punch people in the face. Still have an occasional urge."

"I would suggest that you find yourself some help for that condition."

"Help comes in various forms. Sometimes a couple of jabs to the mouth are exactly the medicine a man needs."

"Are you threatening me, sir?"

DeMarco shrugged. "I have a long history of violence. And history is the mother of philosophy. So maybe if I knock out a few of your teeth I will have a better understanding of the meaning of life."

"I believe it's considered a crime to make such a threat."

"If I were threatening you, and not merely theorizing, it might be called simple assault. Me, if I'm going to break the law, I break it all the way. Like knocking your nose out the other side of your cheek so that you can smell sideways. That would be a law worth breaking."

Gillespie blinked, looked away. His mouth opened slightly as if he wanted to speak, but then he changed his mind, licked his lips, took half a step backward, turned his body to the side.

DeMarco counted to five, then smiled again. "Nice chatting with you," he said.

He returned to his car, climbed in, started the engine, and pulled out of the parking space. Gillespie remained just as he had been a minute earlier, limp and immobile.

DeMarco gave him a friendly *beep beep.* He just couldn't resist.

FIFTY-ONE

Kaitlin came away from the dispersing crowd along with Griffin Lewis and two other students, one white male, one African American female. The four walked the length of the football field together, talking most of the way as they angled toward the parking lot. Jayme followed along the front of the bleachers, staying far enough behind to remain out of their peripheral vision.

As the four closed on the parking lot, the unfamiliar male peeled off from the group and headed toward the far end of the lot. The other three remained in a tight knot as they left the grass and made their way to the second row of cars. Jayme kept an eye on all of them, watched the unfamiliar male climb into a car and speed away. She then approached the group of three.

Kaitlin and the other female stood facing the driver's door on a yellow Mustang, with Griffin Lewis leaning against the door panel. They stopped talking when Jayme approached. "Hi, guys," she said.

Lewis straightened, and Kaitlin went stiff.

"Griffin," Jayme said, "I just want to say again how sorry I am for your loss. It's a terrible thing to have to suffer."

He said, "What are you doing here?"

"My job," she answered. "Trying to find the person responsible for this."

"You couldn't leave us alone for one night?" Kaitlin asked.

"I'm surprised you would want us to take a rest." Jayme turned to the other girl and smiled. "Hi, I'm Jayme Matson. Are you one of Dr. Gillespie's students too?"

Hesitatingly, the girl reached out to take Jayme's hand, but Griffin's hand shot out to push the girl's hand away. "You don't have to talk to her," he said. "She's not the police. And even if she was."

Jayme smiled at the girl. "My partner and I are former Pennsylvania State Police. We're now attached to the Mahoning County Sheriff's Office as special investigators. So yes, we are the police. May I ask your name, please?"

"You don't have to tell her anything," Lewis said.

But the girl answered, though timidly. "Rebecca Sadler," she said. "Becca."

"And are you also one of Dr. Gillespie's students?"

"Last semester I was."

Griffin blew out a breath in disgust. Scowled and shook his head.

"And who is the boy who just now walked away?"

"This is illegal," Griffin said. He turned, reached for his door, and popped it open. "You're not allowed to talk to us without lawyers present."

"That's incorrect," Jayme told. "It's true that you don't have to talk to me if you don't want to. But I'm having a hard time understanding why you wouldn't want to. Aren't you anxious to find out who killed your sister?"

He glared at her for a moment, then turned to the girls. "I'm outta here," he told them. "You need a ride, Becca?"

"I'll take her," Kaitlin said.

"Whatever." He climbed inside and slammed the door. The females stood aside and watched the vehicle pull away. The tires screeched when he turned onto the street.

Jayme said, "Is it me, or is he always angry about something?"

The only response was a quick scowl from Kaitlin.

"Honestly, ladies," Jayme told them, "I

am here to help. All I want to do is to find out who killed your friend."

Becca said, "The same person who killed those two men, right?"

"Probably. And we *will* find out who that person is. Right now we're just trying to collect more pieces to the puzzle."

She smiled first at Kaitlin, then at Becca. "Look, I understand how Griffin must feel. This is a very profound loss for him. For all of you. And I know he sees our questions as an invasion of his grief. I'm sorry about that. But it's a small sacrifice, don't you think? If we can put her killer away forever?"

Becca said, "His name's Connor McBride. The boy who was with us tonight."

"Thank you," Jayme said. "And he's also one of Dr. Gillespie's students?"

Becca nodded. "The semester before me, I think."

"And you all hang out together now?"

"Not usually," Kaitlin said. "Just tonight actually."

"Gotcha," said Jayme. She cocked her head, scratched a place above her right ear. "So Griffin's starting his senior year," she said, thinking aloud, "as Samantha would have. And you're a junior, right, Kaitlin?"

Kaitlin answered with the tiniest of nods.

"And you, Becca?"

"I'll be a sophomore. Same as Connor. Except that he dropped out for a couple of years and then came back."

"And all four of you were Gillespie's students. Samantha makes five. Did you all get an A in his class?"

Kaitlin said, "Becca, I have to get going. So if you want me to drop you off . . ."

"I checked him out on Rate My Professor," Jayme said. "He has an awful lot of negative reviews. What did you think of the course, Becca?"

The young woman had been standing with her eyes down, but now, questioned directly, she quickly looked at Kaitlin. *Deer in the headlights,* Jayme thought.

Kaitlin dug into her jeans pocket, pulled out her keys. "We need to go."

Jayme stepped between Kaitlin and Becca. "So you all took the same course but in different semesters. There are a lot of students on campus, right? How did you all get to know each other?"

Kaitlin looked up at her. Defiant. Then said, "Some lecture or something. What's the difference?"

"I saw he was here tonight too," Jayme said. "He seems to have a special relationship with you four. You want to tell me what's going on?"

Becca stared at the dirty pavement. Kaitlin looked as if she might snarl.

Jayme said, "By the way, Kaitlin, I talked to one of your roommates earlier. She's concerned that she hasn't seen or heard from you in a while. You told her you were going home to be with your parents. Would you like for me to contact them for you, let them know where you've really been staying?"

Kaitlin held Jayme's gaze for three seconds. Then abruptly turned away. "I'm leaving, Becca. With or without you." She walked away without waiting for a response.

"I'm sorry," Becca said, and hurried to catch up with her friend.

Jayme watched them for a few moments, then turned and crossed half the lot to find DeMarco in his vehicle, engine running, his head laid back, eyes closed. She knocked on the hood as she passed the front of the vehicle.

After she had climbed in and closed the door, DeMarco asked, "How'd it go?"

"The one boy split off before I got to them. His name's Connor McBride. He seems a couple years older than the rest of them. Griffin refused to talk to me; he split too. Kaitlin was borderline hostile. And sweet little Rebecca Sadler . . . we need to talk to her alone."

"Can do," he said. "Learn anything else?"

"They were all Gillespie's students. Griffin too. And all so pretty. Even the boys. Petite, delicate features, almost like four little dark-haired dolls. Every single one of them."

"And Samantha Lewis makes five."

"What are the odds, do you think? That five of Gillespie's students would all share those physical similarities?"

"Are you suggesting he's a doll collector?"

She thought for a moment. "What's that saying about there being something fishy in Denmark?"

"Something rotten in Denmark," he said.

"Yeah. Even better."

FIFTY-TWO

On the drive back to Pennsylvania, they shared everything they had learned and suspected from their brief interviews. Gillespie would now know that he was a subject of the investigation; if he truly had something to hide, he would be very nervous, as the students had been. They were all probably talking or texting even now.

"Let them fret," DeMarco said. "The more they communicate, especially by phone, the better for us."

"If and when we have enough information to subpoena the phone records."

"If and when," he said.

"What I can't get a handle on is why Samantha's friends might be involved in this. I mean, to kill her, okay, some kind of group dynamics gone haywire. But what about Brenner and Hufford? We've kind of lost track of them in all this."

DeMarco nodded. "Something's bound

to unravel. We just have to keep pulling at the one thread we have."

"I do feel as if we're getting somewhere finally."

"Though not by leaps and bounds."

"When does it ever happen by leaps and bounds?"

"In novels," he said. "Movies. Made-up stories." *Though not in Chandler's novels. Not in Tom's.* And then he chuckled to himself, amused by the notion that maybe he *was* just a character in a Thomas Huston novel. *Then that would mean that I talked with my own creator. Had lunch with him several times.*

But no, Tom was all too human. Which is to say, imperfect.

On the other hand, he told himself, *what if God is imperfect? Tom had said that a book is never as good as the writer wants it to be, because no writer possesses that level of talent. Maybe the same is true for God. All those fine ideas. All those big plans. Yet they all fell short somehow. The dinosaurs. The hominids. Neanderthal, Cro-Magnon, modern humans. None of it ever quite hit the mark.*

That would explain a lot, DeMarco thought. *Yep. That would explain everything.*

FIFTY-THREE

They entered the house as usual, relocked the door behind them, went about their usual preparations for bed. Both seemed to have settled into solitary contemplation, though there were subjects Jayme still wanted to explore. She wanted to find out if the passing hours had helped Ryan to process his feelings regarding Lathea and her message, and how he felt about Laraine's impromptu visit a day earlier. She wanted to tell him that she, Jayme, still felt strangely troubled that Laraine had showed up unannounced at their door, the way she might feel if she were ticketed for a traffic violation, for making a rolling stop at an intersection, for failing to yield while merging onto a busy street. It was a feeling of embarrassment for being caught, and anger at herself for thinking she could get away without consequences for breaking the rules. And, worst of all, a fear that the visit might signal Laraine's first foray into their lives, an ambush to be followed by more guerilla attacks. Was she using their deceased child and Ryan's guilt to insinuate herself back into his life?

He would probably dismiss her concerns with a simple *Don't be silly. That isn't going to happen.* He was seldom willing to delve beneath the surface of a personal problem, whether hers or his own. When he grew uncomfortable with a subject, uncomfortable with his own emotions, he would make a joke. And she, most times, would let him get away with it. He preferred to sequester his feelings, except the positive ones, under lock and key. That was how he worked. How he held himself together. By relying on the comfort of old habits.

She wondered what would become of them if he never broke from those habits. But if she pushed, might she push him away?

They undressed and took a quick shower together, but for once he did not reach for her in the shower stall, did not stand behind her with his hands cupping her breasts and his body pressed to hers. He soaped her back, as always, and she did the same for him, but then they rinsed clean without further contact, stepped out and toweled dry.

While she combed out her hair, he pulled on a pair of clean basketball shorts and a white V-neck T-shirt, then placed the box containing Huston's notebooks in the middle of the bed, climbed in, and started reading. She joined him there ten minutes later, and resumed her reading as well.

Twenty minutes passed before she spoke. "Can I read something to you?" she asked.

"Of course."

"It's called 'My Child,'" she said, and waited, half expecting that the title might change his mind about hearing it.

"Okay," he said without inflection.

And so she read:

When I first held you, the whole of your body barely covered my chest. But that was all the touch it took to make the magic work — your pure and tiny heart pressed like a kiss to the scars that covered mine, the warmth of your tender skull against my cheek. I would sit like that for hours wanting nothing more than you, needing nothing more, that small shabby room of our house underwater, all of my small life joyfully underwater with you, while the tears of the staggering truth of a love that will always be absolute and infinite washed their blessings into my skin.

She waited for what seemed a long time, hoping that he would hear in Huston's words and in her voice the longing she had to hold her own child to her breast. Then she asked, "Should I mark it as a keeper?"

Another ten seconds passed before he answered. "That's exactly how I felt when Ryan was born."

Only then did she realize her mistake. She had misjudged his reaction to the piece, had hoped to awaken his empathy, but had only awakened a painful memory.

He marked the page in the composition book he had been reading and closed the cover and laid the book back into the box. "I'm too tired to read any more," he said.

"I'll stop too. You want to talk?"

"About what?" he said.

What could she say? *I want to talk about my feelings, not yours. I want you to understand how I feel.* There was no way to not appear selfish.

She closed the cover on her notebook, but instead of returning it to the box, she placed it on her end table, then switched off the light. DeMarco lifted the box off the bed and set it on the floor, then turned out the light on his bed table. He rolled over and kissed her forehead. "Good night, baby girl," he said, then lightly kissed her cheek and her mouth before returning to his place on the bed and rolling onto his side, his back to her.

With each of his kisses, each gentler than the previous one, her chest had ached more. But she concentrated on her breath going slowly in and out, one long, aching breath after another, and remained there on her back with her eyes on the dark ceiling for a quarter of an hour. She could hear the air conditioner humming through the ductwork behind the walls, and she could feel the cool air on her face and the warmth of DeMarco's body next to hers and the weight of the sheet atop her knees and toes.

Only when DeMarco's breathing deepened and she knew that he was sleeping did she allow herself to cry.

FIFTY-FOUR

They slept late the next morning, well past sunrise. When DeMarco awoke, the room was already full of light, the curtains glowing yellow. He rolled his head to the other side and saw Jayme lying there with her cell phone held aloft. "Good morning, beauty," he said.

"Clear and scorching today," she told him.

"How scorching?"

"Ninety-one."

He groaned. "Better than ninety-two, I guess." Then he asked, "How long you been awake?"

"An hour or so. I woke up nauseous. You didn't hear me in the bathroom?"

"No, I'm sorry. Are you okay?"

She laid the phone aside and rolled up against him. "I'm good. I think the salmon on my salad might have been a little off."

"I had the same meal."

"But a different piece of fish. I'm fine now,

babe. What are our plans for the day?"

"Dinner with Ben and Vee tonight. Other than that . . . anything you would like to do?"

"This feels pretty good right here," she said.

"It does, doesn't it? Go back to sleep if you want to."

"So you can slip away and go study your display wall?"

"I'll stay right here. Are you sure you're not coming down with something?"

"Yeah, the skunky salmon blues."

"Sounds serious."

"Shut up and hold me awhile."

She would have liked to tell him about the dream that woke her an hour earlier, but felt she had to keep it to herself. In a few days the case would break open, they would identify a person of interest if not a suspect, and Brinker's team would take over with their warrants and interrogations. Then she and DeMarco could breathe a mutual sigh of relief and focus on their own lives again. Their life together. Their future. Maybe then her troubling dreams would stop too.

In last night's dream she had been sitting on the sofa in the living room, nursing a baby, with the light coming full through the window, bright and warm on her shoulders and head. Then DeMarco walked in from the kitchen and looked at her darkly and said, *Where did that come from?* She placed a hand on the back of the tiny warm head, tried to cover the entire body with her hands and arms. And DeMarco said, *You need to call someone to come get that thing.* He walked to the front door then and flung it open and strode out, and suddenly all the noise of the world came rushing in through the door in a black fog and filled every room with a cacophony as thick and heavy as a thunderstorm, the sounds of sirens and rumbling traffic and dogs barking and horns blaring, of someone pounding a mallet against metal and the heavy booming bass of a car stereo. She bent over her baby to cover it with her body and felt every sound pounding into her like a thousand angry fists. Worried that she was smothering the infant, she drew away to look at its lovely face, but instead saw the painted face of a porcelain doll with its skull smashed in. She awakened with a jolt and lay there gasping in bed, curled rigid and tight into herself with DeMarco's breath slow and deep and regular beside her. Then the nausea hit and she had to scurry into the bathroom as quietly as she could.

She knew that DeMarco would never

react that way to a real baby, that he was a loving and compassionate man. She knew it but didn't want to hear how he would respond to the dream. She didn't want to talk about any of it or even think about it anymore, because if she did she would be sick again. So she kept quiet and laid her hand flat upon his chest and murmured contentedly as if all was right with the world.

FIFTY-FIVE

The Brinkers lived in a large white colonial on a double half-acre lot on Poland Manor Road, a few miles southeast of the city. The sheriff, dressed in blue jeans and loafers and a pale-yellow knit shirt, met them on the front porch.

"Nice crib," DeMarco said.

"Got it in foreclosure," Ben told him. "Sheriff's sale." And gave Jayme a wink.

She handed him a bottle of merlot. "Thank you for having us over."

He held the bottle by the neck and read the label. "Vee's favorite," he said. Then he turned and called through the screen door. "Vee! They brought wine!"

A few seconds later his wife appeared at the door. "In that case, they can stay awhile!"

She was a tall, stately woman, nearly as tall in white espadrille wedge sandals as her husband. She wore a brightly flowered halter-style maxi dress, with large red hoop earrings and a triple-strand necklace of cherry-red beads. She stepped outside and threw her arms around Jayme. "*Akeyi,* my darling. Welcome!"

She squeezed her hard for a moment, then drew away, but held to Jayme's hands. "What a beauty you are! Look at this hair! You deserve a better man than this scoundrel," she said, and jerked her head toward DeMarco.

"Miss Veronica," he said. "It is so nice to see you again."

She released Jayme and embraced De-Marco. "You are the only person who doesn't call me Vee," she said. "And I've always loved that about you."

"I can call you Veronica," Ben said.

"No thank you. It's special for Ryan."

Ben turned to Jayme. "I think she wishes she'd married him instead."

"Not true," Vee said. "I am very happy with the choice I made." Again she took Jayme's hand. "I lack the necessary resources to contend with a man like yours. But I sense that you do not. I have never seen him looking so contented."

"Sometimes I wonder," Jayme said. And Vee squeezed her hand.

DeMarco said, "Could we stop talking

about me, please?"

"I second that," Ben answered, and bumped his shoulder against DeMarco's. "Can't think of a more boring subject. How about a drink, Sergeant? Bourbon okay?"

"Superlative."

"And for the ladies?"

"The merlot, of course," Vee said. "And, Jayme? We have just about every spirit known to man."

"Maybe some water or club soda? With lime or lemon if you have it."

DeMarco raised his eyebrows.

She told him, "You have fun and relax tonight. I'll drive us home."

After the pleasantries they moved to the spacious kitchen, where Jayme and De-Marco were seated at a marble-topped island to watch Ben assemble a cheese-and-fruit plate while Vee tended to the lamb curry and basmati saffron rice with peas and cashews. They talked about Vee's parents' migration from Haiti when Vee was barely three years old, and how Jayme had applied for acceptance to the state police academy "on a whim" four days after receiving her baccalaureate in psychology.

Ben said, "Abnormal psychology, right? Which is how you ended up with him?"

She nodded. "I studied him for my master's thesis. He never knew he was my lab rat."

"And what did you learn?" Vee asked.

Jayme smiled at DeMarco. Took his hand. "That some things will always remain a mystery."

The evening passed quickly. For forty-five minutes the couples traded stories about their pasts, always skirting delicately around any mention of Laraine or Baby Ryan. When Vee asked DeMarco how he was enjoying being back in his hometown, his hesitation before saying "It's great" was just long enough to make Ben cock his head.

"Not your city anymore, huh?" he asked.

DeMarco shrugged. "I guess I've discovered that I'm not really a city kind of guy."

"Isn't there anything you like about the city?" Ben asked.

"Fewer insects," DeMarco said, then thought for a moment, and added with a smile, "but more cockroaches. So that's a wash."

Vee said, "I couldn't live without my Rulli Brothers and Giant Eagle."

"And your Southern Park Mall," Ben said. Then, to DeMarco, "So there's no chance of you two moving back this way?"

When DeMarco didn't answer, Jayme said, "We might hit the road in the RV again. See what the rest of the world has to offer. Right, babe?"

DeMarco nodded, but he had no idea what waited next for them. He only knew that every breath still felt a little too heavy, every room felt a little too small. Even a four-person dinner party made him claustrophobic. He finished his drink and declined a refill, and switched to sparkling water throughout the rest of the meal.

When Vee rose to clear the plates, and Ben stood to help, Jayme insisted that he sit while she helped his wife clear the table.

In the kitchen, with the dishwasher fully loaded, Vee slid a mango sorbet pie from the refrigerator and set it on the counter. "Would you mind pouring the coffee while I slice the pie?" she asked. Then, as Jayme was gathering fresh cups from the cupboard, Vee said, in a half whisper, "So how are you planning to get that man up to the altar?"

Jayme chuckled and set the cups on the counter. She liked this woman. Liked her boldness and sense of humor. Liked her intelligence and style. She answered, "Bigamy is illegal in this state."

"Why are they still married after all these years?"

"You know about the suicide attempt, right?"

"Oh yes. Ben told me that same night he found out."

"Ryan wants a divorce. I think he's just waiting until she's healthier."

"That might be a long wait," Vee said. "And until then, what?"

"I guess we just keep on keeping on. We *are* talking about having a baby, though."

"Who's talking?"

"Me, mostly."

"Does he at least pay attention?"

"It's hard to tell sometimes."

Vee paused with the pie knife poised in the air, and gave Jayme a long look.

Jayme said, "What?"

"He'd better start listening. Am I right?"

Jayme blushed. Said, "Is this a special kind of coffee? It smells really good."

"Direct trade coffee straight from the mountains. Grown in the shade. On the label it says, 'Defense Against the Dark Arts.' Fifteen dollars a pound for the beans. But worth every cent if it keeps the bad juju away."

Jayme grinned. "Do you still have relatives in Haiti?"

"All over the place. Nieces and nephews by the score."

Jayme smiled, nodded, filled the last cup. She said, "Speaking of bad juju, Laraine showed up unannounced at the house the other day."

"Lordee, lordee. Lots of fireworks then, I bet."

"Surprisingly, not so much as a bottle rocket. Ryan was in the shower, so she had a quick look around and left."

"Like a scout before the frontal attack, sounds to me. Looking for the weak spot in the defenses."

"Maybe," Jayme said. "I don't know. Anyway, he called her afterward, and it turned out she knew a psychic who had a message for him from their son."

Vee stood up straight. "From their baby that was killed?"

"Yes, ma'am," Jayme said. "So yesterday we drove up to Erie and had a brief talk with Madame Lathea."

"He actually agreed to that? Oh my my my."

"The message was kind of a scolding," Jayme told her. "He was supposed to quit acting like a baby and let go of all that guilt he has."

" 'Bout time somebody told him that."

"He thinks it was Laraine's doing. That she put Lathea up to it."

"The man doesn't believe in spirits? After all he's been through?"

"That's the thing," Jayme said. "I think he really wants to. He's had a couple of dreams about Ryan as an older boy."

Vee nodded to herself. "He does need to pay attention. When Spirit talks, you better listen. Otherwise, they'll just go away and leave you to flounder in your own ignorance."

"So you believe that it can actually happen?"

"That spirits talk to us? Honey, I don't believe it, I know it. My own grandmother leaves shiny pennies lying around for me to find. Always heads up, every one of them. That's how I know she's still watching over me."

"I hope that's true," Jayme said. "I lost my grandmother not long ago."

"You didn't lose her. There's somebody with us all the time."

Jayme blinked. Smiled. Began setting the cups on the tray. "That's a really nice way of thinking about it."

"Especially because that's the way it is," Vee said.

After devouring most of his pie, DeMarco asked Vee for permission to talk business for a while.

"Thank you for holding out so long," she

teased. "I know it's been difficult for both of you. Ben's been sitting there all night looking like he has to pee."

DeMarco and Jayme took turns filling the sheriff in on their various conversations with Daksh Khatri, the commissioner and Griffin, Professor Gillespie, Samantha's roommate and friends. Ben listened attentively until they finished. Then he nodded, and said, "Well, it's interesting, for sure, that all four kids took Gillespie's class. But it's hardly incriminating."

DeMarco said, "Khatri makes five students. And Samantha makes six."

"And remember," Jayme said, "Samantha's course notebook has disappeared. The only one missing from her bookshelf."

Ben said, "Maybe she lost it a long time ago. Or lent it to another student who never gave it back."

"The room hasn't been touched since she died. That's two weeks of dust on the shelves. You can see it in the photo I took. The notebook should have been at the bottom of the stack, but it's not. And there's hardly any dust where it should have been. It was recently removed."

"Okay," Ben said, "okay. Like I said, it's an interesting coincidence."

"It's a quadruple coincidence," DeMarco

told him.

"But how does it lead to murder?" Ben asked. "How does it even suggest it? And what's its relationship to Brenner and Hufford? A missing notebook. Six students who took the same course. I just don't see the connection. I'm sorry, but I don't."

He delivered these statements with his head down, eyes on the edge of his dessert plate, the tip of his fork pushing a piece of pistachio from the pie crust back and forth.

DeMarco said, "What's going on, Ben?"

Ben looked up, met DeMarco's eyes. Smiled sheepishly. "Okay," he said. "I have what, to me, feels like good news. But you two might not agree."

"Let's hear it," DeMarco said.

"We can finally connect Costa to Talarico."

"How?" Jayme asked.

"Actually, it was your idea about checking the library records. Olcott thought, why not try it for the Torso Murders? Did Talarico's killer maybe do some research about the Torso Murders first? Before he did Talarico and his lawyer?"

DeMarco said, "You're saying Costa did?"

Brinker nodded. "Of course this was before the internet got popular, and before the new library was built. But they still kept records. To check out a book, you wrote your name on a card. Had to take out a library card first if you didn't have one. And believe me, it took some digging. But the records were still there, all packed away in the basement."

"And Costa researched the Torso Murders?"

"Checked out two books. The only ones the library had on the subject."

"So what's the personal connection?" De-Marco asked. "Costa's to the vics?"

"Through an old girlfriend. She was Talarico's secretary at the time."

"Okay," DeMarco said. "And?"

"That's about as far as we've gotten. Haven't been able to locate her yet."

"Then you don't have anything, Ben. Anybody in the world can check out a book. Even if the dates coincide, which I assume they do, reading isn't a motive for murder. We learned that with Khatri. So Costa had an interest in the Torso Murders, plus his girlfriend worked for Talarico. Why are our links coincidences, and yours aren't?"

Ben looked at the palms of his hands, fingers spread. "All I'm saying —" he started, but DeMarco interrupted.

"And besides, even if Costa was responsible for Talarico and Brogan, and it's a big if, how does that tie him to Brenner or Lewis or Hufford? Your guys are still playing that angle, right? The same guy did all five?"

Again the sheriff nodded. "I just wanted to let you guys know, is all. It's a lead. More than we've had in a long time."

Jayme said, "You're not suggesting we give up *our* leads, are you?"

"I wouldn't call them leads exactly," Brinker said.

"There is something funny going on with Gillespie and those kids," she told him. "One of whom is the victim's twin brother. Who has been anything but cooperative. Ditto Kaitlin Mahood. Both of them know something they haven't told us yet."

DeMarco said, "1988 has absolutely nothing to do with now, Ben. You surely know that."

The sheriff wagged his head back and forth. He looked to his wife, who was regarding him with her head cocked, chin tucked, eyebrows raised: it was her *careful what you say* look.

"Okay," he finally said. "You guys keep doing what you're doing. Just please try to wrap it up. Two special consultants don't come cheap. And I have a fairly stingy budget to maintain."

DeMarco continued to frown while staring at a smear of yellow sorbet on his dessert plate. Then, remembering where he was, he smiled and looked up. "Miss Veronica," he said. "This pie is wickedly good."

"I'll send a couple slices home with you."

"Sheriff," Jayme said, "we need a warrant to search Griffin's room. The entire house, in fact."

"You want to search a county commissioner's house?"

"There's something in that missing notebook that somebody doesn't want us to see."

Ben leaned back in his chair. "Bring me something better than that," he said, "and I'll take it to the judge."

FIFTY-SIX

"That was a pleasant evening," Jayme said after buckling up.

DeMarco inched the car out of its space in Ben's driveway, made the turn, and eased onto the street. She told herself, *He only drives this slow when he's lost.*

"Should I not have mentioned the warrant?" she asked.

"That's the thing. I don't know where to go without it."

"Back to the kids maybe? I know we can crack Becca. Probably Kaitlin too eventually. We haven't even talked to Connor McBride yet."

"On the other hand . . . why would they kill their friend? That still bothers me."

"Maybe they're covering for Gillespie."

"Why would they? And why would *he* kill Samantha? And why in the world would he kill Brenner and Hufford?"

She had no answer, except to ask *Why*

does any psychopath kill? But it didn't need to be said. The truth was, she wanted to put Gillespie away for something. He made her skin crawl. But was that any different from Koenig and Fascetti wanting to see Costa locked up?

"Do we really have to know that yet?" she asked. "Do we have to know why?"

"What if Ben's right and we're barking up an empty tree?"

"At least let's keep at it until we know for sure that we're wrong."

He nodded. Squinted into the darkness. And that was another thing he did when he was uncertain; he leaned forward, close to the steering wheel. It reminded her of the cartoon character Mr. Magoo, such an old memory. But an endearing one. Crotchety old Magoo, half-blind and hunched over the wheel of his antique Studebaker. Crotchety old DeMarco. Not so old, though. And not always crotchety.

"Babe?" she said.

He looked her way.

"I love you with all my heart."

He nodded. "Me too."

"You love yourself with all your heart?"

His mouth held a grimace, and for a moment he looked like a six-foot-tall baby with gas. She turned away, smiled sadly at the side window. Watched the darkness going past, the lights flicking by. The sky was black, every star smothered in dark clouds. "It's going to rain tonight," she said.

He glanced at her again, hands tight on the steering wheel, brow furrowed, as if she had spoken in a language he didn't understand. And she wondered, *Is this the way it's always going to be with us?*

She understood, probably better than he did, that he was suffering from PTSD because of Huston's death, Bonnie's slit throat, the murder of Huston's family, and even because of the bullet DeMarco had fired into the murderer's heart. She knew enough about his time in Panama and Iraq to know that he was haunted by those experiences too. And the death of his own son — how could he ever get over that? His mother's suicide. The years of abuse heaped upon him by his father. Yes, she understood the mood swings, the lapses of attention, the insomnia, the cancerous guilt. *But what about us?* she wondered. *Is this the best it's ever going to get?*

Fifty-Seven

DeMarco read only two brief passages that night, each written on a separate sheet of paper in one of Huston's composition books. After reading the second one, he sensed a continuity in the pieces — not a unity of theme, but a unity of purpose, as if each was meant to tell him something important. Something he knew but had forgotten. Or something he needed to know. He read the first one again:

My father used to tell me that nothing worth having comes easily. He probably didn't realize that he was echoing similar pronouncements from the likes of Teddy Roosevelt, Booker T. Washington, and probably millions of other fathers before him. It can be a concise and effective admonition against the inherent laziness of a daydreaming boy. But it's a lie.

Many of the things most worth having

arise spontaneously, through no effort at all, gifts we did not expect, blessings we might not deserve: a child's laugh; a mother's kiss good night; a father's pat on the shoulder; a friendly dog's wet nose pressed against your neck; a butterfly that lands on your knee while you sit reading in the sun; the bliss of your partner's naked body against your own; birdsong; an old friend's hug; sunrise; a summer rain; love; and on and on and on and on . . .

And this time when DeMarco read his friend's words, he felt something like a punch in the stomach, not hard, but hard enough to make him catch his breath. Hard enough to make the room begin to waver around him, and grow watery around the edges, so that he had to blink to clear his eyes to read the second piece again.

Nature waits, but she will not hold her breath for you. Do you think you can ignore her like the old friend whose emails you never answer? Do you think you can turn your back to her as you do with your partner, when you are deep inside yourself and ego-blind to the needs of others?

Nature always waits; never tires of waiting. But if you ignore her correspondence too long, if you turn your back on too many nights and mornings and sweetly scented gloamings, it is you who will grow cold and stiff and numb and dry, not her. And when you become an empty husk, every strand of golden corn silk gone, blowing brittle and lost across last year's stubble, she will watch, will even help you find a dark corner where you can turn to dust, but, like the wife you ignore or the husband you deny, like the old friend who will eventually lose all memory of your face, she will not hold her breath for you; she will not sigh.

And now, too, in the mirror of those words, DeMarco acknowledged his regret, an ache left unsatisfied too long, that boyish pleasure he'd so often sought in the company of trees and meadows, that peculiar elevation of his spirit and the reassurance that he need never feel alone.

There was no apparent connection between the pieces, yet DeMarco felt certain a connection existed, a resonance with particular application to him. He could not have articulated the nature of that resonance, only that he was moved by it, as by a passage of music without words. Debussy's

"Clair de Lune," for example. Mozart's "Lacrimosa."

His rational mind told him that Huston had not intended to connect the pieces or he would have written them on the same page, and probably wrote each of them on a different day. Yet still the pieces cohered for DeMarco, and they were all he wanted to read that night.

He closed the composition book and placed it in the box. Jayme looked his way. He said, smiling softly, "May I make love to you, my beauty?"

She blinked. Then smiled too. Closed the cover on her notebook and placed it in the box.

He set it on the floor. When he turned back to her, she asked, "Did you read something sexy?"

He nodded, and touched her as he spoke. "Your eyes. Your nose. Your mouth. Your neck . . ."

FIFTY-EIGHT

In the morning she awoke to the scents of coffee and fried ham. She found the panties and camisole she had taken off, and pulled them on again. Went to the bathroom, washed her face and hands, brushed her teeth, combed her hair.

Downstairs, the kitchen table was set for breakfast. DeMarco was scooping ice cubes from the freezer and dumping them into a plastic bag. At his feet was his big blue cooler, and in the cooler were clear plastic containers of olives, pickles, cheese, sliced apples and pears, a tray of deep-fried chicken, two sweet rolls, bottles of water, two multigrain hard rolls.

She said, "Did you rob a grocery store?"

"Walmart is open all night," he said.

"You drove to Walmart already?"

He grinned. "Should we take a bottle of wine?"

"To where?"

"I was thinking that if we get to the Kinzua Sky Walk early, we can have it all to ourselves. I haven't been up there since they put in the glass floor. And then maybe a picnic in the woods. Does that sound okay?"

"Sounds wonderful. What brought this on?"

He kept grinning. "Did you hear it raining last night?"

"No. When?"

"Just a soft steady drizzle most of the night. This morning the grass was glinting with a thousand little diamonds."

She cocked her head, her hip. Her look of amazement made him smile. Made him feel something else too, started something moving around inside his blood. It felt like an army of leaf cutter ants converging on the philodendron in his crotch.

He wished he had the words to say how much he adored her, how much he needed her. He adored her more than a thousand words could express. He needed her more than everything Hemingway had ever written between the lines.

He patted his lap. "Get some coffee and have a seat. No work today, okay? Today is a day to just *be.*"

FIFTY-NINE

The work was important; he had no doubt of it. But this was important too, to stand above the treetops, his hand in hers, as the little creek, barely visible through the ground-hugging mist, trickled three hundred feet below. The sky walk ended midway across the gorge. Rusting girders and splintered beams from the fallen half still lay scattered over the gorge and up the far hillside. He looked out across the emptiness, which was not empty at all but full of color and light and scent and birdsong.

He had come here twice as a younger man. First when the railroad bridge was still intact, and if you dared to walk the ties across the gorge you had to be prepared to turn and run if the rails started to vibrate. This was in the winter, a few days after his mother's funeral, when he didn't know whether he would run or not if the trestle began to tremble. If he ran, he would be sent back to Panama, where he had done things he would not have believed he was capable of doing, and had seen things he wished he could scrub from his memory.

Many years later he came again after a second funeral, this one in the fall. A tornado had ripped away half the bridge, leaving broken ties and snapped rails hanging three hundred feet in the air. There were no guardrails back then, only a warning sign, and if you did not care about what might happen, you could make your way out as far as the last intact tie, and you could stand there full of rage and the deepest, blackest grief a human being can know. You could fantasize about stepping off the rails and into the air, and wonder how long you would remain conscious, and whether it would be better to fall feet or head first.

If you are lucky, you feel more rage than despair. Rage will eventually carry you back across the rails to your car. But that is where your luck ends, because it is impossible to leave the rage behind when you drive away, even if it is of negative value in the valley below.

Those times, he hoped, were years long gone. In the interim, a group of people had saved what was left of the bridge and raised enough money to turn it into a tourist attraction. There was a plank floor now and sturdy railing and a glass panel you could stand atop and imagine you were standing on air. The train no longer ran, and the danger of falling to your death was slight unless you made the effort to climb up over the railing and throw yourself off. Eventually someone would do that, because there was never a shortage of despair in this life, never a dearth of sorrow.

Still, he was glad they had come. Jayme clutched his hand the whole way out to the end of the sky walk, squeezed his fingers hard when she stood over the glass pane. He had been right about getting there early. A thin mist still hugged the ground, and the light on the treetops was orange and soothing. Theirs was the only car in the parking lot, their whispered voices the only intrusion.

"My heart is racing," Jayme said. Small black shapes he thought were probably crows were clustered in a high oak maybe a quarter mile away. An invisible jay cackled nearby. A slight breeze stirred only the tops of the trees. Only silence rose up from the stream and the darkness beneath the leaves.

It was often necessary to work day after day with your eyes to the microscope, head bent to the smallest of details as you tried to make sense of mere cells of information, but it was tedious work and it often made you blind to life beyond the glass slide. So it was good to stand above the treetops now and then, to fill your lungs with sky, and to gaze again into the far distance where heaven and earth were joined.

The air was sweet and clean at three hundred feet, and for a few moments he imagined that if he had enough faith he could step into that air and walk across it to the far side of the gorge. As a boy he had often imagined the same thing, that faith was stronger than gravity or any chasm no matter how wide, and faith would hold him aloft, would allow him to fly if only he could call up an unshakable belief.

He leaned over the ledge, peered into the mist at the twisted girders and splintered beams. Yes, it was a long way down, all right. But he had already been a long way down. Almost to the bottom. He had hung there, a few feet above the rest of the rusting wreckage, for most of thirteen years. And never thought he would ever be up in the light again. Yet here he was. All thanks to a strawberry blond who wouldn't take no for an answer.

Not that he expected there would be nothing but light from here on in. He was too much of a realist to believe that. Gravity would eventually seize him again. Sooner or later, the darkness would latch on to his ankles and attempt to drag him down. But he was higher now. He knew what to hold on to. Hell, sometimes she almost made him believe he could levitate.

Thinking of Jayme, smiling to himself, his skin began to tingle. A feeling spread across his skin then, a tingling not from the air or the mist but within, so that he felt it all up and down his arms and into his hands, across his chest and back, upward into his neck and face and downward through every inch of flesh and into his toes. The tingling covered him with chill bumps but warmed him deep inside, made the air appear to sparkle and filled the weeds below and the distant trees with tiny sparkles too, and not as something separate but as a part of him, and him a part of all of it — the earth and everything that grew or lived on it, the sky and every cloud and star and particle of air, the radiance within and without him all the same radiance but with a trillion eyes beholding it. He was both enormous and microscopic and there was nothing wrong with that. It was all fine and right and exactly as it was meant to be.

It was the strangest feeling he had ever

experienced and he did not want it to end. For those few moments, he did not have to reach for Jayme because she was within and without him too, her own field of tiny lights but integral to him as well, and he to her. He stood very still and soaked it all up, did not want to move or speak or do anything else at all, for nothing would ever compare to this wonderment.

And then it began to fade. He tried not to blink or even breathe, yet the twinkling lights faded out one by one, until there was no tingling left and only a soft glow of sunrise backlighting the wall of fog atop the hills. But the reassurance of those few moments lingered. The certainty that everything was okay, that everything was fine and right and always would be.

Then he was just a man again, separate and small. Yet changed, he hoped, forever. He hoped those moments would never leave him. That he would remember them whenever he needed them most.

There was no way to explain any of it to Jayme. No words could capture that feeling.

He turned to her and asked, "Want to see me levitate?"

"I do not," she said. "It sounds dangerous. What do you plan to do — climb up and stand on the railing?"

All he could do was smile. It must have seemed a silly, boyish smile, but that was okay too. He said, "Race you back to the car?"

"Go!" she said, and was off and running, sprinting hard.

He followed along behind her, strolling leisurely, in no hurry. God, how he loved to watch her move.

SIXTY

On the ride home after the morning stroll high in the air, and after a long hike followed by a picnic in the woods, then the nap and slowly waking to lie on the blanket and gaze at the sky through the high mosaic of leaves, after all this, in the late afternoon, they stopped in the little town of Mount Jewett for cappuccinos to go, and spoke of the murder investigation for the first time all day.

"Let's start with the other boy," DeMarco said. "The one we haven't interviewed yet."

"Connor McBride," Jayme said. "You think Olcott would get his address for us? The registrar probably won't give it to a couple of gumshoes like us."

He smiled. "Gumshoes. That makes me think of a pair of Hush Puppies I used to have. Gum soles. The first pair of new shoes I ever bought for myself. 1986, I think."

"Weren't you the fashionista!"

"Hey, they looked good with brown corduroy pants."

She shook her head, her eyes sparkling. "I'll grab the coffee. You call Ollie."

"He's Ollie now?"

"We're tight," she told him. "Almost as close as me and Fascetti."

He was still chuckling when he pressed the telephone icon. Olcott answered during the voice recording. "Sorry!" he said. "Had to get the burgers off the heat."

DeMarco could hear somebody's lawn mower in the background. "Am I interrupting dinner?" he asked.

"Not quite. Just now laid the wieners on. What can I do for you?"

"We found another one of Gillespie's students we'd like to interview. He was at Samantha Lewis's memorial. Any chance you could contact the registrar in the morning, get us his address and phone number?"

"Happy to try," Olcott said. "What's his name?"

"McBride. First name Connor."

"Ha, that's a familiar name around here."

"You know the kid?"

"I know McBride. Quite a family."

"How so?" DeMarco asked.

"Two sisters are well-known escorts, I guess you could say. Three brothers and the old man did stints for solicitation, possession, possession with intent, breaking and entering, you name it. I remember arresting the old man for abuse of a corpse. Kept his wife in the freezer for eight months before somebody reported it."

"Did he kill her?"

"Naw, natural causes. Just couldn't stand the thought of parting with her SSI check."

"Oy," DeMarco said. "Anything on the kid?"

"Not that I know of. Maybe he's the black sheep of the family. Actually trying to make something of himself."

"Let's hope so," DeMarco said.

"Get back to you in the morning, Sergeant. Gotta run. The grill's smoking."

"Many thanks."

Jayme stood nearby, holding two twenty-ounce cappuccinos in paper cups. "How's our boy?" she asked.

"I think his wiener was burning."

"Oh, DeMarco," she said, and headed for the door.

SIXTY-ONE

True to his word, Olcott called DeMarco at 9:07 Monday morning with Connor McBride's address. Olcott had no idea how many other family members shared the residence, or if any of them were related to those McBrides he had dealt with professionally. "There are a ton of McBrides in this city alone," he said. "And no shortage over your way either. No father is listed as contact for the boy. Mother's name is Victoria. I ran both her name and the kid's but they came up clean. No arrests."

"Glad to hear it," DeMarco said.

"Keep us in the loop, okay?"

"The minute we find a loop, you'll be in it. Speaking of things loopy, how's your partner doing these days?"

"Ha," Olcott said. "He sends you his regards."

"Should I have them tested for explosives?"

"Seriously," Olcott said, speaking more softly now, "if you come up with anything conclusive . . ."

"What's this angle you guys are working? Something about an old girlfriend?"

"Turns out Costa used to date a waitress from the restaurant Talarico was known to frequent. Apparently she also did some typing for Talarico from time to time, some kind of secretarial work. Our informant claims that Talarico was doing her on the side, and Costa found out about it."

"You trust your informant?"

"As far as any informant can be trusted."

"No sign of the girlfriend?"

"She's in the wind. Disappeared a few weeks after Talarico's and Brogan's bodies turned up on the golf course."

"In the wind or in the ground," DeMarco said. "Or in the water. Which leaves you where?"

"Pounding pavement."

"I hear you. Next time I sign on for a job, remind me to get paid by the mile. Thanks for the address for the kid."

"No problema. Talk to you later," Olcott said.

Breakfast had been over for most of ninety minutes, dishes cleared and cleaned. De-Marco and Jayme, energized from their day of rest, were ready to get down to business again. He checked that the front door was locked, grabbed two bottles of water from the refrigerator, and joined Jayme on the back porch, where she sat bouncing the car key in her hand while staring at the half-finished brick path to the garage he had started years earlier.

The morning was gray, the air heavy. He inhaled the scent of skunk. "You smell that?" he asked.

"How could I not smell it?" She stood, and waited for him to come down off the porch.

But he remained standing with his back to the open door, scanning his yard for small mounds of disturbed earth. "They come through here and dig for grubs. Spreading around mothballs or cayenne pepper is supposed to keep them away."

"Guess I'll have to stop eating the grass," she said.

He looked down at her. "Ready to roll?"

"Been ready."

He pulled the back door shut, jerked the handle to check the lock, and told her, "Public housing apartment, downtown."

She nodded and started down the brick path. "You ever plan to finish this? We could knock it off together in a day."

"Or plant a For Sale sign in the yard. Less work."

"You're ready to sell?"

"All I need is Laraine's okay."

She turned to look over her shoulder at him. Did he really mean it?

He smiled. "You driving?"

"Of course I'm driving. You're just the water boy."

"And sex toy."

"One of many. You have a plan B in case there's nobody home at the apartment?"

"Always."

"Care to share?"

"We do something else."

"Brilliant," she said. She loved when he was like this, upbeat, ready for action. The problem was, how long would it last?

Sixty-Two

Victoria McBride was at home, but she looked none too happy to be awakened at such a god-awful early hour by the heel of DeMarco's jackhammer fist. After a rap of four thumps, followed by one of seven thumps, followed by one of nine thumps, she yanked open the door.

"For fuck's sake," she said, squinting, her pupils black microdots. "What do you want?"

She was a woman of average height, thin but busty, dressed in black thong panties and a T-shirt that failed to cover her navel or the purple crystal ornament dangling from it. Her only other accoutrements were short, spiky black hair, smeared mascara, and screaming red finger- and toenails so bright that DeMarco felt his pupils shrinking. The edges of her nostrils were inflamed, and she sniffed every ten seconds. Every now and then she used her long fingernails to scratch at her arms or belly.

"Are you Victoria McBride?" he asked.

"How should I know? You couldn't wait for a decent hour to pound a hole in my door?"

Both he and Jayme took out their IDs. De-Marco said, "Would you mind putting on some clothes, please, so we could talk?"

"I'm wearing clothes," she said. "What do you want?"

The building smelled of fried meat and burnt onions. Babies were crying, radios and televisions blaring. Somebody one floor above was either using a pogo stick or stomping out a fire, all while singing in off-key Spanish.

She gave the IDs a quick glance. Then shook her head, sniffed, and slapped herself on the cheek, hard enough to make Jayme wince.

"We're looking for your son, Connor," De-Marco said. "Is he home?"

"I just got out of bed, remember? I'm still trying to wake up. What time is it?"

"A few minutes after ten."

"In the fucking morning?"

"Correct," DeMarco told her. "Is your son at home?"

"What's he supposed to have done?"

"As far as we know, nothing. We'd just like

to talk to him for a minute."

"About what?"

"I'm not at liberty to discuss that with you."

"Well, you'd better get at liberty. Or else you can forget about talking to my boy."

"He's over eighteen, Ms. McBride. We don't need your permission."

She squinted at him for half a minute, then at Jayme for another fifteen seconds. Jayme smiled and said, "I love your belly button jewelry."

Victoria looked down. Gave the dangling crystal a flip. "It's a piece of crap," she said. "I paid twenty dollars for this thing. Supposed to be real quartz and silver, but I think it's turning my skin green." She used the middle finger of each hand to stretch her naval open. "Does that look green to you?"

Jayme squatted down and leaned close. "I don't think so," she said. "Maybe a little blue. More like bruising, I think." She stood. "Can you remember how it might have gotten bruised?"

The woman thought for a moment, then her eyes widened in a silent *Aha!* "That asshole Daryl," she said. "He likes to suck it into his mouth. Not just the crystal but the whole thing! Don't ask me why."

Jayme shook her head and tsked in commiseration.

"Ms. McBride," DeMarco said. "If we could speak to Connor, please?"

She turned slightly and screamed over her shoulder. "Connor!" She listened for a moment, heard no reply, and screamed louder. *"Connor!"* Still no reply. She sniffed, pinched her nostrils, and looked to Jayme again. "What day is this?"

"This is Monday," Jayme said.

"You should've told me that in the first place. He's down at Hot Head's."

"The burrito place?" DeMarco asked.

"Well, what else is called Hot Head's?"

"He works there?"

She rolled her eyes. "Are you done with me here? People have to sleep, you know."

"Have a lovely day," he told her.

She took a step back and flung the door shut. The dead bolt clicked.

DeMarco turned to Jayme. "Well?" he said. "Was her belly button green or not?"

She said, "Now that I know about Daryl and his spit, I guess it could have been mold."

He chuckled, but he was already thinking about Connor. About having to grow up with a mother like that. In an atmosphere like that. But the kid had a job, he was enrolled in college. DeMarco hoped for the best.

SIXTY-THREE

They sat at a table in the front corner, as far away as possible from the serving counter and the other employee. DeMarco sat with his back to the door, facing Connor, with Jayme between them. The room smelled of onions and garlic, fried meat and boiled rice. Connor said, "If we get a rush in here, I need to get back behind the counter."

"You sell a lot of burritos this early?" DeMarco asked.

"You'd be surprised."

"We'll be quick," Jayme told him. "I saw that you were at the memorial for Samantha Lewis."

"Yeah?" he said. He glanced out the window. Then met her gaze again. "Me and a hundred or so other people. So what?"

DeMarco asked, "You were one of her friends?"

The young man was silent for a moment,

then answered. "Hardly even knew her."

"How *did* you know her?" Jayme asked.

He shrugged. "We went to the same school. I just figured, you know, it was the thing to do."

"To show your respect," Jayme said.

"Exactly."

DeMarco said, "You didn't share any classes with her? Dr. Gillespie's, for example?"

"Who's Gillespie?"

Jayme said, "You were with Kaitlin and Becca and Griffin at the memorial. All of them took his class in comparative religion."

"Yippee for them."

The smart-ass attitude was a familiar one to DeMarco. He wondered if he had come off like that to people when he was Connor's age. He said, "Yippee for you too."

"Says who?"

DeMarco smiled. "The registrar. You received an A."

The boy looked out the window again. Watched the street traffic for ten seconds. "We had discussion groups sometimes. Informal. New students, old students, anybody could attend. I said hello to her once. We talked a little bit. That's the extent of it."

DeMarco asked, "Where did these discussion groups meet?"

The young man didn't answer. He continued to watch out the window.

Jayme asked, "Was Dr. Gillespie in attendance as well?"

Finally Connor turned to look at her. "Why don't you ask him that?"

"Because," she said with a smile, "at the moment we are talking to you."

Just then a tall, thin Black man stepped in through the door. He paused and looked toward the counter, but apparently didn't see what he wanted to see there. Then he noticed Connor at the table, and raised his eyebrows in a silent question.

Connor saw him too, but looked away. The customer went back out the door and made a left. Connor said, "I don't remember ever seeing him at one."

Both Jayme and DeMarco had caught his reaction to the customer. She said, "You don't recall ever seeing Dr. Gillespie at one of the discussion groups?"

"Yeah," Connor said. "What difference does it make?"

DeMarco said, "What kind of car do you drive?"

It caught Connor by surprise. "What?" he said.

"I'm just curious. What kind of car do you drive?"

"Who says I even have a car?"

Jayme said, "You drove one to the memorial, didn't you?"

"What does any of this have to do with anything?"

She said, "We won't know until we hear the answers."

"And I'm just supposed to sit here and waste my time feeding you trivial information?"

DeMarco said, "Why is it a waste of your time to help us find a murderer?"

McBride pushed back his chair. "If you want to place an order, come up to the counter. Otherwise I've got better things to do than sit and watch the cars go by."

He stood and walked briskly to the back of the store, then disappeared into the kitchen.

Jayme said, "Kids don't have much respect for authority these days, do they?"

"Permissive parenting," he said. And thought, *Or negligent parenting. Drunken parenting. Hardly any parenting at all.* "What's this generation called, anyway?"

"Generation Z."

" 'Z' as in what? 'Zombie'?"

Jayme pushed back her chair. "Are we

finished here?"

He turned to look at the menu above the counter. "You hungry?"

"Don't tell me you are already?"

"Absolutely not," he said, and stood. "Just thinking of you."

She stood, gave him a look, one eyebrow cocked, and headed for the door. A moment before she stepped outside, he leaned close and whispered, "Eyes left."

The thin Black man was leaning against the corner of the building, smoking. The moment he noticed Jayme, he slid behind the wall, out of sight.

"Oh yeah," she told DeMarco as they walked to the car.

SIXTY-FOUR

"I remember it being orange," Jayme told him. "And longer than most these days." She collected their iced coffees from the fast-food take-out window and handed them to DeMarco. Then drove to the front of the restaurant's lot and parked facing the street.

"Like a Dodge Challenger maybe?"

"Yeah," she said, nodding as the image solidified in her memory. "I'm pretty sure that's what it was."

DeMarco stripped the paper from the plastic straws, jammed a straw into a lid, and handed the cup to Jayme. Then denuded his straw as well. "So he earns minimum wage selling burritos," he said, thinking out loud. "Lives in public housing with his mother. How does he pay for a $30K car? $35K with all the goodies."

"Generous mommy?"

"Generous mommy with a heroin habit?

Seems unlikely."

"So he has another source of revenue. Ergo the non-burrito customer who didn't hang around long enough to be introduced."

"You know," DeMarco said, "once you factor drugs into a situation, anything becomes possible."

"Yeah, but I didn't see any signs in those other kids."

"Smart dealers don't use."

"And you think Gillespie is involved in this somehow? Got his own campus drug ring?"

DeMarco sipped his coffee. Squinted at the sun glaring off the windshield. "What doesn't jibe is the way all those kids look. Why go to the trouble of putting together a crew based on their physical similarities?"

"They're all dark-haired little beauties, that's for sure. I don't think any of them stands over five six. Connor maybe, but he was wearing those hiking shoes with the thick sole."

"Same thing I'm wearing," DeMarco said, and waggled his feet. "They're comfortable."

"But they do add an inch or so, right?"

"What do you expect me to wear — flip-flops?"

"Please, not with your feet."

"Hey. I wore army boots for four years."

She grinned and told him, "Thank you for your service."

"You mind if we get back to the subject at hand? Five kids who all share similar physical traits. All who took the same college course from the same professor."

"And probably all got As," she said.

"Let's see if Olcott can confirm that. Any other similarities?"

"They are all contrarians. The only one who's been the least bit cooperative is Becca. Though we have no idea how Samantha might have been."

"Let's not forget about Khatri," DeMarco told her. "What is he — at least six years older than the rest?"

"Sounds about right."

"So he's the exception to every similarity. Cooperative, tall, older, not especially pretty. And a dropout from Gillespie's course."

"Dropped out or pushed out?"

He shrugged. Shook his head. Said, "One rich kid, half-Asian, fraternal twin of the deceased. One farm-fresh country girl. One Black girl, gentle, shy . . . middle-class suburbanite?"

Jayme sipped her coffee. Then said, "That would be my guess."

"And one welfare boy who is probably selling drugs and whose mother is almost certainly a junkie."

"And one big pompous ass with poor taste in clothing standing right at the center of them all."

DeMarco sipped. Thought. Squinted. Took another sip. "Okay," he said. "Physical appearance? Check. Aced the same course? Check unless facts prove otherwise. Rebellious, at least when it comes to us. Check. And that's it. That's all we've got. We need more connective tissue."

"Becca," Jayme said a few seconds later.

He reached into the back seat for Jayme's laptop, handed it to her. "You hit Facebook, I'll call Olcott."

"Maybe we should try the registrar ourselves this time. We don't want the good detective getting the idea we think he's working for us."

"Smart lady," he said.

"It's called empathy."

"I think I read about that somewhere."

SIXTY-FIVE

With a little pressure and DeMarco's insistence that she call Sheriff Brinker for approval, the registrar pulled up Becca's campus address, home address, and the grade transcripts for her and the other students. And now Jayme and DeMarco stood in the shade outside the administrative building, close to the cool stone wall.

DeMarco gazed into the high leaves of a maple tree, watched the light appear to jump back and forth, playing hide-and-seek behind the leaves. And the word *komorebi* came to him then, a word he had read long ago, probably in a novel by Yukio Mishima, that fine Japanese writer who disemboweled himself. A single word to describe the way sunlight streamed through leaves on a tree. *There should also be a word for the way light through trees makes us suddenly remember a word,* DeMarco thought. *Or the way memo-*

ries pop up out of nowhere for no apparent reason.

Jayme, who had been staring at the ground between her feet, said, "According to Kaitlin's roommate, most everybody gets a C from Gillespie. If they're lucky. But not the doll collection. All As for them. Even though both Connor and Kaitlin have a GPA well under 3.0. I would love to hear Gillespie's explanation for that."

DeMarco had spotted movement between the leaves, and followed it to its resting place near the trunk. *Gray squirrel,* he thought. As he watched the squirrel, he said, "Here's my read on Khatri. He's not just angry at Gillespie for humiliating him. He's hurt. What he really wanted to do at that presentation was to *impress* Gillespie. I'll bet you dollars to doughnuts that Daksh grew up under the thumb of a very critical father. Mother too maybe."

"You think he knows more about Gillespie than he told us?"

"We have to find out. He and Becca are our best shots right now. If either of them gives us something . . ."

"We can use it to apply a little pressure to Kaitlin and Griffin. Connor, I don't know. I sense a lot of resistance in him."

"He sells drugs. He'll be the last nut to

crack, if he ever does."

She was silent for a few moments. Then said, "Does it ever get to you, Ryan? Manipulating people like this? Exploiting their need for approval, love, whatever?"

"People manipulate people every day. And cause a lot more damage than we will. Our job is to catch the bad guys."

She flinched. "I don't mind using bad guys to catch bad guys," she told him. "But you don't know how fragile people like Daksh and Becca might be."

"All right, doc. You tell me how to play it, and that's how I'll play it."

A door banged inside the building, startling her. "Can we go to the car now?" she said, and started walking.

He hurried to catch up. "Hey. What did I do?"

"Nothing," she said.

"You're ticked off at something. And I'm the only something in the vicinity."

She shook her head, handed him the car key, and kept walking fast. He noticed a glimmer of tear in the corner of her eye. What in the world had he done wrong this time?

SIXTY-SIX

They sat in the car with the air conditioner running. He fiddled with the radio for a minute, hoping to find a soothing song, something to accompany an apology, then decided to go it alone, and turned the volume off. "I don't know what I said to upset you," he told her, "but whatever it was, I'm sorry."

She shook her head no. "You're a kind person, I know that. You can be very compassionate."

"What is it then?"

She tried out a smile. "Just one of those days. Feeling a little emotional for some reason. I just don't want people getting hurt."

"I don't either," he said. "Especially you."

She gave him a long look then, her brow wrinkled, mouth tight, and he thought she was about to tell him something. She looked at him a long time, her mouth slightly open.

Then her features relaxed. She turned away from him, pulled out her notebook and flipped to the last page used. Reaching for her phone, she said, "As long as we're in town, how about I give Becca a call? Just in case she's staying on campus this summer. Before we make the drive north to Daksh."

"You okay?" he said.

She nodded, but he could tell that she was fighting back tears. And wondered, *What's going on here?*

She punched in the phone number the registrar had provided, then tapped the speaker icon.

Becca answered on the third ring. "Hello?"

"Hi, Becca. This is Jayme Matson. Any chance Sergeant DeMarco and I could meet up with you for a few minutes?"

There was a long pause. Then, "About what?"

"We just need a few minutes. Are you in the residence hall this summer or at home?"

"At home, but I don't . . . My mother's here."

Jayme laid the notebook on the console for DeMarco to see, and tapped the home address. He read *Farrell, PA,* frowned, then gave an affirmative nod, slipped the gearshift into Drive, and pulled away from the curb.

She told the girl, "Just pick a place for us

to meet. We can be there in . . ."

"Thirty," DeMarco whispered.

"Thirty minutes," Jayme said into the phone. "Does that work for you?"

"I, uh . . . I can't think of a place . . ."

"Tell you what," Jayme said. "We're going to head your way, so why don't you send me a text in ten minutes or so? We can meet in a park, a restaurant, anywhere you feel comfortable."

"Oh," Becca said after another pause. "Okay."

"And Becca, it would be best if you don't let any of your friends know you're going to meet with us. Best for you. You understand?"

A pause. A heavy breath. "Okay."

"See you soon."

Jayme ended the call. "Sorry. I should have checked the address again before making the call."

He shrugged. "It's closer to home. If it turns out we need to see Daksh after all, we'll do it in the morning."

"She's scared," Jayme said.

"I guess that's a good thing."

Eighteen minutes later, just as they were crossing back into Pennsylvania, Jayme received a text. Buhl Park Casino? She showed the text to DeMarco.

"Excellent," he said, but Jayme looked again as if she were going to cry.

He reached across the seat and took her hand. "After this case?" he said. "What say we take our ill-gotten gains and open a coffee shop?"

She nodded and choked back the tears. "Where?"

"Someplace there's a shortage of coffee shops."

"Someplace that's safe for children," she said.

He considered a joke, *Like a deserted island?* But then thought better of it, and kept the joke to himself for fear she would get upset again. She seemed overly sensitive these days, often reacting with a tenderness that surprised him. Was the case getting to her — too much misery and death? Or was it something he had done or said? Probably the latter. Here she was separated from family and friends, with not even the guys in Troop D to horse around with. Isolated and, except for him, alone. All because of their relationship. What an oaf he was to not realize that sooner. He should try to be more social, take her to one of those paint-and-sip classes, encourage her to take up yoga or something. He couldn't blame her for needing more than just his company.

Hell, most of the time even he didn't want to be with himself.

SIXTY-SEVEN

They crossed from the parking lot to the sidewalk fronting the eleven-acre Lake Julia and, on the other side of the lake, the massive Greek Revival–style Buhl Casino. Framed in white pine boards, and with white Tuscan columns supporting the first- and second-floor covered porches on all sides, the huge rectangular building with its low roof stood like a stern schoolmarm watching over her classroom.

From the swimming pool beside the casino, the shouts and screams of three dozen children came floating across the lake, where geese and a pair of swans floated undisturbed, and old men sat on white buckets and fished, and a few small children played on the rocky shore. Joggers, dog walkers, baby walkers, bicyclists, old folks grabbing some shade and gossip, picnickers and Frisbee players were scattered all over the three-hundred-acre park, yet an air of calm pervaded. The park, built by a steel magnate and his wife in the second decade of the previous century, had become the summer focal point for citizens from several local communities.

DeMarco recognized the oasis appeal of the park to urban- and suburbanites alike, but being there brought back old memories and old feelings. He had visited twice as a young man, first on a spontaneous road trip with four other classmates, and again with his neighbor Paul. Neither time had he felt comfortable or welcome in the park. No one had regarded him critically or asked him to leave, yet he felt out of place, a stranger. Everything was too civilized for his taste. The gazebos and picnic shelters, the strategically placed benches, paved walking paths and guided exercise courses, the signs erected to describe the plants and wetlands and bird species — it was all too manufactured and unnatural.

He liked the woods better. Untended and untrimmed. He could lose himself in the woods, lose all self-consciousness, move with purpose and grace. None of that applied here.

On this day there appeared to be the female component of a wedding party, the bride and bridesmaids and fifteen or so mothers and friends, using the casino as a backdrop for photos. Only the bride was being photographed, but even she was casually dressed. She posed in front of the building, on the steps at a railing, peeking out from behind a column, while the photographer and her assistant, carrying a huge circular reflector, cooed and smiled and told her how great she looked.

DeMarco was puzzled by all the shorts and tank tops and T-shirts. "Shouldn't they be in their wedding clothes?"

"It's probably just practice," Jayme told him. "Checking the lighting and such."

"It takes twenty people to do that?"

He had never understood the tendency for women to do everything in a group. In truth, a part of him envied their camaraderie. He acknowledged that it must make a person feel confident and strong to know she can count on such support. He had learned at a very young age that he had better not count on anyone.

Jayme, he noticed, was watching the group intently, a wistful smile on her lips. Did every woman want a large, flamboyant wedding? Did every woman want to pose in an expensive white dress? To have at least one day in her life when every relative and acquaintance tells her how beautiful she is?

Jayme's silence and fifty-yard gaze suggested that she wanted that. And yes, he wanted it for her.

He asked, "What are you thinking?"

She averted her gaze from the group. Blushed a little, and scanned the upper balcony. "I could never figure out why it's called a casino. Was it originally used for gambling?"

"Not to my knowledge. There is a dance floor, I hear. That's a form of gambling."

"For some of us," she said. "Any sign of Becca?"

"Not yet." He told her, "This is the first place I ever played golf. Across the road behind the casino."

"How old?"

"Nineteen. Home from basic training. My neighbor Paul took me. Said he would teach me how to play."

"I'd like to hear about Paul sometime."

"It's still the only free nine-hole golf course in the country. I'm sure that's why Paul took me there. He charged me $10 for gas."

Jayme turned to him. "Poor baby," she said. "But he instilled the love of the game in you, right?"

"I'd rather wrestle an octopus than play golf. But I'd rather play golf than dance."

The trip with Paul had been a fiasco, an excuse for the older man to get a free tank of gas. DeMarco finished only three holes before walking back to the little shed near the parking lot to return his clubs, with Paul smoking and complaining every step of the way. The bugs were fierce, Paul had said, and slapped the back of his neck to prove it. The rough was too deep, the greens looked like crap, but you get what you pay for, right, kid? More often than not, DeMarco's ball had gone scooting off to the right, into bushes or trees or across the street. You look like you never swung a club in your life, Paul had said, and DeMarco answered, I haven't. Well, that's not the way to hit a ball, Paul told him, and DeMarco asked, So what is the way? And Paul said, Not like that.

The only other time DeMarco had come home prior to his mother's suicide, he found her with a yellowing bruise below her eye. His father had been dead for nearly four years, and the only other man in her life was Paul, who lived in the trailer next door. By then DeMarco had come to understand that Paul's favors, as his mother called them, such as driving her to the store, or teaching her son to play golf, were never free. If she had no money, she held off

433

Paul's demands with sex until the next welfare check came in. Once DeMarco became a soldier, he made certain that his mother always had money. A bruise on her face was not part of the bargain. So he spent a few minutes in Paul's trailer, pushing the man's nose toward the whirring garbage disposal in the sink while cold water splashed onto his head.

"Corner pillar," Jayme said, and he realized that he had been staring at the building but not seeing it. "First floor."

A small figure in red shorts and a pale-pink top had stepped out from behind the pillar. Jayme smiled. "Public yet discreet," she said. "Good girl."

There were no chairs or benches anywhere along the porches, as if the building were intended to be seen but not enjoyed. Jayme suggested they stand at the southwestern corner, with enough water, land, and tennis courts between them and the nearest mac-adam path that they could be seen only as two tall Caucasians with a petite African American girl between them. Both Jayme and DeMarco stood sideways to the rail, facing Becca, who faced the water.

"Do you come here a lot?" Jayme asked.

"I used to swim here when I was little. Come to jog sometimes. My friend Christian is trying to teach me tennis."

Jayme asked, "Does Christian go to school with you?"

Becca shook her head. "He works."

Jayme gave DeMarco a little nod.

"So here's the thing, Becca," DeMarco said. "There's you, Kaitlin, Connor, Griffin, and there used to be Samantha. And there's Dr. Gillespie." He spoke slowly, evenly, and watched her face to see the effect of his words. "What's going on?"

A muscle in her jaw tightened. She stared at the water, and was visibly trembling. "What do you mean?"

"You know what I mean."

She looked up at him briefly, then looked away. "No, I don't."

Jayme said, "You don't really want to be a part of their group, do you, Becca? That's what I think. But you're stuck with it now. Is that the way it is?"

Nothing was said for half a minute. Voices from the pool on the opposite side of the building echoed and raced along the porch from one side to the other. Becca said, "It's just that we took the same class is all. We get together sometimes to talk about what we learned. It's interesting."

DeMarco bent toward her, his voice almost a whisper. "And what exactly did you learn? What is so interesting that students who took the course two, three, even four semesters apart are still getting together to talk about it?"

The girl was trembling so violently now that Jayme longed to pull her close and wrap her up with warmth. But she could not. She said, "Somebody is going to talk, Becca. And whoever does, that's the only person we'll be able to protect."

"Protect from what?"

"Let's start with staying in college," De-Marco said. "Not having to explain to your parents and friends why you were expelled. And then there are always the criminal charges to consider."

She jerked her eyes up to Jayme; they were desperate, pleading.

Jayme said, "I can't help you until you help us."

Becca said, "I thought you were supposed to be trying to find out who killed Sammie."

Jayme told her, "That's exactly what we're doing."

"We didn't have anything to do with that! We all loved her! She was always so sweet and kind to me."

"All right," DeMarco said. "Tell us about your group meetings. Who supplies the drugs?"

She would not look at him. Kept her eyes fixed on Jayme. "Why does he say that?"

"Because he's good at putting two and two together," Jayme said. "And because we know that Connor sells drugs. And sooner or later, sweetie, we're going to know everything. And when that happens, people will go to jail."

There were tears in Becca's eyes now. Tears on her cheeks. "It's just weed and chocolate suckers," she said. "Everybody does it."

"You need to be careful," DeMarco told her. "Mushrooms are dangerous."

She turned quickly, looked at him with glittering eyes. "No they're not! They're not dangerous or addictive at all. And they're teaching me so much! You don't understand."

It was the first time he'd seen her assertive. He said, "What are they teaching you?"

"All about myself and who I really am. About reality, and how there's so much more to it than we think there is. And that we can learn about past lives and even talk to beings from other worlds."

DeMarco felt awash with concern for her, but also anger that she was being exploited. He stared into her eyes.

She said, "I told you you wouldn't understand." And she faced the water again, shoulders limp, and leaned against the rail.

"I guess I don't," he told her. "But I do know this. There's something else going on in those meetings too, isn't there, Becca? Maybe something you're not so sure about? Something you don't like?"

For several beats the girl did not move, only sniffed, swallowed, sniffed again. Then suddenly she turned to Jayme and collapsed sobbing in her arms.

And DeMarco felt a punch in his stomach, felt the breath rush out of his lungs, and knew that his suspicions were true. He thought of Gillespie, so smug and narcissistic.

Tense with anger, he turned and moved away from them, shaking his head, reaching for his phone. A minute later Sheriff Brinker answered the call. DeMarco said, "We have a young woman here you're going to want to talk to, Ben."

SIXTY-EIGHT

DeMarco, Fascetti, and Olcott stood in the hallway outside the interrogation room in the Sharon Municipal Police Department, only a few miles from the casino. Through the one-way mirror they watched and listened to Sheriff Brinker interviewing Rebecca Sadler. Jayme leaned in the corner of the room, smiling and nodding at Becca each time she spoke.

They all had secret names, given by Gillespie: he was Dashwood, Samantha had been Venus, Kaitlin was Flora, Becca was Daphne, Griffin was Priapus, and Connor was Dionysus. All but Dashwood were names of gods and goddesses, just as members had been named in the original Lord Dashwood's London Hellfire Club in the 1730s, where members of British nobility and visitors such as Ben Franklin had engaged in political discussions, the intellectual dissection of society, and drunken sex orgies.

The espoused philosophy of Gillespie's group came from Aleister Crowley's doctrine of Thelema, which, Gillespie claimed, was derived from ancient mystery religions, such as the Essenes and Gnostics: to subvert tyrannical authority at every turn and to engage in acts contemptuous of that authority, and to above all else exercise free will, because only through the exercise of that will could a person come to know her True Self.

And yes, Becca admitted, the students had noticed their physical similarities, and the boys had even questioned Gillespie about it, but he waved it off as a coincidence. They were chosen, he assured them, because of their responses to class essays and discussions in which they displayed a great capacity for independence and individuality, a staggering potential to take their rightful places among the world's movers and shakers, their intellectual honesty and passion for life. The drugs and sex were necessary, he explained, to break down inhibitions and cultural programming, and to prove their contempt for the cabal of conformity, and to display their devotion to the mantra of "Do what thou wilt."

Both DeMarco and Olcott were saddened

and more than a little staggered by what they heard. Fascetti, on the other hand, seemed almost happy. "Way to go, De-Marco," he said. "You broke up a college sex ring. Which, incidentally, has nothing to do with anybody's murder."

"You track down Costa's girlfriend yet?" DeMarco asked, and was answered with a scowl. "That's what I thought," he said.

SIXTY-NINE

"It's a difficult situation," Brinker explained later in the conference room. The students were all over eighteen, and apparently had participated willingly in the bimonthly "meetings" in Gillespie's remodeled basement. If the students all testified to that willingness, any charges concerning sexual misbehavior would be impossible to prove. The drugs were another matter. Who brought them to Gillespie's place? Who paid for them? Becca refused to name names, and would concede only that, although she had felt some pressure from both Gillespie and her peers, the choice to participate had been hers alone.

"There was wine too," DeMarco said.

"Which is illegal in Ohio for anybody under twenty-one without parental permission. But it's a slap on the wrist."

Jayme sat there shaking her head. "The man is scum."

"I'm sure the university administration will see it the same way. Thing is, he's tenured. It will be a fight to get rid of him. Officially, nothing happened on campus. And nobody is going to want any of this to go public, least of all the university."

She said, "What about grades for sex? Can he prove that every one of them really deserved their A?"

Brinker shrugged. "That's something for the university to work out."

Fascetti said, "Somebody could leak this to the newspapers. Let the public do the lynching."

"Nobody is leaking anything," said Brinker. "I'm going to lay it all on the DA's desk. After that, it's up to her."

To Jayme, Olcott said, "I'm betting the girl caves. She's admitted to possession. Charge her. Charge them all. Somebody will open up sooner or later."

"She's nineteen," Brinker said. "Never been in any kind of trouble. Kids experiment. Every one of you did, and I did too. It's called growing up. The one I'm concerned about is Connor McBride. We need to catch him in the act. If he's selling drugs on campus . . . that's going to tick me off."

DeMarco said, "Jayme and I need to stick with the murder investigation."

"Which has come to a screeching halt," Fascetti said.

"Unlike your thirty-year investigation," Jayme said.

Fascetti sat up straighter and leaned into the table. "Tell me how any of this ties into Brenner and Hufford or the girl. Any of it."

"Drugs and sex," DeMarco answered. "You've never seen that combination lead to murder?"

"All right, all right," said Brinker. "For now we're just going to wait and see what the DA has to say. Trust me; if she can make anything stick, she'll go for it. Meantime, everybody continue to work your own angles. And for God's sake, bring me something solid."

SEVENTY

They had been reading in bed for nearly a half hour when Jayme spoke. "Want to hear something weird?" she asked.

DeMarco lowered the composition book. "How weird?"

"So I was sort of reflecting a couple of minutes ago, just thinking about Becca and her friends, Lathea and her partners. And it made me feel so, I don't know, out of the loop all of a sudden. I mean . . . did you know that everybody is having rampant polyamorous sex these days?"

"In Portland, Oregon, maybe. Kind of a surprise around here."

"Exactly," she said. "So I was trying to figure out how I felt about it all. Not just morally but, I don't know, in terms of how it affects society. On one hand, if there was even more of it going on, maybe people wouldn't be killing each other all the time. On the other hand, maybe it sometimes *causes* people to kill each other."

DeMarco thought for a moment. "I don't think the problem is sex per se, but human nature. As long as we're wired to be selfish and petty and jealous and greedy, sex and a thousand other things will lead to violence."

She nodded, but said nothing more, only chewed on the corner of her lip.

He asked, "That's the something weird you wanted to tell me?"

"The weird thing," she said, and smiled, "is that when I went back to reading, still with those questions in my head, I flipped the page and read this. It almost seems as if Thomas were responding directly to my questions."

"Read it to me."

"It's fairly long. He starts out with a quote from Walt Whitman: 'After you have exhausted what there is in business, politics, conviviality, love, and so on — have found that none of these finally satisfy, or permanently wear — what remains?' And then he answers that question by talking about his work — writing and teaching — and about his children, and being in nature, and making love. Those are the things, he said, that nurture and sustain him on a deeper level."

DeMarco said, "I'm not seeing how that applies to your questions."

"This paragraph," she told him, and read:

Had Whitman raised a child or two, I bet he would have agreed that that activity, along with writing and nature and sex with a beloved partner, all share the same remarkable characteristic: each can be a deeply spiritual activity. Each connects me to something vast and mysterious that exists both outside and inside myself. It may be a bit too New Agey to say that all these activities put me in touch with God, but it is no exaggeration to say that they do make me feel, however obliquely, the presence of something majestic and infinite — something that never fails to reawaken my appreciation for this mortal, ever-waning state of being, and to crave every moment of it within my reach.

She said, "I could swear he was answering me directly."

"That happens with me sometimes too."

"It's spooky!"

"Although maybe," DeMarco said, "we hear what we want to hear. Or need to hear. Or both."

"Well, what I hear him saying is that anything that makes us feel part of something majestic and infinite is good. And the way I see it, that's Lathea's relationship with her partners. But the one with those kids and Gillespie? There's no godliness in that."

"Sounds like a reasonable interpretation."

"What makes you feel connected to something majestic and infinite?"

"You," he answered.

"I wasn't fishing for a compliment."

"I'm not giving you one. You make me feel that way. About 87 percent of the time."

She chuckled. "And you make me feel that way. About 62 percent of the time. What else?"

"Doing good work. Remembering my boy. Being in the woods. And reading what my friend has written."

"I feel like he's becoming my friend too."

"I'm glad you feel that way. What else?"

"Working with you. Helping people. Family."

"We're lucky," he told her. And took her hand. "I'm sorry I said that thing about being lonely with you."

"That was a week ago."

"Most of the time when I'm with you, I'm not lonely at all."

"It's okay," she told him. "You get lost inside your head sometimes and don't want to come out."

"I'm getting better, though. Right?"

She smiled. Laid her head on his shoulder. "There's been a gradual improvement," she said, and felt a terrible sadness deep in her chest. Was he really getting better? And would it be soon enough?

SEVENTY-ONE

Morning brought a return to the sense of urgency DeMarco had been missing. He was in the shower, soaping his chest, then went still for a few seconds. Then he rushed through the rest of the shower, and was still dripping when he reached for the cell phone and called Sheriff Brinker.

The call went to voicemail. After the beep, he said, "Now that we know about those kids using drugs at Gillespie's place, and have a reasonable suspicion that Connor is a dealer, what say we get a fistful of warrants and do a full-court press? Somebody is paying for those drugs, and my money is on Gillespie. We search Connor's place, Griffin's, Kaitlin's, Becca's, and Gillespie's house and office too. Let's just go whole hog. I think if we find that missing notebook of Samantha's, there's a good chance we might learn something important about who killed her. *Somebody* took that notebook, Ben. Who had access to it? Grieving brother? Grieving father? Maybe the grief isn't all that real. Or maybe it is but it's also mixed up with remorse and guilt? I mean the second option, now that I hear it, it kind of muddies the water in regard to Hufford and Brenner, but I, uh, I don't know . . . Ah hell, Ben. At the very least we might learn who Connor is working for or buying from. Let's just get the freaking warrants, okay?"

He hung up without saying goodbye, a little embarrassed by his excitement and that he was dripping all over the bathroom rug.

SEVENTY-TWO

Four hours later, three teams went out from the justice center to serve the warrants. Jayme, accompanied by two deputies from the sheriff's office, searched the Lewis house in Canfield. DeMarco and his team shook Connor McBride's mother out of bed once again. Olcott took a team to Gillespie's residence, where the professor was found alone in his kitchen, eating eggs Benedict, and then to Kaitlin's apartment in town. Becca had not yet moved into her dorm room for the next semester, so was given a pass for the time being.

Shortly after 1:00 p.m., the team leaders reconvened in a justice center conference room to share the results of their search.

From Victoria's bedroom in the McBride apartment, they seized a heroin smoking kit, including a glass pipe containing trace amounts of powder, Victoria's little black book of her regular customers, less than an ounce of cannabis, and a baggie containing an assortment of uppers and downers, Viagra, mango-flavored edible lubricant, and a tube of penile thickening gel.

In Connor's bedroom, they found nothing of consequence. DeMarco stated to Sheriff Brinker, "Obviously, the kid was expecting us. Cleanest college student's room I've ever seen. The place reeked of lemon-scented Pledge. My guess is, our little visit to his place of employment got him worried. We need to find his car. We're pretty sure it's a late-model Dodge Charger. Thing is, his mother denies any knowledge of the vehicle, or where he might be. So maybe he borrowed the Charger from somebody for the memorial. But from who? We need to find that out. There can't be all that many orange Dodge Chargers in the city."

No signs of drugs or drug paraphernalia were found in Griffin's bedroom in the Lewis home, nothing to tie Griffin to Hufford or Brenner, nothing out of the ordinary for a twentysomething spoiled rich kid.

In Samantha's bedroom, her comparative religion notebook was found in its proper place on the bookshelf. Jayme said, "Griffin claims no knowledge that the notebook was ever missing from his sister's room. He appeared genuinely surprised that it was missing, and was now back in its proper place. When asked if he knew the contents of the notebook, he speculated that it would include all notes pertinent to the coursework. A cursory examination of the contents substantiates this. But he also claims ignorance of the fact that numerous pages appear to be missing from the back of the notebook. It's one of those Mead one-subject spiral notebooks, so it's not readily apparent from just looking at it that there are pages missing. In comparison with her other notebooks, however, it becomes more obvious. I checked online, and that style of notebook contains seventy pages. There are fifty-six in Samantha's."

Nothing appeared to have been removed from the basement of Gillespie's residence, but numerous photos were shot. Olcott told his colleagues, "This guy lives alone in a big house, with three extra bedrooms. So why would he need a finished basement with four couches and a nice Persian-type carpet in it? Plus several little lamps and lamp tables. And maybe half a dozen open jars of those fragrance beads used for air fresheners. The beads kind of disappear over time, and these jars were still full. Looked new to me. He said the place gets to smelling musky from time to time, so he has to keep replacing the jars. There's also a wet bar, and a good supply of red and white wines. Other than that, it looks like a museum showroom — one of those rooms that gets roped off so nobody can actually enter it. Those four plush couches — he called them divans — each one was pushed up against a wall. But indentations in the carpet suggest that the couches were previously arranged in a square facing each other. When I asked him about this, he said he pulls them closer together for study groups when classes are in session. The other thing I noticed was a tiny piece of black poster paper stuck to one of the basement window frames. Upon closer examination, I could feel a sticky residue around all three of the room's little windows. To me that suggests the windows might have previously been covered up with black poster paper."

Sheriff Brinker listened patiently to all this, without commentary or question. Then he said, ticking off each point by unfurling a finger from his left fist and tapping it with his right index finger, "I'll have somebody from the drug task force bring in Victoria McBride. She'll either cooperate and enter rehab, or go to jail. Meantime, Sergeant, we'll track down Connor and that Dodge Charger. I'll keep you apprised.

"As for the Lewises . . . I've already fielded one hysterical call from the commissioner. I'm going to assure him, for now, that everything's cool. Meantime, Jayme, if you could take a long, hard look at that notebook . . .

"In regard to Gillespie . . . I'll pass this all along to the DA, but I know what she's going to say. Until we have verifiable evidence of criminal activity . . ."

Jayme said, "The man was building his own cult."

"So did Jesus," Brinker said. "Brigham Young. L. Ron Hubbard. Jim Jones. The thing is, if people go along with it willingly . . ." He shrugged and held out both hands, palms up. "You get Becca or Kaitlin or Griffin to agree to testify that Gillespie forced them to have sex, or supplied them with drugs or alcohol, and we'll arrest him. Until then . . ."

She said, "You are at least going to contact the university, I hope."

"They deserve a heads-up. And who knows, maybe we'll get lucky and there will already be several complaints on Gillespie's record. I can't imagine that if he's been doing this for a while, nobody has ever reported him for it."

"He's careful," DeMarco said. "Takes his

time screening them. Gets them at their youngest legal age. Plays on their daddy issues, their need for approval, their distrust of authority. Probably has them recruiting each other, year after year."

Jayme said, "We need to see if we can track down any, what do we call them — alumni? Previous members of his cult. Like, how many people can four couches hold?"

Brinker nodded. "It's worth a shot. Thing is, we can't go around arresting people or even harassing them for having sex. Let's not try to rewire human nature to suit our own agenda."

Jayme stood. Leaned forward with both hands flat on the table. "If Gillespie skates," she said, "I am not going to be happy."

DeMarco stood beside her, and offered the group a smile. "And trust me, gentlemen. You do not want to be in the vicinity when my partner is unhappy."

SEVENTY-THREE

Jayme remained silent and furious as they left the justice center. She and DeMarco stood on the sidewalk outside the door, looking toward but not moving to his vehicle parked at the curb. The sun was bright in their eyes and hot on their faces, glaring off every surface of metal and glass. The traffic rumble seemed thunderous and came from all directions. The air stank of exhaust fumes and hot concrete and stung their nostrils with every breath.

She turned to look at him, her mouth hard, and saw the grim set of his jaw, the stiffness of his posture. She said, "Maybe we should walk a little bit before getting in the car."

He nodded. "Let's try to stick to the shade."

There wasn't much shade to be had, no matter which way they turned. After ten minutes they found themselves breathless and sweat-slicked, looking across the street to the parking lot fronting a small strip mall. A Planet Fitness. A Chinese buffet. A kombucha bar. A pawn shop with a large sign in the window that read *We Buy Gold!*

"I need something cold," he said. "What exactly is kombucha?"

"Sweet tea. But it's fermented."

"As long as its liquid and cold."

They waited for the light to change, then crossed the street. They were halfway into the parking lot when a vehicle came speeding into the lot and squealed to a stop in a handicap slot. DeMarco turned in time to watch the driver hang a disable driver placard from his rearview mirror, pop open the door, and stride toward the Planet Fitness building. He was taller than DeMarco and half again as broad, all of it muscle. "Hey!" DeMarco called, and started toward the man.

"Babe!" Jayme said, but he ignored her.

"Is it in your head?" DeMarco asked as he closed on the man.

The guy turned. He was dressed in tight black workout shorts and a red tank top, every inch of exposed skin, from ankles to jaw, bulging with tanned muscle. "Is what in my head?" he asked.

DeMarco came to a stop barely two feet

from him. "Your handicap. It's obviously not physical, so I'm guessing it must be in your head."

"Chill out, man. What's it to you where I park?"

"I don't know, I just have this thing about selfish, inconsiderate assholes. I've never learned to like them much."

The guy leaned forward, grinning. "Maybe it's about time you did."

DeMarco reached for his cell phone. "Naw, I think I'd rather take a photo of your license plate and text it to Sheriff Brinker over in the justice center." He walked away, smiling, toward the rear of the car.

"All right, all right," the guy said. "Talk about assholes." He hurried to the driver's door, yanked it open and jumped inside. DeMarco moved to the left to allow the vehicle to back out of the spot. He waited until it was parked ten feet away, then strode back to Jayme.

She said, "Are you starting to come apart on me?"

"Let's get that kombucha."

She took hold of his arm, made him stop and look at her. "He was half your age and almost twice your size."

"Not even close to twice my size."

"Stop it," she said.

"Tell me what I did wrong. He's not handicapped. He shouldn't park there."

"You can't fix the whole world, Ryan. What if he had just hauled off and punched you?"

He looked into her eyes. Saw her fear. And blinked.

"Please don't have a meltdown on me," she said.

He blinked again. Breathed in the hot air. Let it out through his mouth. Then told her, "He was bigger up close than I thought."

She nodded. Laid a hand against his chest. "Your heart's racing." She could see in his eyes that he was feeling embarrassed now and regretted what he had done. She had never known him to be an impulsive man.

"Let's get that cold drink," she said.

They walked side by side toward the kombucha bar. All she could think about was how out of character his aggression had been. On the other hand, what about his behavior with Richie in Tennessee? Two outbursts of near violence. Had there been other episodes she didn't know about? And if so, what kind of father would he be?

"What we need," he told her, "is a friendly witness. Somebody we can trust."

It took her a moment to switch gears, to recognize that he was talking about the case.

461

They were almost to the door when they stopped at the same time, looked at each other, and said, "Daksh."

SEVENTY-FOUR

The front room was empty when DeMarco and Jayme arrived at the Humane Society facility north of Youngstown, but voices and barking and an occasional scraping sound could be heard coming through the door at the rear of the room. They crossed to the threshold and saw Daksh Khatri returning a listless beagle to its cage while two other workers, one male and one female, both in their late teens or early twenties, stood ready at the next cage. The young man was armed with a short-handled shovel and a cardboard box lined with a black plastic garbage bag, and the young woman held a green garden hose by its spray-gun handle.

When Daksh turned after locking the beagle's cage to see Jayme and DeMarco filling the door, he crossed to the young woman and leaned close to say something otherwise indistinguishable above the barking. She nodded in reply, while cutting a quick look toward DeMarco and Jayme. Then she laid the hose down on the already wet floor, gathered two puppies from their collie-husky mother in a different cage, and headed out the back door.

Daksh held up an index finger to Jayme and DeMarco, gathered up the mother in his arms, then gave them a nod as he too headed out the back door. They followed.

The mother and her pups were placed in a larger kennel outside. The young woman, returning to the cages inside, smiled at Jayme in passing. Daksh secured the door on the larger kennel, and motioned for De-Marco and Jayme to join him at the other end of the enclosure, where the barking from inside was muted.

"I apologize for the odor," he told them. "The cages should have been cleaned this morning, but my regular volunteer did not show up. I telephoned three others before Lisa agreed to come in and help. And then Cory showed up after all."

Jayme smiled. For some reason she found the lilt of his inflection soothing. "So now you have to manage two volunteers as well as all the animals."

"I do not know which is more difficult," he said with a grin.

DeMarco told him, "We won't take up a

lot of your time, Daksh. But we could use your help filling in some details."

"I am pleased to be of assistance."

"The last time we spoke," DeMarco said, "you told us about Dr. Gillespie's 'pets.' We know who those pets are. We know about their secret meetings. About the drugs and the sex."

Daksh's cheeks darkened with a blush. He watched the puppies nipping at each other. "So the rumors are true?"

Jayme nodded. "We need you to keep this conversation confidential, by the way."

"Indeed," he said. "It will be no problem at all. I am not an extroverted individual by nature."

"So here's what we need to know," DeMarco told him. "And I understand that your exposure to Gillespie and his group was limited. But tell me this. Did you attend any of the secret meetings?"

"Oh no, I did not. I was never among his favorites."

"Do you know anybody else who might have attended?"

"I am sorry, no."

Jayme said, "But you witnessed interactions between these students and Gillespie? Whether before, during, or after class? And you apparently heard other students' gossip about them. Would that be correct?"

"Mmm," he said, and bobbed his head back and forth as if trying to remember. "To a small extent. As I said, there were only rumors. But many. Of those I heard . . . I have no memory of the source."

DeMarco scowled, tried to think of where to go with his questions.

Daksh held his right wrist in his left hand, turned the wrist back and forth as if massaging the cobra tattoo. "I was not very happy there. I had no friends. Things are better where I am now."

"What about arguments?" Jayme asked. "Or just general demeanor. How, in your opinion, did the group get along?"

He shook his head. "I possess no knowledge of a group per se," he said. "In my class, there was the girl and her brother. The professor favored her explicitly. He never corrected her when she was wrong, and her answers were often incorrect."

"Not so much her brother?" Jayme asked.

"So-so," Daksh said. "I would say he was tolerated more than the rest of us. But the girl could do no wrong."

DeMarco asked, "Can you think of *anybody* who resented that fact? Was angry enough about it to do her harm?"

Daksh continued to watch the puppies

with their mother, a finger and thumb still encircling his wrist. The puppies clambered over their docile mother, nipping at one another. "She had six in all," he said. "The last two are being difficult to place."

DeMarco and Jayme waited. She smiled at him. He frowned and gave his head a little shake.

"There was only one time," he said, "he seemed to be very angry with the girl. But that is only how it seemed to me. I do not wish to paint an incorrect impression of what I heard."

DeMarco said, "We're talking Professor Gillespie and Samantha Lewis, right?"

"That is correct. I went to the professor's office to inquire of a recent grade. My grades have never been so low in any other class. My work is always of a very high caliber. I work very hard to do my best."

Jayme said, "You strike me as a highly efficient and ambitious young man."

"That is very kind of you to say. It is important for me that I succeed in this country."

"You saw Gillespie angry, you said?" asked DeMarco.

"No sir, no, I did not see this. But I could hear his voice quite clearly through the door. The emotion of it, although not always the words."

"What did you hear?" Jayme asked.

"Again, I hesitate to create a false impression . . ."

"It's okay," Jayme said. "Just tell us what you heard."

"His voice was angry. There is no mistaking the sound of anger. The words? In recollection, it seems that he was jealous of some other man. 'You will not see him!' That is a phrase I heard at least once, quite clearly."

"And how did she respond?"

"I heard crying. Sobbing. She was clearly distraught."

DeMarco said, "How did you know it was Samantha Lewis?"

"I moved farther down the hall," Daksh said, "wishing not to intrude on a private moment. But when the door opened and she came out, I was surprised to see a student, and one I recognized."

"You're sure it was Samantha?" Jayme asked.

"I am indeed quite certain of that."

DeMarco said, "Then what? Did you talk to her about it?"

"I did not intrude," Daksh said. "Perhaps I should have. But it is not my nature to insert myself in other people's business."

"And Gillespie?" DeMarco asked.

"We did not meet that day. He came to the door and saw me standing down the hall. He was still very angry, his face very red. Then he closed the door and went back inside, and I . . . He is not a reasonable man. To make a young woman weep . . ." He shook his head. Watched the puppies. "I did not speak with him that day."

DeMarco and Jayme exchanged a look, hers full of sympathy, his a quizzical one, eyebrows raised.

Daksh said, "I am sorry to be of so little assistance."

DeMarco asked, "Based on what you witnessed in class, or on any rumors you might have heard, do you have any suspicion of who Gillespie was referring to when he said the word 'him'?"

"I do not, sir. I am sorry. She was a very pretty girl. I am sure a lot of the boys were attracted to her."

A few moments passed. Then Jayme said, "Thanks for talking to us, Daksh. If you think of anything else, anything at all, you call me, okay?"

"I have your card you gave me last time," he told her. "I will use it if I can."

A minute later, while standing beside De-Marco's car with the front doors open, waiting again for the air conditioner to soften the greenhouse effect inside the vehicle, Jayme asked, "Any thoughts?"

"Sounds to me like Gillespie didn't like sharing his toys. Unless he controlled the sharing."

"Could be Griffin he was jealous of," she said. "Could be Connor. Could even be her father, for that matter."

"Or any other male in the city."

"How do we narrow it down?"

"There's only one other person who might know."

"True," she said. "On to Canfield?"

"Giddyup."

They climbed into the car and closed the doors with a simultaneous double thud. He said, "Do you mind if we ride with the windows down?"

"What — you don't like the lingering scent of animal feces?"

"I know it's a character flaw in me, but no, I've never learned to appreciate that scent." He started the engine and powered down the windows.

"So I should throw away my bottle of Eau de Kennel?"

He smiled as he backed out of the parking space. "You crack me up, Matson."

She buckled her seat belt. "Those puppies were pretty cute, though, weren't they? I saw the way you were looking at them."

He said nothing, but continued to smile as he drove forward and onto the street. And told himself, *Yeah, they were pretty damn cute.*

Seventy-Five

On the drive to Canfield, Jayme put her phone on speaker and called the Lewis residence. A female voice answered. Jayme introduced herself and asked to speak with Griffin, and the woman said, "Just a minute, please." It wasn't long before the woman returned. "I'm sorry. He isn't available right now."

"With whom am I speaking?" Jayme asked, with a roll of the eyes to DeMarco.

"This is Paulina, the housekeeper."

"Thank you, Paulina. Please tell Griffin that if he doesn't wish to speak with us at the house, we can have a police car pick him up there in a few minutes and bring him to Youngstown for a conversation."

"Oh," the housekeeper said. "Just one minute, please."

When she returned to the phone, she said that Griffin would be happy to receive them at the house.

After Jayme ended the call, she told De-Marco, "I'm so glad we made him happy. Aren't you?"

Paulina led them through the house and to the rear door, which opened onto an extensive flagstone patio that ran half the length of the building and extended thirty feet into the yard, complete with a stone fireplace, oven and grill, a koi pond, and a bonsai garden.

A few yards beyond the striped awning's reach, Griffin, wearing only a pair of tight swim trunks, lay sunning himself on a chaise longue. He did not sit up or even open his eyes when Jayme stepped onto the flagstone, but he did spread a large yellow towel across his chest and stomach. DeMarco grabbed two wicker patio chairs from against the wall, carried them to where the young man lay, and slapped them down atop the pavers. Griffin's flinch from the sudden noise made DeMarco smile.

DeMarco and Jayme sat side by side facing Griffin. Jayme was the first to speak, her tone abrupt and resolute. "All right, listen up," she said. "I've never had much time for spoiled pretty boys, Griffin, and I'm at the end of my patience with you. I couldn't care less if your neocortex is still four years short of maturity. You need to sit up and answer some questions."

Three seconds later, he opened his eyes and slowly rolled his head toward her. And in that moment, DeMarco saw something familiar about the way Griffin's mouth was set, something familiar about the truculence in his eyes. And DeMarco felt, for the first time, sympathy for the young man.

DeMarco said, "Believe it or not, Griffin, I understand this philosophy you ascribe to. It might surprise you to know that I grew up that same way, hating everybody who wanted to tell me what to do. I didn't need a philosophy to make me that way. Life was a bitch, just like it is for you right now. Like it's been, probably, since your mother died. Truth is, I'm still not a big fan of authority. But what it comes down to in the end is trust and mutual benefit. We're trying to help you, Griffin. And your father. And Samantha. We want to find her killer and put him in prison forever. I'm assuming you want the same thing. If you don't . . . then I have to ask myself, why not?"

It took a few beats before the boy's eyes softened. Then he raised his upper body, pulled on the chair's arms and locked them into a higher position. Sitting up, he stared straight ahead, out across the manicured yard, and nodded.

DeMarco said, "We have recently learned that Dr. Gillespie was jealous of Samantha's relationship with some other male. Would you have any idea who that might be?"

Griffin jerked his head around to meet DeMarco's gaze. His surprise was evident. "No, none. Where did you hear that?"

"She didn't have a boyfriend?" Jayme asked.

"No."

"Seems odd for such a pretty young woman."

"She was focused on her schoolwork. That's just how she was."

"From all accounts," DeMarco said, "you two were extremely close. Which seems natural, being twins."

"Are you implying that he was jealous of me?"

"I'm asking," DeMarco said.

"Why would a professor be jealous of a student's brother?"

DeMarco was about to speak when the cell phone in his pocket vibrated, two quick buzzes like a bumblebee trapped in his pants. He ignored it.

He said, "We know about the sex parties at Dr. Gillespie's house, Griffin. We know about the drugs."

The young man's eyes flared open, though with fear, not anger.

"Hey, you're old enough to make your own decisions," DeMarco told him. "We're not here to judge you for anything. We just need to know what was going on between Gillespie and your sister. And apparently some other male."

Thirty seconds passed before Griffin responded. "The meetings we had were . . . rituals. Ceremonies. It wasn't like a free-for-all orgy, if that's what you're thinking."

Jayme said, her own tone softer now, "I know this is going to make you uncomfortable, Griffin, but we need to know who was making Gillespie jealous. If she didn't have a boyfriend outside of the group, that leaves you and Connor McBride. Could she have been interested, romantically, in Connor?"

"That's absurd," Griffin said. But his face was pinched, eyes narrowed as if he were thinking hard, so Jayme and DeMarco waited.

"I mean," Griffin said, "yeah, he was always trying to get with her."

DeMarco said, "And by 'get with her,' you mean . . . ?"

"Hook up with her."

"Outside of the ceremonies?"

"Right."

Jayme asked, "How about during the ceremonies? Was he hooking up with her then?"

Griffin lifted a hand, palm up, as if trying to reach for the right explanation. "Generally it would be me and Connor with Kaitlin and Becca. Gillespie kept Sammy for himself. High priest and priestess, you know? The relationship is sacred. Not that that stopped him from doing the other girls too."

DeMarco suppressed his rising emotions, kept his voice low and even. "But outside of the meetings," he said. "Connor wanted to get with Sammy, but she wasn't interested?"

Griffin nodded. "Plus we weren't supposed to . . . dissipate the sacred energy."

"No sex outside the meetings?" Jayme said.

"Not that she would have hooked up with him anyway."

DeMarco asked, "With Connor?"

"He was only in the group because —" Griffin said, then cut himself off.

DeMarco finished the sentence. "Because he could supply the weed and mushrooms."

Now Griffin lowered his chin and stared at a spot closer to the foot of the chaise longue.

Jayme said, "And I bet that made him

angry, didn't it? That Sammy wouldn't have anything to do with him."

"He's the kind of guy who's always pissed off about something," Griffin said. "But yeah. Like I told you, he was always trying to get with her, and she was always telling him no, no way, not ever. My sister wasn't a slut."

"Nobody suggested she was," DeMarco said. He leaned back in his chair. Cut a look toward Jayme.

She said, "I need to ask you again about those pages missing from your sister's notebook."

"I didn't take them," he told her.

"We know you didn't. But who else might have had the opportunity to take them? Did Connor?"

Griffin shrugged. "He was here a couple times. First time was right after the funeral."

DeMarco asked, "He came here, to your house, the same day as your sister's funeral?"

"Yeah. I didn't want to go to the thing afterward, the reception or whatever. Whatever it's called. Dad said I didn't have to if I didn't want to. And Connor offered to bring some weed and, I don't know, just chill with me and Becca and Kaitlin for a while."

Jayme said, "So there were just the four of

you here at the house? For how long?"

"I don't know, three or four hours."

"And your sister's notebook was where — up in her room?"

"As far as I know."

DeMarco said, "And let me guess. The second time Connor came here was sometime between our first and second search of her room."

Griffin nodded. "Actually it was the day after the first search. And it was just him that time."

Jayme asked, "Sounds to me like he knew we had been here, and that I saw the notebook was gone. How would that have happened?"

Griffin said nothing. His jaw was set, teeth pressed together, lips slightly puckered as if his mouth held something foul his throat refused to swallow.

DeMarco said, "You were all staying in touch with each other, right? All four of you?"

"We were sworn to secrecy about the group. It was like us . . . I don't know."

"You against the world," DeMarco said.

"I guess."

Jayme said, "So Gillespie was kept informed as well?"

"Not by me," Griffin said. "Kaitlin probably."

Jayme asked, "Do you have any idea what kind of information was in the missing pages?"

Again he shrugged. "She took a lot of notes. Probably everything that had anything to do with the course and, you know, the group. She was really into it all. After Mom died . . . Sammy needed something, I guess. Dad was a mess, and not even here most of the time. And I was . . . just a brother. I mean we were close but . . . I guess that wasn't enough."

"So you joined the group because of her?"

"She wanted me there. I doubt it was Gillespie's idea."

The grief was tangible on his face now, and in his sagging body — as visible to both DeMarco and Jayme as a darkening of the sky. She said, "So . . . did your group have a name?"

"Voluntas. It's Latin for 'will,' as in free will."

"And the purpose of the group? Was it just ostension, or something more?"

"I don't know that word," he said.

"A kind of performance. An acting out of a legend or myth. For its own sake."

"Of course we have a purpose," he said.

"And what is it exactly?"

"To exercise free will. To stop being puppets. To wake up to the fact that everybody with any power or authority is trying to keep us asleep."

DeMarco said, "And by everybody, you mean . . . ?"

"The government. Religion. The media. Wall Street, Madison Avenue, you name it. Their goal is to keep us 'unaware and compliant,' just like Hillary Clinton said. So that we won't notice the chem trails, or the black ops, or the UFOs, or how the NSA and Homeland Security are eavesdropping on everything we do, or how Google and Amazon and Facebook have turned us all into data they can sell to the highest bidder.

"Reality is a lie," he told her. "And the only way to shatter that lie is to stand up against it."

And in so doing, DeMarco thought, *you became Gillespie's puppet.* But he kept the thought to himself. He said, "I admire people who think for themselves, Griffin. I admire nonconformists. But if I were in your position, I might ask myself how much of a nonconformist a tenured professor can be, especially when his agenda is to manipulate several young people for his own gratification."

Griffin held DeMarco's gaze for a few seconds, then looked away, first into the sky, and then, again, at the ground. He said, "It's all just a bullshit matrix of lies and illusions. There can be no freedom until we destroy it."

"You keep saying we," DeMarco told him. "But don't you think that true nonconformity is an individual job?"

The boy turned his head, looked DeMarco's way. "What do you mean?"

"If you put five, ten, twenty people in a group, what do you have? People who are conforming to each other. Groupthink. Herd mentality." He put a hand on the boy's shoulder. "Think for yourself, Griffin. Follow your own heart. That's the only group you need."

For a while, nobody spoke. DeMarco slid his hand off Griffin's shoulder, and wondered if his advice sounded as phony to the boy as it did to his own ears. Did he listen to his own heart, or to some less reliable voice?

He held that question in his mind until he became aware of a bird singing in a nearby bush. Its song consisted of a repetition of two tweets in a row, the second pitched lower than the first, both trembling with vibrato. He looked around until he located the bird. A robin. So common, yet somehow anomalous now.

"One last question, Griffin," he finally said. "Do you think Connor would be capable of hurting your sister?"

The young man was leaning forward, arms clutched around his stomach. The towel had fallen off his chest and lay over his arms, and his eyes were wet with tears. He said, "There's nothing you could tell me about him that would surprise me."

Before leaving, DeMarco asked for and received Griffin's promise that he would keep their conversation confidential. Then they departed by walking around the side of the house to the circular driveway out front. Along the way, DeMarco slipped the cell phone from his pocket and read the text he had received earlier. It was from Detective Olcott. DeMarco showed the text to Jayme. Dodge Charger registered to Darlene Lubich, it said. Connor's aunt.

■ ■ ■ ■

III

■ ■ ■ ■

Come dance with me, the darkness says,
and we'll prowl these streets for what we
    crave,
that startled gasp, that taste, that scent —
sweet sustenance for another week,
another month of dull routine —
that smothered cry, that strangled scream.
Come dance with me, the darkness says.
                — from "3 a.m.," Thomas Huston

It was raining the night I did Hufford. I first noticed him in line at Subway, but I didn't pay any attention to him, just wanted to pay and get my sandwich and get back to the car before the rain started. And I made it, just barely. So I'm sitting there eating my sub, I've got the engine running to keep the air conditioner going, and the wipers flipping back and forth because the rain's pouring down in buckets by then. There's thunder booming and lightning popping all over the sky. It's cool to watch, and the smell coming through the vents is good too, clean, like the storm is washing away all the dirt and stink of the city. I could have sat there happy all night, just enjoying the storm and my sandwich.

But pretty soon here comes Hufford out of the store. It's kind of comical the way he's hugging his big bag of subs close to his chest and holding the other hand over his head as he goes hotfooting it down the street. But then the voice says, Go get him, and I say What? No. He's too big. And the voice says, Go! Now!

So I lay my sub up on the dash and wheel the car around and drive up beside him while he's jogging the way big guys do, sort of heavy-footed and running on their heels. I put my window down and say over the pounding of the rain, Hey, man, get in. You're going to drown out there. He stops and bends over and looks in at me, and I point to my sub up on the dash, and then it's like we're brothers or something, I guess, because he goes loping around the front and pops open the door and throws his fat wet self into the seat. He starts thanking me and buckling up and telling me where to turn two blocks ahead, but that's about all he gets to say.

I had the new place picked out ever since the thing with Venus, when I knew I had to do another one, so that's where we went. The stunner didn't work as good on him as it did with Brenner, all that extra cushion to get through, but the storm and the black night worked to my benefit, putting a hush over everything, and later with the cutting as well. Washed us both clean, is the way I like to think of it. Though I didn't much appreciate him getting my seat all wet. I had those three extra subs of his though, one turkey half sub, one meatball half, one spicy Italian foot-long. Kept me fed for the next couple of days.

I am Erebus, son of Khaos.

SEVENTY-SIX

While waiting for a warrant to impound and search the Dodge Charger, if and when it could be located, personnel from the sheriff's office determined that the vehicle was not equipped with an optional tracking system. "It's going to be close to where he lives," DeMarco said. "And probably not in a public parking garage. I'm thinking a covered building of some kind. Privately owned. Within a ten-, fifteen-minute walking radius of the apartment." He didn't want to question Victoria, Connor, or Darlene Lubich, whose name was on the title, as to the vehicle's location, because doing so might give Connor a chance to hide the car or clean out its contents.

A deed search was conducted to determine if any nearby properties were owned by the Lubiches, who lived in a $1200/month town house in a gated community in Vienna Center, approximately fourteen miles north of downtown Youngstown. Their town house came with a two-car garage, which presumably housed their other two vehicles, a Jeep Wrangler and a Nissan Altima. Darlene McBride Lubich's most recent arrest for solicitation was in 2012; Joe Lubich's two arrests, one for pimping and pandering, the other for possession of marijuana with intent to sell, were both in that same decade. The deed search came up with zero properties owned by the Lubiches.

"Word on the street," Olcott said, "is that Darlene caters to a more discreet clientele these days. She's forty-two years old but claims to be thirty-three and apparently gets away with it. Joe works at TopNotch Industrial in Warren, general warehouse duties, makes $16 an hour."

"So that's $32,000 a year gross income," DeMarco said. "A little over $20,000 after taxes. But they own three late-model vehicles and live in a fairly pricey neighborhood. Darlene must be keeping busy."

"The drug task force suspects that Joe is still in the weed business. Maybe other drugs too. At what level, they don't yet know."

"So why buy their nephew a vehicle to drive?" Jayme asked. "Unless maybe he's dealing for Joe?"

"It's a good bet," DeMarco said.

"You know," Olcott said, "old man Mc-Bride was into a lot of bad stuff back in the day. I wonder . . ."

He did another deed search, this one for Bertram McBride, now deceased. And came up with two hits. "A little gas station out on 62," Olcott informed them, "and a house in McGuffey Heights. Both still in his name."

"A lot of abandoned homes in McGuffey Heights," DeMarco said. "And maybe ten minutes by Uber from Connor's apartment. About the same by bicycle."

Olcott grinned. "I know that gas station. It's still operational. Always wondered how a little place like that could stay in business. Let me make a quick call to a guy in Drugs, see if they have that place on their radar. Then I'll grab a deputy and we can go have a look at the house."

"Fascetti won't miss you?" Jayme asked.

"He's in court all day. Aggravated murder case in Austintown."

DeMarco said, "No luck on Costa's girl-friend yet?"

"Not a trace. We have a lifer in OSP, though, who claims to know what happened to her. He's holding out for a fifty-five-inch flat screen with cable hookup, which isn't going to happen anytime soon." Olcott reached for his cell phone. "I'll send a car out to keep watch over the place in McGuffey Heights while we wait for the warrant. If you guys want to go downstairs for some coffee, or to get a bite to eat . . ."

"Coffee sounds good," DeMarco said. "Call us when you're ready to roll."

SEVENTY-SEVEN

One hour and six minutes later, warrant in hand, Olcott pulled his car to the curb outside an abandoned two-story house in the McGuffey Heights neighborhood. De-Marco parked behind him. The municipal police car that had been parked farther down the street, with two uniformed officers inside, now came forward to park facing Olcott's vehicle.

Like other neighborhoods in the city, McGuffey Heights was marked by numerous run-down buildings, razed and overgrown lots, neglected streets and sidewalks. Some of the buildings had fallen in on themselves; others looked as if they had been hit by a bomb. Traffic was sparse, with few people coming or going.

The entire neighborhood was quiet, but with a different kind of quiet than the late-summer-afternoon quiet when kids are worn out from their boisterous day, and mothers are starting to think about what to make for dinner, and fathers are not yet home from the office. There were as many abandoned homes in this neighborhood as occupied, and those who lived in the occupied buildings did so because they were too old or poor to start over somewhere else, and so they kept to the dimness of their rooms throughout the day, watching pirated cable TV or listening to a radio with the volume turned low, and came outside for the evening's coolness only when the air was dark and the despair on their faces did not show.

After releasing her seat belt, Jayme asked DeMarco, "Are we going in armed?"

"With a one in seventeen chance in this neighborhood of being a victim of crime?" he said, and reached over her knees to pop open the glove compartment. "Damn straight we are."

"Do we need to get an okay from Olcott first?"

"He'll tell us if he wants to."

They stepped outside the car, fitted their pocket holsters and weapons into place. In his left hand DeMarco held a small but powerful flashlight similar to the one Olcott carried. The detective, walking toward them, saw the weapons but made no mention of them. "Officer Blanchard says there's been nobody in or out."

"Every window is boarded shut," Jayme noted. She studied the driveway. "When was the last time it rained?"

"Two nights ago," DeMarco told her. "Started around midnight, drizzled most of the night."

"So somebody went into or out of the garage that night. Or else those dirty tread marks would have been washed away."

Olcott, accompanied by Blanchard a few steps behind, went onto the front porch. "Careful," he told the officer. "Some of these floorboards are rotted." He pounded on the front door while Jayme waited in the yard by the side windows, and DeMarco stood at the rear corner of the house, watching the back door. No sound of any kind came from inside the house. A second officer stood in the driveway.

DeMarco moved onto the little rear porch, just a stoop with a shingled awning, and tested the rear door. The screen door had been torn off its frame, splintering the wood, but a cheap hollow metal door remained. The door was locked but it hung crookedly from the hinges, and DeMarco could feel the sloppy fit of the latch moving in the strike plate. He gripped the knob with both hands and pulled the door hard to the right while turning the knob, and this time the latch slipped out of the strike plate and the door swung open.

He went to the side of the building and called, "Back door is open!"

Olcott came off the porch and crossed around to the rear. To Jayme he said, "Blanchard's up front. Can you help Officer Simms keep an eye on the back and the garage?"

"Will do," she said, and slipped her .380 from the holster.

At the back, Olcott said to DeMarco, "It wasn't locked?"

"It was," DeMarco said with a sheepish grin, "but it opened anyway."

Olcott raised his eyebrows, appraised the door for a moment, then turned on his flashlight, pulled his weapon, and stepped inside. DeMarco followed suit.

The kitchen was dim and empty and smelled of mold. All appliances, including the sink and most of the cabinets, had long ago been dragged away. The linoleum floor was buckled and scarred and smeared with dried mud.

They moved into the next room, and the one after that, and the one after that, every room stripped bare and odorous with mold, especially the living room with its dank carpet. Water stains below the windowsills showed where rain had leaked in through the broken windows and past the plywood. Olcott said, "Nobody has lived here in a very long time."

They moved up the stairs with Olcott leading the way. Slowly down the hallway, floorboards creaking. DeMarco checked each room on one side of the hallway, Olcott the other side, their flashlight beams swinging back and forth, briefly painting every corner. Empty. Bare. Dark. The air thick and stale and warm.

"Nothing," DeMarco told Jayme five minutes later, after he and Olcott had emerged from the building and relocked the rear door. Both men ran a hand over their faces and necks as if they had walked through a curtain of cobwebs, and now turned their attention to the detached garage.

The only windows on the garage were near the roof, too high to peer inside. The metal side door was windowless and firmly secured with a relatively new lock. The single stall garage door was solidly in place as well.

DeMarco said, "Let's pop that side door open and see what we've got."

Olcott said, "I think you've popped enough doors for one day. I'll call a locksmith."

"C'mon, man," DeMarco said.

"We break it open, we have to secure it afterward," the detective said. "Did you happen to bring along a hammer and nail and a couple pieces of lumber? And if there's nothing inside, who gets the bill for repairs?"

"Are you always such a killjoy?" DeMarco asked. "I used to think you were the fun guy."

"Ha," Olcott said. "Fascetti wouldn't have even let you in the house."

It took the locksmith a long twenty-five minutes to arrive. During those minutes, Olcott struck up a conversation with the two municipal police officers, Blanchard and Simms. DeMarco and Jayme stood side by side leaning against the side of his car, their feet on the curb.

"What if the car isn't there?" she said. "You think they'll put out a BOLO?"

"Doubtful," DeMarco said. "Olcott and the uniforms probably wouldn't even be here if not for Ben."

"He trusts your instincts."

"I wish I did."

"I trust them too," she said.

DeMarco shrugged, shook his head. "All I know is that nobody removes, how many, fourteen sheets of paper out of a girl's notebook for no reason. We need those pages."

"What if he burned them?"

"Then we're done. Nowhere to go. Ben can deal with Gillespie however he sees fit, but as for the triple homicide, we'll be no further ahead than Fascetti is. And if Ben doesn't pull the plug on us, maybe we should."

She scraped the sole of her shoe back and forth over the concrete. "What keeps tripping me up is the two men," she said. "I can buy a messed-up kid taking his sexual frustration out on Sammy, but what's that have to do with Hufford and Brenner?"

"That's always been the question."

"Do you think there's a chance Connor was selling drugs to them too?"

"That or some other connection we just can't see yet."

They were silent for a while. Then she said, "It's strange how quiet everything is. No birds. No kids riding their bikes or playing ball in the street. Nobody mowing their yard."

"Ghosts," DeMarco said. "Ghosts don't make any noise."

When the sound of the locksmith's truck

reached their ears, everybody turned, smiled, and stood at attention. They could have been kids waiting for the ice cream truck. But no tinny melody emanated from the truck, only a rattle and screech as the vehicle nosed into the driveway and came to a stop.

The driver took his time climbing out, then ambled toward Olcott with a bag of tools in hand. The man was at least eighty years old, DeMarco thought, out of another era. He wore baggy jeans and, despite the heat, a stained, too-small blue chambray shirt rolled to the elbows. He was short and barrel-chested, paunchy, bowlegged and stiff, his gray hair a mess of frizz and limp curls, his hands and forearms thick and hairy.

"It's Norman Mailer," DeMarco said, and started toward the garage. "Let's go get his autograph."

Jayme and the four men gathered around the old man as he worked, trying out one master key after another from his ring of a hundred or so. *Be there,* DeMarco kept thinking. *Be there. Be there. Be there.*

When the lock clicked, the old man left the key in place and stepped back, allowing Olcott to swing the door open. DeMarco shifted position to peer over the detective's shoulder, and saw orange. He blinked and stepped closer.

The Dodge Charger was there, its orange body waxed and shining in the shaft of low light that flooded inside. Olcott allowed Jayme and DeMarco to join him inside, but suggested that they stand against the wall on either side of the door so as not to block the light. The two small windows near the roof were filmed with dust but allowed a soft suffusion of light to enter.

A blue microfiber towel had been stuffed down into the driver's door handle. The only dirt on the vehicle was the dried mud caked in the tire treads. The vehicle was locked, all windows up. An empty Dunkin' Donuts coffee cup standing upright on the passenger floor was the only discernible object inside.

"Nobody touch anything," Olcott said. He turned, saw Blanchard standing just outside the door, and tossed him his car keys. "Black Dragon gloves," he said. "In the console. Bring the whole box. Plus some evidence bags." He pulled out his cell phone, turned back to the vehicle, and clicked off a dozen photos, taken at various distances and angles.

He then turned to Blanchard, who was now waiting with the gloves and evidence bags. Olcott removed a pair of the tight black nitrile gloves and pulled them on. Then removed the small towel from the door handle and placed it in an evidence bag, and passed the bag to Officer Simms.

To the locksmith, Olcott said, "Trunk, please?"

DeMarco kept trying to peer through the car windows, hands at his side. Twice he had to remind himself to take a breath. But nothing was visible on the front seats. Nothing on the rear seats.

The trunk lock clicked, and the locksmith stepped away from the car. "That it?" he asked.

"That's everything, thanks," Olcott said. "We'll leave the interior for forensics."

The locksmith jangled his keys as he returned to his truck.

Now Olcott stepped close to the trunk, slipped a gloved finger beneath the edge of the lid, and lifted it up. Jayme and DeMarco leaned closer. *Be there,* DeMarco thought. He wanted to see a folder, or a large envelope, anything that might hold Samantha's missing pages.

Instead, each time the camera's flash illuminated the inside of the trunk, DeMarco saw something new.

A folded gray blanket. A box of Saran

wrap. An opened box of Curad latex gloves. A coil of yellow polypropylene rope. A plastic container of Pampers wet wipes. A roll of duct tape. A large Dick's Sporting Goods shopping bag, with something inside.

When Olcott finished taking photos, he turned, looked at both Jayme and DeMarco, then handed the phone to Jayme. He said, "Wait till I open up that shopping bag, then take as many as you think are necessary."

He leaned close to the Dick's bag and carefully pulled the mouth open wide to expose a long black plastic box inside. Not until he had lifted the box out of the bag and set it atop the plastic was DeMarco able to see the thick yellow block lettering across the middle of the box. *DeWALT.*

Olcott lifted his hands away from the box, took a step back, turned and looked at De-Marco, both men breathing quickly through their mouths now, eyes wide with surprise and recognition. For the next ten seconds, nothing could be heard but the sound of five people breathing.

DeMarco felt weak and a little woozy. He knew that everyone in the garage felt the same. If the box still held its original contents . . .

Olcott turned toward the open trunk again. Bent forward, clicked up the pair of plastic latches, one on each side of the box's handle. He laid the lid back and stepped away again.

A twenty-volt cordless reciprocating saw, the housing yellow, the handle and tip black. A battery recharger. An assortment of blades.

In that instant, DeMarco envisioned every connection, the ideal scenario. Traces of blood on the Sawzall, all three victims' blood. Connor's DNA on the microfiber towel, the soft drink cup, his fingerprints and DNA on the saw handle and all through the vehicle. What he could not see was the why of it all. Why Hufford? Why Brenner? Why such a world where things like this could happen, and did happen, again and again and again?

"Jayme," Olcott said, his voice barely above a whisper. She came forward. The camera clicked. Nobody spoke. Only Jayme was not motionless, and her movements barely discernible, a half inch to this side, a quarter inch lower. When she finished, she too stood motionless, staring into the trunk. Then she lifted her gaze to Olcott, and their eyes met for several seconds. When she held the phone out to him, her hand was trembling. He took the phone, slipped it back into his pocket.

Every movement seemed slow now, as if somehow restrained, underwater. Breaths were slow and deep, going in, going out.

Olcott was the first to speak. "That's it, then," he said. "That appears to be it."

He turned to DeMarco. "No notebook paper," he said. "Sorry."

DeMarco blinked, was still feeling dazed. "Murder weapon beats paper," he answered, "any day of the week."

Olcott smiled, nodded.

Jayme said, as if to herself, "I can't believe what I'm seeing."

Olcott looked at every face in turn, nodded, and smiled to each of them. Then returned his gaze to Jayme and DeMarco.

"It's been a long day," he said. "All this has to be processed, and then we'll get the vehicle towed out of here. There's no need for you guys to hang around for that. Why don't you go on home and have yourselves a glass of wine or two. You deserve to celebrate a little."

DeMarco said, "As long as we're in town, how about if my partner and I pay another visit to Victoria McBride, just in case her prodigal son has returned?"

"Blanchard and Simms will take care of that. Right, guys?" Olcott said. "Meantime I'll contact the Vienna Center police department to follow up with the Lubiches. If we strike out there, I'll put out an ATL. He can't be far away if he's on foot."

"For all we know," said DeMarco, "he could have been watching us all this time. Might be watching us right now."

"Anything's possible."

"Jayme and I can do a house-to-house if you want."

"I'll get some people here," Olcott said.

Jayme said, "How about calling Uber? See if any driver did a pickup or drop-off near here today."

Olcott nodded. "We'll take care of it. Listen, you guys did great. You did all the heavy lifting. Leave the rest to us, okay? We'll find him. Don't worry."

DeMarco blew out a slow breath. Gave Olcott a slow nod. Then he turned to Jayme. "Call it a day?"

"Yeah," she said after a pause. "Let's do that."

His knees felt stiff, legs weak as they walked to the car. The late-afternoon light seemed somehow strange now, so golden and soft and almost sad, like a candlelit silence. At the car they both paused to look back, saw the detective and the two officers standing there watching them, softly talking. Finally DeMarco clicked the remote to unlock the doors, and they climbed inside, into the stale and smothering heat.

He slipped the key into the ignition, but did not turn the key. The light was coming straight through the windshield now, straight up the street and in through the bug-specked glass.

He said, "Kind of anticlimactic, isn't it?"

She snapped the seat belt into place. "This is what we get for giving up the badge."

He nodded. "You miss it?"

"At times like this I do."

He said nothing. Nodded to himself. After a while, she said, "You want to start the car? Or should I get out and push us home?"

There was a quality to her voice that made him look her way, and a quality to the way he looked at her that made her say, "Don't look at me like that, babe. I already feel like crying."

"About what?" he said.

And she said, "I don't even know."

SEVENTY-EIGHT

It took DeMarco a long time to push the events of the day to the back of his brain, though he knew it was good and even necessary to do so. There wasn't much they could accomplish until Connor was found. The police would visit Gillespie and Kaitlin and Griffin, take them in for questioning, see what stories they spun and how those stories held up over time. Olcott or maybe Ben would call on the university president to inform him of Gillespie's activities with his students, and that thread of the story would take on its own importance, though probably a secretive one, considering how much the university had to lose with such bad publicity. In any case, what remained to do was out of DeMarco and Jayme's hands now. The police would wrap things up.

Thank God for Tom's pages. There was no more effective distraction for DeMarco than to hear his friend's thoughts. He always heard them delivered in Tom's voice too, that rich, practiced baritone that knew just when to pause, inflect, when to quicken the pace or slow down and deepen.

It was a poem that finally took DeMarco away from his own ruminations that night, and into the head and voice of his friend. The poem was titled "Thinking Twice," and DeMarco read it three times, each time a bit more slowly, and feeling more certain each time that the poem had been written about him:

Lying in my narrow bed with the transistor radio on.
Listening to a game as Clemente belts a home run.
Never thinking twice that no morning is guaranteed.

Stretched out in the night grass, watching stars beside some girl.
Touching. Exploring. Bragging about the ways we'll leave our fingerprints on the world.
Never thinking twice that dreams can be so easily undreamed.

Grabbing food out of my mom's refrigerator.

Running out the door yelling, "Catch you
   later!"
Never thinking twice about that door
   slamming shut.

Tucking my babies into bed every night.
Kissing their cheeks, whispering, "Sleep
   tight."
Never thinking twice that the kisses could
   dry up.

Sleeping in the chair with the television
   on.
Waking in a house with everybody gone.

Listening to the dirt fall on a cold metal
   roof.
Drowning in the darkness. Cursing the
   truth.
Thinking twice.

He thought about sharing the poem with
Laraine . . . but then caught himself,
abruptly, and felt a hot rush of guilt, followed by a shiver of recognition of the damage he might have done had he said that
name aloud.

It wasn't the first time he had been reading and momentarily forgot that the woman
beside him was not Laraine. He hadn't read

in bed like this since the first years of his marriage, when Laraine was doing her best to round off his rough edges with literature and drama and poetry. The lapse was always a brief one but jarring nonetheless, and he felt an urge to apologize to Jayme afterward, but had enough sense to keep his mouth shut.

But now he started wondering how Laraine was doing, and if he had done the right thing by leaving her at the hospital. Should he call to speak with her doctor again? Surely somebody from the hospital was keeping tabs on her. Was she going to therapy, other than with a psychic? What kind of safeguards had been implemented so that she wouldn't cut herself again? Drugs, probably. Always the easy choice. And DeMarco hated drugs. He would rather feel his pain, not to wallow in it but to know it better. Only when you knew your pain could you fight it effectively. It was always a two-stage battle. No, make that three-stage. Know your pain; know yourself; engage. And hope you would survive. Survival was the fourth and final stage. From there you eventually circled back to the beginning again, because there was always a new pain or the resurgence of an old one.

That was the thing he and Tom both

understood, the commonality that had brought them together. Both were ambivalent survivors. DeMarco was older, and his wounds, his amputations, were older too, but Tom was a better thinker, better at the kind of self-analysis that might someday yield salubrious results.

That was why reading his reflections, random, fragmentary, and unpredictable as they sometimes were, brought DeMarco not only pleasure but relief. The pleasure of relief. DeMarco could take Tom's thoughts and make them his own. Or at least pick them apart and find a nugget to clutch, to slip into his pocket, so to speak. And now that Tom was gone . . .

His death had altered the balance somehow. Before, Tom had been the younger brother, brighter and handsomer and more successful, and DeMarco had felt a truly brotherly pride in him. But death had made Tom wiser. Older. Bestowed upon him, DeMarco imagined, a more panoramic view. If death couldn't be counted on for that, what good was it?

He was sitting with the back of his skull against the headboard, eyes on the far corner of the ceiling, where the light from his little reading lamp did not reach, when, out of the blue, Jayme startled him with a question. "Does it seem to you that we have a lot of sex?" she asked.

He blinked. Rolled his head against the headboard. Tried to quickly make the adjustment, but her question had jarred him. "Where did that come from?" he asked.

"This piece I just now read. This line in particular: 'when I can no longer find that earthly ecstasy of joining my body with my lover's.'"

"And you think that can happen from too much sex?" he asked. "That it loses its, I don't know, magic?"

"Do you?"

Oh God, he thought. *It's going to be one of those conversations. Watch out for the quicksand.* "I guess it can if you let it," he said. "Are you worried about that happening to us?"

"Not necessarily. Statistically, though, most couples don't have as much sex as we do."

"Are you saying we have too much?"

"I'm asking what is too much. We have it almost every morning. Then almost every night."

"Is it a good thing or a bad thing that you're keeping track?"

"I want to be sure that you're getting enough," she said, "but not too much. Does that make sense? I want to keep you happy."

"I am happy."

"Would more sex make you happier?"

"Honestly?"

"No, babe, lie to me. Of course honestly."

"All right then. There are times. After-noons, especially. Sometimes I'd like to just reach over and touch you and . . . start taking your clothes off."

"Is this one of those times?"

He thought for a moment. No way he could tell her he'd been thinking, if only momentarily, about Laraine. So what was the correct answer? "Sure," he said. "I mean . . . I never lose the desire for you. I just don't want you thinking that it's, you know, all about the sex for me. The only reason I want the sex is because of our feelings for each other."

"So let's say we don't know each other," she said. "We've never seen each other before. Then we happen to get on an eleva-tor together. Just us. I'm wearing that short red skirt you like. And I lean up against you and whisper, 'Please, mister. Take me right now, right here.' Would you do it?"

"That's a trick question if I've ever heard one."

"Would you or wouldn't you?"

He thought for a moment, then asked,

"How many floors?"

She punched his arm. "See? You would! Under the right circumstances, you *would* have sex with me even if you'd never seen me before. Ergo, you're an asshole."

He used his left hand to rub his arm. "I thought we were talking about frequency. What does that have to do with elevators?"

She punched him again.

He winced, tried to think of something funny to say, then decided to say nothing.

She went back to reading, or at least pretending to, snapping the pages and holding them close to her face. And there was something about her pouty petulance that he found arousing, but the arousal made him feel like an oaf because he wanted to touch her again, wanted to lay his hand on her thigh and press his mouth to her neck.

He felt he needed to explain himself before making any physical overtures, tell her why touching and sex were important to him and why they meant more to him than she might think.

"I didn't get a lot of affection when I was young," he said.

She lifted her gaze from the composition book, then turned her head his way.

He said, "You grew up in a big family. A loving family. We're not all that lucky."

She closed the composition book and laid it in her lap.

"Laraine was the first time I felt real love in a woman's touch. Since my mother, I mean."

"I can't believe you didn't have any girlfriends."

"There were girls I dated but . . . I didn't really feel anything for them. And never believed they felt anything real for me."

"I'm sure they did, though. You just had yourself all locked up back then."

He nodded. "For some reason, it was different with Laraine. For a while anyway. Then a few months after Ryan was born, one night after dinner, she was at the sink, cleaning up, and I walked up behind her, put my arms around her waist and sort of pressed up against her, you know?"

"And?" Jayme said.

"She spun around and snapped at me. Said, 'Do you have to be touching me *all the time*?'"

"Oh baby," she said, and laid her hand on his arm.

"I've never forgotten how much that stung. It was worse than a slap in the face."

She stroked his arm. And said, "Make you a deal?"

"Okay," he said.

"If I can touch you anytime I want, you can touch me anytime you want."

"Sounds fair."

"And if one of us just isn't in the mood and reneges on that deal, the other one promises not to be personally offended."

"Like when you have PMS, you mean?"

"That's one example."

"There is also such a thing as male PMS," he told her. "Scientific fact."

"Oh really? You know when I'll believe that? When I see you shove a tampon up the little guy."

"Ouch," he said, and squeezed his thighs together.

She snuggled against him. "You want to get rid of the box for the night?"

"Only if you do."

"I want your hands on me."

"Are you saying that just to be kind?"

She turned her face into his shoulder and bit him through the T-shirt. "Don't make me ask you twice," she said.

SEVENTY-NINE

Over the next two days, either Olcott or Sheriff Brinker kept them apprised of developments. Becca's and Griffin's corroborating testimonies concerning the use of alcohol and psilocybin mushrooms during the meetings in Dr. Gillespie's basement convinced the DA to file charges against the professor for the possession of a Schedule 1 drug, and for its dissemination, along with alcohol, to minors. He was booked and released on bail. The university had been apprised of Dr. Gillespie's activities, and had quietly suspended him pending the outcome of his trial. Kaitlin continued to deny any knowledge of or participation in the monthly meetings, but Sheriff Brinker felt certain she would come around soon; he had suggested to the university that those students who cooperated with the investigation not be suspended or expelled.

The students' Twitter and Facebook and

other social media accounts were all being monitored by the department, as was Gillespie's, in hopes that somebody would slip up and reveal a bit of illuminating information about Connor McBride's whereabouts. Phone records for all involved had been subpoenaed, but it would take weeks to get them. The drug task force was keeping the Lubich-owned service station on route 62 under surveillance; no suspicious activity to report. Ditto the abandoned house and now-empty garage in McGuffey Heights. The police were considering a sting operation to catch Darlene Lubich in an act of prostitution, as a means of getting her to reveal any knowledge of her nephew's whereabouts.

No one knew where Connor McBride had gone. His mother didn't know, Gillespie didn't know, Connor's friends and known associates didn't know, his manager at Hot Heads didn't know. Neither did law enforcement. An Uber driver had picked him up downtown on the day the Charger was found, and, at approximately 2:20 that afternoon, had dropped him off two blocks from the abandoned house in McGuffey Heights, only a hundred yards from where Officers Blanchard and Simms were then parked.

"So he probably saw the patrol car and bolted," Sheriff Brinker said.

DeMarco said, "I'm betting he climbed into another abandoned house and watched the whole operation. Watched us search the house, open up the garage, find his tool kit, and tow the car away."

"So he knows we're looking for him."

"Oh, he knows. He knows."

DeMarco sometimes found himself walking aimlessly through the house, pausing at this window or that window to look out, sometimes even stopping in the middle of a room, his gaze fixed on the floor, or on the edge of the coffee table, or at a nail hole in the wall.

Jayme said, one of those times, "Maybe we should bring Tom's box down here and work our way through it. There's no reason we have to wait till night to read, is there?"

He scrunched up his mouth. "If you don't mind," he said, "I'd rather wait." He was glad she did not ask for an explanation, because he had none. He didn't want to read Tom's secret writing with the sunlight coming harsh and full through the windows. Just didn't want to. It was as simple as that.

Time moved slowly for DeMarco. Crawled on its belly. Progressed slower than a python digesting a piano.

On the third day, a Friday, he was awake early after a restless night. He made coffee, and while it percolated into the carafe, he moved through the kitchen as quietly as possible, opened the back door and stepped out onto the porch. He stood with his toes over the edge of the porch and looked at the sun spilling juice from a blood orange over the eastern horizon. It was a pretty sunrise but something told him it was pretty like the eyes of a viper.

He could sense something hidden behind that sunrise, could feel something coming toward him from every edge of the sky, something ponderous moving in. It wasn't visible, wasn't audible, wasn't yet in any way knowable. It was like a snow leopard crawling through the snow toward its prey, but bigger than that, darker than that. It was like a great black thundercloud full of lightning and drowning rain, but deadlier, angrier. It was the void preceding time, the darkness preceding light.

You're losing your mind, DeMarco told himself. *For chrissakes, man, find something to do.*

EIGHTY

He was on his knees in the yard when Jayme came to the door. Still in his boxers and a T-shirt, a trowel in hand as he lifted bricks from the half-completed path, smoothed out the layer of sand, sometimes added more sand from the bag he had dragged from the garage, then replaced the brick and used the trowel handle to tap it flat and even. Jayme watched him reset half a dozen bricks this way, then called to him. "You want some breakfast?"

When he looked up, his face without expression, as blank as a brick, she thought, *He doesn't even recognize me.*

Then he blinked, smiled sheepishly, and asked, "What time is it?"

"Time for a man in his boxers to come inside."

He looked around, embarrassed. Then climbed to his feet and strode onto the porch.

He cleaned up and dressed while she scrambled eggs and fried a ham steak for them to share. They ate in relative silence, though he told her twice how good the food was and thanked her for making it. The taste registered in her own mouth too but his excessive politeness soured every bite so that it sat heavy in the center of her chest, and the sound of their forks scraping the plates set her teeth on edge. She had something she wanted to say but there was too much sadness in the room, too much uncertainty. The room was full of light but there was no illumination in it.

"You're more than what you do," she told him.

He was bent over his plate, taking one slow forkful of food after another. Now he turned his head to look her way.

She said, "You have to stop being like this."

"Like what?" he asked, not angry or defensively, but gently, so that it sounded almost as if he were encouraging her to criticize him.

"You started out worrying that you weren't doing any good, that one more bad guy in jail didn't matter. And now that it's practically over, you're depressed. Like unless you're chasing after some murderer, your life has no meaning. But that's selfish thinking, Ryan. Can't you see how selfish that is?"

He had listened attentively, and now answered with a little nod. Very quietly he laid the fork on the edge of the plate, leaned back in his chair and let his hands fall into his lap.

She said, "Your father did terrible things to you when you were a boy. The war did terrible things to you. Two wars. Then you lost your boy, your marriage . . . you lost your best friend. Yes, life has done terrible things to you."

"I've done terrible things," he said.

"And it is what it is. Done is done. We all have regrets, Ryan. But no amount of beating yourself up is going to change a second of it."

He said, "You're right. I know you're right. I just don't know what to do about it."

"You can start by being aware of how your moods affect me."

"I am aware. And that's one of the things that makes me so sad."

"You get sad because you blame yourself and go into yourself and don't want to come back out again."

"I know I do. I don't know where else to go."

"In a strange, unhealthy way," she told him, "you only feel good when you're making yourself feel bad." Then she paused and thought for a few moments. She wanted to be gentle, but she also needed things to change. There was change coming whether he liked it or not, and she needed him to make the necessary adjustments to accommodate that change. A moody, silent man was not going to cut it.

She said, "You know that I always put us first — right?"

"I know you do."

"I need for you to do that too."

He nodded.

"Aren't you always saying that people have to take responsibility for themselves? I've heard you say it a dozen times."

Again he nodded.

"If you make yourself think about other people first," she told him, "about how sad your sadness makes *me* feel, you would stop yourself. I know you would."

Several seconds ticked by before he spoke. When he smiled, his mouth looked crooked and pained. "Have you ever been driving along thinking about something, and then you look up and realize you're miles from where you want to be?"

"So you turn around, babe," she told him. "You just hit the damn brakes and turn yourself around. Because if you don't, you are never going to get where you want to be. And where I need you to be."

He lifted his arm, reached out across the table and took her hand. He held to it firmly but delicately, the way a person would hold to a fragile crystal thread when falling out of a plane. "I'll try," he said.

She shook her head, and squeezed his fingers so hard that somebody's knuckle cracked. "No, damn it. You won't *try*, you will *do it*. You will do it or else you will lose me and everything we've made together."

He closed his eyes and nodded, and kept nodding, quick little nods at first but then slower ones as his resolve gelled. Finally he opened his eyes and looked at her and said, "I'll do whatever you want me to do."

"You promise?"

"Just not drugs. Don't ask me to take anything."

"I don't want you taking anything. I don't want you numbed. I want you whole."

"I'm in your hands," he said. This time his smile was not crooked, but the helplessness in it nearly broke her heart.

EIGHTY-ONE

She went online and found the phone number for a local PTSD support group with weekly meet-ups not eight miles away. She punched the number into her phone, and handed the phone to him as he stood on the back porch looking at his unfinished brick walkway.

"It's up to you to press the call button," she told him.

He made an exaggerated grimace. "This is going to hurt."

"So does resetting a fractured bone so that it will heal straight."

"Do I at least get a lollipop afterward?"

"No," she said, and kissed his cheek. "That's all the sweetness you get."

She went back inside then and left him alone to make the call. The man who answered had a gruffer voice than he expected, not polished and condescending but the kind of voice that came with a scruffy beard and dirty tennis shoes and a faded Grateful Dead T-shirt. So DeMarco stayed on the line and listened. And agreed to attend the next meet-up.

He stood there on the edge of the porch then, palming Jayme's phone, and reminded himself of how lucky he was to have her on his side. She had more balls than a pool table, and every one of them was pure ivory.

The sun was bright and the sky clear and the day felt promising. Warm but with a hint of coolness, and now and then even a freshening wisp of breeze. A neighbor two houses down was mowing his yard already, even though the last of the morning's dew had not yet burned away, and the old woman who lived next door on his left was on her hands and knees at a flower bed, pulling weeds and coaxing the summer blossoms to linger awhile longer. Her wide-brimmed straw sun hat made him smile, though he could not have explained why. The top was rounded like a pith helmet, but the brim held a bend in the front like the one in Indiana Jones's fedora, and a wide blue ribbon with a bowknot caught the sunlight and sparkled with the bits of glitter embedded in the cloth.

The woman was eighty-six but still working hard and even dressing to catch the light. He thought about how pretty and saucy his mother would have looked in a hat like that. Told himself to not think about her never owning such a hat, but about how she loved to look her best no matter what. Even on her last night in this world she had fixed herself up first. Did her hair and nails and put on a fresh coat of mascara and lipstick, a pair of nylon stockings and heels and her favorite thrift-store dress. When he thought of her that way, all dolled up, as people used to say, kneeling beside the bathtub and leaning over the rounded edge with her arms in the water, he almost had to laugh. She wanted to look good for the undertaker. How could you not love somebody like that?

And with that thought, another memory rushed forward from out of whatever place in which memories hide. Maybe it was because of the glitter in his neighbor's hat ribbon. The glitter made him remember the Christmas angels.

When he was a boy, there was no room in the trailer for a Christmas tree and no money to buy one even if sufficient room existed, so his mother would set six cardboard Christmas angels on the windowsills every December. They were a dirty white, with cardboard bodies and wings with cotton glued to them, each with a golden halo, all identical, maybe six inches tall. Through the chest of each was a hole in the cardboard so that a branch on the Christmas tree could be poked through, leaving the angel suspended as if hovering in the air. Gold glitter lined the wings and the halos, and if you touched the angel, a bit of glitter would stick to your fingers. His mother would prop the angels up on the narrow windowsills, leaning against the dirty glass, two in the kitchen, two in the living room, and one each in her and Ryan's bedrooms. During the day the light would shine through the gray windows and out the holes in the angels' chests, and at night the darkness would make a black oculus through the very hearts of the angels. Yet DeMarco had loved those cardboard angels, especially during the day. Sometimes at night they frightened him.

It was at night that his father destroyed the angels. Came home drunk and angry, flew into a rage over something DeMarco's mother had said, gathered up all six angels and set them aflame in the sink, filling the trailer with acrid smoke. DeMarco couldn't remember his age that Christmas, probably eight or nine, but he remembered the flames and the stink of smoke and the way his mother had sat at the table and cried after flushing the ashes down the sink.

And now DeMarco stepped down off the porch and started through his yard, meaning to say good morning to his neighbor and tell her how much he admired the hat, how much it reminded him of his mother. But he was only halfway there when Jayme's cell phone vibrated in his hand. He looked at the screen and read the name of the caller. Stopped moving and read the name a second time. Then tapped the phone icon, put the phone to his ear and said, "Daksh. What's up?"

EIGHTY-TWO

"Where is Jayme Matson?" Daksh asked. "I would like to talk to her, please."

"I'm walking toward the house right now. What's going on?"

"It is her number I have. Her phone I call."

"It's okay; you can talk to me," DeMarco said. He stepped onto the porch, pulled open the screen door and stepped inside. Jayme turned away from the sink, saw the look on his face, and cocked her head in question.

He put the call on speaker, then said, "I need you to calm down a little, Daksh. Just tell me what's going on."

"I wish to speak with Jayme Matson," Daksh said. "It is her number I call."

She grabbed a dish towel and quickly dried her hands, then reached for the phone.

"She's right here," DeMarco said, and handed the phone to her.

"Hi, Daksh," she said. "You sound upset. What's going on?"

"You gave me your card and you told me to call you anytime."

"I know I did. Tell me what's wrong."

"It is about the man the police are hunting. I remember him."

"Are you talking about Connor McBride?"

"The one the police want to find, yes. I saw it online this morning."

"And you know him?"

"He was in the class with me."

"Dr. Gillespie's class?"

"I remember his video. It is where he might be. I see his face and remember him and think maybe that is where he might be."

"Okay, wait a minute," Jayme said. "Let's slow down a bit so that I'm sure I'm understanding you. You saw Connor's face on a local news feed, and you recognized him as someone from your class with Dr. Gillespie?"

"Yes, yes, that is exactly correct. I remember his face."

"Okay, good," she said. DeMarco moved closer to her now, didn't want to miss a word. She said, "And what's this video you referred to? For a class project?"

"Yes, exactly. We were to take photos or make a short video with our cell phones."

"Of what specifically?"

"True will. To show the exercise of true will in action. By us or someone else."

"All right, good. And Connor's video showed a particular place?"

"An abandoned building that used to be a hospital, I think."

"In Youngstown? Or Garrettsville, or . . . ?"

"No, not anywhere I have been. But not far away, I think. I remember he said it used to be a hospital. With a woman's name. The city cannot afford to tear it down."

DeMarco leaned close to her and whispered, "St. Margaret's? In Sharpsville?"

She said, "Is it St. Margaret's Hospital, Daksh? In Sharpsville, Pennsylvania?"

"St. Margaret's, yes! That is the name he gave!"

"Okay, great. You're doing so well, Daksh. So why do you think he might be there now?"

"I only thought when I saw his face this morning . . . I remembered when he showed the video. He was very excited about the place. About the people there and what they were doing."

"The people he met at St. Margaret's Hospital? In the abandoned building?"

"Yes! There were rituals, there were people wearing masks. There was magic being

535

practiced there but it was very bad, very bad magic. It was not the kind of true will we were meant to practice."

"I think I understand," Jayme said. "And you believe he might be there now?"

"I do not know," Daksh told her. "I only thought, he is hiding somewhere. Maybe there. This is why I use the card you gave me, and why I call your number."

"You did great, Daksh. You did the right thing."

"I see his face this morning, I remember the class, and I tell myself, you should call and let her know."

"Absolutely the right thing to do," she told him.

"I am glad," he said. "Thank you. Ah, it is a relief to know I made the right decision."

"You absolutely did."

"Thank you. You might also like to know that the puppies will be ready soon to be placed in a new home. I remember how you enjoyed them."

"We'll keep that in mind," she told him, and gave DeMarco a wink.

She was about to tell him goodbye when DeMarco whispered again. "What was Gillespie's reaction to the video?"

"One last thing, Daksh," she said into the phone. "Do you remember how Dr.

Gillespie reacted to Connor's video?"

"Hmm," Daksh said. "I think the professor did not like him much. Some students he was very kind to, but others, like me, Connor McBride, he could be very, very unkind."

"In what way was he unkind to Connor?"

"He was the boy, I think, who always dressed in army pants. I believe I am remembering this correctly. The class was many months ago."

"When you say army pants . . ."

"The kind that are supposed to make a soldier invisible."

"Camo?"

"Yes! Yes, camo. The professor was very brusque to him. Very unkind. He said that a soldier is invisible to everyone but the enemy. That a soldier has no identity of his own. He said that only the weak-minded and frightened want to be invisible. I am remembering it all better now."

"All right, good. Thank you for calling, Daksh. This is all very helpful."

"I am happy that I have spoken to you. And please remember that the puppies are here if you would like to give one a home. I think you would make a very good mother for a puppy."

After she ended the call, she regarded De-

Marco standing motionless, hands in his pockets, his head cocked to the side, eyes fixed on a table leg. "So?" she said.

He shook his head. "There are houses and an apartment building across the street from that hospital. I doubt very much that Connor would be living there. He has to have food, has to have water. Not a good place to survive unnoticed."

"Maybe somebody is taking care of him. Somebody from the group that practiced, or practices, ritual magic there. You want to call Brinker?"

He shrugged. "St. Margaret's is ten minutes away."

"So we go there and take a quick look around. Then we'll know whether or not to call the boss."

"I thought you were the boss," DeMarco said.

She grinned. "I'm *your* boss, mister. And don't you ever forget it."

And they were both happy again, the adrenaline flowing.

EIGHTY-THREE

Movement, DeMarco realized as he drove, was helping him to think. Movement blew the cobwebs out, got the juices running again. Walking was best, walking in the woods, but even driving a car was beneficial. It had something to do with stimulation, he guessed. Blood flow to the brain. More oxygen to the brain. More brain chemicals lighting up more neurons. More endorphins, adrenaline, testosterone, L-DOPA.

Sitting in a car didn't sound like much movement but it involved a complex set of actions: foot from accelerator to brake, hand making fine corrections on the steering wheel, eyes assessing traffic ahead, to the rear, to the side, all of it continuous and synchronous. Taking the wheel with the left hand while putting the right hand out to lay atop a fine, warm leg clothed in tight denim. Yes, it was all so very good for the brain.

And the sunlight warm on the side of his

face, the cooling air from the vents. A good morning, already productive. So why was his chest sore again, every breath heavy? Why the metallic taste in his mouth?

He said, "Didn't Becca say she took Gillespie's class with Connor?"

"She did, didn't she? And that would have been last fall. But she also said that he had dropped out for a while. Took the class when he came back to school."

"Daksh said the class was many months ago. Would you refer to last fall as 'many months ago'?"

"Maybe Connor failed the class the first time and had to repeat it."

"Is that how college works? If you fail a class, you have to take it again?"

"Only if it's a required course. I suspect Gillespie's are electives unless you're a religion major," Jayme said. "So why repeat an elective you already failed?"

"You tell me," he said.

"On the other hand, we know that he dropped out of college for a while. Maybe he never finished the course before dropping out. Then came back and took it again."

"So both Becca and Daksh could be telling the truth."

She nodded. "Which implies that the

subject matter was important enough to Connor that he was willing to face Gillespie's animosity a second time."

"Or maybe he took it to impress Samantha Lewis? According to her brother, Connor was always trying 'to get with' Samantha."

"Could be," Jayme said.

" 'Because the women are watching,' " he said.

"Watching what?"

"It's what T. E. Lawrence said. The guy the movie *Lawrence of Arabia* was about."

"That was a real guy?"

DeMarco nodded. "He was asked once why men go to war. And he said, 'Because the women are watching.' "

"So now we're getting the blame for wars too?"

"You're to blame for everything men do."

"I think it cuts both ways."

"Probably," he told her, happy to be moving again, trying despite the heaviness in his chest to be happy for blue sky and summer's greenery and a woman like her with whom to go to war.

EIGHTY-FOUR

The bank sign they had passed on their way into town five minutes earlier had flashed *10:37,* then *84°.* Now they were moving slowly along the street that ran more or less parallel to the Shenango River. DeMarco had considered making a quick stop at the building on South Walnut to let the local chief of police know what he and Jayme were up to, except that a quick stop would probably stretch into thirty minutes or more. The borough employed only five police officers in total, which meant that three at the most were working the day shift. So now he pulled to the shoulder in front of the old St. Margaret's Hospital and shut off the engine. Almost immediately the cool air inside the vehicle began to warm.

Both he and Jayme looked across the thirty yards of weedy, littered ground to the abandoned building. The old hospital took up four full lots, was flanked by a small macadam parking lot on the eastern side, empty ground to the west and rear of the building, the shallow river fifty yards beyond the rear wall. Two-story frame houses in disrepair lined the rest of the street, with a five-story low-income apartment building directly across the street.

The concrete drive up to the front entrance of St. Margaret's was blocked with a rusty chain and a lopsided sign that read *No Trespassing.* A massive catalpa tree, long untended, stretched twisting arms out across the circle of ground at the end of the drive, shading the weeds with its broad green leaves. Dead leaves and dry brown seed pods blanketed the ground and some of the pavement.

The building was comprised of one main structure, three stories high, and two flat-roofed wings both two stories high, plus a small, detached shed of some kind, all made of 1920s yellow brick. The parking lot was bumpy with frost heaves and broken pavement and was slowly being reclaimed by weeds and wild grass. A naked, rusting flagpole stood in the circle of weeds, a limp length of fraying cord dangling from an eyebolt. Pieces of rotted white soffit and fascia, loosened by bees and termites and water damage, hung below the roof of the building like dirty Tibetan prayer flags.

Jayme said, her arms pimpled with goose bumps, "It's like looking at a decaying corpse in broad daylight."

DeMarco said nothing. Concentrated on trying to fill his lungs, exorcise that soreness in the center of his chest, the distant rumbling in his brain.

When Jayme turned away from the window and looked at him, he nodded toward the glove box. "We're not going to need them," he said, "but let's play it safe."

She popped open the compartment, handed him his weapon and holster, then took out her own. She then removed the two identical flashlights, only four inches long but with powerful LED lights and pebbled black steel handles, and gave one of them to him. He removed the key from the ignition and popped open the door. The wash of heat and humidity hit him like a soft blow, as if by opening the door he had let a huge invisible ball of hot, wet cotton roll atop him. In an instant he felt weakened by the heat, by the dry scent of dirty concrete and the pervasive stink of entropy.

Jayme saw his hand go to his chest, heard his quick, shallow breath. "You okay?" she asked.

"It's just the humidity," he said.

"Are you having trouble breathing?"

"I'm fine. Let's get moving."

He stood up. Closed the door. Fitted the holster onto his pocket. Pulled his shirt down over the weapon.

She climbed out the other side and closed the door. As she fitted the weapon into place and covered it with her shirt, she said, "Let's just wait here a few minutes until we get used to the humidity."

"Stop treating me like a baby," he said, and pushed the door shut, harder than he'd intended.

"Stop acting like one."

He moved away from the car, kept his eyes on the building. "Looks like the front door is boarded shut. I'm going to check the parking lot side. You're welcome to join me, if you wish."

He crossed ahead of her around the end of the chain and onto the paved driveway, breathing with his mouth open, long, purposeful strides, doing his best to appear strong and steady. Seed pods crackled under his feet. And then he was into the shade beneath the catalpa tree, breathed deeper, the air a few delicious degrees cooler. He pretended to be waiting for her, and when she caught up, they moved out into the sun together.

And stopped simultaneously at the sound of laughter. Two kids coming around the side of the building, Black girl, white boy, midteens, both in shorts and tees. They spotted DeMarco and Jayme and suddenly got serious, whispered to each other and slowed down.

"How you doing?" DeMarco said as they approached.

"Doing good," the boy said.

"Can I ask you a question?"

"We was just checking the place out is all. It's pretty cool in there."

"Is it?" Jayme said. "What's it like? We thought we'd check it out too."

Now the boy laughed. "Dude, it's like a bomb went off in there. Lots of bombs."

"It's awesome," the girl added. "Zombie apocalypse awesome. Somebody should make a movie in there."

DeMarco asked, "Is there anybody else inside?"

"Naw, man," the boy told him. "I didn't see nobody. And we went the whole way to the top."

"Just the zombies," the girl said. "Have fun!"

And then they were jogging away and laughing again, across the street and toward the low-income apartments. Jayme and De-

Marco continued around the side of the building, and there found the heavy metal safety door hanging open crookedly, half-torn from the hinges. Part of an old cardboard sign was still tacked to the door:

NO TRESPAS
KEEP O

DeMarco paused on the threshold and peered into the stairwell. The sun was still at his back but coming down at a sharp angle, so that the harsh light did not fully illuminate the small room all the way to the set of interior metal doors.

She came up beside him and squeezed in close. Saw the way the old fallen tiles and ceiling panels had been kicked to the side, leaving a narrow trail that forked at the foot of the stairs and continued to the double doors. "Well-traveled path," she said. "How long has this building been standing here like this?"

"Late nineties," he said. He shined his flashlight up the stairs, saw the landing at the turn jammed with old lockers and metal chairs. "It's blocked off. Probably not safe."

"My God," she said, "this place is a death trap. Why hasn't it been torn down or at least locked up?"

"Money," he answered. "The lack thereof."

Then he said, "Stay close," and pushed forward, in through the double doors. They swung easily for the first twenty or so degrees, then caught on debris piled on the floor. The doors opened onto a wide, dim hallway, brighter light in the distance, where the lobby with its high windows waited.

Smaller rooms opened off the corridor — empty, raided, stripped and ruined rooms sometimes decorated with orange or green graffiti, the quick scrawls of teenagers testing their courage or venting their wrath. Water-damaged drywall was stained with black mold, punched full of ragged holes, some panels torn from the walls. A lot of the drywall lay shattered on the floor or was ground into dust, some of it into a thick wet paste in small puddles of stagnant water. Window screens, wires, cables, pieces of pipe and two-by-fours lay about everywhere. Sometimes a heavy metal desk, an overturned filing cabinet with its files spilling out. Rubble and debris mixed with an occasional beer can, soda can, cigarette butt, even a single Converse tennis shoe, now waterlogged and black with mold.

"The kid was right," Jayme said as she followed DeMarco into the wide lobby. "It looks exactly like a bomb was dropped in here. Is this what it's like to be in a war zone?"

"All that's missing are the bodies," he said, and immediately she regretted her question.

They came to a door with a small plaque that read *Visitor Restroom.* DeMarco turned the knob and opened the door. The tile walls and floor were mostly intact, a toilet still in place but with the seat and tank lid missing, four inches of black water still in the tank, a smashed soap dispenser still attached to the wall. The stink of old urine was unmistakable.

In the next room the entire ceiling had been ripped down, every drop tile on the floor, along with a length of metal rectangular ductwork that, seen from the right angle in the partial light, could be mistaken for a coffin.

Room by room, most of the damage was obviously deliberate, but only some of it purposeful. The place had been readied for demolition, holes cut into the floor, corner beams and I beams exposed — everything in standby for implosion.

"Looks like the money ran out after prepping the building," Jayme said.

"Demolition is expensive. Lots of environmental issues too."

They could find no sign of Connor Mc-
Bride or Satanists or ritualized magic on
the first floor. The trail through the debris
led to another stairwell on the far side of
the lobby. This stairway appeared to be clear
of obstacles. "You want this one?" Jayme
asked. "I'll go back and head up the other
side."

"We need to stay together," he told her.

"Now who's treating who like a baby?"

"It's the smart thing to do."

"The place is empty," she said, "and I
don't plan to stand here breathing this mold
any longer than I have to. See you at the
top." She turned to walk back to the eastern
side of the building.

He said, "Let's both go up these stairs.
Why climb over those desks and stuff? They
could collapse with you on top of them."

She gave him a mischievous grin. "I live
for adventure. Race you to the top!" And
she bolted forward, back into the hallway
and through the lobby.

He wanted to follow her but knew she
would be angry if he did. She would accuse
him of not respecting her abilities. Would
feel diminished by his concern. So he
stepped forward to make his way up the
stairs, but in no hurry to get to the top. It

would be better to let her win. Better for him to emerge on the second floor and find her standing there grinning in victory.

Besides, the air was wet and heavy and moldy. He would take his time getting to the top, right hand gripping the flashlight, left hand tapping his chest.

EIGHTY-FIVE

By keeping most of her weight on the handrail, pulling herself up and over with a few careful steps, Jayme easily scaled the pile of desks and chairs in the middle of the stairway. Ten more stairs and she was at the double doors on the second floor. She used her shoulder to ease the left door open. Scanned what she could see of the hallway beyond, her flashlight beam illuminating more of the same, dangling cables and wires and fallen ceiling panels all the way down to the middle of the hallway. There, a long section of counter plus several metal desks and chairs lay capsized and piled atop one another across the center of the hall.

Nurses' station, she told herself. But why build a thick fence of metal furnishings from wall to wall? It didn't make any sense. On the other hand, it seemed that all the stripping and prep for demolition completed so far had been done in random stages, furnishings dragged halfway down the stairs or to the center of the room, some copper tubing stripped from the walls and some left intact. *ADHD,* she told herself, and chuckled at the idea of an entire crew of demolition workers with attention deficit hyperactivity disorder.

Before stepping through the doors, she leaned in a bit farther so as to look around the door she held open, but was startled when a hand poked around the door and punched into her stomach. Instantly her entire body went rigid, every muscle stretched taut to the point of snapping, and she felt herself falling to the side, rigid and completely paralyzed. She was fully alert but in a random, fragmented way, so that she felt the flashlight slip from her hand and heard it thud against the floor but recognized no connection between the two events, could not have said which happened first or for how long. She felt her other hand falling away from the door but which door, where, and why she could not have said. A part of her brain recognized the stun gun's effect, and another part remembered the police academy training, but, for those moments, the two memories had no knowledge of each other.

She imagined she was screaming *Stop!*

Stop! while reaching for her weapon, but was incapable of speech or the slightest voluntary movement. Someone grabbed her arm as she was falling and yanked her into the hallway, and she was grateful to have her body twisted as she fell, her face saved from bashing into the floor, taking the impact with her left arm, shoulder and hip, separate punches of pain. She smelled the moldy, chalky debris against the side of her face. Smelled the dust rising around her face. The sweaty stink of a body pressing close to hers. She wanted to close her senses to it all but could not.

The stun gun's crackling stopped but her muscles kept twitching. When she saw the hand and knife coming down toward her chest, she recognized the danger and tried without success to roll away from it. The knife was moving not in slow motion but in stop-action jerks, a flip-book hand and knife inching closer. She struggled to raise her hand in defense, to grab the wrist and push it away, but her own actions were flip-booking too, so she pushed harder and felt the wrist slap into her palm, felt her fingers close around the wrist, and then the knife went into her just below the left breast, and she screamed from the pain and heard a woman's scream coming from far away down the hall, and as the knife sliced through her flesh and out of her body she felt herself tumbling backward into a pool of darkness, and she heard breath slipping out of her mouth, and the darkness sucked her in.

EIGHTY-SIX

DeMarco swept the flashlight beam back and forth as he ascended the stairs. For the most part the stairway was clear of debris, but enough shattered drywall lay atop the steps that he picked his way along carefully, reading the graffiti and looking carefully for symbols or phrases that suggested sinister happenings inside the building. All he saw were juvenile scrawlings, names and dates, vulgar epithets, hearts surroundings teenage lovers' names.

He was still five steps from the top when he heard the scream, Jayme's scream, and then abandoned all precision of movement. He took the final steps two at a time, throwing himself forward to burst through the double doors with his pistol drawn. A second later he heard an electrical crackle near his ear and felt something bite into the back of his shoulder. But he was moving as fast as he could and the electrical contact was brief. It buckled his knees and kicked a leg out from under him but his momentum carried him forward, into the wide corridor, where he fell while twisting to see who was behind him, and landed hard against the floor, left hand smashing to the dusty tile as well, flashlight flying away in pieces.

Connor McBride lunged at him, stun gun in his left hand, a long-bladed knife in his right. DeMarco, even as the pain was shooting up his spine and his body was still falling backward, fired three shots. The first went high and into the ceiling, the second creased Connor's shoulder, and the third shattered his right clavicle and exited into the wall.

The boy staggered back into the corner, then twisted sideways and went down on his knees, squealing in pain. DeMarco rolled onto a hip, thought he might have broken his tailbone, but pushed the pain aside, climbed to his feet and crossed to Connor. He had dropped the cell phone stun gun but still gripped the knife, and as DeMarco approached, the boy shrank away from him and screamed "Magus!" The word echoed down the hall, ricocheted through DeMarco's ear canals.

He switched the 9 mm to his left hand and sent Connor reeling to the side with a short jab to the jaw. Surprisingly, the boy, now semiconscious on his back, still clung to the knife. DeMarco took the nine into his gun hand again, then pressed a heel atop the boy's hand until his fingers sprang open, and he kicked the knife across the hallway.

A gunshot popped behind him, the tinny sound of a .380; the bullet sent a puff of dust out of the drywall behind DeMarco. He knew the sound of Jayme's weapon, and then knew that she had been disarmed, and ran forward, zigzagging a little and keeping low, gasping from the pain of each step, using the barricade of desks across the center of the lobby for concealment. Before he reached the barricade, another shot followed, also wide and high. He hunkered down low behind the desks. Whoever was firing at him wasn't a very good shot, probably had little experience with a handgun. DeMarco peered between the pieces of metal, then spotted the figure kneeling behind a supine Jayme, and couldn't believe what he saw.

"I will slice her throat!" Daksh called to him.

DeMarco stood, exposing his chest and shoulders and head.

A shot pinged off the metal. DeMarco flinched but stood his ground. Took aim on

Daksh's moving head. Pulled the trigger.

The shot went high, but not by much. Dust puffed out of the drywall.

Now Daksh went down on his stomach behind Jayme, steadying his hands atop her belly. He fired once. The round pinged and ricocheted close to DeMarco's knee.

DeMarco started pulling at the desks in an attempt to dislodge the barricade. But they were jammed together too solidly. Using knees and elbows and left hand and belly, everything but his gun hand, he crawled over the barricade. "I'm going to rip off your head and kick it down the stairs, Daksh!"

The next shot came so close to DeMarco's middle finger, which was hooked over the edge of a desk, that he thought he had been hit, felt the heat and shock race up his finger and into the palm of his hand. But he didn't stop. Wouldn't stop. Not then or for the next two shots, both of which pinged close to him.

DeMarco returned fire twice, but deliberately high so as to force Daksh to cower even lower. He was too close to Jayme for DeMarco to risk a kill shot. Instead, he threw a leg over the last impediment and had only to bring his other leg forward to be clear of the desks. "Seven shots!" he called out. "You're empty, Daksh!" *And you have two,* DeMarco told himself.

In answer, Daksh pulled the trigger twice more, and heard nothing but clicks. "You will watch her die!" he screamed.

Clear of the desks, DeMarco stood motionless and took aim as close to the top of Daksh's head as he dared. Pulled the trigger. Watched Daksh flatten himself atop Jayme for a moment and knew he had felt the hot breeze crease his hair.

"I have four shots left," DeMarco lied, and walked toward him steadily, keeping his arm and hand steady, gunsight fixed on Daksh's hairline. "Back away from her now or I will blow your brains out. Harm her in any way and I will rip you into a thousand pieces."

Daksh did not move. DeMarco fired again, his final bullet. Daksh slapped a hand to the top of his head, pulled the hand away, and looked for blood. Saw none.

DeMarco calculated the remaining distance at thirty feet. He wanted to look at Jayme's face, wanted to see if her chest was rising and falling. But he dared not. He took long, even strides, was moving as briskly as he dared though a sharp pain shot up his back with every step. "Back away from her!" he called again. "Or the last three go right between your eyes!"

For five long seconds Daksh did not move. Then suddenly he threw himself backward and into the swinging doors, rolled, and scrambled into the stairwell. A second after Daksh moved, DeMarco started running. And as he ran he yanked his cell phone from his pocket, then went sliding to his knees beside Jayme even as Daksh's footsteps were pounding down the stairs.

EIGHTY-SEVEN

He had her in his arms, was walking quickly but stiffly out to the street when the first patrol car screeched to a stop in front of the old hospital. On both sides of the street, people were standing on their porches, in their yards, leaning out their windows. An ambulance siren screamed in the distance, and the local dogs had set up a chorus of howls in reply.

On the second floor of the hospital, the first thing he had done was to press his left palm atop the knife wound under Jayme's breast and, with his other hand holding the cell phone, dialed 911 with his thumb. He put the phone on speaker and laid it on the floor and while shouting at the dispatcher he gently ran his right hand over her body, felt for a second wound or blood or anything broken. Within thirty seconds he had pushed the dispatcher's voice into the background, knew he wasn't going to sit there waiting for the EMTs to arrive, wasn't going to waste those precious minutes. There was also blood between her legs, seeping through her jeans along both thighs, but he could detect no external wound, no entry or exit holes. He ripped off his shirt and pressed it to the knife wound as firmly as possible, and then as he slipped both hands under her and lifted her up he felt for the first time the pain in his back, the whoosh of pain like a flare being lit, searing the whole way up his spine and into the base of his skull. His legs nearly buckled but he would not let it happen, damn it, and shouted to the phone on the floor for the dispatcher to alert the emergency room, alert the trauma team and the operating room and the blood bank that she was coming in. He pushed through the double doors and staggered down the stairs thinking *the golden hour, the golden hour,* and felt every ponderous step send another blast of pain up his back.

As quickly as he could he lumbered across the yard and under the catalpa tree, heard a siren screaming up the street and watched a patrol car come screeching to the curb. She groaned in his arms and pulled her knees up tight and he said "I'm sorry, baby, I'm sorry" and pushed himself to move faster. The fingernails of her left hand bit into the back of his neck and the fingernails of her right hand dug into his ribs. His field of vision had tightened to a small tunnel of brightness and color, so bright that he had to squint and keep blinking, the periphery clouded in charcoal gray. The patrolman on the passenger side of the patrol car jumped out and came toward him saying, "Put her down, sir! Lay her on the ground!"

"The hospital," DeMarco told him, "the golden hour, the golden hour," and kept trying to walk to the street, but now the driver of the patrol car was there too and trying to lift Jayme out of his arms.

Both men kept yelling at him to drop his weapon, put her down, but they did not understand, and he could not remember which way was the hospital. But then the first officer was standing close to him and screaming "Drop your weapon!" while aiming his own weapon at DeMarco's chest, and only then did DeMarco realize that he was still holding the 9 mm, had it in his right hand under Jayme's legs, so he opened his fingers and let it drop into the grass and he said to the officer, "It's empty. It's empty."

The sun was too bright and painful in his eyes and all he knew for certain was that he needed to get her to the hospital now. Then the ambulance with its siren wailing was there with a pair of paramedics, and after another brief struggle he finally let them take her. A patrolman pulled him away and said. "Right over here, sir. You can stay close."

"Alert the trauma team," he said, "the operating room, she's going to need some blood," and a patrolman stood close and told him, "They have it, sir, they have it. You come stand over here with me. I need to talk to you for a minute. Let's just stay here where you can see her and you can tell me what happened in there."

He did not want to stay with the officers but they promised to take him to the hospital in a minute or two. No, he could not ride in the ambulance, there were still some things they needed to know. He nodded and was as clear as he could be but when the ambulance pulled away screaming he kept looking down the street and felt his body wanting to be pulled along behind it.

He told the patrolman about Daksh's phone call to Jayme earlier, and why he and Jayme had gone into the building. Told him that two teenagers had informed them that the building was empty. He was on autopilot and answered all of their questions but wanted only to catch up with the ambulance. When he told them that Connor McBride was on the second floor with a couple of bullets in him, one officer went inside and the other one stayed with De-Marco. Soon the one with DeMarco received a call. He listened briefly and then said, "Okay," and ended the call. He told DeMarco, "He's still breathing," and that another ambulance had been called. He then called the state police to secure the crime scene. DeMarco gave the officer Ben Brinker's number, and, because McBride and his mother resided in the city, the Youngstown chief was called as well.

Then DeMarco looked across the street and noticed the two kids he had seen earlier coming out of the abandoned building, the ones who had told him the building was empty, and he said to the officer, "Those two kids over there. The boy and the girl. You need to talk to them."

The officer left him for several minutes and came back and said, "They got paid twenty dollars to tell you the place was empty. A guy told them he wanted to play a joke on his friends. The way they described him, he's the one you shot. It was the boy who called the police when they heard the shots inside. Both of them are pretty upset about what happened in there. They wanted to give me the twenty dollars to give to you. I told them to keep it. I hope that's okay."

DeMarco nodded but he had not followed all of the officer's story, did not care about the money or about the joke. Only about what the joke had cost him. He kept looking up and down the street in hopes of seeing a sign for the hospital, but everything was so strange and unfamiliar and no matter where he looked, the sun was sharp and fiery in his eyes.

He noticed a car parked down the street a little way and thought it looked a lot like his car but everything looked different now. Everything was too bright and flaming hot, yet dark and blurry around the edges. His back hurt like hell and his mouth and throat were bone dry, and every time he breathed he thought his lungs were going to burst into flame. He could hear his voice and the voices of others when they spoke, but the pressure inside his head made them sound like voices heard through a softly buzzing fog.

And then a state police car was pulling up to the curb and then another ambulance and police car and before long the street was lined with police cars. Officers went into the building, then paramedics went in. He was handed a bottle of cold water and moved to the back seat of one of the police vehicles, where he watched the gurney coming out with Connor McBride strapped to it, and saw the ambulance speed away. An officer came out carrying evidence bags containing a knife and two cell phones.

"One of those phones is mine," he told the officer standing outside the car. "And Jayme's weapon should be there. I don't see her weapon."

The officer walked over to the one with the evidence bags, spoke for a minute, and returned to DeMarco and told him that no other firearms were recovered. "It's a .380 Glock," DeMarco said.

"No other weapons were found, sir. They did a thorough search."

"Daksh," he told him. "Daksh took it with him."

After another twenty minutes or so, he found himself surrounded by familiar faces from Troop D. By then he was thinking a little more clearly though still in a lot of pain, still anxious to get to the hospital, but he told the whole story again and again, and kept pleading for somebody to give him directions to the hospital now, until finally his former station commander, Captain Kyle Bowen, put DeMarco in his own car and drove him to the facility.

EIGHTY-EIGHT

Jayme was still in surgery, he was told by a nurse, who then asked why he was standing so crookedly and why did he have such difficulty walking, and some of those lacerations on his arms looked like they might need stitches. Then he was sitting in a small room atop an examination table lined with crinkly white crepe paper, wearing only his boxers and socks as he shifted uncomfortably from one hip to the other, with a dagger of pain shooting up his spine every time he moved.

Kyle Bowen was with him in the room, standing near the door, watching and telling him not to worry, she was going to be okay. DeMarco asked what time it was and Bowen said, "12:17." DeMarco asked what time the ambulance had picked up Jayme, and Bowen said, "It must have been about an hour ago."

"That doesn't seem possible," DeMarco

told him. "It seems like it was yesterday some time."

Later there was a doctor in the room who asked DeMarco to lie on his stomach while the doctor pressed his fingertips on and around the tailbone. Then the doctor left the room and a nurse came to take his blood pressure and a sample of his blood. The blood on his arms and legs was cleaned away and all the little wounds examined and painted orange-brown with Betadine. Butterfly bandages, gauze patches and tape were applied and a hypodermic needle was pushed into one buttock. Then he was wheeled away for an MRI.

Afterward DeMarco was in a bed and trying not to fall asleep, with Bowen still watching from inside the door and a man who seemed distantly like Ben Brinker leaning close to tell DeMarco everything was going to be okay. And then some time later he opened his eyes to find himself in an enormous soft bed in an all-white room, with the sunlight pleasantly bright and warm and golden through the open windows, a cool breeze smelling of oranges coming through the windows to blow across his face and arms and hands. There were no bandages on his body and no pain anywhere, and finally the dense black rumbling inside his head was gone, and the heaviness in his chest had lifted, and everything was clear now, everything was fine and soft and sleepy, and there was a boy smiling down at him with a smile and blue eyes he had known for a very long time.

Eighty-Nine

It was Ben who told him about the baby. "But she's going to be all right," he kept saying, his broad dark face trying to look happy, but his forehead sweaty and his eyes full of concern. "Everything else is okay, man. I promise you she's okay."

Ben kept talking but all of the sound disappeared when DeMarco heard about the baby. He understood in an instant what Jayme must be feeling, a mother and now not one, and he a father without knowing it, and now not one again. He also understood why she hadn't told him, what a dolt he had been, what an insensitive dolt, and with that knowledge a great black silence descended over him. Ben's voice went silent, the room went silent, DeMarco's own heart fell silent. The silence muffled and suffocated everything but grief, everything but pain. The hospital was engulfed and consumed by the silence, as were the earth

and heaven and every drop of light the
universe held.

NINETY

More time passed in a syrupy, meandering kind of way, twisting out and away from him like brown taffy pulled in all directions. Later he was surprised to realize that he was sitting up in a wheelchair with a deep soft pillow beneath him, and the air in the room turning clearer by the second, but then too bright, and every clang and beep and slam from out in the hallway too loud. He was wearing a new knit shirt, butter yellow, but had no idea where it had come from, no recollection of pulling it on over his head. The skin on his face was tight, as if with sunburn, and the tip of his nose was tender when he touched it. There were a half dozen places on his arms still painted with Betadine or bandaged or wrapped in tape, and his right hand felt swollen and his fingers stiff when he tried to flex them. But even those sensations seemed distant to him, not immediate or fully experienced, more like the memory of an experience than the actual present pain.

Ben was still there, and told him again that Jayme was doing okay. The knife wound did no arterial damage, took twenty-six stitches to close and had put a notch in her fifth rib. Vee had come to the hospital with Ben and was throwing her weight around, Ben said, had handed out the marching orders and didn't care who liked it or didn't. DeMarco had a bruised coccyx and had also been treated for several cuts and bruises acquired while scrambling over the pile of metal desks.

"You couldn't remember when you had your last tetanus shot," Ben told him, "so they gave you a booster. They jabbed you with some morphine too. I told them you'd be pissed but they did it anyway. That was maybe seven or eight hours ago. You're on acetaminophen with codeine now. If you're feeling a little spacey, that's why."

Connor McBride was in ICU, with Fascetti and Olcott standing by, eager to question him. "The FBI is there too," Brinker said, "seeing as how he crossed state lines. So the other guy, Khatri, the one we think McBride called Magus in his journal, he's the feds' problem now."

DeMarco couldn't remember being told

that McBride had a journal or that one belonging to him had been found.

"You were pretty out of it, I guess," Ben said. "But yeah, we found it. About fifty yards upriver from the hospital. No idea what it was doing there."

"Daksh dumped it," DeMarco said.

"Why would he do that?"

"What does it say?"

"Most of it is just McBride rambling about how much he hates everybody. But the good parts," Ben said, "the good parts are all confession."

"He confessed to all three?"

"Tell you what," Ben said. "I need to take another look at it tonight. Then I'll get a copy of it made for you and Jayme. We can talk about it tomorrow."

Only one witness, in addition to the two kids, had come forward so far to report on Daksh's footrace up the river, probably to his parked car, Ben said. "But don't think for a second he's going to get away with this."

DeMarco was interested in what Ben was telling him, but more interested in finding Jayme. He kept trying to get up out of his wheelchair, but every time he did, the pain pulled at him like a thick, searing cord, while Ben's heavy hand on his shoulder pushed down, and the two forces were too much for DeMarco, whose strength seemed to have evaporated.

"I need to see Jayme," he said again, for maybe the thirtieth time, and finally he was wheeled into the room where she lay sedated and sleeping. Vee was sitting in a padded chair on the window side of the bed, holding Jayme's hand and softly praying. DeMarco was pushed up close to the other side, where he slipped one hand under Jayme's and gripped her wrist with his other hand. He thought she looked pale in her powder-blue hospital gown, her hand cold, her beautiful hair brushed back and held in place by an elastic white headband — a way she never wore it. All this troubled him, made him shiver despite the hot flush of fear in his chest. He bent forward to press his lips to the back of her hand, and swore to himself that he would not move from that position until she opened her eyes and returned to him.

NINETY-ONE

The only human sense and the only human emotion that grief cannot blunt is grief itself.

He heard that thought but did not know if it was his own or one of Huston's. He slept bent over with his head on the edge of Jayme's mattress, his body motionless but for when a sharp pain made him twitch. At those times his brain lit up in what he thought of as a loud silent noise, and in that instant between when the light winked out and he woke, a brief passage from Huston's notebooks would whisper to him in his own voice. The first time, he heard:

The end of days did not come as we expected. All of us were surprised.

The first sign was a faint arrow of stars. Not everybody could see it, not even on the darkest night. But we did.

He woke then and lifted his head and saw Jayme sleeping, Vee watching him from across the bed. He smiled at her and laid his head down again. He drifted back into sleep, body still and brain dark. Then another twitch and flare of light, and he heard:

In the fall the novel was always there, but I did not go to it anymore. The air was cold inside and outside the house, and the sky, no matter how bright was always gray.

Throughout the rest of that day and night, he remained in the room with Jayme, sometimes slept and sometimes did not. Just before falling asleep, or just before waking, the anomalous snatches of Huston's words came back to him, disparate fragments. Each time he woke fully, he marveled at the unpredictable nature of memory, and wondered if it had some secret purpose of its own.

From time to time Jayme awoke and looked at him, but her eyes were dull, her smile weak. He might speak to her and she might murmur an answer, their voices soft and hoarse, expressions muted. Food was brought, then taken away untouched.

In the evening when there was no light

outside the window but for artificial light, nothing natural and soothing but for the darkness itself, Jayme sat up and sipped from a glass of warm water, DeMarco from a cardboard cup of cold coffee. He told her all that had happened inside St. Margaret's, but wasn't sure how much she was absorbing, how much she would retain. His own thoughts were still none too coherent. There seemed an odd thickness to every movement, every word, every look, as if the air had gelled all around them.

She apologized in a voice that was gravelly and slow. "I don't know why I trusted him. He played me like a cheap violin."

He apologized in a voice that was weak and strained. "I fell for it too. I never once thought about checking out his story. I'm the senior officer, it's my fault, not yours. I almost got you killed."

"I thought he was trustworthy. I'm sorry, babe. So sorry."

He shook his head through the gelatinous air. "As trustworthy as a cure for baldness," he said. But neither of them laughed. There was no laughter anywhere in the room.

They touched each other's wounds, gazed helplessly at each other's tears. Neither of them referred directly to the miscarriage. But he asked her once, when her eyes came open after a brief sleep, "How are you feeling?"

And she answered, after a long pause for self-assessment, "Empty." They held hands, embraced, yet each felt alone inside an unassailable misery.

Sometime around midnight, or what felt like midnight, she asked if the room's door could be closed and the glass panel covered, and when the nurse said *I'm sorry, we can't do that,* DeMarco walked the hallway, grimacing with every step, until he found a bulletin board and removed two thumbtacks. Back in Jayme's room he covered the glass with a towel, pushed the thumbtacks into the thin wooden frame, closed the door, and took his seat beside her again.

When she slept, he closed his eyes too. He dreamed of Panama. He was facedown in a muddy pit, at the bottom of a stack of rotting bodies, twisted sideways so that his right arm extended up through the stack, one hand in the fetid air. Standing up there atop the bodies was a barefoot blue-eyed boy in brown shorts, feet and legs covered with blood-reddened mud, his face and arms charred by the flamethrowers. He had taken hold of two fingers on DeMarco's hand, one finger clutched in each tiny fist, and the boy kept pulling and screaming, pulling and screaming, *No respires, señor! Do not breathe! The stink of death will consume you!*

Ninety-Two

Saturday morning came and slowly passed. They took turns washing up in her hospital room's little bathroom, and when he finished and came back to her bed, she was fully dressed in a pair of blue scrubs and sitting in the chair by the window. She had her back to the glass, wasn't looking out, wasn't looking at anything in particular, eyes cast to the floor. What difference did the weather make, or the world outside?

She was wearing a pair of pink hospital socks with tiny rubber bumps on the soles and heels. *So she won't slip,* he thought, and then realized that his brain still wasn't working clearly, was still surrounded by a dulling haze, just as hers must have been.

He said, "I'm sorry. I should have brought you some clean clothes."

"This is fine," she said, and pushed the hair away from her eyes with a slow, heavy swipe. "Do you know where my shoes are?"

He found them in the little closet, slipped them on her feet and tied the laces. So far they had spoken of the baby only in a few hushed whispers. *Did Ben tell you yet? Yes, my love, he did. I'm so very, very sorry.* He resolved to say no more about it until she wanted to talk. If she wanted to talk. He knew very well the wall of isolation that grief builds around a person. What he did not know was how to breach that wall. Or even if he could, buried as he was under his own mountain of dead.

A few minutes before nine, Vee and Ben showed up with fresh coffee and croissant breakfast sandwiches in a white paper bag. "Did you have breakfast yet?" Ben asked.

"I'm sorry, Ben," Jayme said. "The smell of food makes me nauseated."

He held the bag toward DeMarco. "You?" he asked, and DeMarco, though he was starving, hadn't eaten anything since the morning of the attack, shook his head no.

Ben removed the cups of coffee from the bag, set them on the tray table beside the bed, then took the sandwiches out to the nurses' station. When he returned, De-Marco was sipping from one of the cups. Ben asked, "When do you get sprung?"

"After the doctor stops by," she said.

Ben nodded. Turned to DeMarco. Said,

"You guys want an update, or . . . ?"

DeMarco looked to Jayme. She said, "Sure. Go ahead."

"We got a little more out of McBride this morning. He's still groggy but stabilized, and I'm pretty sure he's going to flip like a shiny penny. I mean we have his journal, which is as good as a confession already. Plus, those FBI boys painted a pretty picture for him of his cell in Chillicothe. Told him how it took Dennis McGuire twenty-five minutes to die back in 2014. You should've seen the look on the kid's face."

DeMarco asked, "Any sign of Daksh?"

"Every two-, four-, and one-lane road in three states is being watched. Turns out there's no vehicle registered in his name. But he didn't walk to Pennsylvania, that's for certain."

Jayme asked, "You think he had some help getting away?"

The sheriff shrugged. "Either that or he did the Indian rope trick and disappeared into the clouds." Then he looked to his wife, who had her head cocked and was frowning. "What?" he asked. "Was that racist of me?"

She clicked her tongue, shook her head.

Jayme and DeMarco shared the smallest of smiles.

Vee said, "How about you boys go bring the car around. Give me a couple minutes with Jayme before the doctor comes. We'll catch up with you in the lobby."

NINETY-THREE

Going down in the elevator, DeMarco had to put a hand to the shiny wall. Moments of dizziness came and went; moments of confusion. A minute later, walking out through the lobby, he asked, "How'd you get my car here?"

"You gave me the key yesterday," Ben said.

"Oh. Yeah," DeMarco said, though he had no recollection of the transaction.

Ben took the car key from his pocket, held it out. "You okay to drive?"

"I'm fine. Thanks." DeMarco palmed the key. "Thanks for everything, Ben."

"I've got something else for you too," he said, and reached back to his right hip pocket, pulled forth a roll of printer paper held together with a rubber band. He clutched it like a runner's baton, ready to pass it off. "You listen to my phone message yet? The one I left you last night?"

"Phone's still off," DeMarco told him. "I

haven't thought to turn it on yet."

"Okay, well," Ben said, and tapped the edge of the roll against his left palm, "you should maybe listen to it before you look at these papers. Photocopies from Connor's journal. It's only six pages or so, just the relevant parts. But some of it, I think, is going to surprise you."

"How so?" DeMarco asked, but there was a flatness in his voice, a lack of interest.

"Don't worry about it for now." Ben extended the papers to him. "Whenever you guys want to take a look."

DeMarco waited until he had unlocked the car and opened the door, then he took the papers and climbed inside and tossed the roll of papers up against the windshield.

Ben followed him to the edge of the car door, stood there with his hand on the doorframe, holding it open. "One other thing," he said, but then looked back toward the hospital, over the roofs of a field of parked cars. DeMarco waited.

Ben's gaze came back to him. "Jayme was talking to Vee, and Vee thought you should know."

"Know what?"

"Jayme's afraid you're going to think she tricked you somehow. That she did it on purpose."

DeMarco slid sideways on the seat, his knees toward the sheriff. "What are you talking about, Ben?"

"Back in Kentucky. She was worried crazy about you when you took off in the RV by yourself. Angry as hell too, yeah, but mostly worried sick about you. And then not a word from you in what, three days?"

"My phone was dead."

"I know, I know. And you were shot at, injured, everything else that happened to you. Jayme told Vee all about it . . . and Vee told me. Thing is, Jayme didn't know any of that until you got back. She said she was a zombie the whole time you were gone. Couldn't eat, couldn't sleep, couldn't think straight. You know what it's like, man. You've been there, I know."

DeMarco nodded. "You're saying she forgot to take her pills."

"It wasn't deliberate, that's the thing. People make mistakes. Especially when they love somebody, and that somebody's gone. You can't hold it against her."

"I don't."

"She already blames herself. Both for getting pregnant, and then losing it."

DeMarco's eyes were on the dirty pavement now, his head going back and forth, his throat thick.

"She's afraid you're going to hate her for it," Ben said.

DeMarco looked up at him, his eyes wet, as were Ben's. "That's never going to happen."

Ben nodded. Sniffed. "Vee told her that. We just thought you should know where her head is right now."

"I appreciate it," DeMarco said. He remained still for a few moments, then slid around to face the steering wheel.

Ben said, "You mind if I follow you guys partway home? Just to make sure you're keeping it between the lines?"

"I don't mind," DeMarco said, and tried for an appreciative smile, but felt as if he might throw up.

NINETY-FOUR

Twenty-five minutes later, DeMarco and Jayme were alone in his car, heading east. Ben's car followed to within a mile of De-Marco's house, then Ben flashed his high beams in DeMarco's rearview mirror, slowed and made a U-turn, and headed for the interstate and Ohio.

Both DeMarco and Jayme were wearing sunglasses, the sun bright in their eyes, the glare still sharp and jagged through tinted glass. He thought she had glanced a couple of times at the roll of paper lying up against the windshield behind the instrument panel, but she didn't ask any questions, so he didn't volunteer any answers. She held a small pink cloth bag on her lap, the one Vee had carried into the room earlier that morning — held it in a puzzling way, he thought, with both hands cupped beneath it. Originally he had assumed the bag held some kind of gift, a tea mug and bags of chamomile tea, a small box of chocolates, maybe a book full of aphorisms and inspirational verses. But the way she held it, cradling it, suggested something else.

She saw him looking at the bag, and said, "Vee gave this to me before I left the room."

There was such a solemn quality to the tone of her voice, at once full of both sorrow and something else, maybe gratitude, that he took another quick glance at the bag, then into her eyes. His foot, by its own volition, eased off the accelerator. "What is it?" he asked.

She put out a hand, laid it atop his thigh. "Our baby," she said.

A brief, cold shiver seized him. He heard his own sharp inhalation. Then let his right hand fall from the steering wheel to cover hers. Got his breathing under control. And asked, "How does that work?"

"It doesn't look like a baby," she told him. "Just like a tiny seed. You can see it if you want to."

He wasn't sure if he wanted to or not. Wasn't sure if she should have seen it. "So, what, uh . . ."

"Vee said it's helpful sometimes, you know? To have a little ceremony for it? Just you and me. Though she said they would come if we want them to."

"A burial?" he said.

She nodded. "Vee did it with her first baby. I don't know if Ben told you or not. That she had a miscarriage too."

He shook his head no. Swallowed what felt like a small stone of calcified spit. Felt that stone lodge in the center of his chest, cold and sharp, stealing his breath.

She said, "I'm so glad Vee was there for me. Otherwise the hospital would have just . . . I can't stand the thought of that. I don't care how small it is. It's still our baby, isn't it?"

He nodded. Swallowed again. "Do you think it will help?" he asked. "If we have a burial for it?"

She nodded. Slid her left hand away from his and cupped the bottom of the bag again. Protecting it. "I think it would."

"Then we should do that," he told her, and laid his hand on her thigh. "Let's do that."

She lifted the small cloth bag a bit, held it against her belly. He blinked, tried to clear his vision. Tried his best to see the road ahead.

■ ■ ■ ■

CODA

■ ■ ■ ■

At times I will awaken in the stillness of
  the night, ensconced in darkness,
and I will thank the silence for all that I
  have, and for the gift of another day,
and I will find myself wrapped in emotions
  that should not exist together but do,
and I will know in those moments the
  very essence of our Creator:
an insatiable longing; an unassailable
  grief;
a profound gratitude; a transcendent joy.
  — from the notebooks of Thomas Huston

NINETY-FIVE

There was always a letdown after a case got solved. After all the congratulations and backslapping. All the figurative applause. But this time was different. After what had happened to Jayme, and what had almost happened to her . . . There was no letdown this time. There was a crash.

Jayme went straight to bed when they returned home on Saturday. Put on a pair of silky pajamas and swallowed two tablets from the little orange vial that had been in the pink bag, crawled under the sheet and took a small wooden box out of the bag and tucked it against her side. DeMarco lay with her for a while, the small box between them, but he could not sleep. He thought about all the ways he could put himself to sleep, all of his old remedies, but rejected every one of them as a form of cheating. It was fine for Jayme to sleep, but his job was to stand guard against the darkness, even at one in the afternoon.

Both he and Jayme had turned off their phones in the hospital, so he, after a long shower — first warm in an unsuccessful attempt to wash out the chill beneath his skin, and then cold as an act of defiance against that chill — sat on the edge of the back porch and turned his phone on again. Immediately the notices for missed calls, phone messages and texts beeped in, many from numbers he did not recognize. He listened only to the messages from people he knew, guys from Troop D, from Ben and Olcott and even Fascetti. For some reason Fascetti's halting, awkward message nearly brought him to tears.

"Hey, brother. I just wanted to say . . . you know, you guys did a hell of a job. Above and beyond. I owe you a beer. Couple of beers. When you're feeling up to it, I'd like to take you and your partner out to dinner. I've got a wife who will come too. Bet you didn't know I'm married, did you? Probably thought nobody could stand me, huh? Anyway, the reason I called. I'm betting if we all put our heads together, we can wrap up the Talarico case too while we're at it. Our guy in OSP, I know we can make him sing. Track down the girlfriend, make her an offer she can't refuse. And you'll see that I was right too. Costa did it. Not a doubt in the world. It's a thought anyway. We'd be glad to have you and your lady giving us a hand. So anyway . . . I mean Jesus Christ, man. I'm so freaking sorry about what happened to Jayme. Sheriff thought we needed to know; I hope you don't mind. Don't blame him if you do, okay? You know I think she's a hell of woman. Just don't tell her I said so. Ha. She's going to be okay, though, don't you worry. She's tough as nails. You probably know that already. Okay, man. That's all. That's all I have to say."

The rest of the calls were more of the same, equally awkward, equally touching. Only the second message from Ben was matter-of-fact.

"Listen, I didn't want to bring this up at the hospital, but I informed the victims' families that you got the guy. The guy who actually, physically, did it all. And all three families agree. With or without Khatri — who we're going to get sooner or later, you can take that to the bank — they want you and Jayme to have the reward money. You deserve every penny of it. Three families, Ryan. Three families are going to sleep a little easier tonight because of what you and Jayme did. I just wanted you guys to know that."

Hearing that statement — *The guy who actually, physically, did it all* — DeMarco remembered Ben's admonition in the hospital parking lot; he remembered the rolled-up papers still in his car. He stood and walked as briskly across the yard as he could, his feet in white socks, no shoes, opened the door and climbed in, unfurled the pages and read. Sweat beaded on his forehead and dripped down his neck. Connor's description of killing Brenner. Connor's description of killing Hufford. And the final piece, out of sequence, Connor's description of Samantha Lewis's death:

Okay, I'm going to write about Venus now. Not as an example of True Will, though. Not mine anyway. Just the opposite. But maybe if I make myself write about it, I'll stop remembering it all the time. I have to get it out of my head one way or another. Magus said the best way is to write it all down.

So Dashwood came across some article a while back about how peak experiences in altered consciousness will actually show decreased brain activity, not more. So we'd been playing around with that idea ever since. We started out with just the mushrooms and sex, then started doing the elevator while on shrooms, and then having sex while we were still spacey from doing the elevator.

Here DeMarco stopped reading, took out his phone and asked it, "What does it mean to do the elevator?"

He scrolled through several irrelevant responses before happening upon a bit of conversation in a forum on erotic asphyxiation: "I had to ask myself the same thing, bro. But once you do it, you'll want to every time. It's not as intense as being choked but tons safer. I hear it's not particularly good for the brain cells, but what is? I mean, we've all heard stories about people dying from it, but who knows if they're true or not? Anyway, you just pull everybody into a huddle, then you all squat down and stand up again, squat and stand, squat and stand in a steady rhythm, hyperventilating the whole time, everybody all synced up. Eventually the huddle will fall apart and you'll be laying there on the floor feeling like you're floating through deep space."

DeMarco's face got twisted. He blew out a breath, shook his head back and forth. "What the hell is wrong with people?" he muttered, and then went back to reading Connor's entry:

Then a couple of us, actually everybody except Becca, tried using plastic bags over our heads during sex. Dashwood kept ramping things up, coming up with new things to try. He never forced anybody to do something they didn't want to do, but he'd let you know you were falling short if you didn't at least try it a couple of times. Venus would do anything he wanted.

So one night I get a call from Dashwood to bring him over a bag of shrooms, just enough for him and Venus. I get there and he has her laid out on the sofa bed, naked and spread-eagled. Usually I give him the shrooms and he tells me to hit the road, but this night he says hang around, he's going to need an extra set of hands. Which tells me he's ramping things up again. What he wants is for me to hold a bag closed around his throat while he's holding one closed around hers.

I hated watching his big ugly body having sex with her. I wanted to be the one giving her pleasure. Maybe that's why I started squeezing a little too hard, because of the wanting and the hating, and maybe that caused him to squeeze harder too. It kills me to think I might be responsible for what he did to her. All I know is that as soon as he went over on his side, I ripped off his bag and then went for hers. But she was too still. I mean her chest wasn't moving at all, whereas Dashwood was laying there moaning and pulling his dick trying to make himself cum. It was one of the ugliest things I'd ever seen. Cutting up Brenner didn't even compare to how ugly this was. Pretty soon I'm screaming at him and punching him and he gets up on his feet eventually and knocks me against the wall. And then I don't know how many minutes passed with us just breathing and not moving a muscle, just trying to wrap our heads around what had happened and what we were going to do about it.

He had me help carry her upstairs and put her in the shower. He soaped her up from head to toe, washed every inch of her clean. Didn't want any trace of himself left on her. When he had her out and on the bathroom floor and getting her dried, he told me to bring her clothes up from the basement so we could dress her. His plan was to drive her car somewhere, and put her in it with the bag over her head as if she'd done it to herself. But while I was down in the basement I called Magus and told him what happened. I just wanted him to tell me to get the hell out of there and never go back. But he surprised me. He said I had to clean up my own messes. He said to make it look like the job I did on Brenner. To get some hair or something of Dashwood's and plant it with the plastic bag on her body after laying Venus out and cutting her up where somebody would find her. I didn't want to do any of it. Not to her. But Magus said it was the only way. Two murders, both pointing to Dashwood. Magus had always planned on at least two anyway, and then he'd tip off the police to Dashwood's little cult, and get him sent away forever.

It didn't take much to convince Dashwood that making it look just like Brenner's was the way to go. Anything to keep himself out of the picture, or so he thought. He even said he was proud of me for thinking it up. He asked if I could get hold of a saw somewhere, and said if I had to buy one he would pay me back whatever it cost. I just wanted to spit in his ugly face. I had to settle for pulling some hairs out of his brush in the bathroom.

Thing is, when push came to shove, I couldn't dishonor Venus by stripping her naked and ripping her apart. I started, I tried, but I couldn't go through with it. I just couldn't. And when I went back to Magus's place that night and told him, I was ready

604

to take a beating if I had to. Anything would have been easier than cutting her up. He just looked at me, those dark eyes of his full of disgust, and said I owed him another body. I had to do it all again, and soon, if I had any hope of earning back his trust. And that's why I did Hufford. Cutting him up was the easiest thing in the world. I didn't want to stop.

NINETY-SIX

Jayme awoke early in the evening. He opened a can of chicken noodle soup, sat with her while she ate a third of it, and filled her in on all the good wishes from the phone messages. "Ben said he had to make a statement to the press, asked if we wanted to be there for it. I sent him a text, told him to count us out. I hope that's okay."

"Absolutely," she said.

"There will probably be something on the news tonight if you want to watch it."

She shook her head no. Swallowed a spoonful of cloudy broth. Then asked, "How are you feeling? Are you in pain?"

He shrugged. "What's a human being doing with a tailbone anyway? I mean we've been standing upright for how long now? Two, three million years? And we're still part animal?"

She smiled, said nothing, swallowed another spoonful of broth.

He considered asking if she wanted to know how the case was playing out, but she seemed to have little interest in anything at all, every smile and blink and movement slowed. It could wait, he decided. Everything could wait.

Later she slept with her head in his lap as he sat on the sofa watching an old movie on TCM. Bogart was holding Bette Davis and Leslie Howard hostage in a diner in the Petrified Forest. Howard is a penniless, disillusioned writer; Bette's a lonely waitress. Bogart is a ruthless killer, of course, and all of them are stuck in the desert during the Great Depression. There are other characters too, there are always other characters, but the story is about those three. In the end, Howard orchestrates his own death at the hands of Bogart so that Bette can join her negligent mother in France. DeMarco thought it an overly talky story, noir existentialism stirred up with sappy romanticism. All the loose ends tied up with a bow. Final justice for the bad guys, and happiness for those who deserve it.

DeMarco didn't buy it. He found the movie as entertaining as a bruised tailbone.

But even after he turned the TV off, even after he half carried a half-sleeping Jayme back to the bed, he remembered a couple of lines he liked, spoken by the disillusioned writer. "Any woman's worth everything that any man has to give . . . that's the whole excuse for our existence. It's what makes the whole thing possible and tolerable."

DeMarco lay in bed and felt Jayme's warmth beside him, and mumbled the lines over and over again, repeating them like a mantra that might eventually lull him to sleep.

NINETY-SEVEN

Sunday morning. DeMarco lay in bed, uncovered, sweating despite the air conditioner. The sunlight coming through the curtains was bright and too warm, as if that wasn't morning light on the other side of the glass but a raging fire, the entire world combusting, and now the flames were about to break through and engulf them too.

He knew she was awake. He could feel it. Knew she was lying there with her eyes open, staring at the ceiling, feeling what she must be feeling. He knew that emptiness, the one that comes after too much sedation, and the one that comes after loss. The first kind was a good one to know, he supposed, so that you could learn to avoid it. But the second one . . . He would never wish it on anybody, least of all on her. He didn't want it to change her, but knew that it would. Knew there was nothing he could do to erase it from her. And *that* helplessness, that knowledge — it felt like a hundred extra pounds of misery in his bones.

Get up, he told himself, but could not move.

You're worthless, he told himself. *Get up!*

And managed to roll onto his side, face the curtains, dare the fire to incinerate him.

He sat up finally. Set his bare feet on the floor.

"You okay?" she asked.

The hoarseness of her voice stabbed his heart. And the fact that her first thought was for him. God, he just wanted to fall onto the floor. Crawl under the bed and never come out.

The curtains shimmered behind a veil of water, but his tears did nothing to extinguish the fire. Without turning, he reached a hand backward, touched her arm. She took his hand and gripped it hard. "I'll make us some coffee," he said.

She held tight to his hand. "Don't go yet, babe."

And now he turned, and slid off the bed to kneel facing her, and leaned forward across the bed, pressed his mouth to her hand still holding his.

Then he lifted his eyes to hers. Her eyes were red, inflamed, and shimmering. Yet she smiled. And in so doing, she weakened and emptied and strengthened and filled him with that smile.

"We need to move," he told her. "We need to get out of here as soon as we can. Out of this house, out of this state."

"I'm with you. Where do you want to go?"

"Someplace where people aren't always hurting each other."

"Like maybe a grocery store?" she said. "The fruit section?"

His laughter hurt, felt like something broken inside his chest. "No good," he said. "I've seen people come to blows over a mango."

"Who ended up with it — you or her?"

"She was wiry for an old woman."

They smiled at each other, a matching pair of smiles, equally fraudulent. He pulled his body forward a bit more, took her into his arms. Pulled his legs and feet back onto the bed. She curled into him, cried quietly against his chest.

He said nothing, only held her. Was willing to do so forever if that was what she needed.

But a few minutes later, she drew a hand over her face, wiped off the tears. Turned to sit with her head on his shoulder. She said, "Can we talk about that reward money for a minute?"

"I don't want it," he said.

"I don't either. Let's give it away. We can start with the victims' families."

He nodded. "We'll make a list." He had a hand just above her stomach, fingers spread. Her stomach rose and fell as she breathed. Beneath his thumb, her heart continued to beat. Or maybe it was his own pulse beating in his thumb. Maybe both hearts were beating to the same rhythm.

She asked, "Can we do something today?"

"Anything you want."

She moved her hand to the side, felt around for the little wooden box, and finally found it beneath the sheet. She pulled it forth and set it atop the back of his hand, where she held it in place. She said, "I want to put our baby to rest somewhere."

He tried to keep his voice calming and steady. "It's already at rest."

She shook her head no. "I want it to be with somebody who will watch over it and always take care of it. But I don't know who. Who's going to watch over our baby's soul?"

He sniffed, felt his head and chest fill with congestion, felt his eyes sting and his throat tighten, felt her heart and his hammering with grief. He lifted her hand momentarily, turned his own hand underneath the box until it was resting in the palm of his hand, then brought her hand down again to hold the box from the top. "Don't worry," he told her. "I know just the right place."

Ninety-Eight

DeMarco came down the stairs that morning and saw the white envelope on the foyer floor and stopped on the fourth step from the bottom of the stairs. There was no mail delivery on Sundays. Somebody had slipped the envelope through the mail slot while he and Jayme were still in bed.

He looked back over his shoulder to make sure she wasn't close behind. No, he could hear water running in the bathroom; she had stepped into the shower. He came down the last three steps, stood over the envelope, looking down.

A white card envelope, faceup on the cool tile. There was no return address, no stamp. No bulges. Nothing to indicate it was anything other than a card from a well-wisher. Yet it oozed darkness. It made the dim air feel even heavier.

He picked it up by one corner, just in case, careful to touch no other part of its surface. Carried it, dangling from his finger and thumb, into the kitchen. Using his free hand, he tore a paper towel from the roll on the dispenser, laid the towel on the kitchen table, and dropped the card atop it. He gathered another paper towel and, from the knife block, a paring knife. Used the second paper towel to hold the envelope flat while he sliced it open. Used the tip of the knife to slide the sheet of yellow stationery, folded twice, out of the envelope and onto the first paper towel. Used both the knife and the paper towel to unfold the letter. And read the neatly typed message that filled both sides of the page. The font was small and made him squint:

TO: Sergeant Detective Ryan DeMarco
So now you know. From the TV news I learned that our Mr. McBride, my Erebus, still lives and is cooperating with your police. I had hoped and planned otherwise. Had you and Miss Jayme come up the same stairs, Erebus would have attacked one of you and been killed by the other. His journal would have been dis-

covered, the killer identified, and all settled but for the identity of the mysterious Magus. Why did Miss Jayme leave your side? Who mounts a barricade in the middle of the stairs? Obviously, I misjudged both her and your tenacity. You always appeared so tame to me. I hope that characterisation does not offend you. I did imagine you less capable. That was my error, and one I will not make again. Also, I promise to become more proficient with a firearm — now that I have one of my own. A knife is more intimate, of course, but intimacy has never been my objective.

You might imagine that you have won the war by routing your enemy, but you are mistaken. I know that Erebus will entertain you with all he knows, but do not think that I have been careless with what I have allowed him to know. Also he will lie to you to save himself. That you can count on. I know him well and used him well. He was a spear for me, nothing more. And when a spear breaks, the warrior throws it away and rearms himself with a new one. I have many spears. I need only reach out to seize another one, for they surround me wherever I go, eager to be of service. In this way the war continues, and is now more imperative than ever.

I invite you to look around — at this town where you live, the city where you grew up, the country you fought dumbly for not once but twice, all the damage you and those like you have wrought. Yes, I watched as your sheriff praised you before the insatiable cameras. I wonder why you and your wounded mistress were not there puffing up your chests and basking in the praise. I am glad I did not kill her. To die is to be free of this prison, and it is not yet time for either of you to be free. You must first learn who you truly are and who is pulling your strings. Your country is spreading its pollution around the entire planet now, and only absolute chaos can cleanse it. There are dark, chilling currents running through your history and your culture, but how many of you are willing to acknowledge them? Have you paused to notice how many of your countrymen and women are addicted to alcohol and tobacco and prescription drugs? Cannabis, once meant to be employed only as part of the rituals of healing and divine connection, is now sold like bags of cotton candy in many of your states. How many ways must you find to narcotise your souls? Your people are obese and cancerous with sloth. You sedate yourselves with noise and artificial light, rendering the stars invisible and the celestial hum impossible to hear. There is no city in your country where the stink of smog and the insane clamour of man cannot be heard. Your leaders are thieves and deceivers, hysterical in their idiocy, vile and foul in their avarice, putrefying in their desire to subvert individual will for their own gain. Your children are raised addicted to the opium of the little screens, one worthless generation after another, multiplying like fevered beasts, filling subdivision after subdivision, ghetto after ghetto. You have made technology your god, but technology is a product and function of ego. Ego must be subverted, not apotheosised, if you hope to ever evolve. It would be better to see a thousand of you fall than to see another tree felled. You have divorced yourself from Aranyani to such an extent that she no longer speaks a word to you, no longer cares for your continuance, but pleads to the Source for your extinction. All this is the faeces you have spread across the planet, not like a fertile manure but like bile and vomit, so perversely have you interrupted the natural cycle by which life sanitises and perpetuates itself. You protect and nurture that which is too weak to survive on its own, and in so doing you weaken all life. Conflict and suffering are essential to growth. A dog with only eight teats does not attempt to nurture nine puppies; she devours the runt of the lit- ter, and thereby assures her own survival as well as that of the other eight puppies. Every animal down to the simplest bacterium behaves this way, because they have not lost their native intel- ligence. They understand that the weak will weaken all of them. But your society has forgotten this. You attempt to sanitise it from conflict and suffering. You waste your energy and resources by sustaining that which should be allowed to die. You coddle the weak, and in so doing weaken all of your society. This you call morality. This you call compassion. There can be no growth for mankind, no evolution, without suffering. The weak will die cradling the weaker in their arms!

These are dangerous times indeed. You must remain aware of this now and never lose sight of what you have done. That reason alone is why I am happy I did not kill you and you did not kill me. Because now everything I do will remind you of this truth. Every time a citizen is run down by a truck or shot dead in the street, you will think of me. Every time a fire erupts in an apartment building for no reason, you will think of me. Every time a child disappears from one of your odorous amusement parks, you will think of me.

Only chaos can cleanse you, my friend. The spectre of death will drive many of you even deeper into your bottles and drugs and the insentience of fear, but those not yet wholly weak of mind and will can be saved by it. Like me they will awaken to the truth, will detoxify their bodies and purify their minds of your culture's putrescence. Perhaps you and I will meet again in this incarnation, but whether or not the universe chooses for this to happen, I will always be with you now. I am multitudinous. I will be everywhere you look, and especially in those places where you fail to look. Like Khaos, I surround you, and like Shiva, I am here to destroy you, arouse you from your stupor, and give you new form.

I am Magus, the Redeemer.

DeMarco's hands were shaking as he pulled a plastic bag from the box in a kitchen drawer, and as he slipped both the letter and the envelope into that bag. He then stood very still and cocked an ear; water was still trickling though the pipes upstairs. He went out the back door, sat on the edge of the porch, and took out his phone.

NINETY-NINE

"For the love of God," Ben said after being informed of the contents of the letter. "Well, I guess we need to get it to the FBI. You want to meet me in Erie?"

"Jayme and I have some plans for the morning. I'd rather not have to cancel them."

"Want me to come get the letter?"

"Could you? I hate to ask you to make the drive."

"Where's a safe place you could leave it for me?"

"I'll put it in the top drawer in the china closet in the dining room. The house key will be, uh . . . back porch. Under a bag of sand against the wall."

"Got it," Ben said. "Has Jayme seen the letter?"

"No, and I don't want her to. Not just yet anyway. I don't want her to know how close that son of a bitch was to us last night. Can you ask the FBI to not release any information about how they came by the letter, or who it was addressed to?"

"I'll insist. Not that I carry much weight with the feds, but I'll insist anyway. To release it to the press would just incite panic and play right into that lunatic's hands."

"Thanks, Ben," DeMarco said. "I owe you one."

"You don't owe me diddly, brother. Just do what you have planned for the day, and this conversation never happened."

"What have you learned about Khatri?"

"That's not his real name, for one thing."

"What is?"

"Still a mystery. The feds are doing fingerprint and facial recognition searches, but they're coming up empty."

"Then they need to expand the search. He came from somewhere on this planet."

"I hear you, Ryan. I hear you. By the way, his bosses at the Dairy Queen and Humane Society had nothing but praise for him. Said he was an exemplary employee. Smart, reliable, a natural-born leader."

"Who apparently knows how to fake or get hold of fake documents. Didn't anybody do a background check? Call for references?"

"To serve ice cream and shovel up dog

doo-doo? There's a high turnover rate for both of those job skills, I'm afraid."

"What about the colleges? Was he a registered student at either one?"

"No record of that. McBride says he audited Gillespie's class. Has no knowledge of him attending any other classes. Said Khatri claimed to have 'released' a dozen or more souls so far, but he wouldn't say when or where."

"There's probably no way to disprove or corroborate that."

"Not with over forty thousand sets of unidentified human remains gathering dust in this country alone."

DeMarco shook his head, could think of nothing to say.

Brinker asked, "Did you have a chance to read those pages from McBride's journal?"

"I did. I haven't showed them to Jayme yet."

"Whatever you decide is fine with me. Just so you know, though, McBride's been filling in some important details for us."

"What details?"

"Khatri was in the car with him for Brenner and Hufford."

"Jesus," DeMarco said. "He helped kill them?"

"Kept them secured and subdued anyway.

The little coward hid in the back, then used his stun gun on them. It was Khatri's car they used, which is why no DNA turned up in McBride's. McBride says he wasn't allowed to write any of that in his journal. Wasn't allowed to mention Khatri's name. Khatri kept tabs on it. Read everything he wrote."

"It was his insurance policy. Plan A was to pin everything on Gillespie. If that failed, plan B was to pin it all on McBride."

"I bet he did a happy dance when Gillespie accidentally killed the girl."

"Then found out we were looking for McBride. Probably knew the kid would turn on him sooner or later. So he lured us to the hospital expecting McBride wouldn't survive it. Plant the journal, killer dead, case closed."

"Except that your aim was too good."

"Nobody aims to wound, Ben. You know that. I sure as hell didn't."

"Well, it's a good thing he's still alive. Works out better for us."

"Except that I played right into Khatri's hands," DeMarco said. "Almost did his dirty work for him." The thought that he had allowed himself to be duped by Khatri made a bubble of nausea rise in his stomach. And with it, his anger rose too.

"We'll get him sooner or later. It's only a matter of time. Most people go through life trying to convince themselves they're not as boring or homely or incompetent or stupid or cowardly as they fear they are. Only the fools succeed at that task. And Khatri is a fool if thinks he can hide from the FBI."

"And how many people will he kill in the meantime?"

Brinker must have noticed the alteration in tone, the self-blame; he changed the subject. "How's our girl doing today?"

"Sleeps, mostly. Otherwise in a kind of daze. Makes it easier to keep her away from the news. She doesn't even seem curious about any of the developments."

"That won't last."

"I *am* going to tell her. Sooner or later. But when she's stronger."

"Tell her what?" Ben said. "I don't even know what you're talking about."

"Huh," DeMarco said, the best laugh he could muster.

"And how are you doing, my friend? Holding up okay?"

"Scraping by all right," DeMarco said. "Like a glacier."

"There's a lot of power behind a glacier."

"Gravity, Ben. That's all it is."

"I hear that, I surely do. Well . . . enjoy

your Sunday, man. Best that you can."

Afterward DeMarco sat awhile longer on the edge of the back porch. Sat looking at his yard and the alley and the garage and the spread of town and land and sky beyond. More than anything, he wanted out of there. Wanted to lift Jayme off the ground and carry her away somewhere. Wanted to stand with her on a hill so high that they could look down on the planets and stars and black holes and the whole angry sea of pain and wherever the hell God was hiding.

He needed to tell her that. He stood. Hid a house key behind the bag of sand on the porch. Then placed the plastic bag containing Khatri's letter in the china closet in the dining room. Then went upstairs and into the bedroom.

She was still in the bathroom, its door closed, though the shower was silent now. He reached for the doorknob but paused when he heard a sharp inhalation, followed by a shallow exhalation and soft "hunh." She was sobbing.

Of course she is, he told himself, and put his hand on the doorknob. But the door was locked. She never locked the bathroom door. What should he do?

He turned and looked into the bedroom. Should he sit and wait? Allow her the privacy she obviously wanted?

He crossed to her side of the bed, sat on the edge. Heard another convulsive sob, and stood. Then told himself, *No, she locked the door. Let her be.*

Walked around to his side of the bed. Saw the box of Huston's papers on the floor. *What should I do?* he asked. *Should I talk to her through the door?*

This was all unfamiliar territory to him. He had viewed it from afar but had never lived it before. Never inhabited the very heart of it like this.

He eased himself down onto his knees beside the box. Pushed the top layer of composition books aside and squeezed the edge of one near the bottom. Pulled it up through the others and laid it atop the bed, one hand flat atop it. "Help me, Tom," he said.

After a few moments, he opened the book at random. *Verso and recto,* he told himself. Left and right pages. Laraine had taught him that. That and a lot more, not all of it about literature.

The choice was easy; the verso page was blank.

On the recto page, he read:

Everyone is angry today. Everyone is

bilious with social or political or moral outrage. What a waste that is! What a waste of your precious time on this earth!

The piece seemed to have been written for Huston's students, and went on to talk about the need to ignore the ubiquitous media attempts to inflame and manipulate their passions. It talked about spending time alone in the woods, and meditating, in learning to find joy in even the most banal of activities, and in always nurturing a dream, a goal. DeMarco struggled to find any relevance in the material to his own life. Then he came to the final paragraphs:

Of what value is a life spent in anger? Of what value is a day spent without hope, without a dream?

These lives we are living now might someday prove to have been computer simulations or holograms, as contemporary science theorizes. Time itself might prove to have been nothing but an illusion. But we cannot live that way now. We must live as if every day is real, and as if every minute of every day is significant. We must give ourselves meaning even when everybody else is attempting to strip us of meaning. To fill your life with the negative charge of nihilism is to deny the very real beauty and joy of life that exists all around you.

A positive life, a meaningful life, is one that is lived inside that beauty and joy, even if you have to work hard from time to time to remain inside. Don't look for beauty to be flamboyant or loud or startling; it usually isn't. Look for it in the meals your mother sets before you, and in the warmth of your father's hand on your shoulder. Look for it in a baby's smile, or in the way your dog greets you at the door. In your friends' laughter, or the tears they share with you. Look for it in the good work you do, and in the satisfaction of knowing, at the end of each day, that you performed to the best of your ability. Be that beauty and that joy. When you do that, your life becomes art. Be the artist of your own life.

DeMarco laughed softly to himself, and closed the book, and laid his forehead against the edge of the mattress, and wept.

One Hundred

DeMarco patted the dirt back into the small hole he had made with the trowel he had brought along, and in which Jayme had placed the two bunches of marigolds purchased at a small nursery on the edge of town. Both filled their hands with topsoil from the bag beside the headstone, then smoothed the dirt and wiped their hands on the grass, then knelt there together for a while holding hands, looking down at the tiny grave atop Ryan Jr.'s grave, looking down at the bright-yellow flowers.

Vee had saved the tiny remains inside a gauze pad wrapped in half, and then had placed the pad in a zippered plastic bag, and had placed the bag in the small wooden box. DeMarco was glad she had done that for Jayme, was glad to have the Brinkers as friends. Daksh's letter had been, and still was, unsettling, but he was determined to not allow it to dominate his thoughts or cast this time with Jayme into shadow. The air was fresh and clean here, and the sun was warm on his shoulders and the top of his head, and what he felt for Jayme was stronger and more resilient than any madman's curse.

"Can you say something?" she asked.

"You mean . . . a prayer?"

"To your son. He doesn't know me."

Maybe he did, maybe he didn't. DeMarco wished he knew the answer to that and a lot of other questions. Speaking out loud to his son would make him feel foolish, but if that was what Jayme wanted, what she needed . . .

"This is your little brother or sister, my son."

"Sister," Jayme said.

He turned to look at her.

"I just know," she told him. "When I close my eyes, I see pink."

Okay; he did too. Right from the start, from the very moment Ben gave him the news. He always saw Jayme with a pink bundle in her arms. Again, maybe it meant something, maybe it didn't. But that was a discussion for another day.

"This is your little sister, Ryan. Please love her and take care of her. Until we're all together again."

Jayme smiled and nodded and pressed her hand flat atop the replanted sod. After a while she turned to look at him with the saddest eyes he had ever seen, eyes he wanted to shine again, to flicker with the flame of her spirit and the fury of her love. They were brimming with tears now, her mouth quivering. "Does a baby this small, this early, even have a soul?"

"Of course," he told her.

"How do you know?"

He had no answer.

"Ryan. How do you *know*"

"We have to believe it does," he said.

"Then what happens to it? To the soul of a baby that was never even born?"

"I wish I could answer that for you, sweetheart."

He was certain that she was going to break down sobbing, would stretch herself across the grass and never want to leave. Instead, her eyes turned hopeful. "Do you think Lathea would know?"

He was quiet for a while, felt the dampness of the ground on his knees. Felt the warmth of the sun on his face and the coolness of the tears on his cheeks. He smelled the grass he had overturned and the dirt drying on his hands. He must not let that fire in her emerald eyes go out.

He pushed himself to his feet and brushed the dirt from his palms. Then he looked down at her and smiled and extended a hand. "Let's go for a drive and find out."

ABOUT THE AUTHOR

Randall Silvis's fiction and nonfiction books have appeared on Best of the Year lists from the *New York Times,* the *Toronto Globe & Mail,* SfSite.com, and the International Association of Crime Writers, as well as on several editors' and booksellers' pick lists. Also a prizewinning playwright, a produced screenwriter, and a prolific essayist, his literary awards include the Drue Heinz Literature Prize, two literature fellowships from the National Endowment for the Arts, a Fulbright Senior Scholar Research Fellowship, and a Doctor of Letters degree from Indiana University of Pennsylvania for distinguished literary achievement.

Cohost of the popular podcast series *The Writer's Hangout* (thewritershangout.com), Silvis lives in western Pennsylvania.